The Gypsies

Charles G. Leland

Contents

THE GYPSIES

BY

Charles G. Leland

PREFACE.

The reader will find in this book sketches of experiences among gypsies of different nations by one who speaks their language and is conversant with their ways. These embrace descriptions of the justly famed musical gypsies of St. Petersburg and Moscow, by whom the writer was received literally as a brother; of the Austrian gypsies, especially those composing the first Romany orchestra of that country, selected by Liszt, and who played for their friend as they declared they had never played before for any man; and also of the English, Welsh, Oriental, and American brethren of the dark blood and the tents. I believe that the account of interviews with American gypsies will possess at least the charm of novelty, but little having as yet been written on this extensive and very interesting branch of our nomadic population. To these I have added a characteristic letter in the gypsy language, with translation by a lady, legendary stories, poems, and finally the substance of two papers, one of which I read before the British Philological Society, and the other before the Oriental Congress at Florence, in 1878. Those who study ethnology will be interested to learn from these papers, subsequently combined in an article in the "Saturday Review," that I have definitely determined the existence in India of a peculiar tribe of gypsies, who are *par eminence* the Romanys of the East, and whose language is there what it is in England, the same in vocabulary, and the chief slang of the roads. This I claim as a discovery, having learned it from a Hindoo who had been himself a gypsy in his native land. Many writers have suggested the Jats, Banjars, and others as probable ancestors or type-givers of the race; but the existence of the ***Rom himself*** in India, bearing the distinctive name of Rom, has never before been set forth in any book or by any other writer. I have also given what may in reason be regarded as settling the immensely disputed origin of the word "Zingan," by the gypsies' own account of its etymology, which was beyond all question brought by them from India.

In addition to this I have given in a chapter certain conversations with men of note, such as Thomas Carlyle, Lord Lytton, Mr. Roebuck, and others, on gypsies; an account of the first and family names and personal characteristics of English and American Romanys, prepared for me by a very famous old gypsy; and finally a chapter on the "Shelta Thari," or Tinkers' Language, a very curious jargon or language, never mentioned before by any writer except Shakespeare. What this tongue may be, beyond the fact that it is purely Celtic, and that it does not seem to be identical with any other Celtic dialect, is unknown to me. I class it with the gypsy, because all who speak it are also acquainted with Romany.

For an attempt to set forth the tone or feeling in which the sketches are conceived, I refer the reader to the Introduction.

When I published my "English Gypsies and their Language," a reviewer declared that I "had added nothing to our" (that is, his) "knowledge on the subject." As it is always pleasant to meet with a man of superior information, I said nothing. And as I had carefully read everything ever printed on the Romany, and had given a very respectable collection of what was new to me as well as to all my Romany rye colleagues in Europe, I could only grieve to think that such treasures of learning should thus remain hidden in the brain of one who had never at any time or in any other way manifested the possession of any remarkable knowledge. Nobody can tell in this world what others may know, but I modestly suggest that what I have set forth in this work, on the origin of the gypsies, though it may be known to the reviewer in question, has at least never been set before the public by anybody but myself, and that it deserves further investigation. No account of the tribes of the East mentions the Rom or Trablus, and yet I have personally met with and thoroughly examined one of them. In like manner, the "Shelta Thari" has remained till the present day entirely unknown to all writers on either the languages or the nomadic people of Great Britain. If we are so ignorant of the wanderers among us, and at our very doors, it is not remarkable that we should be ignorant of those of India.

INTRODUCTION.

I have frequently been asked, "Why do you take an interest in gypsies?"

And it is not so easy to answer. Why, indeed? In Spain one who has been fascinated by them is called one of the *aficion*, or affection, or "fancy;" he is an *aficionado*, or affected unto them, and people there know perfectly what it means, for every Spaniard is at heart a Bohemian. He feels what a charm there is in a wandering life, in camping in lonely places, under old chestnut-trees, near towering cliffs, *al pasar del arroyo*, by the rivulets among the rocks. He thinks of the wine skin and wheaten cake when one was hungry on the road, of the mules and tinkling bells, the fire by night, and the *cigarito*, smoked till he fell asleep. Then he remembers the gypsies who came to the camp, and the black-eyed girl who told him his fortune, and all that followed in the rosy dawn and ever onward into starry night.

> "Y se alegre el alma llena
> De la luz de esos luceros."

And his heart is filled with rapture
At the light of those lights above.

This man understands it. So, too, does many an Englishman. But I cannot
tell you why. Why do I love to wander on the roads to hear the birds; to
see old church towers afar, rising over fringes of forest, a river and a
bridge in the foreground, and an ancient castle beyond, with a modern
village springing up about it, just as at the foot of the burg there lies
the falling trunk of an old tree, around which weeds and flowers are
springing up, nourished by its decay? Why love these better than
pictures, and with a more than fine-art feeling? Because on the roads,
among such scenes, between the hedge-rows and by the river, I find the
wanderers who properly inhabit not the houses but the scene, not a part
but the whole. These are the gypsies, who live like the birds and hares,
not of the house-born or the town-bred, but free and at home only with
nature.

I am at some pleasant watering-place, no matter where. Let it be
Torquay, or Ilfracombe, or Aberystwith, or Bath, or Bournemouth, or
Hastings. I find out what old churches, castles, towns, towers, manors,
lakes, forests, fairy-wells, or other charms of England lie within twenty
miles. Then I take my staff and sketch-book, and set out on my day's
pilgrimage. In the distance lie the lines of the shining sea, with ships
sailing to unknown lands. Those who live in them are the Bohemians of
the sea, homing while roaming, sleeping as they go, even as gypsies dwell
on wheels. And if you look wistfully at these ships far off and out at
sea with the sun upon their sails, and wonder what quaint mysteries of
life they hide, verily you are not far from being affected or elected
unto the Romany. And if, when you see the wild birds on the wing,
wending their way to the South, and wish that you could fly with
them,--anywhere, anywhere over the world and into adventure,--then you
are not far in spirit from the kingdom of Bohemia and its seven castles,

in the deep windows of which AEolian wind-harps sing forever.

Now, as you wander along, it may be that in the wood and by some grassy nook you will hear voices, and see the gleam of a red garment, and then find a man of the roads, with dusky wife and child. You speak one word, "Sarishan!" and you are introduced. These people are like birds and bees, they belong to out-of-doors and nature. If you can chirp or buzz a little in their language and know their ways, you will find out, as you sit in the forest, why he who loves green bushes and mossy rocks is glad to fly from cities, and likes to be free of the joyous citizenship of the roads, and everywhere at home in such boon company.

When I have been a stranger in a strange town, I have never gone out for a long walk without knowing that the chances were that I should meet within an hour some wanderer with whom I should have in common certain acquaintances. These be indeed humble folk, but with nature and summer walks they make me at home. In merrie England I could nowhere be a stranger if I would, and that with people who cannot read; and the English-born Romany rye, or gentleman speaking gypsy, would in like manner be everywhere at home in America. There was a gypsy family always roaming between Windsor and London, and the first words taught to their youngest child were "Romany rye!" and these it was trained to address to me. The little tot came up to me,--I had never heard her speak before,--a little brown-faced, black-eyed thing, and said, "How-do, Omany 'eye?" and great was the triumph and rejoicing and laughter of the mother and father and all the little tribe. To be familiar with these wanderers, who live by dale and down, is like having the bees come to you, as they did to the Dacian damsel, whose death they mourned; it is like the attraction of the wild deer to the fair Genevieve; or if you know them to be dangerous outlaws, as some are, it is like the affection of serpents and other wild things for those whom nature has made their friends, and who handle them without fear. They are human, but in their lives they are between man as he lives in houses and the bee and bird and fox, and I cannot help believing that those who have no sympathy with them have none for the forest and road, and cannot be rightly familiar with the witchery of wood and wold. There are many ladies and gentlemen who can well-nigh die of a sunset, and be enraptured with "bits" of color, and captured with scenes, and to whom all out-of-doors is as perfect as though it were painted by Millais, yet to whom the bee and bird and gypsy and red Indian ever remain in their true inner life strangers. And just as strange to them, in one sense, are the scenes in which these creatures dwell; for those who see in them only pictures, though they be by Claude and Turner, can never behold in them the fairy-land of childhood. Only in Ruysdael and Salvator Rosa and the great unconscious artists lurks the spell of the Romany, and this spell is unfelt by Mr. Cimabue Brown. The child and the gypsy have no words in which to express their sense of nature and its charm, but they have this sense, and there are very, very few who, acquiring culture, retain it. And it is gradually disappearing from the world, just as the old delicately sensuous, naive, picturesque type of woman's beauty--the perfection of natural beauty--is rapidly vanishing in every country, and being replaced by the mingled real and unreal attractiveness of "cleverness," intellect, and fashion. No doubt the newer tend to higher forms of culture, but it is not without pain that he who has been "in the spirit" in the old Sabbath of the soul, and in its quiet, solemn sunset, sees it all vanishing. It will all be gone in a few years. I doubt very much whether it will be possible for the most unaffectedly natural writer to preserve any of its hieroglyphics for future Champollions of sentiment to interpret. In the coming days, when man shall have developed new senses, and when the blessed sun himself shall perhaps have been supplanted by some tremendous electrical light, and the moon be expunged altogether as interfering with the new arrangements for gravity, there will doubtless be a new poetry, and art become to the very last degree self-conscious of its cleverness, artificial and impressional; yet even then weary scholars will sigh from time to time, as they read in our books of the ancient purple seas, and how the sun went down of old into cloud-land, gorgeous land, and then how all dreamed away into night!

Gypsies are the human types of this vanishing, direct love of nature, of this mute sense of rural romance, and of *al fresco* life, and he who does not recognize it in them, despite their rags and dishonesty, need not pretend to appreciate anything more in Callot's etchings than the skillful management of the needle and the acids. Truly they are but rags themselves; the last rags of the old romance which connected man with nature. Once romance was a splendid mediaeval drama, colored and gemmed with chivalry, minnesong, bandit-flashes, and waving plumes; now there remain but a few tatters. Yes, we were young and foolish then, but there are perishing with the wretched fragments of the red Indian tribes mythologies as beautiful as those of the Greek or Norseman; and there is also vanishing with the gypsy an unexpressed mythology, which those who are to come after us would gladly recover. Would we not have been pleased if one of the thousand Latin men of letters whose works have been preserved had told us how the old Etruscans, then still living in mountain villages, spoke and habited and customed? But oh that there had ever lived of old one man who, noting how feelings and sentiments changed, tried to so set forth the souls of his time that after-comers might understand what it was which inspired their art!

In the Sanskrit humorous romance of "Baital Pachisi," or King Vikram and the Vampire, twenty-five different and disconnected trifling stories serve collectively to illustrate in the most pointed manner the highest lesson of wisdom. In this book the gypsies, and the scenes which surround them, are intended to teach the lesson of freedom and nature. Never were such lessons more needed than at present. I do not say that culture is opposed to the perception of nature; I would show with all my power that the higher our culture the more we are really qualified to appreciate beauty and freedom. But gates must be opened for this, and unfortunately the gates as yet are very few, while Philistinism in every form makes it a business of closing every opening to the true fairy-land of delight.

The gypsy is one of many links which connect the simple feeling of nature with romance. During the Middle Ages thousands of such links and symbols united nature with religion. Thus Conrad von Wurtzburg tells in his "Goldene Schmiede" that the parrot which shines in fairest grass-green hue, and yet like common grass is never wet, sets forth the Virgin, who bestowed on man an endless spring, and yet remained unchanged. So the parrot and grass and green and shimmering light all blended in the ideal of the immortal Maid-Mother, and so the bird appears in pictures by Van Eyck and Durer. To me the gypsy-parrot and green grass in lonely lanes and the rain and sunshine all mingle to set forth the inexpressible purity and sweetness of the virgin parent, Nature. For the gypsy is parrot-like, a quaint pilferer, a rogue in grain as in green; for green was his favorite garb in olden time in England, as it is to-day in Germany, where he who breaks the Romany law may never dare on heath to wear that fatal fairy color.

These words are the key to the following book, in which I shall set forth a few sketches taken during my rambles among the Romany. The day is coming when there will be no more wild parrots nor wild wanderers, no wild nature, and certainly no gypsies. Within a very few years in the city of Philadelphia, the English sparrow, the very cit and cad of birds, has driven from the gardens all the wild, beautiful feathered creatures whom, as a boy, I knew. The fire-flashing scarlet tanager and the humming-bird, the yellow-bird, blue-bird, and golden oriole, are now almost forgotten, or unknown to city children. So the people of self-conscious culture and the mart and factory are banishing the wilder sort, and it is all right, and so it must be, and therewith *basta*. But as a London reviewer said when I asserted in a book that the child was perhaps born who would see the last gypsy, "Somehow we feel sorry for that child."

THE RUSSIAN GYPSIES.

It is, I believe, seldom observed that the world is so far from having quitted the romantic or sentimental for the purely scientific that, even in science itself, whatever is best set forth owes half its charm to something delicately and distantly reflected from the forbidden land of fancy. The greatest reasoners and writers on the driest topics are still "genial," because no man ever yet had true genius who did not feel the inspiration of poetry, or mystery, or at least of the unusual. We are not rid of the marvelous or curious, and, if we have not yet a science of curiosities, it is apparently because it lies for the present distributed about among the other sciences, just as in small museums illuminated manuscripts are to be found in happy family union with stuffed birds or minerals, and with watches and snuff-boxes, once the property of their late majesties the Georges. Until such a science is formed, the new one of ethnology may appropriately serve for it, since it of all presents most attraction to him who is politely called the general reader, but who should in truth be called the man who reads the most for mere amusement. For Ethnology deals with such delightful material as primeval kumbo-cephalic skulls, and appears to her votaries arrayed, not in silk attire, but in strange fragments of leather from ancient Irish graves, or in cloth from Lacustrine villages. She glitters with the quaint jewelry of the first Italian race, whose ghosts, if they wail over the "find," "speak in a language man knows no more." She charms us with etchings or scratchings of mammoths on mammoth-bone, and invites us to explore mysterious caves, to picnic among megalithic monuments, and speculate on pictured Scottish stones. In short, she engages man to investigate his ancestry, a pursuit which presents charms even to the illiterate, and asks us to find out facts concerning works of art which have interested everybody in every age.

Ad interim, before the science of curiosities is segregated from that
of ethnology, I may observe that one of the marvels in the latter is
that, among all the subdivisions of the human race, there are only two
which have been, apparently from their beginning, set apart, marked and
cosmopolite, ever living among others, and yet reserved unto themselves.
These are the Jew and the gypsy. From time whereof history hath naught
to the contrary, the Jew was, as he himself holds in simple faith, the
first man. Red Earth, Adam, was a Jew, and the old claim to be a
peculiar people has been curiously confirmed by the extraordinary genius
and influence of the race, and by their boundless wanderings. Go where
we may, we find the Jew--has any other wandered so far?

Yes, one. For wherever Jew has gone, there, too, we find the gypsy. The
Jew may be more ancient, but even the authentic origin of the Romany is
lost in ancient Aryan record, and, strictly speaking, his is a
prehistoric caste. Among the hundred and fifty wandering tribes of India
and Persia, some of them Turanian, some Aryan, and others mixed, it is of
course difficult to identify the exact origin of the European gypsy. One
thing we know: that from the tenth to the twelfth century, and probably
much later on, India threw out from her northern half a vast multitude of
very troublesome indwellers. What with Buddhist, Brahman, and Mohammedan
wars,--invaders outlawing invaded,--the number of out-*castes* became
alarmingly great. To these the Jats, who, according to Captain Burton,
constituted the main stock of our gypsies, contributed perhaps half their
entire nation. Excommunication among the Indian professors of
transcendental benevolence meant social death and inconceivable cruelty.
Now there are many historical indications that these outcasts, before
leaving India, became gypsies, which was the most natural thing in a
country where such classes had already existed in very great numbers from
early times. And from one of the lowest castes, which still exists in
India, and is known as the Dom, {19} the emigrants to the West probably

derived their name and several characteristics. The Dom burns the dead, handles corpses, skins beasts, and performs other functions, all of which were appropriated by, and became peculiar to, gypsies in several countries in Europe, notably in Denmark and Holland, for several centuries after their arrival there. The Dom of the present day also sells baskets, and wanders with a tent; he is altogether gypsy. It is remarkable that he, living in a hot climate, drinks ardent spirits to excess, being by no means a "temperate Hindoo," and that even in extreme old age his hair seldom turns white, which is a noted peculiarity among our own gypsies of pure blood. I know and have often seen a gypsy woman, nearly a hundred years old, whose curling hair is black, or hardly perceptibly changed. It is extremely probable that the Dom, mentioned as a caste even in the Shastras, gave the name to the Rom. The Dom calls his wife a Domni, and being a Dom is "Domnipana." In English gypsy, the same words are expressed by *Rom*, *romni*, and *romnipen*. D, be it observed, very often changes to *r* in its transfer from Hindoo to Romany. Thus *doi*, "a wooden spoon," becomes in gypsy *roi*, a term known to every tinker in London. But, while this was probably the origin of the word Rom, there were subsequent reasons for its continuance. Among the Cophts, who were more abundant in Egypt when the first gypsies went there, the word for man is *romi*, and after leaving Greece and the Levant, or *Rum*, it would be natural for the wanderers to be called *Rumi*. But the Dom was in all probability the parent stock of the gypsy race, though the latter received vast accessions from many other sources. I call attention to this, since it has always been held, and sensibly enough, that the mere fact of the gypsies speaking Hindi-Persian, or the oldest type of Urdu, including many Sanskrit terms, does not prove an Indian or Aryan origin, any more than the English spoken by American negroes proves a Saxon descent. But if the Rom can be identified with the Dom--and the circumstantial evidence, it must be admitted, is very strong--but little remains to seek, since, according to the Shastras, the Doms are Hindoo.

Among the tribes whose union formed the European gypsy was, in all probability, that of the *Nats*, consisting of singing and dancing girls and male musicians and acrobats. Of these, we are told that not less than ten thousand lute-players and minstrels, under the name of *Luri*, were once sent to Persia as a present to a king, whose land was then without music or song. This word *Luri* is still preserved. The saddle-makers and leather-workers of Persia are called Tsingani; they are, in their way, low caste, and a kind of gypsy, and it is supposed that from them are possibly derived the names Zingan, Zigeuner, Zingaro, etc., by which gypsies are known in so many lands. From Mr. Arnold's late work on "Persia," the reader may learn that the *Eeli*, who constitute the majority of the inhabitants of the southern portion of that country, are Aryan nomads, and apparently gypsies. There are also in India the Banjari, or wandering merchants, and many other tribes, all spoken of as gypsies by those who know them.

As regards the great admixture of Persian with Hindi in good Romany, it is quite unmistakable, though I can recall no writer who has attached sufficient importance to a fact which identifies gypsies with what is almost preeminently the land of gypsies. I once had the pleasure of taking a Nile journey in company with Prince S---, a Persian, and in most cases, when I asked my friend what this or that gypsy word meant, he gave me its correct meaning, after a little thought, and then added, in his imperfect English, "What for you want to know such word?--that *old* word--that no more used. Only common people--old peasant-woman--use that word--*gentleman* no want to know him." But I did want to know "him" very much. I can remember that one night, when our *bon prince* had thus held forth, we had dancing girls, or Almeh, on board, and one was very young and pretty. I was told that she was gypsy, but she spoke no Romany. Yet her panther eyes and serpent smile and *beaute du diable* were not Egyptian, but of the Indian, *kalo-ratt*,--the dark blood, which, once known, is known forever. I forgot her, however, for a long time, until I went to Moscow, when she was recalled by dancing and smiles, of which I will speak anon.

I was sitting one day by the Thames, in a gypsy tent, when its master, Joshua Cooper, now dead, pointing to a swan, asked me for its name in gypsy. I replied, "*Boro pappin*."

"No, *rya*. *Boro pappin* is 'a big goose.' *Sakku* is the real gypsy word. It is very old, and very few Romany know it."

A few days after, when my Persian friend was dining with me at the Langham Hotel, I asked him if he knew what Sakku meant. By way of reply, he, not being able to recall the English word, waved his arms in wonderful pantomime, indicating some enormous winged creature; and then, looking into the distance, and pointing as if to some far-vanishing object, as boys do when they declaim Bryant's address "To a Water-Fowl," said,--

"Sakku--one ver' big bird, like one *swen*--but he *not* swen. He like the man who carry too much water up-stairs {22} his head in Constantinople. That bird all same that man. He *sakkia* all same wheel that you see get water up-stairs in Egypt."

This was explanatory, but far from satisfactory. The prince, however, was mindful of me, and the next day I received from the Persian embassy the word elegantly written in Persian, with the translation, "*a pelican*." Then it was all clear enough, for the pelican bears water in the bag under its bill. When the gypsies came to Europe they named animals after those which resembled them in Asia. A dog they called *juckal*, from a jackal, and a swan *sakku*, or pelican, because it so greatly resembles it. The Hindoo *bandarus*, or monkey, they have changed to *bombaros*, but why Tom Cooper should declare that it is *pugasah*, or *pukkus-asa*, I do not know. {23} As little can I conjecture the meaning of the prefix *mod*, or *mode*, which I learned on the road near Weymouth from a very ancient tinker, a man so battered, tattered, seamed, riven, and wrinkled that he looked like a petrifaction. He had so bad a barrow, or wheel, that I wondered what he could do with it, and regarded him as the very poorest man I had ever seen in England, until his mate came up, an *alter ego*, so excellent in antiquity, wrinkles, knobbiness, and rags that he surpassed the vagabond pictures not only of Callot, Dore, and Goya, but even the unknown Spanish maker of a picture which I met with not long since for sale, and which for infinite poverty defied anything I ever saw on canvas. These poor men, who seemed at first amazed that I should speak to them at all, when I spoke Romany at once called me "brother." When I asked the younger his name, he sank his voice to a whisper, and, with a furtive air, said,--

"*Kamlo*,--Lovel, you know."

"What do you call yourself in the way of business?" I asked. "*Katsamengro*, I suppose."

Now *Katsamengro* means scissors-master.

"That is a very good word. But *chivo* is deeper."

"*Chivo* means a knife-man?"

"Yes. But the deepest of all, master, is *Modangarengro*. For you see that the right word for coals isn't *wongur*, as Romanys generally say, but *Angara*."

Now *angara*, as Pott and Benfey indicate, is pure Sanskrit for coals, and *angarengro* is a worker in coals, but what *mod* means I know not, and should be glad to be told.

I think it will be found difficult to identify the European gypsy with any one stock of the wandering races of India. Among those who left that country were men of different castes and different color, varying from the pure northern invader to the negro-like southern Indian. In the Danubian principalities there are at the present day three kinds of gypsies: one very dark and barbarous, another light brown and more intelligent, and the third, or *elite*, of yellow-pine complexion, as American boys characterize the hue of quadroons. Even in England there are straight-haired and curly-haired Romanys, the two indicating not a difference resulting from white admixture, but entirely different original stocks.

It will, I trust, be admitted, even from these remarks, that Romanology, or that subdivision of ethnology which treats of gypsies, is both practical and curious. It deals with the only race except the Jew, which has penetrated into every village which European civilization has ever touched. He who speaks Romany need be a stranger in few lands, for on every road in Europe and America, in Western Asia, and even in Northern Africa, he will meet those with whom a very few words may at once establish a peculiar understanding. For, of all things believed in by this widely spread brotherhood, the chief is this,--that he who knows the *jib*, or language, knows the ways, and that no one ever attained these without treading strange paths, and threading mysteries unknown to the Gorgios, or Philistines. And if he who speaks wears a good coat, and appears a gentleman, let him rest assured that he will receive the greeting which all poor relations in all lands extend to those of their kin who have risen in life. Some of them, it is true, manifest the winsome affection which is based on great expectations, a sentiment largely developed among British gypsies; but others are honestly proud that a gentleman is not ashamed of them. Of this latter class were the musical gypsies, whom I met in Russia during the winter of 1876 and 1877, and some of them again in Paris during the Exposition of 1878.

ST. PETERSBURG.

There are gypsies and gypsies in the world, for there are the wanderers
on the roads and the secret dwellers in towns; but even among the
aficionados, or Romany ryes, by whom I mean those scholars who are fond
of studying life and language from the people themselves, very few have
dreamed that there exist communities of gentlemanly and lady-like gypsies
of art, like the Bohemians of Murger and George Sand, but differing from
them in being real "Bohemians" by race. I confess that it had never
occurred to me that there was anywhere in Europe, at the present day,
least of all in the heart of great and wealthy cities, a class or caste
devoted entirely to art, well-to-do or even rich, refined in manners,
living in comfortable homes, the women dressing elegantly; and yet with
all this obliged to live by law, as did the Jews once, in Ghettos or in a
certain street, and regarded as outcasts and *cagots*. I had heard there
were gypsies in Russian cities, and expected to find them like the
kerengri of England or Germany,--house-dwellers somewhat reformed from
vagabondage, but still reckless semi-outlaws, full of tricks and lies; in
a word, *gypsies*, as the world understands the term. And I certainly
anticipated in Russia something *queer*,--the gentleman who speaks Romany
seldom fails to achieve at least that, whenever he gets into an unbroken
haunt, an unhunted forest, where the Romany rye is unknown,--but nothing
like what I really found. A recent writer on Russia {26} speaks with
great contempt of these musical Romanys, their girls attired in dresses
by Worth, as compared with the free wild outlaws of the steppes, who,
with dark, ineffable glances, meaning nothing more than a wild-cat's,
steal poultry, and who, wrapped in dirty sheep-skins, proudly call
themselves *Mi dvorane Polaivii*, Lords of the Waste. The gypsies of

Moscow, who appeared to me the most interesting I have ever met, because most remote from the Surrey ideal, seemed to Mr. Johnstone to be a kind of second-rate Romanys or gypsies, gypsified for exhibition, like Mr. Barnum's negro minstrel, who, though black as a coal by nature, was requested to put on burnt cork and a wig, that the audience might realize that they were getting a thoroughly good imitation. Mr. Johnstone's own words are that a gypsy maiden in a long *queue*, "which perhaps came from Worth," is "horrible," "*corruptio optimi pessima est*;" and he further compares such a damsel to a negro with a cocked hat and spurs. As the only negro thus arrayed who presents himself to my memory was one who lay dead on the battle-field in Tennessee, after one of the bravest resistances in history, and in which he and his men, not having moved, were extended in "stark, serried lines" ("ten cart-loads of dead niggers," said a man to me who helped to bury them), I may be excused for not seeing the wit of the comparison. As for the gypsies of Moscow, I can only say that, after meeting them in public, and penetrating to their homes, where I was received as one of themselves, even as a Romany, I found that this opinion of them was erroneous, and that they were altogether original in spite of being clean, deeply interesting although honest, and a quite attractive class in most respects, notwithstanding their ability to read and write. Against Mr. Johnstone's impressions, I may set the straightforward and simple result of the experiences of Mr. W. R. Ralston. "The gypsies of Moscow," he says, "are justly celebrated for their picturesqueness and for their wonderful capacity for music. All who have heard their women sing are enthusiastic about the weird witchery of the performance."

When I arrived in St. Petersburg, one of my first inquiries was for gypsies. To my astonishment, they were hard to find. They are not allowed to live in the city; and I was told that the correct and proper way to see them would be to go at night to certain *cafes*, half an hour's sleigh-ride from the town, and listen to their concerts. What I wanted, however, was not a concert, but a conversation; not gypsies on exhibition, but gypsies at home,--and everybody seemed to be of the opinion that those of "Samarcand" and "Dorot" were entirely got up for effect. In fact, I heard the opinion hazarded that, even if they spoke Romany, I might depend upon it they had acquired it simply to deceive. One gentleman, who had, however, been much with them in other days, assured me that they were of pure blood, and had an inherited language of their own. "But," he added, "I am sure you will not understand it. You may be able to talk with those in England, but not with ours, because there is not a single word in their language which resembles anything in English, German, French, Latin, Greek, or Italian. I can only recall," he added, "one phrase. I don't know what it means, and I think it will puzzle you. It is *me kamava tut*."

If I experienced internal laughter at hearing this it was for a good reason, which I can illustrate by an anecdote: "I have often observed, when I lived in China," said Mr. Hoffman Atkinson, author of "A Vocabulary of the Yokohama Dialect," "that most young men, particularly the gay and handsome ones, generally asked me, about the third day after their arrival in the country, the meaning of the Pidgin-English phrase, 'You makee too muchee lov-lov-pidgin.' Investigation always established the fact that the inquirer had heard it from 'a pretty China girl.' Now *lov-pidgin* means love, and *me kamava tut* is perfectly good gypsy anywhere for 'I love you;' and a very soft expression it is, recalling *kama-deva*, the Indian Cupid, whose bow is strung with bees, and whose name has two strings to it, since it means, both in gypsy and Sanskrit, Love-God, or the god of love. 'It's *kama-duvel*, you know, *rya*, if you put it as it ought to be,' said Old Windsor Froggie to me once; 'but I think that Kama-*devil* would by rights come nearer to it, if Cupid is what you mean.'"

I referred the gypsy difficulty to a Russian gentleman of high position, to whose kindness I had been greatly indebted while in St. Petersburg. He laughed.

"Come with me to-morrow night to the *cafes*, and see the gypsies; I know them well, and can promise that you shall talk with them as much as you like. Once, in Moscow, I got together all in the town--perhaps a hundred and fifty--to entertain the American minister, Curtin. That was a very hard thing to do,--there was so much professional jealousy among them, and so many quarrels. Would you have believed it?"

I thought of the feuds between sundry sturdy Romanys in England, and felt that I could suppose such a thing, without dangerously stretching my faith, and I began to believe in Russian gypsies.

"Well, then, I shall call for you to-morrow night with a *troika*; I will come early,--at ten. They never begin to sing before company arrive at eleven, so that you will have half an hour to talk to them."

It is on record that the day on which the general gave me this kind invitation was the coldest known in St. Petersburg for thirty years, the thermometer having stood, or rather having lain down and groveled that morning at 40 degrees below zero, Fahr. At the appointed hour the *troika*, or three-horse sleigh, was before the Hotel d'Europe. It was, indeed, an arctic night, but, well wrapped in fur-lined *shubas*, with immense capes which fall to the elbow or rise far above the head, as required, and wearing fur caps and fur-lined gloves, we felt no cold. The beard of our *istvostshik*, or driver, was a great mass of ice, giving him the appearance of an exceedingly hoary youth, and his small horses, being very shaggy and thoroughly frosted, looked in the darkness like immense polar bears. If the general and myself could only have been considered as gifts of the slightest value to anybody, I should have regarded our turn-out, with the driver in his sheep-skin coat, as coming within a miracle of resemblance to that of Santa Claus, the American Father Christmas.

On, at a tremendous pace, over the snow, which gave out under our runners
that crunching, iron sound only heard when the thermometer touches zero.
There is a peculiar fascination about the *troika*, and the sweetest,
saddest melody and most plaintive song of Russia belong to it.

THE TROIKA.

Vot y'dit troika udalaiya.

> Hear ye the troika-bell a-ringing,
> And see the peasant driver there?
> Hear ye the mournful song he's singing,
> Like distant tolling through the air?
>
> "O eyes, blue eyes, to me so lonely,
> O eyes--alas!--ye give me pain;
> O eyes, that once looked at me only,
> I ne'er shall see your like again.
>
> "Farewell, my darling, now in heaven,
> And still the heaven of my soul;
> Farewell, thou father town, O Moscow,
> Where I have left my life, my all!"
>
> And ever at the rein still straining,
> One backward glance the driver gave;
> Sees but once more a green low hillock,
> Sees but once more his loved one's grave.

"*Stoi*!"--Halt! We stopped at a stylish-looking building, entered a

hall, left our *skubas*, and I heard the general ask, "Are the gypsies
here?" An affirmative being given, we entered a large room, and there,
sure enough, stood six or eight girls and two men, all very well dressed,
and all unmistakably Romany, though smaller and of much slighter or more
delicate frame than the powerful gypsy "travelers" of England. In an
instant every pair of great, wild eyes was fixed on me. The general was
in every way a more striking figure, but I was manifestly a fresh
stranger, who knew nothing of the country, and certainly nothing of
gypsies or gypsydom. Such a verdant visitor is always most interesting.
It was not by any means my first reception of the kind, and, as I
reviewed at a glance the whole party, I said within myself:--

"Wait an instant, you black snakes, and I will give you something to make
you stare."

This promise I kept, when a young man, who looked like a handsome light
Hindoo, stepped up and addressed me in Russian. I looked long and
steadily at him before I spoke, and then said:--

"*Latcho divvus prala*!" (Good day, brother.)

"What is *that*?" he exclaimed, startled.

"*Tu jines latcho adosta*." (You know very well.) And then, with the
expression in his face of a man who has been familiarly addressed by a
brazen statue, or asked by a new-born babe, "What o'clock is it?" but
with great joy, he cried:--

"*Romanichal*!"

In an instant they were all around me, marveling greatly, and earnestly
expressing their marvel, at what new species of gypsy I might be; being
in this quite unlike those of England, who, even when they are astonished

"out of their senses" at being addressed in Romany by a gentleman, make the most red-Indian efforts to conceal their amazement. But I speedily found that these Russian gypsies were as unaffected and child-like as they were gentle in manner, and that they compared with our own prize-fighting, sturdy-begging, always-suspecting Romany roughs and *rufianas* as a delicate greyhound might compare with a very shrewd old bull-dog, trained by an unusually "fly" tramp.

That the girls were first to the fore in questioning me will be doubted by no one. But we had great trouble in effecting a mutual understanding. Their Romany was full of Russian; their pronunciation puzzled me; they "bit off their words," and used many in a strange or false sense. Yet, notwithstanding this, I contrived to converse pretty readily with the men,--very readily with the captain, a man as dark as Ben Lee, to those who know Benjamin, or as mahogany, to those who know him not. But with the women it was very difficult to converse. There is a theory current that women have a specialty of tact and readiness in understanding a foreigner, or in making themselves understood; it may be so with cultivated ladies, but it is my experience that, among the uneducated, men have a monopoly of such quick intelligence. In order fully to convince them that we really had a tongue in common, I repeated perhaps a hundred nouns, giving, for instance, the names of various parts of the body, of articles of apparel and objects in the room, and I believe that we did not find a single word which, when pronounced distinctly by itself, was not intelligible to us all. I had left in London a Russo-Romany vocabulary, once published in "The Asiatic Magazine," and I had met with Bohtlinghk's article on the dialect, as well as specimens of it in the works of Pott and Miklosich, but had unfortunately learned nothing of it from them. I soon found, however, that I knew a great many more gypsy words than did my new friends, and that our English Romany far excels the Russian in *copia verborum*.

"But I must sit down." I observed on this and other occasions that

Russian gypsies are very naif. And as it is in human nature to prefer
sitting by a pretty girl, these Slavonian Romanys so arrange it according
to the principles of natural selection--or natural politeness--that, when
a stranger is in their gates, the two prettiest girls in their possession
sit at his right and left, the two less attractive next again, *et
seriatim*. So at once a damsel of comely mien, arrayed in black silk
attire, of faultless elegance, cried to me, pointing to a chair by her
side, "*Bersh tu alay*, *rya*!" (Sit down, sir),--a phrase which would
be perfectly intelligible to any Romany in England. I admit that there
was another damsel, who is generally regarded by most people as the true
gypsy belle of the party, who did not sit by me. But, as the one who had
"voted herself into the chair," by my side, was more to my liking, being
the most intelligent and most gypsy, I had good cause to rejoice.

I was astonished at the sensible curiosity as to gypsy life in other
lands which was displayed, and at the questions asked. I really doubt if
I ever met with an English gypsy who cared a farthing to know anything
about his race as it exists in foreign countries, or whence it came.
Once, and once only, I thought I had interested White George, at East
Moulsey, in an account of Egypt, and the small number of Romanys there;
but his only question was to the effect that, if there were so few
gypsies in Egypt, wouldn't it be a good place for him to go to sell
baskets? These of Russia, however, asked all kinds of questions about
the manners and customs of their congeners, and were pleased when they
recognized familiar traits. And every gypsyism, whether of word or way,
was greeted with delighted laughter. In one thing I noted a radical
difference between these gypsies and those of the rest of Europe and of
America. There was none of that continually assumed mystery and Romany
freemasonry, of superior occult knowledge and "deep" information, which
is often carried to the depths of absurdity and to the height of humbug.
I say this advisedly, since, however much it may give charm to a novel or
play, it is a serious impediment to a philologist. Let me give an
illustration.

Once, during the evening, these Russian gypsies were anxious to know if there were any books in their language. Now I have no doubt that Dr. Bath Smart, or Prof. E. H. Palmer, or any other of the initiated, will perfectly understand when I say that by mere force of habit I shivered and evaded the question. When a gentleman who manifests a knowledge of Romany among gypsies in England is suspected of "dixonary" studies, it amounts to *lasciate ogni speranza*,--give up all hope of learning any more.

"I'm glad to see you here, *rya*, in my tent," said the before-mentioned Ben Lee to me one night, in camp near Weybridge, "because I've heard, and I know, you didn't pick up *your* Romany out of books."

The silly dread, the hatred, the childish antipathy, real or affected, but always ridiculous, which is felt in England, not only among gypsies, but even by many gentlemen scholars, to having the Romany language published is indescribable. Vambery was not more averse to show a lead pencil among Tartars than I am to take notes of words among strange English gypsies. I might have spared myself any annoyance from such a source among the Russian Romanys. They had not heard of Mr. George Borrow; nor were there ugly stories current among them to the effect that Dr. Smart and Prof. E. H. Palmer had published works, the direct result of which would be to facilitate their little paths to the jail, the gallows, and the grave.

"Would we hear some singing?" We were ready, and for the first time in my life I listened to the long-anticipated, far-famed magical melody of Russian gypsies. And what was it like? May I preface my reply to the reader with the remark that there are, roughly speaking, two kinds of music in the world,--the wild and the tame,--and the rarest of human beings is he who can appreciate both. Only one such man ever wrote a book, and his *nomen et omen* is Engel, like that of the little English slaves who were ***non Angli***, ***sed angeli***. I have in my time been deeply moved by the choruses of Nubian boatmen; I have listened with great pleasure to Chinese and Japanese music,--Ole Bull once told me he had done the same; I have delighted by the hour in Arab songs; and I have felt the charm of our red-Indian music. If this seems absurd to those who characterize all such sound and song as "caterwauling," let me remind the reader that in all Europe there is not one man fonder of music than an average Arab, a Chinese, or a red Indian; for any of these people, as I have seen and know, will sit twelve or fifteen hours, without the least weariness, listening to what cultivated Europeans all consider as a mere charivari. When London gladly endures fifteen-hour concerts, composed of ***morceaux*** by Wagner, Chopin, and Liszt, I will believe that art can charm as much as nature.

The medium point of intelligence in this puzzle may be found in the extraordinary fascination which many find in the monotonous tum-tum of the banjo, and which reappears, somewhat refined, or at least somewhat Frenchified, in the ***Bamboula*** and other Creole airs. Thence, in an ascending series, but connected with it, we have old Spanish melodies, then the Arabic, and here we finally cross the threshold into mystery, midnight, and "caterwauling." I do not know that I can explain the fact why the more "barbarous" music is, the more it is beloved of man; but I think that the principle of the ***refrain***, or repetition in music, which as yet governs all decorative art and which Mr. Whistler and others are endeavoring desperately to destroy, acts in music as a sort of animal magnetism or abstraction, ending in an ***extase***. As for the fascination which such wild melodies exert, it is beyond description. The most enraptured audience I ever saw in my life was at a Coptic wedding in Cairo, where one hundred and fifty guests listened, from seven P.M. till three A.M., and Heaven knows how much later, to what a European would call absolute jangling, yelping, and howling.

The real medium, however, between what I have, for want of better words, called wild and tame music exists only in that of the Russian gypsies. These artists, with wonderful tact and untaught skill, have succeeded, in all their songs, in combining the mysterious and maddening charm of the true, wild Eastern music with that of regular and simple melody, intelligible to every Western ear. I have never listened to the singing or playing of any distinguished artist--and certainly never of any far-famed amateur--without realizing that neither words nor melody was of the least importance, but that the man's manner of performance or display was everything. Now, in enjoying gypsy singing, one feels at once as if the vocalists had entirely forgotten self, and were carried away by the bewildering beauty of the air and the charm of the words. There is no self-consciousness, no vanity,--all is real. The listener feels as if he were a performer; the performer is an enraptured listener. There is no soulless "art for the sake of art," but art for direct pleasure.

"We intend to sing only Romany for *you*, *rya*," said the young lady to my left, "and you will hear our real gypsy airs. The *Gaji* [Russians] often ask for songs in our language, and don't get them. But you are a Romanichal, and when you go home, far over the *baro kalo pani* [the broad black water, that is, the ocean], you shall tell the Romany how we can sing. Listen!"

And I listened to the strangest, wildest, and sweetest singing I ever had heard,--the singing of Lurleis, of sirens, of witches. First, one damsel, with an exquisitely clear, firm voice, began to sing a verse of a love-ballad, and as it approached the end the chorus stole in, softly and unperceived, but with exquisite skill, until, in a few seconds, the summer breeze, murmuring melody over a rippling lake, seemed changed to a midnight tempest, roaring over a stormy sea, in which the *basso* of the *kalo shureskro* (the black captain) pealed like thunder. Just as it died away a second girl took up the melody, very sweetly, but with a little more excitement,--it was like a gleam of moonlight on the still agitated waters, a strange contralto witch-gleam; and then again the chorus and the storm; and then another solo yet sweeter, sadder, and stranger,--the movement continually increasing, until all was fast, and wild, and mad,--a locomotive quickstep, and then a sudden silence--sunlight--the storm had blown away.

Nothing on earth is so like magic and elfin-work as when women burst forth into improvised melody. The bird only "sings as his bill grew," or what he learned from the elders; yet when you hear birds singing in woodland green, throwing out to God or the fairies irrepressible floods of what seems like audible sunshine, so well does it match with summer's light, you think it is wonderful. It is mostly when you forget the long training of the prima donna, in her ease and apparent naturalness, that her song is sweetest. But there is a charm, which was well known of old, though we know it not to-day, which was practiced by the bards and believed in by their historians. It was the feeling that the song was born of the moment; that it came with the air, gushing and fresh from the soul. In reading the strange stories of the professional bards and scalds and minstrels of the early Middle Age, one is constantly bewildered at the feats of off-hand composition which were exacted of the poets among Celts or Norsemen. And it is evident enough that in some mysterious way these singers knew how to put strange pressure on the Muse, and squeeze strains out of her in a manner which would have been impossible at present.

Yet it lingers here and there on earth among wild, strange people,--this art of making melody at will. I first heard it among Nubian boatmen on the Nile. It was as manifest that it was composed during the making as that the singers were unconscious of their power. One sung at first what may have been a well-known verse. While singing, another voice stole in, and yet another, softly as shadows steal into twilight; and ere I knew it all were in a great chorus, which fell away as mysteriously, to become duos, trios,--changing in melody in strange, sweet, fitful wise, as the faces seen in the golden cloud in the visioned aureole of God blend, separate, burn, and fade away ever into fresher glory and tints incarnadined.

Miss C. F. Gordon Cumming, after informing us that "it is utterly impossible to give you the faintest shadow of an idea of the fascination of Tahitian *himenes*," proceeds, as men in general and women in particular invariably do, to give what the writer really believes is a very good description indeed. 'T is ever thus, and thus 't will ever be, and the description of these songs is so good that any person gifted with imagination or poetry cannot fail to smile at the preceding disavowal of her ability to give an idea.

These *himenes* are not--and here such of my too expectant young lady-readers as are careless in spelling will be sadly disappointed--in any way connected with weddings. They are simply the natural music of Tahiti, or strange and beautiful part-songs. "Nothing you have ever heard in any other country," says our writer, "bears the slightest resemblance to these wild, exquisite glees, faultless in time and harmony, though apparently each singer introduces any variations which may occur to him or to her. Very often there is no leader, and apparently all sing according to their own sweet will. One voice commences; it may be that of an old native, with genuine native words (the meaning of which we had better not inquire), or it may be with a Scriptural story, versified and sung to an air originally from Europe, but so completely Tahitianized that no mortal could recognize it, which is all in its favor, for the wild melodies of this isle are beyond measure fascinating.

"After one clause of solo, another strikes in--here, there, everywhere--in harmonious chorus. It seems as if one section devoted themselves to pouring forth a rippling torrent of 'Ra, ra, ra--ra--ra!' while others burst into a flood of 'La, la--la--la--la!' Some confine their care to sound a deep, booming bass in a long-continued drone,

somewhat suggestive (to my appreciative Highland ear) of our own
bagpipes. Here and there high falsetto notes strike in, varied from
verse to verse, and then the choruses of La and Ra come bubbling in
liquid melody, while the voices of the principal singers now join in
unison, now diverge as widely as it is possible for them to do, but all
combine to produce the quaintest, most melodious, rippling glee that ever
was heard."

This is the ***himene***; such the singing which I heard in Egypt in a more
regular form; but it was exactly as the writer so admirably sets it forth
(and your description, my lady traveler, is, despite your disavowal,
quite perfect and a ***himene*** of itself) that I heard the gypsy girls of
St. Petersburg and of Moscow sing. For, after a time, becoming jolly as
flies, first one voice began with "La, la, la--la--la!" to an unnamed,
unnamable, charming melody, into which went and came other voices, some
bringing one verse or no verse, in unison or alone, the least expected
doing what was most awaited, which was to surprise us and call forth gay
peals of happy laughter, while the "La, la, la--la--la!" was kept up
continuously, like an accompaniment. And still the voices, basso,
soprano, tenor, baritone, contralto, rose and fell, the moment's
inspiration telling how, till at last all blended in a locomotive-paced
La, and in a final roar of laughter it ended.

I could not realize at the time how much this exquisite part-singing was
extemporized. The sound of it rung in my head--I assure you, reader, it
rings there yet when I think of it--like a magic bell. Another day,
however, when I begged for a repetition of it, the girls could recall
nothing of it. They could start it again on any air to the unending
strain of "La--la--la;" but ***the*** "La--la--la" of the previous evening
was ***avec les neiges d'antan***, with the smoke of yesterday's fire, with
the perfume and bird-songs. "La, la, la--la--la!"

In Arab singing, such effects are applied simply to set forth erotomania;

in negro minstrelsy, they are degraded to the lowest humor; in higher
European music, when employed, they simply illustrate the skill of
composer and musician. The spirit of gypsy singing recalled by its
method and sweetness that of the Nubian boatmen, but in its *general*
effect I could think only of those strange fits of excitement which
thrill the red Indian and make him burst into song. The Abbe Domenech
{42} has observed that the American savage pays attention to every sound
that strikes upon his ear when the leaves, softly shaken by the evening
breeze, seem to sigh through the air, or when the tempest, bursting forth
with fury, shakes the gigantic trees that crack like reeds. "The
chirping of the birds, the cry of the wild beasts, in a word, all those
sweet, grave, or imposing voices that animate the wilderness, are so many
musical lessons, which he easily remembers." In illustration of this,
the missionary describes the singing of a Chippewa chief, and its wild
inspiration, in a manner which vividly illustrates all music of the class
of which I write.

"It was," he says, "during one of those long winter nights, so monotonous
and so wearisome in the woods. We were in a wigwam, which afforded us
but miserable shelter from the inclemency of the season. The storm raged
without; the tempest roared in the open country; the wind blew with
violence, and whistled through the fissures of the cabin; the rain fell
in torrents, and prevented us from continuing our route. Our host was an
Indian, with sparkling and intelligent eyes, clad with a certain
elegance, and wrapped majestically in a large fur cloak. Seated close to
the fire, which cast a reddish gleam through the interior of his wigwam,
he felt himself all at once seized with an irresistible desire to imitate
the convulsions of nature, and to sing his impressions. So, taking hold
of a drum which hung near his bed, he beat a slight rolling, resembling
the distant sounds of an approaching storm; then, raising his voice to a
shrill treble, which he knew how to soften when he pleased, he imitated
the whistling of the air, the creaking of the branches dashing against
one another, and the particular noise produced by dead leaves when

accumulated in compact masses on the ground. By degrees the rollings of the drum became more frequent and louder, the chants more sonorous and shrill, and at last our Indian shrieked, howled, and roared in a most frightful manner; he struggled and struck his instrument with extraordinary rapidity. It was a real tempest, to which nothing was wanting, not even the distant howling of the dogs, nor the bellowing of the affrighted buffaloes."

I have observed the same musical inspiration of a storm upon Arabs, who, during their singing, also accompanied themselves on a drum. I once spent two weeks in a Mediterranean steamboat, on board of which were more than two hundred pilgrims, for the greater part wild Bedouins, going to Mecca. They had a minstrel who sang and played on the *darabuka*, or earthenware drum, and he was aided by another with a simple *nai*, or reed-whistle; the same orchestra, in fact, which is in universal use among all red Indians. To these performers the pilgrims listened with indescribable pleasure; and I soon found that they regarded me favorably because I did the same, being, of course, the only Frank on board who paid any attention to the singing--or any money for it. But it was at night and during storms that the spirit of music always seemed to be strongest on the Arabs, and then, amid roaring of wild waters and thundering, and in dense darkness, the rolling of the drum and the strange, bewildering ballads never ceased. It was the very counterpart, in all respects, of the Chippewa storm song.

After the first gypsy lyric there came another, to which the captain especially directed my attention as being what Sam Petulengro calls "reg'lar Romany." It was ***I rakli adro o lolo gad*** (The girl in the red chemise), as well as I can recall his words,--a very sweet song, with a simple but spirited chorus; and as the sympathetic electricity of excitement seized the performers we were all in a minute "going down the rapids in a spring freshet."

"*Bagan tu rya*, *bagan*!" (Sing, sir,--sing) cried my handsome neighbor, with her black gypsy eyes sparkling fire. "*Jines hi bagan eto--eto latcho Romanes*." (You can sing that,--it's real Romany.) It was evident that she and all were singing with thorough enjoyment, and with a full and realizing consciousness of gypsyism, being greatly stimulated by my presence and sympathy. I felt that the gypsies were taking unusual pains to please the Romany rye from the *dur' tem*, or far country, and they had attained the acme of success by being thoroughly delighted with themselves, which is all that can be hoped for in art, where the aim is pleasure and not criticism.

There was a pause in the performance, but none in the chattering of the young ladies, and during this a curious little incident occurred. Wishing to know if my pretty friend could understand an English gypsy lyric, I sang in an undertone a ballad, taken from George Borrow's "Lavengro," and which begins with these words:--

> "Pende Eomani chai ke laki dye;
> 'Miri diri dye, mi shom kameli.'"

I never knew whether this was really an old gypsy poem or one written by Mr. Borrow. Once, when I repeated it to old Henry James, as he sat making baskets, I was silenced by being told, "That ain't no real gypsy *gilli*. That's one of the kind made up by gentlemen and ladies." However, as soon as I repeated it, the Russian gypsy girl cried eagerly, "I know that song!" and actually sang me a ballad which was essentially the same, in which a damsel describes her fall, owing to a Gajo (Gorgio, a Gentile,--not gypsy) lover, and her final expulsion from the tent. It was adapted to a very pretty melody, and as soon as she had sung it, *sotto voce*, my pretty friend exclaimed to another girl, "Only think, the *rye* from America knows *that* song!" Now, as many centuries must have passed since the English and Russian gypsies parted from the parent stock, the preservation of this song is very remarkable, and its

antiquity must be very great. I did not take it down, but any resident
in St. Petersburg can, if so inclined, do so among the gypsies at Dorat,
and verify my statement.

Then there was a pretty dance, of a modified Oriental character, by one
of the damsels. For this, as for the singing, the only musical
instrument used was a guitar, which had seven strings, tuned in Spanish
fashion, and was rather weak in tone. I wished it had been a powerful
Panormo, which would have exactly suited the *timbre* of these voices.
The gypsies were honestly interested in all I could tell them about their
kind in other lands; while the girls were professionally desirous to hear
more Anglo-Romany songs, and were particularly pleased with one beginning
with the words:--

> "'Me shom akonyo,' gildas yoi,
> Men buti ruzhior,
> Te sar i chiriclia adoi
> Pen mengy gilior.'"

Though we "got on" after a manner in our Romany talk, I was often obliged
to have recourse to my friend the general to translate long sentences
into Russian, especially when some sand-bar of a verb or some log of a
noun impeded the current of our conversation. Finally, a formal request
was made by the captain that I would, as one deep beyond all their
experience in Romany matters, kindly tell them what kind of people they
really were, and whence they came. With this demand I cheerfully
complied, every word being listened to with breathless interest. So I
told them what I knew or had conjectured relative to their Indian origin:
how their fathers had wandered forth through Persia; how their travels
could be traced by the Persian, Greek, or Roumanian words in the
language; how in 1417 a band of them appeared in Europe, led by a few men
of great diplomatic skill, who, by crafty dealing, obtained from the
Pope, the Emperor of Germany, and all the kings of Europe, except that of

England, permission to wander for fifty years as pilgrims, declaring that they had been Christians, but, having become renegades, the King of Hungary had imposed a penance on them of half a century's exile. Then I informed them that precisely the same story had been told by them to the rulers in Syria and Egypt, only that in the Mohammedan countries they pretended to be good followers of Islam. I said there was reason to believe that some of their people had been in Poland and the other Slavonic countries ever since the eleventh century, but that those of England must have gone directly from Eastern Europe to Great Britain; for, although they had many Slavic words, such as *krallis* (king) and *shuba*, there were no French terms, and very few traces of German or Italian, in the English dialect. I observed that the men all understood the geographical allusions which I made, knowing apparently where India, Persia, and Egypt were situated--a remarkable contrast to our own English "travelers," one of whom once informed me that he would like to go "on the road" in America, "because you know, sir, as America lays along into France, we could get our French baskets cheaper there."

I found, on inquiry, that the Russian gypsies profess Christianity; but, as the religion of the Greek church, as I saw it, appears to be practically something very little better than fetich-worship, I cannot exalt them as models of evangelical piety. They are, however, according to a popular proverb, not far from godliness in being very clean in their persons; and not only did they appear so to me, but I was assured by several Russians that, as regarded these singing gypsies, it was invariably the case. As for morality in gypsy girls, their principles are very peculiar. Not a whisper of scandal attaches to these Russian Romany women as regards transient amours. But if a wealthy Russian gentleman falls in love with one, and will have and hold her permanently, or for a durable connection, he may take her to his home if she likes him, but must pay monthly a sum into the gypsy treasury; for these people apparently form an *artel*, or society-union, like all other classes of Russians. It may be suggested, as an explanation of this apparent incongruity, that gypsies all the world over regard steady cohabitation, or agreement, as marriage, binding themselves, as it were, by *Gand-harbavivaha*, as the saint married Vasantasena, which is an old Sanskrit way of wedding. And let me remark that if one tenth of what I heard in Russia about "morals" in the highest or lowest or any other class be true, the gypsies of that country are shining lights and brilliant exemplars of morality to all by whom they are surrounded. Let me also add that never on any occasion did I hear or see among them anything in the slightest degree improper or unrefined. I knew very well that I could, if I chose, talk to such *naive* people about subjects which would shock an English lady, and, as the reader may remember, I did quote Mr. Borrow's song, which he has not translated. But a European girl who would have endured allusions to tabooed subjects would have at all times shown vulgarity or coarseness, while these Russian Romany girls were invariably lady-like. It is true that the St. Petersburg party had a dissipated air; three or four of them looked like second-class French or Italian theatrical artistes, and I should not be astonished to learn that very late hours and champagne were familiar to them as cigarettes, or that their flirtations among their own people were neither faint, nor few, nor far between. But their conduct in my presence was irreproachable. Those of Moscow, in fact, had not even the apparent defects of their St. Petersburg sisters and brothers, and when among them it always seemed to me as if I were simply with nice gentle creoles or Cubans, the gypsy manner being tamed down to the Spanish level, their great black eyes and their guitars increasing the resemblance.

The indescribably wild and thrilling character of gypsy music is thoroughly appreciated by the Russians, who pay very high prices for Romany performances. From five to eight or ten pounds sterling is usually given to a dozen gypsies for singing an hour or two to a special party, and this is sometimes repeated twice or thrice of an evening. "A Russian gentleman, when he is in funds," said the clerk of the Slavansky Bazaar in Moscow to me, "will make nothing of giving the Zigani a hundred-ruble note," the ruble rating at half a crown. The result is that good singers among these lucky Romanys are well to do, and lead soft lives, for Russia.

MOSCOW.

I had no friends in Moscow to direct me where to find gypsies *en famille*, and the inquiries which I made of chance acquaintances simply convinced me that the world at large was as ignorant of their ways as it was prejudiced against them. At last the good-natured old porter of our hotel told me, in his rough Baltic German, how to meet these mysterious minstrels to advantage. "You must take a sleigh," he said, "and go out to Petrovka. That is a place in the country, where there are grand *cafes* at considerable distances one from the other. Pay the driver three rubles for four hours. Enter a *cafe*, call for something to drink, listen to the gypsies singing, and when they pass round a plate put some money in it. That's all." This was explicit, and at ten o'clock in the evening I hired a sleigh and went.

If the cold which I had experienced in the general's troika in St. Petersburg might be compared to a moderate rheumatism, that which I encountered in the sleigh outside the walls of Moscow, on Christmas Eve, 1876, was like a fierce gout. The ride was in all conscience Russian enough to have its ending among gypsies, Tartars, or Cossacks. To go at a headlong pace over the creaking snow behind an *istvostshik*, named Vassili, the round, cold moon overhead, church-spires tipped with great inverted golden turnips in the distance, and this on a night when the frost seemed almost to scream in its intensity, is as much of a sensation in the suburbs of Moscow as it could be out on the steppes. A few wolves, more or less, make no difference,--and even they come sometimes within three hours' walk of the Kremlin. *Et ego inter lupos*,--I too have been among wolves in my time by night, in Kansas, and thought nothing of such rides compared to the one I had when I went gypsying from Moscow.

In half an hour Vassili brought me to a house, which I entered. A "proud porter," a vast creature, in uniform suggestive of embassies and kings' palaces, relieved me of my *shuba*, and I found my way into a very large and high hall, brilliantly lighted as if for a thousand guests, while the only occupants were four couples, "spooning" *sans gene*, one in each corner and a small party of men and girls drinking in the middle. I called a waiter; he spoke nothing but Russian, and Russian is of all languages the most useless to him who only talks it "a little." A little Arabic, or even a little Chippewa, I have found of great service, but a fair vocabulary and weeks of study of the grammar are of no avail in a country where even men of gentlemanly appearance turn away with childish *ennui* the instant they detect the foreigner, resolving apparently that they cannot and *will not* understand him. In matters like this the ordinary Russian is more impatient and less intelligent than any Oriental or even red Indian. The result of my interview with the waiter was that we were soon involved in the completest misunderstanding on the subject of gypsies. The question was settled by reference to a fat and fair damsel, one of the "spoons" already referred to, who spoke German. She explained to me that as it was Christmas Eve no gypsies would be there, or at any other *cafe*. This was disappointing. I called Vassili, and he drove on to another "garden," deeply buried in snow.

When I entered the rooms at this place, I perceived at a glance that matters had mended. There was the hum of many voices, and a perfume like that of tea and many *papiross*, or cigarettes, with a prompt sense of society and of enjoyment. I was dazzled at first by the glare of the lights, and could distinguish nothing, unless it was that the numerous company regarded me with utter amazement; for it was an "off night," when no business was expected,--few were there save "professionals" and their friends,--and I was manifestly an unexpected intruder on Bohemia. As luck would have it, that which I believed was the one worst night in the year to find the gypsy minstrels proved to be the exceptional occasion when they were all assembled, and I had hit upon it. Of course this struck me pleasantly enough as I looked around, for I knew that at a touch the spell would be broken, and with one word I should have the warmest welcome from all. I had literally not a single speaking acquaintance within a thousand miles, and yet here was a room crowded with gay and festive strangers, whom the slightest utterance would convert into friends.

I was not disappointed. Seeking for an opportunity, I saw a young man of gentlemanly appearance, well dressed, and with a mild and amiable air. Speaking to him in German, I asked the very needless question if there were any gypsies present.

"You wish to hear them sing?" he inquired.

"I do not. I only want to talk with one,--with *any* one."

He appeared to be astonished, but, pointing to a handsome, slender young lady, a very dark brunette, elegantly attired in black silk, said,--

"There is one."

I stepped across to the girl, who rose to meet me. I said nothing for a few seconds, but looked at her intently, and then asked,--

"*Rakessa tu Romanes*, *miri pen*?" (Do you talk Romany, my sister?)

She gave one deep, long glance of utter astonishment, drew one long breath, and, with a cry of delight and wonder, said,--

"*Romanichal*!"

That word awoke the entire company, and with it they found out who the intruder was. "Then might you hear them cry aloud, 'The Moringer is here!'" for I began to feel like the long-lost lord returned, so warm was my welcome. They flocked around me; they cried aloud in Romany, and one good-natured, smiling man, who looked like a German gypsy, mounting a chair, waved a guitar by its neck high in the air as a signal of discovery of a great prize to those at a distance, repeating rapidly,--

"*Av'akai*, *ava'kai*, *Romanichal*!" (Come here; here's a gypsy!)

And they came, dark and light, great and small, and got round me, and shook hands, and held to my arms, and asked where I came from, and how I did, and if it wasn't jolly, and what would I take to drink, and said how glad they were to see me; and when conversation flagged for an instant, somebody said to his next neighbor, with an air of wisdom, "American Romany," and everybody repeated it with delight. Then it occurred to the guitarist and the young lady that we had better sit down. So my first acquaintance and discoverer, whose name was Liubasha, was placed, in right of preemption, at my right hand, the **belle des belles**, Miss Sarsha, at my left, a number of damsels all around these, and then three or four circles of gypsies, of different ages and tints, standing up, surrounded us all. In the outer ring were several fast-looking and pretty Russian or German blonde girls, whose mission it is, I believe, to dance--and flirt--with visitors, and a few gentlemanly-looking Russians, **vieuz garcons**, evidently of the kind who are at home behind the scenes, and who knew where to come to enjoy themselves. Altogether there must have been about fifty present, and I soon observed that every word I uttered was promptly repeated, while every eye was fixed on me.

I could converse in Romany with the guitarist, and without much difficulty; but with the charming, heedless young ladies I had as much trouble to talk as with their sisters in St. Petersburg. The young gentleman already referred to, to whom in my fancy I promptly gave the Offenbachian name of Prince Paul, translated whenever there was a misunderstanding, and in a few minutes we were all intimate. Miss Sarsha, who had a slight cast in one of her wild black eyes, which added something to the gypsiness and roguery of her smiles, and who wore in a ring a large diamond, which seemed as if it might be the right eye in the wrong place, was what is called an earnest young lady, with plenty to say and great energy wherewith to say it. What with her eyes, her diamond, her smiles, and her tongue, she constituted altogether a fine specimen of irrepressible fireworks, and Prince Paul had enough to do in facilitating conversation. There was no end to his politeness, but it was an impossible task for him now and then promptly to carry over a long sentence from German to Russian, and he would give it up like an invincible conundrum, with the patient smile and head-wag and hand-wave of an amiable Dundreary. Yet I began to surmise a mystery even in him. More than once he inadvertently betrayed a knowledge of Romany, though he invariably spoke of his friends around in a patronizing manner as "these gypsies." This was very odd, for in appearance he was a Gorgio of the Gorgios, and did not seem, despite any talent for languages which he might possess, likely to trouble himself to acquire Romany while Russian would answer every purpose of conversation. All of this was, however, explained to me afterward.

Prince Paul again asked me if I had come out to hear a concert. I said, "No; that I had simply come out to see my brothers and sisters and talk with them, just as I hoped they would come to see me if I were in my own country." This speech produced a most favorable impression, and there was, in a quiet way, a little private conversation among the leaders, after which Prince Paul said to me, in a very pleasant manner, that "these gypsies," being delighted at the visit from the gentleman from a distant country, would like to offer me a song in token of welcome. To this I answered, with many thanks, that such kindness was more than I had expected, for I was well aware of the great value of such a compliment from singers whose fame had reached me even in America. It was evident that my grain of a reply did not fall upon stony ground, for I never was among people who seemed to be so quickly impressed by any act of politeness, however trifling. A bow, a grasp of the hand, a smile, or a glance would gratify them, and this gratification their lively black eyes expressed in the most unmistakable manner.

So we had the song, wild and wonderful like all of its kind, given with that delightful *abandon* which attains perfection only among gypsies. I had enjoyed the singing in St. Petersburg, but there was a *laisser aller*, a completely gay spirit, in this Christmas-Eve gypsy party in Moscow which was much more "whirling away." For at Dorot the gypsies had been on exhibition; here at Petrovka they were frolicking *en famille* with a favored guest,--a Romany rye from a far land to astonish and delight,--and he took good care to let them feel that they were achieving a splendid success, for I declared many times that it was *butsi shukar*, or very beautiful. Then I called for tea and lemon, and after that the gypsies sang for their own amusement, Miss Sarsha, as the incarnation of fun and jollity, taking the lead, and making me join in. Then the crowd made way, and in the space appeared a very pretty little girl, in the graceful old gypsy Oriental dress. This child danced charmingly indeed, in a style strikingly like that of the Almeh of Egypt, but without any of the erotic expressions which abound in Eastern pantomime. This little Romany girl was to me enchanting, being altogether unaffected and graceful. It was evident that her dancing, like the singing of her elder sisters, was not an art which had been drilled in by instruction. They had come into it in infancy, and perfected themselves by such continual practice that what they did was as natural as walking or talking. When the dancing was over, I begged that the little girl would come to me, and, kissing her tiny gypsy hand, I said, "*Spassibo tute kamli*, *eto hi*

butsi shukar" (Thank you, dear; that is very pretty), with which the rest were evidently pleased. I had observed among the singers, at a little distance, a very remarkable and rather handsome old woman,--a good study for an artist,--and she, as I also noticed, had sung with a powerful and clear voice. "She is our grandmother," said one of the girls. Now, as every student of gypsies knows, the first thing to do in England or Germany, on entering a tent-gypsy encampment, is to be polite to "the old woman." Unless you can win her good opinion you had better be gone. The Russian city Roms have apparently no such fancies. On the road, however, life is patriarchal, and the grandmother is a power to be feared. As a fortune-teller she is a witch, ever at warfare with the police world; she has a bitter tongue, and is quick to wrath. This was not the style or fashion of the old gypsy singer; but, as soon as I saw the ***puri babali dye***, I requested that she would shake hand with me, and by the impression which this created I saw that the Romany of the city had not lost all the feelings of the road.

I spoke of Waramoff's beautiful song of the "Krasneya Sarafan," which Sarsha began at once to warble. The characteristic of Russian gypsy-girl voices is a peculiarly delicate metallic tone,--like that of the two silver bells of the Tower of Ivan Velikoi when heard from afar,--yet always marked with fineness and strength. This is sometimes startling in the wilder effects, but it is always agreeable. These Moscow gypsy girls have a great name in their art, and it was round the shoulders of one of them--for aught I know it may have been Sarsha's great-grandmother--that Catalani threw the cashmere shawl which had been given to her by the Pope as "to the best singer in the world." "It is not mine by right," said the generous Italian; "it belongs to the gypsy."

The gypsies were desirous of learning something about the songs of their kindred in distant lands, and, though no singer, I did my best to please them, the guitarist easily improvising accompaniments, while the girls joined in. As all were in a gay mood faults were easily excused, and the airs were much liked,--one lyric, set by Virginia Gabriel, being even more admired in Moscow than in St. Petersburg, apropos of which I may mention that, when I afterward visited the gypsy family in their own home, the first request from Sarsha was, "***Eto gilyo, rya!***" (*That* song, sir), referring to "Romany," which has been heard at several concerts in London. And so, after much discussion of the affairs of Egypt, I took my leave amid a chorus of kind farewells. Then Vassili, loudly called for, reappeared from some nook with his elegantly frosted horse, and in a few minutes we were dashing homeward. Cold! It was as severe as in Western New York or Minnesota, where the thermometer for many days every winter sinks lower than in St. Petersburg, but where there are no such incredible precautions taken as in the land of double windows cemented down, and fur-lined ***shubas***. It is remarkable that the gypsies, although of Oriental origin, are said to surpass the Russians in enduring cold; and there is a marvelous story told about a Romany who, for a wager, undertook to sleep naked against a clothed Muscovite on the ice of a river during an unusually cold night. In the morning the Russian was found frozen stiff, while the gypsy was snoring away unharmed. As we returned, I saw in the town something which recalled this story in more than one ***moujik***, who, well wrapped up, lay sleeping in the open air, under the lee of a house. Passing through silent Moscow on the early Christmas morn, under the stars, as I gazed at the marvelous city, which yields neither to Edinburgh, Cairo, nor Prague in picturesqueness, and thought over the strange evening I had spent among the gypsies, I felt as if I were in a melodrama with striking scenery. The pleasing ***finale*** was the utter amazement and almost speechless gratitude of Vassili at getting an extra half-ruble as an early Christmas gift.

As I had received a pressing invitation from the gypsies to come again, I resolved to pay them a visit on Christmas afternoon in their own house, if I could find it. Having ascertained that the gypsy street was in a distant quarter, called the ***Grouszini***, I engaged a sleigh, standing

before the door of the Slavanski-Bazaar Hotel, and the usual close
bargain with the driver was effected with the aid of a Russian gentleman,
a stranger passing by, who reduced the ruble (one hundred kopecks) at
first demanded to seventy kopecks. After a very long drive we found
ourselves in the gypsy street, and the *istvostshik* asked me, "To what
house?"

"I don't know," I replied. "Gypsies live here, don't they?"

"Gypsies, and no others."

"Well, I want to find a gypsy."

The driver laughed, and just at that instant I saw, as if awaiting me on
the sidewalk, Sarsha, Liubasha, and another young lady, with a
good-looking youth, their brother.

"This will do," I said to the driver, who appeared utterly amazed at
seeing me greeted like an old friend by the Zigani, but who grinned with
delight, as all Russians of the lower class invariably do at anything
like sociability and fraternity. The damsels were faultlessly attired in
Russian style, with full fur-lined, glossy black-satin cloaks and fine
Orenberg scarfs, which are, I believe, the finest woolen fabrics in the
world. The party were particularly anxious to know if I had come
specially to visit *them*, for I have passed over the fact that I had
also made the acquaintance of another very large family of gypsies, who
sang at a rival *cafe*, and who had also treated me very kindly. I was
at once conducted to a house, which we entered in a rather gypsy way, not
in front, but through a court, a back door, and up a staircase, very much
in the style of certain dwellings in the Potteries in London. But,
having entered, I was led through one or two neat rooms, where I saw
lying sound asleep on beds, but dressed, one or two very dark Romanys,
whose faces I remembered. Then we passed into a sitting-room, which was

very well furnished. I observed hanging up over the chimney-piece a good
collection of photographs, nearly all of gypsies, and indicating that
close resemblance to Hindoos which comes out so strongly in such
pictures, being, in fact, more apparent in the pictures than in the
faces; just as the photographs of the old Ulfilas manuscript revealed
alterations not visible in the original. In the centre of the group was
a cabinet-size portrait of Sarsha, and by it another of an Englishman of
very high rank. I thought this odd, but asked no questions.

My hosts were very kind, offering me promptly a rich kind of Russian
cake, begging to know what else I would like to eat or drink, and
apparently deeply concerned that I could really partake of nothing, as I
had just come from luncheon. They were all light-hearted and gay, so
that the music began at once, as wild and as bewitching as ever. And
here I observed, even more than before, how thoroughly sincere these
gypsies were in their art, and to what a degree they enjoyed and were
excited by their own singing. Here in their own home, warbling like
birds and frolicking like children, their performance was even more
delightful than it had been in the concert-room. There was evidently a
great source of excitement in the fact that I must enjoy it far more than
an ordinary stranger, because I understood Romany, and sympathized with
gypsy ways, and regarded them not as the ***Gaji*** or Gentiles do, but as
brothers and sisters. I confess that I was indeed moved by the simple
kindness with which I was treated, and I knew that, with the wonderfully
keen perception of character in which gypsies excel, they perfectly
understood my liking for them. It is this ready intuition of feelings
which, when it is raised from an instinct to an art by practice, enables
shrewd old women to tell fortunes with so much skill.

I was here introduced to the mother of the girls. She was a neat,
pleasant-looking woman, of perhaps forty years, in appearance and manners
irresistibly reminding me of some respectable Cuban lady. Like the
others, she displayed an intelligent curiosity as to my knowledge of

Romany, and I was pleased at finding that she knew much more of the language than her children did. Then there entered a young Russian gentleman, but not "Prince Paul." He was, however, a very agreeable person, as all Russians can be when so minded; and they are always so minded when they gather, from information or conjecture, the fact that the stranger whom they meet is one of education or position. This young gentleman spoke French, and undertook the part of occasional translator.

I asked Liubasha if any of them understood fortune-telling.

"No; we have quite lost the art of ***dorriki***. {61} None of us know anything about it. But we hear that you Romanichals over the Black Water understand it. Oh, ***rya***," she cried, eagerly, "you know so much,--you're such a deep Romany,--can't ***you*** tell fortunes?"

"I should indeed know very little about Romany ways," I replied, gravely, "if I could not ***pen dorriki***. But I tell you beforehand, ***terni pen***, '***dorrikipen hi hokanipen***,' little sister, fortune-telling is deceiving. Yet what the lines say I can read."

In an instant six as pretty little gypsy hands as I ever beheld were thrust before me, and I heard as many cries of delight. "Tell ***my*** fortune, ***rya***! tell mine! and ***mine***!" exclaimed the damsels, and I complied. It was all very well to tell them there was nothing in it; they knew a trick worth two of that. I perceived at once that the faith which endures beyond its own knowledge was placed in all I said. In England the gypsy woman, who at home ridicules her own fortune-telling and her dupes, still puts faith in a ***gusveri mush***, or some "wise man," who with crystal or magical apparatus professes occult knowledge; for she thinks that her own false art is an imitation of a true one. It is really amusing to see the reverence with which an old gypsy will look at the awful hieroglyphics in Cornelius Agrippa's "Occult Philosophy," or, better still, "Trithemius," and, as a gift, any ordinary fortune-telling

book is esteemed by them beyond rubies. It is true that they cannot read
it, but the precious volume is treasured like a fetich, and the owner is
happy in the thought of at least possessing darksome and forbidden lore,
though it be of no earthly use to her. After all the kindness they had
shown me, I could not find it in my heart to refuse to tell these gentle
Zingari their little fortunes. It is not, I admit, exactly in the order
of things that the chicken should dress the cook, or the Gorgio tell
fortunes to gypsies; but he who wanders in strange lands meets with
strange adventures. So, with a full knowledge of the legal penalties
attached in England to palmistry and other conjuration, and with the then
pending Slade case knocking heavily on my conscience, I proceeded to
examine and predict. When I afterward narrated this incident to the late
G. H. Lewes, he expressed himself to the effect that to tell fortunes to
gypsies struck him as the very *ne plus ultra* of cheek,--which shows how
extremes meet; for verily it was with great modesty and proper diffidence
that I ventured to foretell the lives of these little ladies, having an
antipathy to the practice of chiromancing as to other romancing.

I have observed that as among men of great and varied culture, and of
extensive experience, there are more complex and delicate shades and
half-shades of light in the face, so in the palm the lines are
correspondingly varied and broken. Take a man of intellect and a
peasant, of equal excellence of figure according to the literal rules of
art or of anatomy, and this subtle multiplicity of variety shows itself
in the whole body in favor of the "gentleman," so that it would almost
seem as if every book we read is republished in the person. The first
thing that struck me in these gypsy hands was the fewness of the lines,
their clearly defined sweep, and their simplicity. In every one the line
of life was unbroken, and, in fine, one might think from a drawing of the
hand, and without knowing who its owner might be, that he or she was of a
type of character unknown in most great European cities,--a being gifted
with special culture, and in a certain simple sense refined, but not
endowed with experience in a thousand confused phases of life. The hands

of a true genius, who has passed through life earnestly devoted to a single art, however, are on the whole like these of the gypsies. Such, for example, are the hands of Fanny Janauschek, the lines of which agree to perfection with the laws of chiromancy. The art reminds one of Cervantes's ape, who told the past and present, but not the future. And here "tell me what thou hast been, and I will tell what thou wilt be" gives a fine opportunity to the soothsayer.

To avoid mistakes I told the fortunes in French, which was translated into Russian. I need not say that every word was listened to with earnest attention, or that the group of dark but young and comely faces, as they gathered around and bent over, would have made a good subject for a picture. After the girls, the mother must needs hear her *dorriki* also, and last of all the young Russian gentleman, who seemed to take as earnest an interest in his future as even the gypsies. As he alone understood French, and as he appeared to be *un peu gaillard*, and, finally, as the lines of his hand said nothing to the contrary, I predicted for him in detail a fortune in which *bonnes fortunes* were not at all wanting. I think he was pleased, but when I asked him if he would translate what I had said of his future into Russian, he replied with a slight wink and a scarcely perceptible negative. I suppose he had his reasons for declining.

Then we had singing again, and Christopher, the brother, a wild and gay young gypsy, became so excited that while playing the guitar he also danced and caroled, and the sweet voices of the girls rose in chorus, and I was again importuned for the *Romany* song, and we had altogether a very Bohemian frolic. I was sorry when the early twilight faded into night, and I was obliged, notwithstanding many entreaties to the contrary, to take my leave. These gypsies had been very friendly and kind to me in a strange city, where I had not an acquaintance, and where I had expected none. They had given me of their very best; for they gave me songs which I can never forget, and which were better to me than all

the opera could bestow. The young Russian, polite to the last, went
bareheaded with me into the street, and, hailing a sleigh-driver, began
to bargain for me. In Moscow, as in other places, it makes a great
difference in the fare whether one takes a public conveyance from before
the first hotel or from a house in the gypsy quarter. I had paid seventy
kopecks to come, and I at once found that my new friend and the driver
were engaged in wild and fierce dispute whether I should pay twenty or
thirty to return.

"Oh, give him thirty!" I exclaimed. "It's little enough."

"*Non*," replied the Russian, with the air of a man of principles. "*Il
ne faut pas gater ces gens-la*." But I gave the driver thirty, all the
same, when we got home, and thereby earned the usual shower of blessings.

A few days afterward, while going from Moscow to St. Petersburg, I made
the acquaintance of a young Russian noble and diplomat, who was well
informed on all current gossip, and learned from him some curious facts.
The first young gentleman whom I had seen among the Romanys of Moscow was
the son of a Russian prince by a gypsy mother, and the very noble
Englishman whose photograph I had seen in Sarsha's collection had not
long ago (as rumor averred) paid desperate attentions to the belle of the
Romanys without obtaining the least success. My informant did not know
her name. Putting this and that together, I think it highly probable
that Sarsha was the young lady, and that the *latcho bar*, or diamond,
which sparkled on her finger had been paid for with British gold, while
the donor had gained the same "unluck" which befell one of his type in
the Spanish gypsy song as given by George Borrow:--

> "Loud sang the Spanish cavalier,
> And thus his ditty ran:
> 'God send the gypsy maiden here,
> But not the gypsy man.'

"On high arose the moon so bright,
The gypsy 'gan to sing,
'I gee a Spaniard coming here,
I must be on the wing.'"

AUSTRIAN GYPSIES.

I.

In June, 1878, I went to Paris, during the great Exhibition. I had been invited by Monsieur Edmond About to attend as a delegate the Congres Internationale Litteraire, which was about to be held in the great city. How we assembled, how M. About distinguished himself as one of the most practical and common-sensible of men of genius, and how we were all finally harangued by M. Victor Hugo with the most extraordinary display of oratorical sky-rockets, Catherine-wheels, blue-lights, fire-crackers, and pin-wheels by which it was ever my luck to be amused, is matter of history. But this chapter is only autobiographical, and we will pass over the history. As an Anglo-American delegate, I was introduced to several great men gratis; to the greatest of all I introduced myself at the expense of half a franc. This was to the Chinese giant, Chang, who was on exhibition at a small cafe garden near the Trocadero. There were no other visitors in his pavilion when I entered. He received me with politeness, and we began to converse in fourth-story English, but gradually went down-stairs into Pidgin, until we found ourselves fairly in the kitchen of that humble but entertaining dialect. It is a remarkable sensation to sit alone with a mild monster, and feel like a little boy. I do not distinctly remember whether Chang is eight, or ten or twelve feet high; I only know that, though I am, as he said, "one velly big piecee man," I sat and lifted my eyes from time to time at the usual level, forgetfully expecting to meet his eyes, and beheld instead the buttons on his breast. Then I looked up--like Daruma to Buddha--and up, and saw far above me his "lights of the soul" gleaming down on me as it were from the top of a lofty beacon.

I soon found that Chang, regarding all things from a giant's point of view, esteemed mankind by their size and looks. Therefore, as he had complimented me according to his lights, I replied that he was a "numpa one too muchee glanti handsome man, first chop big."

Then he added, "You belongy Inklis man?"

"No. My one piecee *fa-ke-kwok*; {69} my Melican, galaw. You dlinkee ale some-tim?"

The giant replied that *pay-wine*, which is Pidgin for beer, was not ungrateful to his palate or foreign to his habits. So we had a quart of Alsopp between us, and drank to better acquaintance. I found that the giant had exhibited himself in many lands, and taken great pains to learn the language of each, so that he spoke German, Italian, and Spanish well enough. He had been at a mission-school when he used to "stop China-side," or was in his native land. I assured him that I had perceived it from the first, because he evidently "talked ink," as his countrymen say of words which are uttered by a scholar, and I greatly gratified him by citing some of my own "beautiful verses," which are reversed from a Chinese original:--

"One man who never leadee {69a}

> Like one dly {69b} inkstan be:
> You turn he up-side downy,
> No ink lun {69c} outside he."

So we parted with mutual esteem. This was the second man by the name of
Chang whom I had known, and singularly enough they were both exhibited as
curiosities. The other made a living as a Siamese twin, and his brother
was named Eng. They wrote their autographs for me, and put them wisely
at the very top of the page, lest I should write a promise to pay an
immense sum of money, or forge a free pass to come into the exhibition
gratis over their signatures.

Having seen Chang, I returned to the Hotel de Louvre, dined, and then
went forth with friends to the Orangerie. This immense garden, devoted
to concerts, beer, and cigars, is said to be capable of containing three
thousand people; before I left it it held about five thousand. I knew
not why this unwonted crowd had assembled; when I found the cause I was
astonished, with reason. At the gate was a bill, on which I read "Les
Bohemiennes de Moscow."

"Some small musical comedy, I suppose," I said to myself. "But let us
see it." We pressed on.

"Look there!" said my companion. "Those are certainly gypsies."

Sure enough, a procession of men and women, strangely dressed in gayly
colored Oriental garments, was entering the gates. But I replied,
"Impossible. Not here in Paris. Probably they are performers."

"But see. They notice you. That girl certainly knows you. She's
turning her head. There,--I heard her say O Romany rye!"

I was bewildered. The crowd was dense, but as the procession passed me at a second turn I saw they were indeed gypsies, and I was grasped by the hand by more than one. They were my old friends from Moscow. This explained the immense multitude. There was during the Exhibition a great *furor* as regarded *les zigains*. The gypsy orchestra which performed in the Hungarian cafe was so beset by visitors that a comic paper represented them as covering the roofs of the adjacent houses so as to hear something. This evening the Russian gypsies were to make their debut in the Orangerie, and they were frightened at their own success. They sang, but their voices were inaudible to two thirds of the audience, and those who could not hear roared, "Louder!" Then they adjourned to the open air, where the voices were lost altogether on a crowd calling, "*Garcon--vite--une tasse cafe*!" or applauding. In the intervals scores of young Russian gentlemen, golden swells, who had known the girls of old, gathered round the fair ones like moths around tapers. The singing was not the same as it had been; the voices were the same, but the sweet wild charm of the Romany caroling, bird-like, for pleasure was gone.

But I found by themselves and unnoticed two of the troupe, whom I shall not soon forget. They were two very handsome youths,--one of sixteen years, the other twenty. And with the first words in Romany they fairly jumped for joy; and the artist who could have caught their picture then would have made a brave one. They were clad in blouses of colored silk, which, with their fine dark complexions and great black eyes, gave them a very picturesque air. These had not seen me in Russia, nor had they heard of me; they were probably from Novogorod. Like the girls they were children, but in a greater degree, for they had not been flattered, and kind words delighted them so that they clapped their hands. They began to hum gypsy songs, and had I not prevented it they would have run at once and brought a guitar, and improvised a small concert for me *al fresco*. I objected to this, not wishing to take part any longer in such a very public exhibition. For the *gobe-mouches* and starers, noticing a stranger talking with *ces zigains*, had begun to gather in a dense crowd around us, and the two ladies and the gentleman who were with us were seriously inconvenienced. We endeavored to step aside, but the multitude stepped aside also, and would not let us alone. They were French, but they might have been polite. As it was, they broke our merry conference up effectively, and put us to flight.

"Do let us come and see you, *rya*," said the younger boy. "We will sing, for I can really sing beautifully, and we like you so much. Where do you live?"

I could not invite them, for I was about to leave Paris, as I then supposed. I have never seen them since, and there was no adventure and no strange scenery beyond the thousands of lights and guests and trees and voices speaking French. Yet to this day the gay boyishness, the merry laughter, and the child-like *naivete* of the promptly-formed liking of those gypsy youths remains impressed on my mind with all the color and warmth of an adventure or a living poem. Can you recall no child by any wayside of life to whom you have given a chance smile or a kind word, and been repaid with artless sudden attraction? For to all of us,--yes, to the coldest and worst,--there are such memories of young people, of children, and I pity him who, remembering them, does not feel the touch of a vanished hand and hear a chord which is still. There are adventures which we can tell to others as stories, but the best have no story; they may be only the memory of a strange dog which followed us, and I have one such of a cat who, without any introduction, leaped wildly towards me, "and would not thence away." It is a good life which has many such memories.

I was walking a day or two after with an English friend, who was also a delegate to the International Literary Congress, in the Exhibition, when we approached the side gate, or rear entrance of the Hungarian cafe. Six or seven dark and strange-looking men stood about, dressed in the uniform of a military band. I caught their glances, and saw that they were

Romany.

"Now you shall see something queer," I said to my friend.

So advancing to the first dark man I greeted him in gypsy.

"I do not understand you," he promptly replied--or lied.

I turned to a second.

"You have more sense, and you do understand. ***Adro miro tem penena mande
o baro rai***." (In my country the gypsies call me the great gentleman.)

This phrase may be translated to mean either the "tall gentleman" or the
"great lord." It was apparently taken in the latter sense, for at once
all the party bowed very low, raising their hands to their foreheads, in
Oriental fashion.

"Hallo!" exclaimed my English friend, who had not understood what I had
said. "What game is this you are playing on these fellows?"

Up to the front came a superior, the leader of the band.

"Great God!" he exclaimed, "what is this I hear? This is wonderful. To
think that there should be anybody here to talk with! I can only talk
Magyar and Romanes."

"And what do you talk?" I inquired of the first violin.

"***Ich spreche nur Deutsch***!" he exclaimed, with a strong Vienna accent
and a roar of laughter. "I only talk German."

This worthy man, I found, was as much delighted with my German as the

leader with my gypsy; and in all my experience I never met two beings so
charmed at being able to converse. That I should have met with them was
of itself wonderful. Only there was this difference: that the Viennese
burst into a laugh every time he spoke, while the gypsy grew more sternly
solemn and awfully impressive. There are people to whom mere talking is
a pleasure,--never mind the ideas,--and here I had struck two at once. I
once knew a gentleman named Stewart. He was the mayor, first physician,
and postmaster of St. Paul, Minnesota. While camping out, *en route*,
and in a tent with him, it chanced that among the other gentlemen who had
tented with us there were two terrible snorers. Now Mr. Stewart had
heard that you may stop a man's snoring by whistling. And here was a
wonderful opportunity. "So I waited," he said, "until one man was coming
down with his snore, *diminuendo*, while the other was rising,
crescendo, and at the exact point of intersection, *moderato*, I blew
my car-whistle, and so got both birds at one shot. I stopped them both."
Even as Mayor Stewart had winged his two birds with one ball had I hit my
two peregrines.

"We are now going to perform," said the gypsy captain. "Will you not
take seats on the platform, and hear us play?"

I did not know it at the time, but I heard afterwards that this was a
great compliment, and one rarely bestowed. The platform was small, and
we were very near our new friends. Scarcely had the performance begun
ere I perceived that, just as the gypsies in Russia had sung their best
in my honor, these artists were exerting themselves to the utmost, and,
all unheeding the audience, playing directly at me and into me. When any
tour was deftly made the dark master nodded to me with gleaming eyes,
as if saying, "What do you think of *that*, now?" The Viennese laughed
for joy every time his glance met mine, and as I looked at the various
Lajoshes and Joshkas of the band, they blew, beat, or scraped with
redoubled fury, or sank into thrilling tenderness. Hurrah! here was
somebody to play to who knew gypsy and all the games thereof; for a very

little, even a word, reveals a great deal, and I must be a virtuoso, at least by Romany, if not by art. It was with all the joy of success that the first piece ended amid thunders of applause.

"That was not the *racoczy*," I said. "Yet it sounded like it."

"No," said the captain. "But *now* you shall hear the *racoczy* and the *czardas* as you never heard them before. For we can play that better than any orchestra in Vienna. Truly, you will never forget us after hearing it."

And then they played the *racoczy*, the national Hungarian favorite, of gypsy composition, with heart and soul. As these men played for me, inspired with their own music, feeling and enjoying it far more than the audience, and all because they had got a gypsy gentleman to play to, I appreciated what a *life* that was to them, and what it should be; not cold-blooded skill, aiming only at excellence or preexcellence and at setting up the artist, but a fire and a joy, a self-forgetfulness which whirls the soul away as the soul of the Moenad went with the stream adown the mountains,--*Evoe Bacchus*! This feeling is deep in the heart of the Hungarian gypsy; he plays it, he feels it in every air, he knows the rush of the stream as it bounds onwards,--knows that it expresses his deepest desire; and so he has given it words in a song which, to him who has the key, is one of the most touching ever written:--

>"Dyal o pani repedishis,
>M'ro pirano hegedishis;

>"Dyal o pani tale vatra,
>M'ro pirano klanetaha.

>"Dyal o pani pe kishai
>M'ro pirano tsino rai."

"The stream runs on with rushing din
As I hear my true love's violin;

"And the river rolls o'er rock and stone
As he plays the flute so sweet alone.

"Runs o'er the sand as it began,
Then my true love lives a gentleman."

Yes, music whirling the soul away as on a rushing river, the violin notes falling like ripples, the flute tones all aflow among the rocks; and when it sweeps *adagio* on the sandy bed, then the gypsy player is at heart equal to a lord, then he feels a gentleman. The only true republic is art. There all earthly distinctions pass away; there he is best who lives and feels best, and makes others feel, not that he is cleverer than they, but that he can awaken sympathy and joy.

The intense reality of musical art as a comforter to these gypsies of Eastern Europe is wonderful. Among certain inedited songs of the Transylvanian gypsies, in the Kolosvarer dialect, I find the following:--

"Na janav ko dad m'ro as,
Niko mallen mange as,
Miro gule dai merdyas
Pirani me pregelyas.
Uva tu o hegedive
Tu sal mindik pash mange."

"I've known no father since my birth,
I have no friend alive on earth;
My mother's dead this many day,
The girl I loved has gone her way;

Thou violin with music free
Alone art ever true to me."

It is very wonderful that the charm of the Russian gypsy girls' singing was destroyed by the atmosphere or applause of a Paris concert-room, while the Hungarian Romanys conquered it as it were by sheer force, and by conquering gave their music the charm of intensity. I do not deny that in this music, be it of voice or instruments, there is much which is perhaps imagined, which depends on association, which is plain to John but not to Jack; but you have only to advance or retreat a few steps to find the same in the highest art. This, at least, we know: that no performer at any concert in London can awake the feeling of intense enjoyment which these wild minstrels excite in themselves and in others by sympathy. Now it is a question in many forms as to whether art for enjoyment is to die, and art for the sake of art alone survive. Is joyous and healthy nature to vanish step by step from the heart of man, and morbid, egoistic pessimism to take its place? Are over-culture, excessive sentiment, constant self-criticism, and all the brood of nervous curses to monopolize and inspire art? A fine alliance this they are making, the ascetic monk and the atheistic pessimist, to kill Nature! They will never effect it. It may die in many forms. It may lose its charm, as the singing of Sarsha and of Liubasha was lost among the rustling and noise of thousands of Parisian **badauds** in the Orangerie. But there will be stronger forms of art, which will make themselves heard, as the Hungarian Romanys heeded no din, and bore all away with their music.

"*Latcho divvus miri pralia*!--*miduvel atch pa tumende*!" (Good-day, my brothers. God rest on you) I said, and they rose and bowed, and I went forth into the Exhibition. It was a brave show, that of all the fine things from all parts of the world which man can make, but to me the most interesting of all were the men themselves. Will not the managers of the next world show give us a living ethnological department?

Of these Hungarian gypsies who played in Paris during the Exhibition much was said in the newspapers, and from the following, which appeared in an American journal, written by some one to me unknown, the reader may learn that there were many others to whom their music was deeply thrilling or wildly exciting:--

> "The Hungarian Tziganes (Zigeuner) are the rage just now at Paris. The story is that Liszt picked out the individuals composing the band one by one from among the gypsy performers in Hungary and Bohemia. Half-civilized in appearance, dressed in an unbecoming half-military costume, they are nothing while playing Strauss' waltzes or their own; but when they play the Radetsky Defile, the Racoksky March, or their marvelous czardas, one sees and hears the battle, and it is easy to understand the influence of their music in fomenting Hungarian revolutions; why for so long it was made treasonable to play or listen to these czardas; and why, as they heard them, men rose to their feet, gathered together, and with tears rolling down their faces, and throats swelling with emotion, departed to do or die."

And when I remember that they played for me as they said they had played for no other man in Paris, "into the ear,"--and when I think of the gleam in their eyes, I verily believe they *told* the truth,--I feel glad that I chanced that morning on those dark men and spoke to them in Romany.

* * * * *

Since the above was written I have met in an entertaining work called "Unknown Hungary," by Victor Tissot, with certain remarks on the Hungarian gypsy musicians which are so appropriate that I cite them in full:--

"The gypsy artists in Hungary play by inspiration, with inimitable *verve* and spirit, without even knowing their notes, and nothing whatever of the rhymes and rules of the masters. Liszt, who has closely studied them, says, The art of music being for them a sublime language, a song, mystic in itself, though dear to the initiated, they use it according to the wants of the moment which they wish to express. They have invented their music for their own use, to sing about themselves to themselves, to express themselves in the most heartfelt and touching monologues.

"Their music is as free as their lives; no intermediate modulation, no chords, no transition, it goes from one key to another. From ethereal heights they precipitate you into the howling depths of hell; from the plaint, barely heard, they pass brusquely to the warrior's song, which bursts loudly forth, passionate and tender, at once burning and calm. Their melodies plunge you into a melancholy reverie, or carry you away into a stormy whirlwind; they are a faithful expression of the Hungarian character, sometimes quick, brilliant, and lively, sometimes sad and apathetic.

"The gypsies, when they arrived in Hungary, had no music of their own; they appropriated the Magyar music, and made from it an original art which now belongs to them."

I here break in upon Messieurs Tissot and Liszt to remark that, while it is very probable that the Roms reformed Hungarian music, it is rather boldly assumed that they had no music of their own. It was, among other callings, as dancers and musicians that they left India and entered Europe, and among them were doubtless many descendants of the ten thousand Indo-Persian Luris or Nuris. But to resume quotation:--

"They made from it an art full of life, passion, laughter, and tears. The instrument which the gypsies prefer is the violin, which they

call **bas' alja**, 'the king of instruments.' They also play the
viola, the cymbal, and the clarionet.

"There was a pause. The gypsies, who had perceived at a table a
comfortable-looking man, evidently wealthy, and on a pleasure
excursion in the town, came down from their platform, and ranged
themselves round him to give him a serenade all to himself, as is
their custom. They call this 'playing into the ear.'

"They first asked the gentleman his favorite air, and then played it
with such spirit and enthusiasm and overflowing richness of variation
and ornament, and with so much emotion, that it drew forth the
applause of the whole company. After this they executed a czardas,
one of the wildest, most feverish, harshest, and, one may say,
tormenting, as if to pour intoxication into the soul of their
listener. They watched his countenance to note the impression
produced by the passionate rhythm of their instruments; then,
breaking off suddenly, they played a hushed, soft, caressing measure;
and again, almost breaking the trembling cords of their bows, they
produced such an intensity of effect that the listener was almost
beside himself with delight and astonishment. He sat as if
bewitched; he shut his eyes, hung his head in melancholy, or raised
it with a start, as the music varied; then jumped up and struck the
back of his head with his hands. He positively laughed and cried at
once; then, drawing a roll of bank-notes from his pocket-book, he
threw it to the gypsies, and fell back in his chair, as if exhausted
with so much enjoyment. And in **this** lies the triumph of the gypsy
music; it is like that of Orpheus, which moved the rocks and trees.
The soul of the Hungarian plunges, with a refinement of sensation
that we can understand, but cannot follow, into this music, which,
like the unrestrained indulgence of the imagination in fantasy and
caprice, gives to the initiated all the intoxicating sensations
experienced by opium smokers."

The Austrian gypsies have many songs which perfectly reflect their character. Most of them are only single verses of a few lines, such as are sung everywhere in Spain; others, which are longer, seem to have grown from the connection of these verses. The following translation from the Roumanian Romany (Vassile Alexandri) gives an idea of their style and spirit:--

GYPSY SONG.

The wind whistles over the heath,
The moonlight flits over the flood;
And the gypsy lights up his fire,
In the darkness of the wood.
Hurrah!
In the darkness of the wood.

Free is the bird in the air,
And the fish where the river flows;
Free is the deer in the forest,
And the gypsy wherever he goes.
Hurrah!
And the gypsy wherever he goes.

A GORGIO GENTLEMAN SPEAKS.

Girl, wilt thou live in my home?
I will give thee a sable gown,
And golden coins for a necklace,
If thou wilt be my own.

GYPSY GIRL.

No wild horse will leave the prairie
For a harness with silver stars;
Nor an eagle the crags of the mountain,
For a cage with golden bars;

Nor the gypsy girl the forest,
Or the meadow, though gray and cold,
For garments made of sable,
Or necklaces of gold.

THE GORGIO.

Girl, wilt thou live in my dwelling,
For pearls and diamonds true? {82}
I will give thee a bed of scarlet,
And a royal palace, too.

GYPSY GIRL.

My white teeth are my pearlins,
My diamonds my own black eyes;
My bed is the soft green meadow,
My palace the world as it lies.

Free is the bird in the air,
And the fish where the river flows;
Free is the deer in the forest,
And the gypsy wherever he goes.
Hurrah!
And the gypsy wherever he goes.

There is a deep, strange element in the gypsy character, which finds no sympathy or knowledge in the German, and very little in other Europeans, but which is so much in accord with the Slavonian and Hungarian that he who truly feels it with love is often disposed to mingle them together. It is a dreamy mysticism; an indefinite semi-supernaturalism, often passing into gloom; a feeling as of Buddhism which has glided into Northern snows, and taken a new and darker life in winter-lands. It is strong in the Czech or Bohemian, whose nature is the worst understood in the civilized world. That he should hate the German with all his heart and soul is in the order of things. We talk about the mystical Germans, but German self-conscious mysticism is like a problem of Euclid beside the natural, unexpressed dreaminess of the Czech. The German mystic goes to work at once to expound his "system" in categories, dressing it up in a technology which in the end proves to be the only mystery in it. The Bohemian and gypsy, each in their degrees of culture, form no system and make no technology, but they feel all the more. Now the difference between true and imitative mysticism is that the former takes no form; it is even narrowed by religious creeds, and wing-clipt by pious "illumination." Nature, and nature alone, is its real life. It was from the Southern Slavonian lands that all real mysticism, and all that higher illumination which means freedom, came into Germany and Europe; and after all, Germany's first and best mystic, Jacob Bohme, was Bohemian by name, as he was by nature. When the world shall have discovered who the as yet unknown Slavonian German was who wrote all the best part of "Consuelo," and who helped himself in so doing from "Der letzte Taborit," by Herlossohn, we shall find one of the few men who understood the Bohemian.

Once in a while, as in Fanny Janauschek, the Czech bursts out into art, and achieves a great triumph. I have seen Rachel and Ristori many a time, but their best acting was shallow compared to Janauschek's, as I have seen it in by-gone years, when she played Iphigenia and Medea in German. No one save a Bohemian could ever so ***intuit*** the gloomy profundity and unearthly fire of the Colchian sorceress. These are the things required to perfect every artist,--above all, the tragic artist,--that the tree of his or her genius shall not only soar to heaven among the angels, but also have roots in the depths of darkness and fire; and that he or she shall play not only to the audience, and in sympathy with them, but also unto one's self and down to one's deepest dreams.

No one will accuse me of wide discussion or padding who understands my drift in this chapter. I am speaking of the gypsy, and I cannot explain him more clearly than by showing his affinities with the Slavonian and Magyar, and how, through music and probably in many other ways, he has influenced them. As the Spaniard perfectly understands the objective vagabond side of the Gitano, so the Southeastern European understands the musical and wild-forest yearnings of the Tsigane. Both to gypsy and Slavonian there is that which makes them dream so that even debauchery has for them at times an unearthly inspiration; and as smoking was inexpressibly sacred to the red Indians of old, so that when the Guatemalan Christ harried hell, the demons offered him cigars; in like manner tipsiness is often to the gypsy and Servian, or Czech, or Croat, something so serious and impressive that it is a thing not to be lightly thought of, but to be undertaken with intense deliberation and under due appreciation of its benefits.

Many years ago, when I had begun to feel this strange element I gave it expression in a poem which I called "The Bohemian," as expressive of both gypsy and Slavonian nature:--

THE BOHEMIAN.

Chces li tajnou vec aneb pravdu vyzvedeti
Blazen, dite opily clovek o tom umeji povodeti.

Wouldst thou know a truth or mystery,
A drunkard, fool, or child may tell it thee

BOHEMIAN PROVERB.

And now I'll wrap my blanket o'er me,
And on the tavern floor I'll lie,
A double spirit-flask before me,
And watch my pipe clouds, melting, die.

They melt and die, but ever darken
As night comes on and hides the day,
Till all is black; then, brothers, hearken,
And if ye can write down my lay.

In yon long loaf my knife is gleaming,
Like one black sail above the boat;
As once at Pesth I saw it beaming,
Half through a dark Croatian throat.

Now faster, faster, whirls the ceiling,
And wilder, wilder, turns my brain;
And still I'll drink, till, past all feeling,
My soul leaps forth to light again.

Whence come these white girls wreathing round me?
Barushka!--long I thought thee dead;
Katchenka!--when these arms last bound thee
Thou laid'st by Rajrad, cold as lead.

And faster, faster, whirls the ceiling,
And wilder, wilder, turns my brain;
And from afar a star comes stealing

Straight at me o'er the death-black plain.

Alas! I sink. My spirits miss me.
I swim, I shoot from shore to shore!
Klara! thou golden sister--kiss me!
I rise--I'm safe--I'm strong once more.

And faster, faster, whirls the ceiling,
And wilder, wilder, whirls my brain;
The star!--it strikes my soul, revealing
All life and light to me again.

* * * * *

Against the waves fresh waves are dashing,
Above the breeze fresh breezes blow;
Through seas of light new light is flashing,
And with them all I float and flow.

Yet round me rings of fire are gleaning,--
Pale rings of fire, wild eyes of death!
Why haunt me thus, awake or dreaming?
Methought I left ye with my breath!

Ay, glare and stare, with life increasing,
And leech-like eyebrows, arching in;
Be, if ye must, my fate unceasing,
But never hope a fear to win.

He who knows all may haunt the haunter,
He who fears naught hath conquered fate;
Who bears in silence quells the daunter,
And makes his spoiler desolate.

O wondrous eyes, of star-like lustre,
How have ye changed to guardian love!
Alas! where stars in myriads cluster,
Ye vanish in the heaven above.

* * * * *

I hear two bells so softly ringing;
How sweet their silver voices roll!
The one on distant hills is ringing,
The other peals within my soul.

I hear two maidens gently talking,
Bohemian maids, and fair to see:
The one on distant hills is walking,
The other maiden,--where is she?

Where is she? When the moonlight glistens
O'er silent lake or murmuring stream,
I hear her call my soul, which listens,
"Oh, wake no more! Come, love, and dream!"

She came to earth, earth's loveliest creature;
She died, and then was born once more;
Changed was her race, and changed each feature,
But yet I loved her as before.

We live, but still, when night has bound me
In golden dreams too sweet to last,
A wondrous light-blue world around me,
She comes,--the loved one of the past.

I know not which I love the dearest,
For both the loves are still the same:
The living to my life is nearest,
The dead one feeds the living flame.

And when the sun, its rose-wine quaffing,
Which flows across the Eastern deep,
Awakes us, Klara chides me, laughing,
And says we love too well in sleep.

And though no more a Voivode's daughter,
As when she lived on earth before,
The love is still the same which sought her,
And I am true, and ask no more.

* * * * *

Bright moonbeams on the sea are playing,
And starlight shines upon the hill,
And I should wake, but still delaying
In our old life I linger still.

For as the wind clouds flit above me,
And as the stars above them shine,
My higher life's in those who love me,
And higher still, our life's divine.

And thus I raise my soul by drinking,
As on the tavern floor I lie;
It heeds not whence begins our thinking
If to the end its flight is high.

E'en outcasts may have heart and feeling,

The blackest wild Tsigan be true,
And love, like light in dungeons stealing,
Though bars be there, will still burst through.

It is the reecho of more than one song of those strange lands, of more
than one voice, and of many a melody; and those who have heard them,
though not more distinctly than Francois Villon when he spoke of flinging
the question back by silent lake and streamlet lone, will understand me,
and say it is true to nature.

In a late work on Magyarland, by a lady Fellow of the Carpathian Society,
I find more on Hungarian gypsy music, which is so well written that I
quote fully from it, being of the opinion that one ought, when setting
forth any subject, to give quite as good an opportunity to others who are
in our business as to ourselves. And truly this lady has felt the charm
of the Tsigan music and describes it so well that one wishes she were a
Romany in language and by adoption, like unto a dozen dames and damsels
whom I know.

> "The Magyars have a perfect passion for this gypsy music, and there
> is nothing that appeals so powerfully to their emotions, whether of
> joy or sorrow. These singular musicians are, as a rule, well taught,
> and can play almost any music, greatly preferring, however, their own
> compositions. Their music, consequently, is highly characteristic.
> It is the language of their lives and strange surroundings, a wild,
> weird banshee music: now all joy and sparkle, like sunshine on the
> plains; now sullen, sad, and pathetic by turns, like the wail of a
> crushed and oppressed people,--an echo, it is said, of the minstrelsy
> of the *hegedosok* or Hungarian bards, but sounding to our ears like
> the more distant echo of that exceeding bitter cry, uttered long
> centuries ago by their forefathers under Egyptian bondage, and borne
> over the time-waves of thousands of years, breaking forth in their
> music of to-day."

Here I interrupt the lady--with all due courtesy--to remark that I cannot
agree with her, nor with her probable authority, Walter Simson, in
believing that the gypsies are the descendants of the mixed races who
followed Moses out of Egypt. The Rom in Egypt is a Hindoo stranger now,
as he ever was. But that the echo of centuries of outlawry and
wretchedness and wildness rises and falls, like the ineffable discord in
a wind-harp, in Romany airs is true enough, whatever its origin may have
been. But I beg pardon, madam,--I interrupted you.

"The soul-stirring, madly exciting, and martial strains of the
Racoczys--one of the Revolutionary airs--has just died upon the ear.
A brief interval of rest has passed. Now listen with bated breath to
that recitative in the minor key,--that passionate wail, that
touching story, the gypsies' own music, which rises and falls on the
air. Knives and forks are set down, hands and arms hang listless,
all the seeming necessities of the moment being either suspended or
forgotten,--merged in the memories which those vibrations, so akin to
human language, reawaken in each heart. Eyes involuntarily fill with
tears, as those pathetic strains echo back and make present some
sorrow of long ago, or rouse from slumber that of recent time. . . .

"And now, the recitative being ended, and the last chord struck, the
melody begins, of which the former was the prelude. Watch the
movements of the supple figure of the first violin, standing in the
centre of the other musicians, who accompany him softly. How every
nerve is *en rapport* with his instrument, and how his very soul is
speaking through it! See how gently he draws the bow across the
trembling strings, and how lovingly he lays his cheek upon it, as if
listening to some responsive echo of his heart's inmost feeling, for
it is his mystic language! How the instrument lives and answers to
his every touch, sending forth in turn utterances tender, sad, wild,
and joyous! The audience once more hold their breath to catch the

dying tones, as the melody, so rich, so beautiful, so full of pathos,
is drawing to a close. The tension is absolutely painful as the
gypsy dwells on the last lingering note, and it is a relief when,
with a loud and general burst of sound, every performer starts into
life and motion. *Then* what crude and wild dissonances are made to
resolve themselves into delicious harmony! What rapturous and fervid
phrases, and what energy and impetuosity, are there in every motion
of the gypsies' figures, as their dark eyes glisten and emit flashes
in unison with the tones!"

The writer is gifted in giving words to gypsy music. One cannot say, as
the inexhaustible Cad writes of Niagara ten times on a page in the
Visitors' Book, that it is indescribable. I think that if language means
anything this music has been very well described by the writers whom I
have cited. When I am told that the gypsies' impetuous and passionate
natures make them enter into musical action with heart and soul, I feel
not only the strains played long ago, but also hear therein the horns of
Elfland blowing,--which he who has not heard, of summer days, in the
drone of the bee, by reedy rustling stream, will never know on earth in
any wise. But once heard it comes ever, as I, though in the city, heard
it last night in the winter wind, with Romany words mingled in wild
refrain:--

"*Kamava tute*, *miri chelladi*!"

II. AUSTRIAN GYPSIES IN PHILADELPHIA.

It was a sunny Sunday afternoon, and I was walking down Chestnut Street,
Philadelphia, when I met with three very dark men.

Dark men are not rarities in my native city. There is, for instance, Eugene, who has the invaluable faculty of being able to turn his hand to an infinite helpfulness in the small arts. These men were darker than Eugene, but they differed from him in this, that while he is a man of color, they were not. For in America the man of Aryan blood, however dark he may be, is always "off" color, while the lightest-hued quadroon is always on it. Which is not the only paradox connected with the descendants of Africans of which I have heard.

I saw at a glance that these dark men were much nearer to the old Aryan stock than are even my purely white readers. For they were more recently from India, and they could speak a language abounding in Hindi, in pure old Sanskrit, and in Persian. Yet they would make no display of it; on the contrary, I knew that they would be very likely at first to deny all knowledge thereof, as well as their race and blood. For they were gypsies; it was very apparent in their eyes, which had the Gitano gleam as one seldom sees it in England. I confess that I experienced a thrill as I exchanged glances with them. It was a long time since I had seen a Romany, and, as usual, I knew that I was going to astonish them. They were singularly attired, having very good clothes of a quite theatrical foreign fashion, bearing silver buttons as large as and of the shape of hen's eggs. Their hair hung in black ringlets down their shoulders, and I saw that they had come from the Austrian Slavonian land.

I addressed the eldest in Italian. He answered fluently and politely. I changed to Ilirski or Illyrian and to Serb, of which I have a few phrases in stock. They spoke all these languages fluently, for one was a born Illyrian and one a Serb. They also spoke Nemetz, or German; in fact, everything except English.

"Have you got through all your languages?" I at last inquired.

"Tutte, signore,--all of them."

"Isn't there *one* left behind, which you have forgotten? Think a minute."

"No, signore. None."

"What, not *one*! You know so many that perhaps a language more or less makes no difference to you."

"By the Lord, signore, you have seen every egg in the basket."

I looked him fixedly in the eyes, and said, in a low tone,--

"*Ne rakesa tu Romanes miro prala*?"

There was a startled glance from one to the other, and a silence. I had asked him if he could not talk Romany. And I added,--

"*Won't* you talk a word with a gypsy brother?"

That moved them. They all shook my hands with great feeling, expressing intense joy and amazement at meeting with one who knew them.

"*Mishto hom me dikava tute*." (I am glad to see you.) So they told me how they were getting on, and where they were camped, and how they sold horses, and so on, and we might have got on much farther had it not been for a very annoying interruption. As I was talking to the gypsies, a great number of men, attracted by the sound of a foreign language, stopped, and fairly pushed themselves up to us, endeavoring to make it all out. When there were at least fifty, they crowded in between me and the foreigners, so that I could hardly talk to them. The crowd did not consist of ordinary people, or snobs. They were well dressed,--young clerks, at least,--who would have fiercely resented being told that they were impertinent.

"Eye-talians, ain't they?" inquired one man, who was evidently zealous in pursuit of knowledge.

"Why don't you tell us what they are sayin'?"

"What kind of fellers air they, any way?"

I was desirous of going with the Hungarian Roms. But to walk along Chestnut Street with an augmenting procession of fifty curious Sunday promenaders was not on my card. In fact, I had some difficulty in tearing myself from the inquisitive, questioning, well-dressed people. The gypsies bore the pressure with the serene equanimity of cosmopolite superiority, smiling at provincial rawness. Even so in China and Africa the traveler is mobbed by the many, who, there as here, think that "I want to know" is full excuse for all intrusiveness. **Q'est tout comme chez nous**. I confess that I was vexed, and, considering that it was in my native city, mortified.

A few days after I went out to the *tan* where these Roms had camped. But the birds had flown, and a little pile of ashes and the usual debris of a gypsy camp were all that remained. The police told me that they had some very fine horses, and had gone to the Northwest; and that is all I ever saw of them.

I have heard of a philanthropist who was turned into a misanthrope by attempting to sketch in public and in galleries. Respectable strangers, even clergymen, would stop and coolly look over his shoulder, and ask questions, and give him advice, until he could work no longer. Why is it that people who would not speak to you for life without an introduction should think that their small curiosity to see your sketches authorizes them to act as aquaintances? Or why is the pursuit of knowledge assumed among the half-bred to be an excuse for so much intrusion? "I want to know." Well, and what if you do? The man who thinks that his desire for knowledge is an excuse for impertinence--and there are too many who act on this in all sincerity--is of the kind who knocks the fingers off statues, because "he wants them" for his collection; who chips away tombstones, and hews down historic trees, and not infrequently steals outright, and thinks that his pretense of culture is full excuse for all his mean deeds. Of this tribe is the man who cuts his name on all walls and smears it on the pyramids, to proclaim himself a fool to the world; the difference being that, instead of wanting to know anything, he wants everybody to know that His Littleness was once in a great place.

I knew a distinguished artist, who, while in the East, only secured his best sketch of a landscape by employing fifty men to keep off the multitude. I have seen a strange fellow take a lady's sketch out of her hand, excusing himself with the remark that he was so fond of pictures. Of course my readers do not act thus. When they are passing through the Louvre or British Museum they never pause and overlook artists, despite the notices requesting them not to do so. Of course not. Yet I once knew a charming young American lady, who scouted the idea as nonsense that she should not watch artists at work. "Why, we used to make up parties for the purpose of looking at them!" she said. "It was half the fun of going there. I'm sure the artists were delighted to get a chance to talk to us." Doubtless. And yet there are really very few artists who do not work more at their ease when not watched, and I have known some to whom such watching was misery. They are not, O intruder, painting for *your* amusement!

This is not such a far cry from my Romanys as it may seem. When I think of what I have lost in this life by impertinence coming between me and gypsies, I feel that it could not be avoided. The proportion of men, even of gentlemen, or of those who dress decently, who cannot see another well-dressed man talking with a very poor one in public, without at once

surmising a mystery, and endeavoring to solve it, is amazing. And they
do not stop at a trifle, either.

It is a marked characteristic of all gypsies that they are quite free
from any such mean intrusiveness. Whether it is because they themselves
are continually treated as curiosities, or because great knowledge of
life in a small way has made them philosophers, I will not say, but it is
a fact that in this respect they are invariably the politest people in
the world. Perhaps their calm contempt of the *galerly*, or green
Gorgios, is founded on a consciousness of their superiority in this
matter.

The Hungarian gypsy differs from all his brethren of Europe in being more
intensely gypsy. He has deeper, wilder, and more original feeling in
music, and he is more inspired with a love of travel. Numbers of
Hungarian Romany chals--in which I include all Austrian gypsies--travel
annually all over Europe, but return as regularly to their own country.
I have met with them exhibiting bears in Baden-Baden. These Ricinari, or
bear-leaders, form, however, a set within a set, and are in fact more
nearly allied to the gypsy bear-leaders of Turkey and Syria than to any
other of their own people. They are wild and rude to a proverb, and
generally speak a peculiar dialect of Romany, which is called the
Bear-leaders' by philologists. I have also seen Syrian-gypsy Ricinari in
Cairo. Many of the better caste make a great deal of money, and some are
rich. Like all really pure-blooded gypsies, they have deep feelings,
which are easily awakened by kindness, but especially by sympathy and
interest.

ENGLISH GYPSIES.

I. OATLANDS PARK.

Oatlands Park (between Weybridge and Walton-upon-Thames) was once the property of the Duke of York, but now the lordly manor-house is a hotel. The grounds about it are well preserved and very picturesque. They should look well, for they cover a vast and wasted fortune. There is, for instance, a grotto which cost forty thousand pounds. It is one of those wretched and tasteless masses of silly rock-rococo work which were so much admired at the beginning of the present century, when sham ruins and sham caverns were preferred to real. There is, also, close by the grotto, a dogs' burial-ground, in which more than a hundred animals, the favorites of the late duchess, lie buried. Over each is a tombstone, inscribed with a rhyming epitaph, written by the titled lady herself, and which is in sober sadness in every instance doggerel, as befits the subject. In order to degrade the associations of religion and church rites as effectually as possible, there is attached to these graves the semblance of a ruined chapel, the stained-glass window of which was taken from a church. {97} I confess that I could never see either grotto or grave-yard without sincerely wishing, out of regard to the memory of both duke and duchess, that these ridiculous relics of vulgar taste and affected sentimentalism could be completely obliterated. But, apart from them, the scenes around are very beautiful; for there are grassy slopes and pleasant lawns, ancient trees and broad gravel walks, over which, as the dry leaves fall on the crisp sunny morning, the feet are tempted to walk on and on, all through the merry golden autumn day.

The neighborhood abounds in memories of olden time. Near Oatlands is a modernized house, in which Henry the Eighth lived in his youth. It belonged then to Cardinal Wolsey; now it is owned by Mr. Lindsay,--a sufficient cause for wits calling it Lindsay-Wolsey, that being also a "fabric." Within an hour's walk is the palace built by Cardinal Wolsey, while over the river, and visible from the portico, is the little old Gothic church of Shepperton, and in the same view, to the right, is the old Walton Bridge, by Cowie Stakes, supposed to cover the exact spot where Caesar crossed. This has been denied by many, but I know that the field adjacent to it abounds in ancient British jars filled with burned bones, the relics of an ancient battle,--probably that which legend states was fought on the neighboring Battle Island. Stout-hearted Queen Bessy has also left her mark on this neighborhood, for within a mile is the old Saxon-towered church of Walton, in which the royal dame was asked for her opinion of the sacrament when it was given to her, to which she replied:--

> "Christ was the Word who spake it,
> He took the bread and brake it;
> And what that Word did make it,
> That I believe, and take it."

In memory of this the lines were inscribed on the massy Norman pillar by which she stood. From the style and cutting it is evident that the inscription dates from the reign of Elizabeth. And very near Oatlands, in fact on the grounds, there are two ancient yew-trees, several hundred yards apart. The story runs that Queen Elizabeth once drew a long bow and shot an arrow so far that, to commemorate the deed, one of these trees was planted where she stood, and the other where the shaft fell. All England is a museum of touching or quaint relics; to me one of its most interesting cabinets is this of the neighborhood of Weybridge and Walton-upon-Thames.

I once lived for eight months at Oatlands Park, and learned to know the neighborhood well. I had many friends among the families in the vicinity, and, guided by their advice, wandered to every old church and manor-house, ruin and haunted rock, fairy-oak, tower, palace, or shrine within a day's ramble. But there was one afternoon walk of four miles, round by the river, which I seldom missed. It led by a spot on the bank, and an old willow-tree near the bridge, which spot was greatly haunted by the Romany, so that, excepting during the hopping-season of autumn, when they were away in Kent, I seldom failed to see from afar a light rising smoke, and near it a tent and a van, as the evening shadows blended with the mist from the river in phantom union.

It is a common part of gypsy life that the father shall be away all day, lounging about the next village, possibly in the *kitchema* or ale-house, or trying to trade a horse, while the wife trudges over the country, from one farm-house or cottage to another, loaded with baskets, household utensils, toys, or cheap ornaments, which she endeavors, like a true Autolyca, with wily arts and wheedling tones, to sell to the rustics. When it can be managed, this hawking is often an introduction to fortune-telling, and if these fail the gypsy has recourse to begging. But it is a weary life, and the poor *dye* is always glad enough to get home. During the day the children have been left to look out for themselves or to the care of the eldest, and have tumbled about the van, rolled around with the dog, and fought or frolicked as they chose. But though their parents often have a stock of cheap toys, especially of penny dolls and the like, which they put up as prizes for games at races and fairs, I have never seen these children with playthings. The little girls have no dolls; the boys, indeed, affect whips, as becomes incipient jockeys, but on the whole they never seemed to me to have the same ideas as to play as ordinary house-children. The author of "My Indian Garden" has made the same observation of Hindoo little ones, whose ways are not as our ways were when we were young. Roman and Egyptian children had their dolls; and there is something sadly sweet to me in the sight of these barbarous and naive facsimiles of miniature humanity, which come up like little spectres out of the dust of ancient days. They are so rude and queer, these Roman puppets; and yet they were loved once, and had pet names, and their owl-like faces were as tenderly kissed as their little mistresses had been by their mothers. So the Romany girl, unlike the Roman, is generally doll-less and toy-less. But the affection between mother and child is as warm among these wanderers as with any other people; and it is a touching sight to see the gypsy who has been absent all the weary day returning home. And when she is seen from afar off there is a race among all the little dark-brown things to run to mother and get kissed, and cluster and scramble around her, and perhaps receive some little gift which mother's thoughtful love has provided. Knowing these customs, I was wont to fill my pockets with chestnuts or oranges, and, distributing them among the little ones, talk with them, and await the sunset return of their parents. The confidence or love of all children is delightful; but that of gypsy children resembles the friendship of young foxes, and the study of their artless-artful ways is indeed attractive. I can remember that one afternoon six small Romany boys implored me to give them each a penny. I replied,--

"If I had sixpence, how would you divide it?"

"That would be a penny apiece," said the eldest boy.

"And if threepence?"

"A ha'penny apiece."

"And three ha'pence?"

"A farden all round. And then it couldn't go no furder, unless we bought tobacco an' diwided it."

"Well, I have some tobacco. But can any of you smoke?"

They were from four to ten years of age, and at the word every one pulled out the stump of a blackened pipe,--such depraved-looking fragments I never saw,--and holding them all up, and crowding closely around, like hungry poultry with uplifted bills, they began to clamor for *tuvalo*, or tobacco. They were connoisseurs, too, and the elder boy, as he secured his share, smelled it with intense satisfaction, and said, "That's *rye's tuvalo*;" that is, "gentleman's tobacco," or best quality.

One evening, as the shadows were darkening the day, I met a little gypsy boy, dragging along, with incredible labor, a sack full of wood, which one needed not go far afield to surmise was neither purchased nor begged. The alarmed and guilty or despairing look which he cast at me was very touching. Perhaps he thought I was the gentleman upon whose property he had "found" the wood; or else a magistrate. How he stared when I spoke to him in Romany, and offered to help him carry it! As we bore it along I suggested that we had better be careful and avoid the police, which remark established perfect confidence between us. But as we came to the tent, what was the amazement of the boy's mother to see him returning with a gentleman helping him to carry his load! And to hear me say in Romany, and in a cheerful tone, "Mother, here is some wood we've been stealing for you."

Gypsies have strong nerves and much cheek, but this was beyond her endowment; she was appalled at the unearthly strangeness of the whole proceeding, and when she spoke there was a skeleton rattle in her words and a quaver of startled ghastliness in her laugh. She had been alarmed for her boy, and when I appeared she thought I was a swell bringing him in under arrest; but when I announced myself in Romany as an accomplice, emotion stifled thought. And I lingered not, and spoke no more, but walked away into the woods and the darkness. However, the legend went forth on the roads, even unto Kingston, and was told among the rollicking Romanys of 'Appy Ampton; for there are always a merry, loafing lot of

them about that festive spot, looking out for excursionists through the
months when the gorse blooms, and kissing is in season--which is always.
And he who seeks them on Sunday may find them camped in Green Lane.

When I wished for a long ramble on the hedge-lined roads--the sweet roads
of old England--and by the green fields, I was wont to take a day's walk
to Netley Abbey. Then I could pause, as I went, before many a quiet,
sheltered spot, adorned with arbors and green alleys, and protected by
trees and hawthorn hedges, and again surrender my soul, while walking, to
tender and vague reveries, in which all definite thoughts swim
overpowered, yet happy, in a sea of voluptuous emotions inspired by
clouds lost in the blue sea of heaven and valleys visioned away into the
purple sky. What opium is to one, what hasheesh may be to another, what
kheyf or mere repose concentrated into actuality is to the Arab, that
is Nature to him who has followed her for long years through poets and
mystics and in works of art, until at last he pierces through dreams and
pictures to reality.

The ruins of Netley Abbey, nine or ten miles from Oatlands Park, are
picturesque and lonely, and well fitted for the dream-artist in shadows
among sunshine. The priory was called Newstead or De Novo Loco in Norman
times, when it was founded by Ruald de Calva, in the day of Richard Coeur
de Lion. The ruins rise gray, white, and undressed with ivy, that they
may contrast the more vividly with the deep emerald of the meadows
around. "The surrounding scenery is composed of rivers and
rivulets,"--for seven streams run by it, according to Aubrey,--"of
foot-bridge and fords, plashy pools and fringed, tangled hollows, trees
in groups or alone, and cattle dotted over the pastures:" an English Cuyp
from many points of view, beautiful and English-home-like from all. Very
near it is the quaint, out-of-the-way, darling little old church of
Pirford, up a hill, nestling among trees, a half-Norman, decorated
beauty, out of the age, but altogether in the heart. As I came near, of
a summer afternoon, the waving of leaves and the buzzing of bees without,

and the hum of the voices of children at school within the adjoining building, the cool shade and the beautiful view of the ruined Abbey beyond, made an impression which I can never forget. Among such scenes one learns why the English love so heartily their rural life, and why every object peculiar to it has brought forth a picture or a poem. I can imagine how many a man, who has never known what poetry was at home, has wept with yearning inexpressible, when sitting among burning sands and under the palms of the East, for such scenes as these.

But Netley Abbey is close by the river Wey, and the sight of that river and the thought of the story of the monks of the olden time who dwelt in the Abbey drive away sentiment as suddenly as a north wind scatters sea-fogs. For the legend is a merry one, and the reader may have heard it; but if he has not I will give it in one of the merriest ballads ever written. By whom I know not,--doubtless many know. I sing, while walking, songs of olden time.

THE MONKS OF THE WEY.

A TRUE AND IMPORTANT RELATION OF THE WONDERFUL TUN-NELL OF NEWARKE ABBEY

AND OF THE UNTIMELY ENDE OF SEVERALL OF YE GHOSTLY BRETH'REN.

The monks of the Wey seldom sung any psalms,
And little they thought of religion or qualms;
Such rollicking, frolicking, ranting, and gay,
And jolly old boys were the monks of the Wey.

To the sweet nuns of Ockham devoting their cares,
They had little time for their beads and their prayers;
For the love of these maidens they sighed night and day,
And neglected devotion, these monks of the Wey.

And happy i' faith might these brothers have been
If the river had never been rolling between
The abbey so grand and the convent so gray,
That stood on the opposite side of the Wey.

For daily they sighed, and then nightly they pined
But little to anchorite precepts inclined,
So smitten with beauty's enchantments were they,
These rollicking, frolicking monks of the Wey.

But scandal was rife in the country near,
They dared not row over the river for fear;
And no more could they swim it, so fat were they,
These oily and amorous monks of the Wey.

Loudly they groaned for their fate so hard,
From the love of these beautiful maidens debarred,
Till a brother just hit on a plan which would stay
The woe of these heart-broken monks of the Wey.

"Nothing," quoth he, "should true love sunder;
Since we cannot go over, then let us go under!
Boats and bridges shall yield to clay,
We'll dig a long tunnel clean under the Wey."

So to it they went with right good will,
With spade and shovel and pike and bill;

And from evening's close till the dawn of day
They worked like miners all under the Wey.

And at vesper hour, as their work begun,
Each sung of the charms of his favorite nun;
"How surprised they will be, and how happy!" said they,
"When we pop in upon them from under the Wey!"

And for months they kept grubbing and making no sound
Like other black moles, darkly under the ground;
And no one suspected such going astray,
So sly were these mischievous monks of the Wey.

At last their fine work was brought near to a close
And early one morn from their pallets they rose,
And met in their tunnel with lights to survey
If they'd scooped a free passage right under the Wey.

But alas for their fate! As they smirked and they smiled.
To think how completely the world was beguiled,
The river broke in, and it grieves me to say
It drowned all the frolicksome monks of the Wey.

* * * * *

O churchmen beware of the lures of the flesh,
The net of the devil has many a mesh!
And remember whenever you're tempted to stray,
The fate that befell the poor monks of the Wey.

It was all long ago, and now there are neither monks nor nuns; the
convent has been converted, little by little, age by age, into cottages,
even as the friars and nuns themselves may have been organically changed

possibly into violets, but more probably into the festive sparrows which flit and hop and flirt about the ruins with abrupt startles, like pheasants sudden bursting on the wing. There is a pretty little Latin epigram, written by a gay monk, of a pretty little lady, who, being very amorous, and observing that sparrows were like her as to love, hoped that she might be turned into one after death; and it is not difficult for a dreamer in an old abbey, of a golden day to fancy that these merry, saucy birdies, who dart and dip in and out of the sunshine or shadow, chirping their shameless ditties *pro et con*, were once the human dwellers in the spot, who sang their gaudrioles to pleasant strains.

I became familiar with many such scenes for many miles about Oatlands, not merely during solitary walks, but by availing myself of the kind invitations of many friends, and by hunting afoot with the beagles. In this fashion one has hare and hound, but no horse. It is not needed, for while going over crisp stubble and velvet turf, climbing fences and jumping ditches, a man has a keen sense of being his own horse, and when he accomplishes a good leap of being intrinsically well worth 200 pounds. And indeed, so long as anybody can walk day in and out a greater distance than would tire a horse, he may well believe he is really worth one. It may be a good thing for us to reflect on the fact that if slavery prevailed at the present day as it did among the polished Greeks the average price of young gentlemen, and even of young ladies, would not be more than what is paid for a good hunter. Divested of diamonds and of Worth's dresses, what would a girl of average charms be worth to a stranger? Let us reflect!

It was an October morning, and, pausing after a run, I let the pack and the "course-men" sweep away, while I sat in a pleasant spot to enjoy the air and scenery. The solemn grandeur of groves and the quiet dignity of woodland glades, barred with rays of solid-seeming sunshine, such as the saint of old hung his cloak on, the brook into which the overhanging chestnuts drop, as if in sport, their creamy golden little boats of leaves, never seem so beautiful or impressive as immediately after a rush and cry of many men, succeeded by solitude and silence. Little by little the bay of the hounds, the shouts of the hunters, and the occasional sound of the horn grew fainter; the birds once more appeared, and sent forth short calls to their timid friends. I began again to notice who my neighbors were, as to daisies and heather which resided around the stone on which I sat, and the exclusive circle of a fairy-ring at a little distance, which, like many exclusive circles, consisted entirely of mushrooms.

As the beagle-sound died away, and while the hounds were "working around" to the road, I heard footsteps approaching, and looking up saw before me a gypsy woman and a boy. She was a very gypsy woman, an ideal witch, nut-brown, tangle-haired, aquiline of nose, and fierce-eyed; and fiercely did she beg! As amid broken Gothic ruins, overhung with unkempt ivy, one can trace a vanished and strange beauty, so in this worn face of the Romany, mantled by neglected tresses, I could see the remains of what must have been once a wonderful though wild loveliness. As I looked into those serpent eyes; trained for a long life to fascinate in fortune-telling simple dove-girls, I could readily understand the implicit faith with which many writers in the olden time spoke of the "fascination" peculiar to female glances. "The multiplication of women," said the rabbis, "is the increase of witches," for the belles in Israel were killing girls, with arrows, the bows whereof are formed by pairs of jet-black eyebrows joined in one. And thus it was that these black-eyed beauties, by *mashing* {108} men for many generations, with shafts shot sideways and most wantonly, at last sealed their souls into the corner of their eyes, as you have heard before. Cotton Mather tells us that these witches with peaked eye-corners could never weep but three tears out of their long-tailed eyes. And I have observed that such tears, as they sweep down the cheeks of the brunette witches, are also long-tailed, and recall by their shape and glitter the eyes from which they fell, even as the daughter recalls the mother. For all love's witchcraft lurks in flashing eyes,--*lontan del occhio lontan dal' cuor*.

It is a great pity that the pigeon-eye-peaks, so pretty in young witches, become in the old ones crow's-feet and crafty. When I greeted the woman, she answered in Romany, and said she was a Stanley from the North. She lied bravely, and I told her so. It made no difference in any way, nor was she hurt. The brown boy, who seemed like a goblin, umber-colored fungus, growing by a snaky black wild vine, sat by her and stared at me. I was pleased, when he said *tober*, that she corrected him, exclaiming earnestly, "Never say *tober* for road; that is *canting*. Always say *drom*; that is good Romanes." There is always a way of bringing up a child in the way he should go,--though it be a gypsy one,--and *drom* comes from the Greek *dromos*, which is elegant and classical. Then she began to beg again, to pass the time, and I lectured her severely on the sin and meanness of her conduct, and said, with bitterness, "Do dogs eat dogs, or are all the Gorgios dead in the land, that you cry for money to me? Oh, you are a fine Stanley! a nice Beshaley you, to sing mumpin and mongerin, when a half-blood Matthews has too much decency to trouble the rye! And how much will you take? Whatever the gentleman pleases, and thank you, my kind sir, and the blessings of the poor gypsy woman on you. Yes, I know that, *givelli*, you mother of all the liars. You expect a sixpence, and here it is, and may you get drunk on the money, and be well thrashed by your man for it. And now see what I had in my hand all the time to give you. A lucky half crown, my deary; but that's not for you now. I only give a sixpence to a beggar, but I stand a *pash-korauna* to any Romany who's a pal and amal."

This pleasing discourse made us very good friends, and, as I kept my eyes sharply fixed on her viper orbs with an air of intense suspicion, everything like ill-feeling or distrust naturally vanished from her mind; for it is of the nature of the Romanys and all their kind to like those whom they respect, and respect those whom they cannot deceive, and to measure mankind exactly by their capacity of being taken in, especially by themselves. As is also the case, in good society, with many ladies and some gentlemen,--and much good may it do them!

There was a brief silence, during which the boy still looked wistfully into my face, as if wondering what kind of gentleman I might be, until his mother said,--

"How do you do with them *ryas* [swells]? What do you tell 'em--about--what do they think--you know?"

This was not explicit, but I understood it perfectly. There is a great deal of such loose, disjointed conversation among gypsies and other half-thinkers. An educated man requires, or pretends to himself to require, a most accurately-detailed and form-polished statement of anything to understand it. The gypsy is less exacting. I have observed among rural Americans much of this lottery style of conversation, in which one man invests in a dubious question, not knowing exactly what sort of a prize or blank answer he may draw. What the gypsy meant effectively was, "How do you account to the Gorgios for knowing so much about us, and talking with us? Our life is as different from yours as possible, and you never acquired such a knowledge of all our tricky ways as you have just shown without much experience of us and a double life. You are related to us in some way, and you deceive the Gorgios about it. What is your little game of life, on general principles?"

For the gypsy is so little accustomed to having any congenial interest taken in him that he can clearly explain it only by consanguinity. And as I was questioned, so I answered,--

"Well, I tell them I like to learn languages, and am trying to learn yours; and then I'm a foreigner in the country, anyhow, and they don't know my *droms* [ways], and they don't care much what I do,--don't you see?"

This was perfectly satisfactory, and as the hounds came sweeping round the corner of the wood she rose and went her way, and I saw her growing less and less along the winding road and up the hill, till she disappeared, with her boy, in a small ale-house. "Bang went the sixpence."

When the last red light was in the west I went down to the river, and as I paused, and looked alternately at the stars reflected and flickering in the water and at the lights in the little gypsy camp, I thought that as the dancing, restless, and broken sparkles were to their serene types above, such were the wandering and wild Romany to the men of culture in their settled homes. It is from the house-dweller that the men of the roads and commons draw the elements of their life, but in that life they are as shaken and confused as the starlight in the rippling river. But if we look through our own life we find that it is not the gypsy alone who is merely a reflection and an imitation of the stars above him, and a creature of second-hand fashion.

I found in the camp an old acquaintance, named Brown, and also perceived at the first greeting that the woman Stanley had told Mrs. Brown that I would not be *mongerdo*, or begged from, and that the latter, proud of her power in extortion, and as yet invincible in mendicancy, had boasted that she would succeed, let others weakly fail. And to lose no time she went at me with an abruptness and dramatic earnestness which promptly betrayed the secret. And on the spot I made a vow that nothing should get a farthing from me, though I should be drawn by wild horses. And a horse was, indeed, brought into requisition to draw me, or my money, but without success; for Mr. Brown, as I very well knew,--it being just then the current topic in the best society on the road,--had very recently been involved in a tangled trouble with a stolen horse. This horse had been figuratively laid at his door, even as a "love-babe" is sometimes placed on the front steps of a virtuous and grave citizen,--at least, this is what White George averred,--and his very innocence and purity had, like a shining mark, attracted the shafts of the wicked. He had come out unscathed, with a package of papers from a lawyer, which established his character above par; but all this had cost money, beautiful golden money, and brought him to the very brink of ruin! Mrs. Brown's attack was a desperate and determined effort, and there was more at stake on its success than the reader may surmise. Among gypsy women skill in begging implies the possession of every talent which they most esteem, such as artfulness, cool effrontery, and the power of moving pity or provoking generosity by pique or humor. A quaint and racy book might be written, should it only set forth the manner in which the experienced matrons give straight-tips or suggestions to the maidens as to the manner and lore of begging; and it is something worth hearing when several sit together and devise dodges, and tell anecdotes illustrating the noble art of mendicity, and how it should be properly practiced.

Mrs. Brown knew that to extort alms from me would place her on the pinnacle as an artist. Among all the Cooper clan, to which she was allied, there was not one who ever begged from me, they having all found that the ripest nuts are those which fall from the tree of their own accord, or are blown earthward by the soft breezes of benevolence, and not those which are violently beaten down. She began by pitiful appeals; she was moving, but I did not budge. She grew pathetic; she touched on the stolen horse; she paused, and gushed almost to tears, as much as to say, If it must be, you *shall* know all. Ruin stared them in the face; poverty was crushing them. It was well acted,--rather in the Bernhardt style, which, if M. Ondit speaks the truth, is also employed rather extensively for acquiring "de monish." I looked at the van, of which the Browns are proud, and inquired if it were true that it had been insured for a hundred pounds, as George had recently boasted. Persuasion having failed, Mrs. Brown tried bold defiance, saying that they needed no company who were no good to them, and plainly said to me I might be gone. It was her last card, thinking that a threat to dissolve our acquaintance

would drive me to capitulate, and it failed. I laughed, went into the
van, sat down, took out my brandy flask, and then accepted some bread and
ale, and, to please them, read aloud all the papers acquitting George
from all guilt as concerned the stolen horse,--papers which, he declared,
had cost him full five pounds. This was a sad come-down from the story
first told. Then I seriously rated his wife for begging from me. "You
know well enough," I said, "that I give all I can spare to your family
and your people when they are sick or poor. And here you are, the
richest Romanys on the road between Windsor and the Boro Gav, begging a
friend, who knows all about you, for money! Now, here is a shilling.
Take it. Have half a crown? Two of 'em! No! Oh, you don't want it
here in your own house. Well, you have some decency left, and to save
your credit I won't make you take it. And you scandalize me, a gentleman
and a friend, just to show this tramp of a Stanley *juva*, who hasn't
even got a drag [wagon], that you can beat her *a mongerin mandy*
[begging me]."

Mrs. Brown assented volubly to everything, and all the time I saw in her
smiling eyes, ever agreeing to all, and heard from her voluble lips
nothing but the *lie*,--that lie which is the mental action and inmost
grain of the Romany, and especially of the *diddikai*, or half-breed.
Anything and everything--trickery, wheedling or bullying, fawning or
threatening, smiles, or rage, or tears--for a sixpence. All day long
flattering and tricking to tell fortunes or sell trifles, and all life
one greasy lie, with ready frowns or smiles: as it was in India in the
beginning, as it is in Europe, and as it will be in America, so long as
there shall be a rambler on the roads, amen!

Sweet peace again established, Mrs. Brown became herself once more, and
acted the hospitable hostess, exactly in the spirit and manner of any
woman who has "a home of her own," and a spark of decent feeling in her
heart. Like many actors, she was a bad lot on the boards, but a very
nice person off them. Here in her rolling home she was neither a beggar

nor poor, and she issued her orders grandly. "Boil some tea for the *rye*--cook some coffee for the *rye*--wait a few minutes, my darling gentleman, and I'll brile you a steak--or here's a fish, if you'd like it?" But I declined everything except the corner of a loaf and some ale; and all the time a little brown boy, with great black eyes, a perfect Murillo model, sat condensed in wondrous narrow space by the fire, baking small apples between the bars of the grate, and rolling up his orbs at me as if wondering what could have brought me into such a circle,--even as he had done that morning in the greenwood.

Now if the reader would know what the interior of a gypsy van, or "drag," or *wardo*, is like, he may see it in the following diagram.

[Picture: Interior of gypsy van]

A is the door; *B* is the bed, or rather two beds, each six feet long, like berths, with a vacant space below; *C* is a grate cooking-stove; *D* is a table, which hangs by hinges from the wall; *E* is a chest of drawers; *f* and *f* are two chairs. The general appearance of a well-kept van is that of a state-room. Brown's is a very good van, and quite clean. They are admirably well adapted for slow traveling, and it was in such vans, purchased from gypsies, that Sir Samuel Baker and his wife explored the whole of Cyprus.

Mrs. Brown was proud of her van and of her little treasures. From the great recess under the bed she raked out as a rare curiosity an old Dolly Varden or damasked skirt, not at all worn, quite pretty, and evidently of considerable value to a collector. This had belonged to Mrs. Brown's grandmother, an old gypsy queen. And it may be observed, by the way, that the claims of every Irishman of every degree to be descended from one of the ancient kings of Ireland fade into nothing before those of the gypsy women, all of whom, with rare exception, are the own daughters of royal personages, granddaughterhood being hardly a claim to true

nobility. Then the bed itself was exhibited with pride, and the princess
sang its praises, till she affirmed that the *rye* himself did not sleep
on a better one, for which George reprimanded her. But she vigorously
defended its excellence, and, to please her, I felt it and declared it
was indeed much softer than the one I slept on, which was really
true,--thank Heaven--and was received as a great compliment, and
afterwards proclaimed on the roads even unto the ends of Surrey.

"Yes," said Brown, as I observed some osiers in the cupboard, "when I
feels like it I sometimes makes a pound a day a-making baskets."

"I should think," I said, "that it would be cheaper to buy French baskets
of Bulrose [Bulureaux] in Houndsditch, ready made."

"So one would think; but the *ranyor* [osiers] costs nothin', and so it's
all profit, any way."

Then I urged the greater profit of living in America, but both assured me
that so long as they could make a good living and be very comfortable, as
they considered themselves, in England, it would be nonsense to go to
America.

For all things are relative, and many a gypsy whom the begged-from pity
sincerely, is as proud and happy in a van as any lord in the land. A
very nice, neat young gypsy woman, camped long before just where the
Browns were, once said to me, "It isn't having everything fine and
stylish that makes you happy. Now we've got a van, and have everything
so elegant and comfortable, and sleep warm as anybody; and yet I often
say to my husband that we used to be happier when we used to sleep under
a hedge with, may be, only a thin blanket, and wake up covered with
snow." Now this woman had only a wretched wagon, and was always tramping
in the rain, or cowering in a smoky, ragged tent and sitting on the
ground, but she had food, fire, and fun, with warm clothes, and believed

herself happy. Truly, she had better reason to think so than any old maid with a heart run to waste on church gossip, or the latest engagements and marriages; for it is better to be a street-boy in a corner with a crust than one who, without it, discusses, in starvation, with his friend the sausages and turtle-soup in a cook-shop window, between which and themselves there is a great pane of glass fixed, never to be penetrated.

II. WALKING AND VISITING.

I never shall forget the sparkling splendor of that frosty morning in December when I went with a younger friend from Oatlands Park for a day's walk. I may have seen at other times, but I do not remember, such winter lace-work as then adorned the hedges. The gossamer spider has within her an inward monitor which tells if the weather will be fine; but it says nothing about sudden changes to keen cold, and the artistic result was that the hedges were hung with thousands of Honiton lamp-mats, instead of the thread fly-catchers which their little artists had intended. And on twigs and dead leaves, grass and rock and wall, were such expenditures of Brussels and Spanish point, such a luxury of real old Venetian run mad, and such deliria of Russian lace as made it evident that Mrs. Jack Frost is a very extravagant fairy, but one gifted with exquisite taste. When I reflect how I have in my time spoken of the taste for lace and diamonds in women as entirely without foundation in nature, I feel that I sinned deeply. For Nature, in this lace-work, displays at times a sympathy with humanity,--especially womanity,--and coquets and flirts with it, as becomes the subject, in a manner which is merrily awful. There was once in Philadelphia a shop the windows of which were always filled with different kinds of the richest and rarest lace, and one cold morning I found that the fairies had covered the panes with literal frost fac-similes of the exquisite wares which hung behind. This was no fancy; the copies were as accurate as photographs. Can it be that in the invisible world there are Female Fairy Schools of Design, whose scholars combine in this graceful style Etching on Glass and Art Needlework?

We were going to the village of Hersham to make a call. It was not at any stylish villa or lordly manor-house,--though I knew of more than one in the vicinity where we would have been welcome,--but at a rather disreputable-looking edifice, which bore on its front the sign of "Lodgings for Travellers." Now "traveller" means, below a certain circle of English life, not the occasional, but the habitual wanderer, or one who dwells upon the roads, and gains his living thereon. I have in my possession several cards of such a house. I found them wrapped in a piece of paper, by a deserted gypsy camp, where they had been lost:--

A NEW HOUSE.

Good Lodging for Travellers. With a Large Private Kitchen.

THE CROSS KEYS,
WEST STREET . . . MAIDENHEAD.

BY J. HARRIS.

The "private kitchen" indicates that the guests will have facilities for doing their own cooking, as all of them bring their own victuals in perpetual picnic. In the inclosure of the house in Hersham, the tops of two or three gypsy vans could always be seen above the high fence, and there was that general air of mystery about the entire establishment which is characteristic of all places haunted by people whose ways are not as our ways, and whose little games are not as our little games. I had become acquainted with it and its proprietor, Mr. Hamilton, in that irregular and only way which is usual with such acquaintances. I was walking by the house one summer day, and stopped to ask my way. A handsome dark-brown girl was busy at the wash-tub, two or three older women were clustered at the gate, and in all their faces was the manner of the **diddikai** or **chureni**, or half-blood gypsy. As I spoke I dropped my voice, and said, inquiringly,--

"Romanes?"

"Yes," was the confidential answer.

They were all astonished, and kept quiet till I had gone a few rods on my way, when the whole party, recovering from their amazement, raised a gentle cheer, expressive of approbation and sympathy. A few days after, walking with a lady in Weybridge, she said to me,--

"Who is that man who looked at you so closely?"

"I do not know."

"That's very strange. I am quite sure I heard him utter two words in a strange language, as you passed, as if he only meant them for you. They sounded like **sarshaun baw**." Which means, "How are you, sir?" or friend. As we came up the street, I saw the man talking with a well-dressed, sporting-looking man, not quite a gentleman, who sat cheekily in his own jaunty little wagon. As I passed, the one of the wagon said to the other, speaking of me, and in pure Romany, evidently thinking I did not understand,--

"**Dikk'adovo Giorgio**, **adoi**!" (Look at that Gorgio, there!)

Being a Romany rye, and not accustomed to be spoken of as a Gorgio, I looked up at him, angrily, when he, seeing that I understood him, smiled, and bowed politely in apology. I laughed and passed on. But I thought

it a little strange, for neither of the men had the slightest indication
of gypsiness. I met the one who had said *sarishan ba* again, soon
after. I found that he and the one of the wagon were not of gypsy blood,
but of a class not uncommon in England, who, be they rich or poor, are
affected towards gypsies. The wealthy one lived with a gypsy mistress;
the poorer one had a gypsy wife, and was very fond of the language.
There is a very large class of these mysterious men everywhere about the
country. They haunt fairs; they pop up unexpectedly as Jack-in-boxes in
unsuspected guise; they look out from under fatherly umbrellas; their
name is Legion; their mother is Mystery, and their uncle is Old Tom,--not
of Virginia, but of Gin. Once, in the old town of Canterbury, I stood in
the street, under the Old Woman with the Clock, one of the quaintest
pieces of drollery ever imagined during the Middle Ages. And by me was a
tinker, and as his wheel went *siz-'z-'z-'z*, *uz-uz-uz-z-z*! I talked
with him, and there joined us a fat, little, elderly, spectacled,
shabby-genteel, but well-to-do-looking sort of a punchy, small tradesman.
And, as we spoke, there went by a great, stout, roaring Romany woman,--a
scarlet-runner of Babylon run to seed,--with a boy and a hand-cart to
carry the seed in. And to her I cried, "*Hav akai te mandy'll del tute a
shaori*!" (Come here, and I'll stand a sixpence!) But she did not
believe in my offer, but went her way, like a Burning Shame, through the
crowd, and was lost evermore. I looked at the little old gentleman to
see what effect my outcry in a strange language had upon him. But he
only remarked, soberly, "Well, now, I *should* 'a' thought a sixpence
would 'a' brought her to!" And the wheel said, "Suz-zuz-zuz-z-z I should
'a' suz-suz 'a' thought a suz-z-zixpence would 'a' suz-zuz 'a' brought
her, too-z-z-z!" And I looked at the Old Woman with the Clock, and she
ticked,
"A--six--pence--would--have--brought--*me*--two--three--four"--and I
began to dream that all Canterbury was Romany.

We came to the house, the landlord was up-stairs, ill in bed, but would
be glad to see us; and he welcomed us warmly, and went deeply into Romany

family matters with my friend, the Oxford scholar. Meanwhile, his daughter, a nice brunette, received and read a letter; and he tried to explain to me the mystery of the many men who are not gypsies, yet speak Romany, but could not do it, though he was one of them. It appeared from his account that they were "a kind of mixed, you see, and dusted in, you know, and on it, out of the family, it peppers up; but not exactly, you understand, and that's the way it is. And I remember a case in point, and that was one day, and I had sold a horse, and was with my boy in a *moramengro's buddika* [barber's shop], and my boy says to me, in Romanes, 'Father, I'd like to have my hair cut.' 'It's too dear here, my son,' said I, Romaneskes; 'for the bill says threepence.' And then the barber, he ups and says, in Romany, 'Since you're Romanys, I'll cut it for *two*pence, though it's clear out of all my rules.' And he did it; but why that man *rakkered Romanes* I don't know, nor how it comes about; for he hadn't no more call to it than a pig has to be a preacher. But I've known men in Sussex to take to diggin' truffles on the same principles, and one Gorgio in Hastings that adopted sellin' fried fish for his livin', about the town, because he thought it was kind of romantic. That's it."

Over the chimney-piece hung a large engraving of Milton and his daughters. It was out of place, and our host knew it, and was proud. He said he had bought it at an auction, and that it was a picture of Middleton,--a poet, he believed; "anyhow, he was a writing man." But, on second thought, he remembered that the name was not Middleton, but Millerton. And on further reflection, he was still more convinced that Millerton *was* a poet.

I once asked old Matthew Cooper the Romany word for a poet. And he promptly replied that he had generally heard such a man called a *givellengero* or *gilliengro*, which means a song-master, but that he himself regarded *shereskero-mush*, or head-man, as more elegant and deeper; for poets make songs out of their heads, and are also ahead of all other men in head-work. There is a touching and unconscious tribute to the art of arts in this definition which is worth recording. It has been said that, as people grow polite, they cease to be poetical; it is certain that in the first circles they do not speak of their poets with such respect as this.

Out again into the fresh air and the frost on the crisp, crackling road and in the sunshine. At such a time, when cold inspires life, one can understand why the old poets and mystics believed that there was fire in ice. Therefore, Saint Sebaldus, coming into the hut of a poor and pious man who was dying of cold, went out, and, bringing in an armful of icicles, laid them on the andirons and made a good fire. Now this fire was the inner glowing glory of God, and worked both ways,--of course you see the connection,--as was shown in Adelheid von Sigolsheim, the Holy Nun of Unterlinden, who was so full of it that she passed the night in a freezing stream, and then stood all the morning, ice-clad, in the choir, and never caught cold. And the pious Peroneta, to avoid a sinful suitor, lived all winter, up to her neck, in ice-water, on the highest Alp in Savoy. {125} These were saints. But there was a gypsy, named Dighton, encamped near Brighton, who told me nearly the same story of another gypsy, who was no saint, and which I repeat merely to show how extremes meet. It was that this gypsy, who was inspired with anything but the inner glowing glory of God, but who was, on the contrary, cram full of pure cussedness, being warmed by the same,--and the devil,--when chased by the constable, took refuge in a river full of freezing slush and broken ice, where he stood up to his neck and defied capture; for he verily cared no more for it than did Saint Peter of Alcantara, who was both ice and fire proof. "Come out of that, my good man," said the gentleman, whose hen he had stolen, "and I'll let you go." "No, I won't come out," said the gypsy. "My blood be on your head!" So the gentleman offered him five pounds, and then a suit of clothes, to come ashore. The gypsy reflected, and at last said, "Well, if you'll add a drink of spirits, I'll come; but it's only to oblige you that I budge."

Then we walked in the sober evening, with its gray gathering shadows, as the last western rose light rippled in the river, yet fading in the sky,--like a good man who, in dying, speaks cheerfully of earthly things, while his soul is vanishing serenely into heaven. The swans, looking like snowballs, unconscious of cold were taking their last swim towards the reedy, brake-tangled islets where they nested, gossiping as they went. The deepening darkness, at such a time, becomes more impressive from the twinkling stars, just as the subduing silence is noted only by the far-borne sounds from the hamlet or farm-house, or the occasional whispers of the night-breeze. So we went on in the twilight, along the Thames, till we saw the night-fire of the Romanys and its gleam on the *tan*. A *tan* is, strictly speaking, a tent, but a tent is a dwelling, or stopping-place; and so from earliest Aryan time, the word *tan* is like Alabama, or "here we rest," and may be found in *tun*, the ancestor of town, and in *stan*, as in Hindostan,--and if I blunder, so much the better for the philological gentlemen, who, of all others, most delight in setting erring brothers right, and never miss a chance to show, through others' shame, how much they know.

There was a bark of a dog, and a voice said, "The Romany rye!" They had not seen us, but the dog knew, and they knew his language.

"*Sarishan ryor*!"

"*O boro duvel atch' pa leste*!" (The great Lord be on you!) This is not a common Romany greeting. It is of ancient days and archaic. Sixty or seventy years ago it was current. Old Gentilla Cooper, the famous fortune-teller of the Devil's Dike, near Brighton, knew it, and when she heard it from me she was moved,--just as a very old negro in London was, when I said to him, "*Sady*, uncle." I said it because I had recognized by the dog's bark that it was Sam Smith's tan. Sam likes to be considered as *deep* Romany. He tries to learn old gypsy words, and he affects old gypsy ways. He is pleased to be called Petulengro, which means Smith. Therefore, my greeting was a compliment.

In a few minutes we were in camp and at home. We talked of many things, and among others of witches. It is remarkable that while the current English idea of a witch is that of an old woman who has sold herself to Satan, and is a distinctly marked character, just like Satan himself, that of the witch among gypsies is general and Oriental. There is no Satan in India. Mrs. Smith--since dead--held that witches were to be found everywhere. "You may know a natural witch," she said, "by certain signs. One of these is straight hair which curls at the ends. Such women have it in them."

It was only recently, as I write, that I was at a very elegant art reception, which was fully reported in the newspapers. And I was very much astonished when a lady called my attention to another young and very pretty lady, and expressed intense disgust at the way the latter wore her hair. It was simply parted in the middle, and fell down on either side, smooth as a water-fall, and then broke into curls at the ends, just as water, after falling, breaks into waves and rapids. But as she spoke, I felt it all, and saw that Mrs. Petulengro was in the right. The girl with the end-curled hair was uncanny. Her hair curled at the ends,--so did her eyes; she *was* a witch.

"But there's a many witches as knows clever things," said Mrs. Petulengro. "And I learned from one of them how to cure the rheumatiz. Suppose you've got the rheumatiz. Well, just you carry a potato in your pocket. As the potato dries up, your rheumatiz will go away."

Sam Smith was always known on the roads as Fighting Sam. Years have passed, and when I have asked after him I have always heard that he was either in prison or had just been let out. Once it happened that, during a fight with a Gorgio, the Gorgio's watch disappeared, and Sam was arrested under suspicion of having got up the fight in order that the watch might disappear. All of his friends declared his innocence. The next trouble was for ***chorin a gry***, or stealing a horse, and so was the next, and so on. As horse-stealing is not a crime, but only "rough gambling," on the roads, nobody defended him on these counts. He was, so far as this went, only a sporting character. When his wife died he married Athalia, the widow of Joshua Cooper, a gypsy, of whom I shall speak anon. I always liked Sam. Among the travelers, he was always spoken of as genteel, owing to the fact, that whatever the state of his wardrobe might be, he always wore about his neck an immaculate white woolen scarf, and on ***jours de fete***, such as horse-races, sported a ***boro stardi***, or chimney-pot hat. O my friend, Colonel Dash, of the club! Change but the name, this fable is of thee!

"There's to be a ***walgoro***, ***kaliko i sala***--a fair to-morrow morning, at Cobham," said Sam, as he departed.

"All right. We'll be there."

As I went forth by the river into the night, and the stars looked down like loving eyes, there shot a meteor across the sky, one long trail of light, out of darkness into darkness, one instant bright, then dead forever. And I remembered how I once was told that stars, like mortals, often fall in love. O love, forever in thy glory go! And that they send their starry angels forth, and that the meteors are their messengers. O love, forever in thy glory go! For love and light in heaven, as on earth, were ever one, and planets speak with light. Light is their language; as they love they speak. O love, forever in thy glory go!

III. COBHAM FAIR.

The walk from Oatlands Park Hotel to Cobham is beautiful with memorials of Older England. Even on the grounds there is a quaint brick gateway, which is the only relic of a palace which preceded the present pile. The grandfather was indeed a stately edifice, built by Henry VIII., improved and magnified, according to his lights, by Inigo Jones, and then destroyed during the civil war. The river is here very beautiful, and the view was once painted by Turner. It abounds in "short windings and reaches." Here it is, indeed, the Olerifera Thamesis, as it was called by Guillaume le Breton in his "Phillipeis," in the days of Richard the Lion Heart. Here the eyots and banks still recall Norman days, for they are "wild and were;" and there is even yet a wary otter or two, known to the gypsies and fishermen, which may be seen of moonlight nights plunging or swimming silently in the haunted water.

Now we pass Walton Church, and look in, that my friend may see the massy Norman pillars and arches, the fine painted glass, and the brasses. One of these represents John Selwyn, who was keeper of the royal park of Oatlands in 1587. Tradition, still current in the village, says that Selwyn was a man of wondrous strength and of rare skill in horsemanship. Once, when Queen Elizabeth was present at a stag hunt, he leaped from his horse upon the back of the stag, while both were running at full speed, kept his seat gracefully, guided the animal towards the queen, and stabbed him so deftly that he fell dead at her majesty's feet. It was daintily done, and doubtless Queen Bess, who loved a proper man, was well pleased. The brass plate represents Selwyn as riding on the stag, and there is in the village a shop where the neat old dame who presides, or her daughter, will sell you for a penny a picture of the plate, and tell you the story into the bargain. In it the valiant ranger sits on the stag, which he is stabbing through the neck with his ***couteau de chasse***,

looking meanwhile as solemn as if he were sitting in a pew and listening
to ***De profundis***. He who is great in one respect seldom fails in some
other, and there is in the church another and a larger brass, from which
it appears that Selwyn not only had a wife, but also eleven children, who
are depicted in successive grandeur or gradation. There are monuments by
Roubiliac and Chantrey in the church, and on the left side of the altar
lies buried William Lilly, the great astrologer, the Sidrophel of
Butler's "Hudibras." And look into the chancel. There is a tablet to
his memory, which was put up by Elias Ashmole, the antiquary, who has
left it in print that this "fair black marble stone" cost him 6 pounds
4*s*. 6*d*. When I was a youth, and used to pore in the old Franklin
Library of Philadelphia over Lilly, I never thought that his grave would
be so near my home. But a far greater literary favorite of mine lies
buried in the church-yard without. This is Dr. Maginn, the author of
"Father Tom and the Pope," and many another racy, subtle jest. A fellow
of infinite humor,--the truest disciple of Rabelais,--and here he lies
without a monument!

Summon the sexton, and let us ask him to show us the scold's, or
gossip's, bridle. This is a rare curiosity, which is kept in the vestry.
It would seem, from all that can be learned, that two hundred years ago
there were in England viragoes so virulent, women so gifted with gab and
so loaded and primed with the devil's own gunpowder, that all moral
suasion was wasted on them, and simply showed, as old Reisersberg wrote,
that ***fatue agit qui ignem conatur extinguere sulphure*** ('t is all
nonsense to try to quench fire with brimstone). For such diavolas they
had made--what the sexton is just going to show you--a muzzle of thin
iron bars, which pass around the head and are padlocked behind. In front
a flat piece of iron enters the mouth and keeps down the tongue. On it
is the date 1633, and certain lines, no longer legible:--

> "Chester presents Walton with a bridle,
> To curb women's tongues that talk too idle."

A sad story, if we only knew it all! What tradition tells is that long ago there was a Master Chester, who lost a fine estate through the idle, malicious clack of a gossiping, lying woman. "What is good for a bootless bene?" What he did was to endow the church with this admirable piece of head-gear. And when any woman in the parish was unanimously adjudged to be deserving of the honor, the bridle was put on her head and tongue, and she was led about town by the beadle as an example to all the scolding sisterhood. Truly, if it could only be applied to the women and men who repeat gossip, rumors reports, *on dits*, small slanders, proved or unproved, to all gobe-mouches, club-gabblers, tea-talkers and tattlers, chatterers, church-twaddlers, wonderers if-it-be-true-what-they-say; in fine, to the entire sister and brother hood of tongue-waggers, I for one would subscribe my mite to have one kept in every church in the world, to be zealously applied to their vile jaws. For verily the mere Social Evil is an angel of light on this earth as regards doing evil, compared to the Sociable Evil,--and thus endeth the first lesson.

We leave the church, so full of friendly memories. In this one building alone there are twenty things known to me from a boy. For from boyhood I have held in my memory those lines by Queen Elizabeth which she uttered here, and have read Lilly and Ashmole and Maginn; and this is only one corner in merrie England! Am I a stranger here? There is a father-land of the soul, which has no limits to him who, far sweeping on the wings of song and history, goes forth over many lands.

We have but a little farther to go on our way before we come to the quaint old manor-house which was of old the home of President Bradshaw, the grim old Puritan. There is an old sailor in the village, who owns a tavern, and he says, and the policeman agrees with him, that it was in this house that the death-warrant of King Charles the First was signed. Also, that there is a subterranean passage which leads from it to the

Thames, which was in some way connected with battle, murder, plots, Puritans, sudden death, and politics; though how this was is more than legend can clearly explain. Whether his sacred majesty was led to execution through this cavity, or whether Charles the Second had it for one of his numerous hiding-places, or returned through it with Nell Gwynn from his exile, are other obscure points debated among the villagers. The truth is that the whole country about Walton is subterrened with strange and winding ways, leading no one knows whither, dug in the days of the monks or knights, from one long-vanished monastery or castle to the other. There is the opening to one of these hard by the hotel, but there was never any gold found in it that ever I heard of. And all the land is full of legend, and ghosts glide o' nights along the alleys, and there is an infallible fairy well at hand, named the Nun, and within a short walk stands the tremendous Crouch oak, which was known of Saxon days. Whoever gives but a little of its bark to a lady will win her love. It takes its name from *croix* (a cross), according to Mr. Kemble, {134} and it is twenty-four feet in girth. Its first branch, which is forty-eight feet long, shoots out horizontally, and is almost as large as the trunk. Under this tree Wickliffe preached, and Queen Elizabeth dined.

It has been well said by Irving that the English, from the great prevalence of rural habits throughout every class of society, have been extremely fond of those festivals and holidays which agreeably interrupt the stillness of country life. True, the days have gone when burlesque pageant and splendid procession made even villages magnificent. Harp and tabor and viol are no longer heard in every inn when people would be merry, and men have forgotten how to give themselves up to headlong roaring revelry. The last of this tremendous frolicking in Europe died out with the last yearly *kermess* in Amsterdam, and it was indeed wonderful to see with what utter *abandon* the usually stolid Dutch flung themselves into a rushing tide of frantic gayety. Here and there in England a spark of the old fire, lit in mediaeval times, still flickers, or perhaps flames, as at Dorking in the annual foot-ball play, which is carried on with such vigor that two or three thousand people run wild in it, while all the windows and street lamps are carefully screened for protection. But notwithstanding the gradually advancing republicanism of the age, which is dressing all men alike, bodily and mentally, the rollicking democracy of these old-fashioned festivals, in which the peasant bonneted the peer without ceremony, and rustic maids ran races *en chemise* for a pound of tea, is entirely too leveling for culture. There are still, however, numbers of village fairs, quietly conducted, in which there is much that is pleasant and picturesque, and this at Cobham was as pretty a bit of its kind as I ever saw. These are old-fashioned and gay in their little retired nooks, and there the plain people show themselves as they really are. The better class of the neighborhood, having no sympathy with such sports or scenes, do not visit village fairs. It is, indeed, a most exceptional thing to see any man who is a "gentleman," according to the society standard, in any fair except Mayfair in London.

Cobham is well built for dramatic display. Its White Lion Inn is of the old coaching days, and the lion on its front is a very impressive monster, one of the few relics of the days when signs were signs in spirit and in truth. In this respect the tavern keeper of to-day is a poor snob, that he thinks a sign painted or carven is degenerate and low, and therefore announces, in a line of letters, that his establishment is the Pig and Whistle, just as his remote predecessor thought it was low, or slow, or old-fashioned to dedicate his ale-shop to Pigen Wassail or Hail to the Virgin, and so changed it to a more genteel and secular form. In the public place were rows of booths arranged in streets forming *imperium in imperio*, a town within a town. There was of course the traditional gilt gingerbread, and the cheering but not inebriating ginger-beer, dear to the youthful palate, and not less loved by the tired pedestrian, when, mixed half and half with ale, it foams before him as *shandy gaff*. There, too, were the stands, presided over by jaunty,

saucy girls, who would load a rifle for you and give you a prize or a
certain number of shots for a shilling. You may be a good shot, but the
better you shoot the less likely will you be to hit the bull's-eye with
the rifle which that black-eyed Egyptian minx gives you; for it is
artfully curved and false-sighted, and the rifle was made only to rifle
your pocket, and the damsel to sell you with her smiles, and the doll is
stuffed with sawdust, and life is not worth living for, and Miching
Mallocko says it,--albeit I believe he lives at times as if there might
be moments when it was forgot.

And we had not been long on the ground before we were addressed furtively
and gravely by a man whom it required a second glance to recognize as
Samuel Petulengro, so artfully was he disguised as a simple-seeming
agriculturalist of the better lower-class. But that there remained in
Sam's black eyes that glint of the Romany which nothing could disguise,
one would have longed to buy a horse of him. And in the same quiet way
there came, one by one, out of the crowd, six others, all speaking in
subdued voices, like conspirators, and in Romany, as if it were a sin.
And all were dressed rustically, and the same with intent to deceive, and
all had the solemn air of very small farmers, who must sell that horse at
any sacrifice. But when I saw Sam's horses I marked that his disguise of
himself was nothing to the wondrous skill with which he had converted his
five-pound screws into something comparatively elegant. They had been
curried, clipped, singed, and beautified to the last resource, and the
manner in which the finest straw had been braided into mane and tail was
a miracle of art. This was *jour de fete* for Sam and his *diddikai*, or
half-blood pals; his foot was on his native heath in the horse-fair,
where all inside the ring knew the gypsy, and it was with pride that he
invited us to drink ale, and once in the bar-room, where all assembled
were jockeys and sharps, conversed loudly in Romany, in order to exhibit
himself and us to admiring friends. A Romany rye, on such occasions, is
to a Sam Petulengro what a scion of royalty is to minor aristocracy when
it can lure him into its nets. To watch one of these small horse-dealers

at a fair, and to observe the manner in which he conducts his bargains, is very curious. He lounges about all day, apparently doing nothing; he is the only idler around. Once in a while somebody approaches him and mutters something, to which he gives a brief reply. Then he goes to a tap-room or stable-yard, and is merged in a mob of his mates. But all the while he is doing sharp clicks of business. There is somebody talking to another party about *that horse*; somebody telling a farmer that he knows a young man as has got a likely 'oss at 'arf price, the larst of a lot which he wants to clear out, and it may be 'ad, but if the young man sees 'im [the farmer] he may put it on 'eavy.

Then the agent calls in one of the disguised Romanys to testify to the good qualities of the horse. They look at it, but the third *deguise*, who has it in charge, avers that it has just been sold to a gentleman. But they have another. By this time the farmer wishes he had bought the horse. When any coin slips from between our fingers, and rolls down through a grating into the sewer, we are always sure that it was a sovereign, and not a half-penny. Yes, and the fish which drops back from the line into the river is always the biggest take--or mistake--of the day. And this horse was a bargain, and the three in disguise say so, and wish they had a hundred like it. But there comes a Voice from the depths, a casual remark, offering to bet that 'ere gent won't close on that hoss. "Bet yer ten bob he will." "Done." "How do yer know he don't take the hoss?" "He carn't; he's too heavy loaded with Bill's mare. Says he'll sell it for a pound better." The farmer begins to see his way. He is shrewd; it may be that he sees through all this myth of "the gentleman." But his attention has been attracted to the horse. Perhaps he pays a little more, or "the pound better;" in greater probability he gets Sam's horse for the original price. There are many ways among gypsies of making such bargains, but the motive power of them all is *taderin*, or drawing the eye of the purchaser, a game not unknown to Gorgios. I have heard of a German *yahud* in Philadelphia, whose little boy Moses would shoot from the door with a pop-gun or squirt at

passers-by, or abuse them vilely, and then run into the shop for shelter.
They of course pursued him and complained to the parent, who immediately
whipped his son, to the great solace of the afflicted ones. And then the
afflicted seldom failed to buy something in that shop, and the corrected
son received ten per cent. of the profit. The attention of the public
had been drawn.

As we went about looking at people and pastimes, a Romany, I think one of
the Ayres, said to me,--

"See the two policemen? They're following you two gentlemen. They saw
you pallin' with Bowers. That Bowers is the biggest blackguard on the
roads between London and Windsor. I don't want to hurt his charackter,
but it's no bad talkin' nor *dusherin* of him to say that no decent
Romanys care to go with him. Good at a mill? Yes, he's that. A reg'lar
wastimengro, I call him. And that's why it is."

Now there was in the fair a vast institution which proclaimed by a
monstrous sign and by an excessive eruption of advertisement that it was
THE SENSATION OF THE AGE. This was a giant hand-organ in connection with
a forty-bicycle merry-go-round, all propelled by steam. And as we walked
about the fair, the two rural policemen, who had nothing better to do,
shadowed or followed us, their bucolic features expressing the intensest
suspicion allied to the extremest stupidity; when suddenly the Sensation
of the Age struck up the Gendarme's chorus, "We'll run 'em in," from
Genevieve de Brabant, and the arrangement was complete. Of all airs ever
composed this was the most appropriate to the occasion, and therefore it
played itself. The whole formed quite a little opera-bouffe, gypsies not
being wanting. And as we came round, in our promenade, the pretty girl,
with her rifle in hand, implored us to take a shot, and the walk wound up
by her finally letting fly herself and ringing the bell.

That pretty girl might or might not have a touch of Romany blood in her veins, but it is worth noting that among all these show-men and show-women, acrobats, exhibitors of giants, purse-droppers, gingerbread-wheel gamblers, shilling knife-throwers, pitch-in-his-mouths, Punches, Cheap-Jacks, thimble-rigs, and patterers of every kind there is always a leaven and a suspicion of gypsiness. If there be not descent, there is affinity by marriage, familiarity, knowledge of words and ways, sweethearting and trafficking, so that they know the children of the Rom as the house-world does not know them, and they in some sort belong together. It is a muddle, perhaps, and a puzzle; I doubt if anybody quite understands it. No novelist, no writer whatever, has as yet *clearly* explained the curious fact that our entire nomadic population, excepting tramps, is not, as we thought in our childhood, composed of English people like ourselves. It is leavened with direct Indian blood; it has, more or less modified, a peculiar *morale*. It was old before the Saxon heptarchy.

I was very much impressed at this fair with the extensive and unsuspected amount of Romany existent in our rural population. We had to be satisfied, as we came late into the tavern for lunch, with cold boiled beef and carrots, of which I did not complain, as cold carrots are much nicer than warm, a fact too little understood in cookery. There were many men in the common room, mostly well dressed, and decent even if doubtful looking. I observed that several used Romany words in casual conversation. I came to the conclusion at last that all who were present knew something of it. The greatly reprobated Bowers was not himself a gypsy, but he had a gypsy wife. He lived in a cottage not far from Walton, and made baskets, while his wife roamed far and near, selling them; and I have more than once stopped and sent for a pot of ale, and shared it with Bill, listening meantime to his memories of the road as he caned chairs or "basketed." I think his reputation came rather from a certain Bohemian disregard of *convenances* and of appearances than from any deeply-seated sinfulness. For there are Bohemians even among gypsies; everything in this life being relative and socially-contractive.

When I came to know the disreputable William well, I found in him the principles of Panurge, deeply identified with the *morale* of Falstaff; a wondrous fund of unbundled humor, which expressed itself more by tones than words; a wisdom based on the practices of the prize-ring; and a perfectly sympathetic admiration of my researches into Romany. One day, at Kingston Fair, as I wished to depart, I asked Bill the way to the station. "I will go with you and show you," he said. But knowing that he had business in the fair I declined his escort. He looked at me as if hurt.

"*Does tute pen mandy'd chore tute*?" (Do you think I would rob *you* or pick your pockets?) For he believed I was afraid of it. I knew Bill better. I knew that he was perfectly aware that I was about the only man in England who had a good opinion of him in any way, or knew what good there was in him. When a *femme incomprise*, a woman not as yet found out, discovers at last the man who is so much a master of the art of flattery as to satisfy somewhat her inordinate vanity, she is generally grateful enough to him who has thus gratified her desires to refrain from speaking ill of him, and abuse those who do, especially the latter. In like manner, Bill Bowers, who was every whit as interesting as any *femme incomprise* in Belgravia, or even Russell Square, believing that I had a little better opinion of him than anybody else, would not only have refrained from robbing me, but have proceeded to lam with his fists anybody else who would have done so,--the latter proceeding being, from his point of view, only a light, cheerful, healthy, and invigorating exercise, so that, as he said, and as I believe truthfully, "I'd rather be walloped than not fight." Even as my friend H. had rather lose than not play "farrer."

This was a very pretty little country fair at Cobham; pleasant and purely English. It was very picturesque, with its flags, banners, gayly bedecked booths, and mammoth placards, there being, as usual, no lack of color or objects. I wonder that Mr. Frith, who has given with such idiomatic genius the humors of the Derby, has never painted an old-fashioned rural fair like this. In a few years the last of them will have been closed, and the last gypsy will be there to look on.

There was a pleasant sight in the afternoon, when all at once, as it seemed to me, there came hundreds of pretty, rosy-cheeked children into the fair. There were twice as many of them as of grown people. I think that, the schools being over for the day, they had been sent a-fairing for a treat. They swarmed in like small bee-angels, just escaped from some upset celestial hive; they crowded around the booths, buying little toys, chattering, bargaining, and laughing, when my eye caught theirs, as though to be noticed was the very best joke in the whole world. They soon found out the Sensation of the Age, and the mammoth steam bicycle was forthwith crowded with the happy little creatures, raptured in all the glory of a ride. The cars looked like baskets full of roses. It was delightful to see them: at first like grave and stolid little Anglo-Saxons, occupied seriously with the new Sensation; then here and there beaming with thawing jollity; then smiling like sudden sun-gleams; and then laughing, until all were in one grand chorus, as the speed became greater, and the organ roared out its notes as rapidly as a runaway musical locomotive, and the steam-engine puffed in time, until a high-pressure scream told that the penn'orth of fun was up.

As we went home in the twilight, and looked back at the trees and roofs of the village, in dark silhouette against the gold-bronze sky, and heard from afar and fitfully the music of the Great Sensation mingled with the beat of a drum and the shouts of the crowd, rising and falling with the wind, I felt a little sad, that the age, in its advancing refinement, is setting itself against these old-fashioned merry-makings, and shrinking like a weakling from all out-of-doors festivals, on the plea of their being disorderly, but in reality because they are believed to be vulgar. They come down to us from rough old days; but they are relics of a time when life, if rough, was at least kind and hearty. We admire that life on the stage, we ape it in novels, we affect admiration and appreciation of its rich picturesqueness and vigorous originality, and we lie in so doing; for there is not an aesthetic prig in London who could have lived an hour in it. Truly, I should like to know what Francois Villon and Chaucer would have thought of some of their modern adorers, or what the lioness Fair-sinners of the olden time would have had to say to the nervous weaklings who try to play the genial blackguard in their praise! It is to me the best joke of the age that those who now set themselves up for priests of the old faith are the men, of all others, whom the old gods would have kicked, ***cum magna injuria***, out of the temple. When I sit by Bill Bowers, as he baskets, and hear the bees buzz about his marigolds, or in Plato Buckland's van, or with a few hearty and true men of London town of whom I wot, ***then*** I know that the old spirit liveth in its ashes; but there is little of it, I trow, among its penny prig-trumpeters.

IV. THE MIXED FORTUNES.

"Thus spoke the king to the great Master: 'Thou didst bless and ban the people; thou didst give benison and curse, luck and sorrow, to the evil or the good.'

"And the Master said, 'It may be so.'

"And the king continued, 'There came two men, and one was good and the other bad. And one thou didst bless, thinking he was good; but he was wicked. And the other thou didst curse, and thought him bad; but he was good.'

"The Master said, 'And what came of it?'

"The king answered, 'All evil came upon the good man, and all happiness to the bad.'

"And the Master said, 'I write letters, but I am not the messenger; I hunt the deer, but I am not the cook; I plant the vine, but I do not pour the wine to the guests; I ordain war, yet do not fight; I send ships forth on the sea, but do not sail them. There is many a slip between cup and lip, as the chief of the rebel spirits said when he was thrown out of heaven, and I am not greater nor wiser than he was before he fell. Hast thou any more questions, O son?'

"And the king went his way."

One afternoon I was walking with three ladies. One was married, one was a young widow, and one, no longer very young, had not as yet husbanded her resources. And as we went by the Thames, conversation turned upon many things, and among them the mystery of the future and mediums; and the widow at last said she would like to have her fortune told.

"You need not go far to have it done," I said. "There is a gypsy camp not a mile away, and in it one of the cleverest fortune-tellers in England."

"I am almost afraid to go," said the maiden lady. "It seems to me to be really wrong to try to look into the awful secrets of futurity. One can never be certain as to what a gypsy may not know. It's all very well, I dare say, to declare it's all rubbish, but then you know you never can tell what may be in a rubbish-heap, and they may be predicting true things all the time while they think they're humbugging you. And they do often foretell the most wonderful things; I know they do. My aunt was told that she would marry a man who would cause her trouble, and, sure enough, she did; and it was such a shame, she was such a sweet-tempered, timid woman, and he spent half her immense fortune. Now wasn't that wonderful?"

It would be a curious matter for those who like studying statistics and chance to find out what proportion in England of sweet-tempered, timid women of the medium-middle class, in newly-sprouted families, with immense fortunes, do *not* marry men who only want their money. Such heiresses are the natural food of the noble shark and the swell sucker, and even a gypsy knows it, and can read them at a glance. I explained this to the lady; but she knew what she knew, and would not know otherwise.

So we came along the rippling river, watching the darting swallows and light water-gnats, as the sun sank afar into the tawny, golden west, and Night, in ever-nearing circles, wove her shades around us. We saw the little tents, like bee-hives,--one, indeed, not larger than the hive in which Tyll Eulenspiegel slept his famous nap, and in which he was carried away by the thieves who mistook him for honey and found him vinegar. And the outposts, or advanced pickets of small, brown, black-eyed elves, were tumbling about as usual, and shouted their glad greeting; for it was only the day before that I had come down with two dozen oranges, which by chance proved to be just one apiece for all to eat except for little Synfie Cooper, who saved hers up for her father when he should return.

I had just an instant in which to give the gypsy sorceress a "straight tip," and this I did, saying in Romany that one of the ladies was married and one a widow. I was indeed quite sure that she must know the married lady as such, since she had lived near at hand, within a mile, for months. And so, with all due solemnity, the sorceress went to her work.

"You will come first, my lady, if you please," she said to the married dame, and led her into a hedge-corner, so as to be remote from public view, while we waited by the camp.

The hand was inspected, and properly crossed with a shilling, and the seeress began her prediction.

"It's a beautiful hand, my lady, and there's luck in it. The line o' life runs lovely and clear, just like a smooth river from sea to sea, and that means you'll never be in danger before you die, nor troubled with much ill. And it's written that you'll have another husband very soon."

"But I don't want another," said the lady.

"Ah, my dear lady, so you'll say till you get him, but when he comes you'll be glad enough; so do you just get the first one out of your head as soon as you can, for the next will be the better one. And you'll cross the sea and travel in a foreign land, and remember what I told you to the end of your life days."

Then the widow had her turn.

"This is a lucky hand, and little need you had to have your fortune told. You've been well married once, and once is enough when it's all you need. There's others as is never satisfied and wants everything, but you've had the best, and more you needn't want, though there'll be many a man who'll be in love with you. Ay, indeed, there's fair and dark as will feel the favor of your beautiful eyes, but little good will it do them, and barons and lords as would kiss the ground you tread on; and no wonder, either, for you have the charm which nobody can tell what it is. But it will do 'em no good, nevermore."

"Then I'm never to have another husband," said the widow.

"No, my lady. He that you married was the best of all, and, after him, you'll never need another; and that was written in your hand when you

were born, and it will be your fate, forever and ever: and that is the
gypsy's production over the future, and what she has produced will come
true. All the stars in the fermentation of heaven can't change it. But
if you ar'n't satisfied, I can set a planet for you, and try the cards,
which comes more expensive, for I never do that under ten shillings."

There was a comparing of notes among the ladies and much laughter, when
it appeared that the priestess of the hidden spell, in her working, had
mixed up the oracles. Jacob had manifestly got Esau's blessing. It was
agreed that the ***bonnes fortunes*** should be exchanged, that the shillings
might not be regarded as lost, and all this was explained to the
unmarried lady. She said nothing, but in due time was also ***dukkered*** or
fortune-told. With the same mystery she was conducted to the secluded
corner of the hedge, and a very long, low-murmuring colloquy ensued.
What it was we never knew, but the lady had evidently been greatly
impressed and awed. All that she would tell was that she had heard
things that were "very remarkable, which she was sure no person living
could have known," and in fact that she believed in the gypsy, and even
the blunder as to the married lady and the widow, and all my assurances
that chiromancy as popularly practiced was all humbug, made no
impression. There was once "a disciple in Yabneh" who gave a hundred and
fifty reasons to prove that a reptile was no more unclean than any other
animal. But in those days people had not been converted to the law of
turtle soup and the gospel of Saint Terrapin, so the people said it was a
vain thing. And had I given a hundred and fifty reasons to this lady,
they would have all been vain to her, for she wished to believe; and when
our own wishes are served up unto us on nice brown pieces of the
well-buttered toast of flattery, it is not hard to induce us to devour
them.

It is written that when Ashmedai, or Asmodeus, the chief of all the
devils of mischief, was being led a captive to Solomon, he did several
mysterious things while on the way, among others bursting into

extravagant laughter, when he saw a magician conjuring and predicting.
On being questioned by Benaiah, the son of Jehoiada, why he had seemed so
much amused, Ashmedai answered that it was because the seer was at the
very time sitting on a princely treasure, and he did not, with all his
magic and promising fortune to others, know this. Yet, if this had been
told to all the world, the conjurer's business would not have suffered.
Not a bit of it. ***Entre Jean***, ***passe Jeannot***: one comes and goes,
another takes his place, and the poor will disappear from this world
before the too credulous shall have departed.

It was on the afternoon of the following day that I, by chance, met the
gypsy with a female friend, each with a basket, by the roadside, in a
lonely, furzy place, beyond Walton.

"You are a nice fortune-teller, aren't you now?" I said to her. "After
getting a tip, which made it all as clear as day, you walk straight into
the dark. And here you promise a lady two husbands, and she married
already; but you never promised me two wives, that I might make merry
withal. And then to tell a widow that she would never be married again!
You're a ***bori chovihani*** [a great witch],--indeed, you aren't."

"***Rye***," said the gypsy, with a droll smile and a shrug,--I think I can
see it now,--"the ***dukkerin*** [prediction] was all right, but I pet the
right ***dukkerins*** on the wrong ladies."

And the Master said, "I write letters, but I am not the messenger." His
orders, like the gypsy's, had been all right, but they had gone to the
wrong shop. Thus, in all ages, those who affect superior wisdom and
foreknowledge absolute have found that a great practical part of the real
business consisted in the plausible explanation of failures. The great
Canadian weather prophet is said to keep two clerks busy, one in
recording his predictions, the other in explaining their failures; which
is much the case with the rain-doctors in Africa, who are as ingenious

and fortunate in explaining a miss as a hit, as, indeed, they need be, since they must, in case of error, submit to be devoured alive by ants,--insects which in Africa correspond in several respects to editors and critics, particularly the stinging kind. "*Und ist man bei der Prophezeiung angestellt*," as Heine says; "when a man has a situation in a prophecy-office," a great part of his business is to explain to the customers why it is that so many of them draw blanks, or why the trains of fate are never on time.

V. HAMPTON RACES.

On a summer day, when waking dreams softly wave before the fancy, it is pleasant to walk in the noon-stillness along the Thames, for then we pass a series of pictures forming a gallery which I would not exchange for that of the Louvre, could I impress them as indelibly upon the eye-memory as its works are fixed on canvas. There exists in all of us a spiritual photographic apparatus, by means of which we might retain accurately all we have ever seen, and bring out, at will, the pictures from the pigeon-holes of the memory, or make new ones as vivid as aught we see in dreams, but the faculty must be developed in childhood. So surely as I am now writing this will become, at some future day, a branch of education, to be developed into results of which the wildest imagination can form no conception, and I put the prediction on record. As it is, I am sorry that I was never trained to this half-thinking, half-painting art, since, if I had been, I should have left for distant days to come some charming views of Surrey as it appears in this decade.

The reedy eyots and the rising hills; the level meadows and the little villes, with their antique perpendicular Gothic churches, which form the points around which they have clustered for centuries, even as groups of boats in the river are tied around their mooring-posts; the bridges and trim cottages or elegant mansions with their flower-bordered grounds sweeping down to the water's edge, looking like rich carpets with new baize over the centre, make the pictures of which I speak, varying with every turn of the Thames; while the river itself is, at this season, like a continual regatta, with many kinds of boats, propelled by stalwart young Englishmen or healthy, handsome damsels, of every rank, the better class by far predominating. There is a disposition among the English to don quaint holiday attire, to put on the picturesque, and go to the very limits which custom permits, which would astonish an American. Of late years this is becoming the case, too, in Trans-Atlantis, but it has always been usual in England, to mark the fete day with a festive dress, to wear gay ribbons, and to indulge the very harmless instinct of youth to be gallant and gay.

I had started one morning on a walk by the Thames, when I met a friend, who asked,--

"Aren't you going to-day to the Hampton races?"

"How far is it?"

"Just six miles. On Molesy Hurst."

Six miles, and I had only six shillings in my pocket. I had some curiosity to see this race, which is run on the Molesy Hurst, famous as the great place for prize-fighting in the olden time, and which has never been able to raise itself to respectability, inasmuch as the local chronicler says that "the course attracts considerable and not very reputable gatherings." In fact, it is generally spoken of as the Costermonger's race, at which a mere welsher is a comparatively respectable character, and every man in a good coat a swell. I was nicely attired, by chance, for the occasion, for I had come out, thinking of a ride, in a white hat, new corduroy pantaloons and waistcoat, and a velveteen coat, which dress is so greatly admired by the gypsies that it may almost be regarded as their "national costume."

There was certainly, to say the least, a rather **bourgeois** tone at the race, and gentility was conspicuous by its absence; but I did not find it so outrageously low as I had been led to expect. I confess that I was not encouraged to attempt to increase my little hoard of silver by betting, and the certainty that if I lost I could not lunch made me timid. But the good are never alone in this world, and I found friends whom I dreamed not of. Leaving the crowd, I sought the gypsy vans, and by one of these was old Liz Buckland.

"**Sarishan rye**! And glad I am to see you. Why didn't you come down into Kent to see the hoppin'? Many a time the Romanys says they expected to see their **rye** there. Just the other night, your Coopers was a-lyin' round their fire, every one of 'em in a new red blanket, lookin' so beautiful as the light shone on 'em, and I says, 'If our **rye** was to see you, he'd just have that book of his out, and take all your pictures.'"

After much gossip over absent friends, I said,--

"Well, **dye**, I stand a shilling for beer, and that's all I can do to-day, for I've come out with only **shove trin-grushi**."

Liz took the shilling, looked at it and at me with an earnest air, and shook her head.

"It'll never do, **rye**,--never. A gentleman wants more than six shillin's to see a race through, and a reg'lar Romany rye like you ought to slap down his **lovvo** with the best of 'em for the credit of his people. And if you want a **bar** [a pound] or two, I'll lend you the money, and never fear about your payment."

It was kind of the old *dye*, but I thought that I would pull through on my five shillings, before I would draw on the Romany bank. To be considered with sincere sympathy, as an object of deserving charity, on the lowest race-ground in England, and to be offered eleemosynary relief by a gypsy, was, indeed, touching the hard pan of humiliation. I went my way, idly strolling about, mingling affably with all orders, for my watch was at home. *Vacuus viator cantabit*. As I stood by a fence, I heard a gentlemanly-looking young man, who was evidently a superior pickpocket, or "a regular fly gonoff," say to a friend,--

"She's on the ground,--a great woman among the gypsies. What do they call her?"

"Mrs. Lee."

"Yes. A swell Romany she is."

Whenever one hears an Englishman, not a scholar, speak of gypsies as "Romany," he may be sure that man is rather more on the loose than becomes a steady citizen, and that he walks in ways which, if not of darkness, are at least in a shady *demi-jour*, with a gentle down grade. I do not think there was anybody on the race-ground who was not familiar with the older word.

It began to rain, and before long my new velveteen coat was very wet. I looked among the booths for one where I might dry myself and get something to eat, and, entering the largest, was struck by the appearance of the landlady. She was a young and decidedly pretty woman, nicely dressed, and was unmistakably gypsy. I had never seen her before, but I knew who she was by a description I had heard. So I went up to the bar and spoke:--

"How are you, Agnes?"

"Bloomin'. What will you have, sir?"

"*Dui curro levinor*, *yeck for tute*, *yeck for mandy*." (Two glasses
for ale,--one for you, one for me.)

She looked up with a quick glance and a wondering smile, and then said,--

"You must be the Romany rye of the Coopers. I'm glad to see you. Bless
me, how wet you are. Go to the fire and dry yourself. Here, Bill, I
say! Attend to this gentleman."

There was a tremendous roaring fire at the farther end of the booth, at
which were pieces of meat, so enormous as to suggest a giant's roast or a
political barbecue rather than a kitchen. I glanced with some interest
at Bill, who came to aid me. In all my life I never saw a man who looked
so thoroughly the regular English bull-dog bruiser of the lowest type,
but battered and worn out. His nose, by oft-repeated pummeling, had
gradually subsided almost to a level with his other features, just as an
ancient British grave subsides, under the pelting storms of centuries,
into equality with the plain. His eyes looked out from under their
bristly eaves like sleepy wild-cats from a pig-pen, and his physique was
tremendous. He noticed my look of curiosity.

"Old Bruisin' Bill, your honor. I was well knowed in the prize-ring
once. Been in the newspapers. Now, you mus'n't dry your coat that way!
New welweteen ought always to be wiped afore you dry it. I was a
gamekeeper myself for six years, an' wore it all that time nice and
proper, I did, and know how may be you've got a thrip'ny bit for old
Bill. Thanky."

I will do Mrs. Agnes Wynn the credit to say that in her booth the best and most abundant meal that I ever saw for the price in England was given for eighteen pence. Fed and dried, I was talking with her, when there came up a pretty boy of ten, so neat and well dressed and altogether so nice that he might have passed current for a gentleman's son anywhere.

"Well, Agnes. You're Wynn by name and winsome by nature, and all the best you have has gone into that boy. They say you gypsies used to steal children. I think it's time to turn the tables, and when I take the game up I'll begin by stealing your *chavo*."

Mrs. Wynn looked pleased. "He is a good boy, as good as he looks, and he goes to school, and don't keep low company."

Here two or three octoroon, duodecaroon, or vigintiroon Romany female friends of the landlady came up to be introduced to me, and of course to take something at my expense for the good of the house. This they did in the manner specially favored by gypsies; that is to say, a quart of ale, being ordered, was offered first to me, in honor of my social position, and then passed about from hand to hand. This rite accomplished, I went forth to view the race. The sun had begun to shine again, the damp flags and streamers had dried themselves in its cheering rays, even as I had renewed myself at Dame Wynn's fire, and I crossed the race-course. The scene was lively, picturesque, and thoroughly English. There are certain pleasures and pursuits which, however they may be perfected in other countries, always seem to belong especially to England, and chief among these is the turf. As a fresh start was made, as the spectators rushed to the ropes, roaring with excitement, and the horses swept by amid hurrahs, I could realize the sympathetic feeling which had been developed in all present by ancient familiarity and many associations with such scenes. Whatever the moral value of these may be, it is certain that anything so racy with local color and so distinctly fixed in popular affection as the *race* will always appeal to the artist and the student of national scenes.

I found Old Liz lounging with Old Dick, her husband, on the other side. There was a canvas screen, eight feet high, stretched as a background to stop the sticks hurled by the players at "coker-nuts," while the nuts themselves, each resting on a stick five feet high, looked like disconsolate and starved spectres, waiting to be cruelly treated. In company with the old couple was a commanding-looking, eagle-eyed Romany woman, in whom I at once recognized the remarkable gypsy spoken of by the pickpocket.

"My name is Lee," she said, in answer to my greeting. "What is yours?"

"Leland."

"Yes, you have added land to the lee. You are luckier than I am. I'm a Lee without land."

As she spoke she looked like an ideal Meg Merrilies, and I wished I had her picture. It was very strange that I made the wish at that instant, for just then she was within an ace of having it taken, and therefore arose and went away to avoid it. An itinerant photographer, seeing me talking with the gypsies, was attempting, though I knew it not, to take the group. But the keen eye of the Romany saw it all, and she went her way, because she was of the real old kind, who believe it is unlucky to have their portraits taken. I used to think that this aversion was of the same kind as that which many good men evince in a marked manner when requested by the police to sit for their photographs for the rogues' gallery. But here I did the gypsies great injustice; for they will allow their likenesses to be taken if you will give them a shoe-string. That this old superstition relative to the binding and loosing of ill-luck by the shoe-string should exist in this connection is of itself curious. In the earliest times the shoe-latchet brought luck, just as the shoe itself did, especially when filled with corn or rice, and thrown after the

bride. It is a great pity that the ignorant Gentiles, who are so careful
to do this at every wedding, do not know that it is all in vain unless
they cry aloud in Hebrew, "*Peru urphu*!" {159} with all their might when
the shoe is cast, and that the shoe should be filled with rice.

She went away, and in a few minutes the photographer came in great glee
to show a picture which he had taken.

"'Ere you are, sir. An elegant photograph, surroundin' sentimental
scenery and horiental coker-nuts thrown in,--all for a diminitive little
shillin'."

"Now that time you missed it," I said; "for on my honor as a gentleman, I
have only ninepence in all my pockets."

"A gent like you with only ninepence!" said the artist.

"If he hasn't got money in his pocket now," said Old Liz, speaking up in
my defense, "he has plenty at home. He has given pounds and pounds to us
gypsies."

"*Dovo's a huckaben*," I said to her in Romany. "*Mandy kekker delled
tute kumi'n a trin-grushi*." (That is untrue. I never gave you more
than a shilling.)

"Anyhow," said Liz, "ninepence is enough for it." And the man,
assenting, gave it to me. It was a very good picture, and I have since
had several copies taken of it.

"Yes, *rya*," said Old Liz, when I regretted the absence of my Lady Lee,
and talked with her about shoe-strings and old shoes, and how necessary
it was to cry out "*Peru urphu*!" when you throw them,--"yes. That's the
way the Gorgis always half does things. You see 'em get a horse-shoe off

the roads, and what do they do with it! Goes like ***dinneli*** idiots and nails it up with the p'ints down, which, as is well beknown, brings all the bad luck there is flyin' in the air into the house, and ***taders chovihanees*** [draws witches] like anise-seed does rats. Now common sense ought to teach that the shoe ought to be put like horns, with the p'ints up. For if it's lucky to put real horns up, of course the horse-shoe goes the same ***drom*** [road]. And it's lucky to pick up a red string in the morning,--yes, or at any time; but it's sure love from a girl if you do,--specially silk. And if so be she gives you a red string or cord, or a strip of red stuff, ***that*** means she'll be bound to you and loves you."

VI. STREET SKETCHES.

London, during hot weather, after the close of the wise season, suggests to the upper ten thousand, and to the lower twenty thousand who reflect their ways, and to the lowest millions who minister to them all, a scene of doleful dullness. I call the time which has passed wise, because that which succeeds is universally known as the silly season. Then the editors in town have recourse to the American newspapers for amusing murders, while their rural brethren invent great gooseberries. Then the sea-serpent again lifts his awful head. I am always glad when this sterling inheritance of the Northern races reappears; for while we have ***him*** I know that the capacity for swallowing a big bouncer, or for inventing one, is not lost. He is characteristic of a fine, bold race. Long may he wave! It is true that we cannot lie as gloriously as our ancestors did about him. When the great news-dealer of Norse times had no home-news he took his lyre, and either spun a yarn about Vinland such as would smash the "Telegraph," or else sung about "that sea-snake tremendous curled, whose girth encircles half the world." It is wonderful, it is awful, to consider how true we remain to the traditions of the older time. The French boast that they invented the *canard*. Let them boast. They also invented the shirt-collar; but hoary legends say that an Englishman invented the shirt for it, as well as the art of washing it. What the shirt is to the collar, that is the glorious, tough old Northern *saga*, or maritime spun yarn, to the *canard*, or duck. The yarn will wash; it passes into myth and history; it fits exactly, because it was made to order; its age and glory illustrate the survival of the fittest.

I have, during three or four summers, remained a month in London after the family had taken flight to the sea-side. I stayed to finish books promised for the autumn. It is true that nearly four million of people remain in London during the later summer; but it is wonderful what an influence the absence of a few exerts on them and on the town. Then you realize by the long lines of idle vehicles in the ranks how few people in this world can afford a cab; then you find out how scanty is the number of those who buy goods at the really excellent shops; and then you may finally find out by satisfactory experience, if you are inclined to grumble at your lot in life or your fortune, how much better off you are than ninety-nine in a hundred of your fellow-murmurers at fate.

It was my wont to walk out in the cool of the evening, to smoke my cigar in Regent's Park, seated on a bench, watching the children as they played about the clock-and-bull fountain,--for it embraces these objects among its adornments,--presented by Cowasie Jehanguire, who added to these magnificent Persian names the prosaic English postscript of Ready Money. In this his name sets forth the history of his Parsee people, who, from being heroic Ghebers, have come down to being bankers, who can "do" any Jew, and who might possibly tackle a Yankee so long as they kept out of New Jersey. One evening I walked outside of the Park, passing by the Gloucester Bridge to a little walk or boulevard, where there are a few benches. I was in deep moon-shadow, formed by the trees; only the ends

of my boots shone like eyes in the moonlight as I put them out. After a
while I saw a nice-looking young girl, of the humble-decent class, seated
by me, and with her I entered into casual conversation. On the bench
behind us were two young Italians, conversing in strongly marked
Florentine dialect. They evidently thought that no one could understand
them; as they became more interested they spoke more distinctly, letting
out secrets which I by no means wished to hear.

At that instant I recalled the famous story of Prince Bismarck and the
Esthonian young ladies and the watch-key. I whispered to the girl,--

"When I say something to you in a language which you do not understand,
answer '*Si*' as distinctly as you can."

The damsel was quick to understand. An instant after I said,--

"*Ha veduto il mio 'havallo la sera?*"

"*Si.*"

There was a dead silence, and then a rise and a rush. My young friend
rolled her eyes up at me, but said nothing. The Italians had departed
with their awful mysteries. Then there came by a man who looked much
worse. He was a truculent, untamable rough, evidently inspired with gin.
At a glance I saw by the manner in which he carried his coat that he was
a traveler, or one who lived on the roads. Seeing me he stopped, and
said, grimly,--"Do you love your Jesus?" This is certainly a pious
question; but it was uttered in a tone which intimated that if I did not
answer it affirmatively I might expect anything but Christian treatment.
I knew why the man uttered it. He had just come by an open-air preaching
in the Park, and the phrase had, moreover, been recently chalked and
stenciled by numerous zealous and busy nonconformists all over
northwestern London. I smiled, and said, quietly,--

"*Pal, mor rakker sa drovan. Ja pukenus on the drum.*" (Don't talk so loud, brother. Go away quietly.)

The man's whole manner changed. As if quite sober, he said,--

"*Mang your shunaben*, rye. *But tute jins chomany. Kushti ratti*!" (Beg your pardon, sir. But you *do* know a thing or two. Good-night!)

"I was awfully frightened," said the young girl, as the traveler departed. "I'm sure he meant to pitch into us. But what a wonderful way you have, sir, of sending people away! I wasn't so much astonished when you got rid of the Italians. I suppose ladies and gentlemen know Italian, or else they wouldn't go to the opera. But this man was a common, bad English tramp; yet I'm sure he spoke to you in some kind of strange language, and you said something to him that changed him into as peaceable as could be. What was it?"

"It was gypsy, young lady,--what the gypsies talk among themselves."

"Do you know, sir, I think you're the most mysterious gentleman I ever met."

"Very likely. Good-night."

"Good night, sir."

I was walking with my friend the Palmer, one afternoon in June, in one of the several squares which lie to the west of the British Museum. As we went I saw a singular-looking, slightly-built man, lounging at a corner. He was wretchedly clad, and appeared to be selling some rudely-made, but curious contrivances of notched sticks, intended to contain flowerpots. He also had flower-holders made of twisted copper wire. But the greatest curiosity was the man himself. He had such a wild, wasted, wistful expression, a face marked with a life of almost unconscious misery. And most palpable in it was the unrest, which spoke of an endless struggle with life, and had ended by goading him into incessant wandering. I cannot imagine what people can be made of who can look at such men without emotion.

"That is a gypsy," I said to the Palmer. "*Sarishan, pal*!"

The wanderer seemed to be greatly pleased to hear Romany. He declared that he was in the habit of talking it so much to himself when alone that his ordinary name was Romany Dick.

"But if you come down to the Potteries, and want to find me, you mus'n't ask for Romany Dick, but Divius Dick." "That means Wild Dick." "Yes." "And why?" "Because I wander about so, and can never stay more than a night in any one place. I can't help it. I must keep going." He said this with that wistful, sad expression, a yearning as for something which he had never comprehended. Was it *rest*?

"And so I *rakker* Romany [talk gypsy to myself], when I'm alone of a night, when the wind blows. It's better company than talkin' Gorginess. More sociable. *He* says--no--*I* say more sensible things Romaneskas than in English. You understand me?" he exclaimed suddenly, with the same wistful stare.

"Perfectly. It's quite reasonable. It must be like having two heads instead of one, and being twice as knowing as anybody else."

"Yes, that's it. But everybody don't know it."

"What do you ask for one of those flower-stands, Dick?"

"A shillin', sir."

"Well, here is my name and where I live, on an envelope. And here are two shillings. But if you *chore mandy* [cheat me] and don't leave it at the house, I'll look you up in the Potteries, and *koor tute* [whip you]."

He looked at me very seriously. "Ah, yes. You could *koor me kenna* [whip me now]. But you couldn't have *koored* my *dadas* [whipped my father]. Leastways not afore he got his leg broken fightin' Lancaster Sam. You must have heard of my father,--Single-stick Dick. But if your're comin' down to the Potteries, don't come next Sunday. Come Sunday three weeks. My brother is *stardo kenna* for *chorin* a *gry* [in prison for horse-stealing]. In three weeks he'll be let out, and we're goin' to have a great family party to welcome him, and we'll be glad to see you. Do come."

The flower-stand was faithfully delivered, but another engagement prevented an acceptance of the invitation, and I have never seen Dick since.

* * * * *

I was walking along Marylebone Road, which always seems to be a worn and wind-beaten street, very pretty once, and now repenting it; when just beyond Baker Street station I saw a gypsy van hung all round with baskets and wooden-ware. Smoke issued from its pipe, and it went along smoking like any careless pedestrian. It always seems strange to think of a family being thus conveyed with its dinner cooking, the children playing about the stove, over rural roads, past common and gorse and hedge, in and out of villages, and through Great Babylon itself, as if the family had a *pied a terre*, and were as secluded all the time as though they lived in Little Pedlington or Tinnecum. For they have just the same narrow range of gossip, and just the same set of friends, though the set are always on the move. Traveling does not make a cosmopolite.

By the van strolled the lord and master, with his wife. I accosted him.

"*Sarishan*?"

"*Sarishan rye*!"

"Did you ever see me before? Do you know me?"

"No, sir."

"I'm sorry for that. I have a nice velveteen coat which I have been keeping for your father. How's your brother Frank? Traveling about Kingston, I suppose. As usual. But I don't care about trusting the coat to anybody who don't know me."

"I'll take it to him, safe enough, sir."

"Yes, I dare say. On your back. And wear it yourself six months before you see him."

Up spoke his wife: "That he shan't. I'll take good care that the *pooro mush* [the old man] gets it all right, in a week."

"Well, *dye*, I can trust you. You remember me. And, Anselo, here is my address. Come to the house in half an hour."

In half an hour the housekeeper, said with a quiet smile,--

"If you please, sir, there's a gentleman--a *gypsy* gentleman--wishes to see you."

It is an English theory that the master can have no "visitors" who are not gentlemen. I must admit that Anselo's dress was not what could be called gentlemanly. From his hat to his stout shoes he looked the impenitent gypsy and sinful poacher, unaffected and natural. There was a cutaway, sporting look about his coat which indicated that he had grown to it from boyhood "in woodis grene." He held a heavy-handled whip, a regular Romany *tchupni* or **chuckni**, which Mr. Borrow thinks gave rise to the word "jockey." I thought the same once, but have changed my mind, for there were "jockeys" in England before gypsies. Altogether, Anselo (which comes from Wenceslas) was a determined and vigorous specimen of an old-fashioned English gypsy, a type which, with all its faults, is not wanting in sundry manly virtues.

I knew that Anselo rarely entered any houses save ale-houses, and that he had probably never before been in a study full of books, arms, and bric-a-brac. And he knew that I was aware of it. Now, if he had been more of a fool, like a red Indian or an old-fashioned fop, he would have affected a stoical indifference, for fear of showing his ignorance. As it was, he sat down in an arm-chair, glanced about him, and said just the right thing.

"It must be a pleasant thing, at the end of the day, after one has been running about, to come home to such a room as this, so full of fine things, and sit down in such a comfortable chair." "Will I have a glass of old ale? Yes, I thank you." "That is **kushto levinor** [good ale]. I never tasted better." "Would I rather have wine or spirits? No, I thank you; such ale as this is fit for a king."

Here Anselo's keen eye suddenly rested on something which he understood.

"What a beautiful little rifle! That's what I call a **rinkno yag-engree** [pretty gun]."

"Has it been a ***wafedo wen*** [hard winter], Anselo?"

"It has been a dreadful winter, sir. We have been hard put to it sometimes for food. It's dreadful to think of. I've acti'lly seen the time when I was almost desperated, and if I'd had such a gun as that I'm afraid, if I'd been tempted, I could a-found it in my heart to knock over a pheasant."

I looked sympathetically at Anselo. The idea of his having been brought to the very brink of such a terrible temptation and awful crime was touching. He met the glance with the expression of a good man, who had done no more than his duty, closed his eyes, and softly shook his head. Then he took another glass of ale, as if the memory of the pheasants or something connected with the subject had been too much for him, and spoke:--

"I came here on my horse. But he's an ugly old white punch. So as not to discredit you, I left him standing before a gentleman's house, two doors off."

Here Anselo paused. I acknowledged this touching act of thoughtful delicacy by raising my glass. He drank again, then resumed:--

"But I feel uneasy about leaving a horse by himself in the streets of London. He'll stand like a driven nail wherever you put him--but there's always plenty of claw-hammers to draw such nails."

"Don't be afraid, Anselo. The park-keeper will not let anybody take him through the gates. I'll pay for him if he goes."

But visions of a stolen horse seemed to haunt Anselo. One would have thought that something of the kind had been familiar to him. So I sent for the velveteen coat, and, folding it on his arm, he mounted the old white horse, while waving an adieu with the heavy-handled whip, rode away in the mist, and was seen no more.

Farewell, farewell, thou old brown velveteen! I had thee first in by-gone years, afar, hunting ferocious fox and horrid hare, near Brighton, on the Downs, and wore thee well on many a sketching tour to churches old and castles dark or gray, when winter went with all his raines wete. Farewell, my coat, and benedicite! I bore thee over France unto Marseilles, and on the steamer where we took aboard two hundred Paynim pilgrims of Mahound. Farewell, my coat, and benedicite! Thou wert in Naples by great Virgil's tomb, and borest dust from Posilippo's grot, and hast been wetted by the dainty spray from bays and shoals of old Etrurian name. Farewell, my coat, and benedicite! And thou wert in the old Egyptian realm: I had thee on that morning 'neath the palms when long I lingered where of yore had stood the rose-red city, half as old as time. Farewell, my coat, and benedicite! It was a lady called thee into life. She said, Methinks ye need a velvet coat. It is a seemly guise to ride to hounds. Another gave me whip and silvered spurs. Now all have vanished in the darkening past. Ladies and all are gone into the gloom. Farewell, my coat, and benedicite. Thou'st had a venturous and traveled life, for thou wert once in Moscow in the snow. A true Bohemian thou hast ever been, and as a right Bohemian thou wilt die, the garment of a roving Romany. Fain would I see and hear what thou'rt to know of reckless riding and the gypsy *tan*, of camps in dark green lanes, afar from towns. Farewell, mine coat, and benedicite!

VII. OF CERTAIN GENTLEMEN AND GYPSIES.

One morning I was walking with Mr. Thomas Carlyle and Mr. Froude. We went across Hyde Park, and paused to rest on the bridge. This is a remarkable place, since there, in the very heart of London, one sees a view which is perfectly rural. The old oaks rise above each other like green waves, the houses in the distance are country-like, while over the trees, and far away, a village-looking spire completes the picture. I think that it was Mr. Froude who called my attention to the beauty of the view, and I remarked that it needed only a gypsy tent and the curling smoke to make it in all respects perfectly English.

"You have paid some attention to gypsies," said Mr. Carlyle. "They're not altogether so bad a people as many think. In Scotland, we used to see many of them. I'll not say that they were not rovers and reivers, but they could be honest at times. The country folk feared them, but those who made friends wi' them had no cause to complain of their conduct. Once there was a man who was persuaded to lend a gypsy a large sum of money. My father knew the man. It was to be repaid at a certain time. The day came; the gypsy did not. And months passed, and still the creditor had nothing of money but the memory of it; and ye remember '*nessun maggior dolore*,'--that there's na greater grief than to remember the siller ye once had. Weel, one day the man was surprised to hear that his frien' the gypsy wanted to see him--interview, ye call it in America. And the gypsy explained that, having been arrested, and unfortunately detained, by some little accident, in preeson, he had na been able to keep his engagement. 'If ye'll just gang wi' me,' said the gypsy, 'aw'll mak' it all right.' 'Mon, aw wull,' said the creditor,--they were Scotch, ye know, and spoke in deealect. So the gypsy led the way to the house which he had inhabited, a cottage which belonged to the man himself to whom he owed the money. And there he lifted up the hearthstone; the hard-stane they call it in Scotland, and it is called so in the prophecy of Thomas of Ercildowne. And under the hard-stane there was an iron pot. It was full of gold, and out of that gold the gypsy carle paid his creditor. Ye wonder how 't was come by? Well, ye'll have heard it's best to let sleeping dogs lie."

"Yes. And what was said of the Poles who had, during the Middle Ages, a reputation almost as good as that of gypsies? ***Ad secretas Poli, curas extendere noli.***" (Never concern your soul as to the secrets of a Pole.)

Mr. Carlyle's story reminds me that Walter Simpson, in his history of them, says that the Scottish gypsies have ever been distinguished for their gratitude to those who treated them with civility and kindness, anent which he tells a capital story, while other instances sparkle here and there with many brilliant touches in his five hundred-and-fifty-page volume.

I have more than once met with Romanys, when I was in the company of men who, like Carlyle and Bilderdijk, "were also in the world of letters known," or who might say, "We have deserved to be." One of the many memories of golden days, all in the merrie tyme of summer song in England, is of the Thames, and of a pleasure party in a little steam-launch. It was a weenie affair,--just room for six forward outside the cubby, which was called the cabin; and of these six, one was Mr. Roebuck,--"the last Englishman," as some one has called him, but as the late Lord Lytton applies the same term to one of his characters about the time of the Conquest, its accuracy may be doubted. Say the last type of a certain phase of the Englishman; say that Roebuck was the last of the old iron and oak men, the ***triplex aes et robur*** chiefs of the Cobbet kind, and the phrase may pass. But it will only pass over into a new variety of true manhood. However frequently the last Englishman may die, I hope it will be ever said of him, ***Le roi est mort,--vive le roi***! I have had talks with Lord Lytton on gypsies. He, too, was once a Romany rye in a small way, and in the gay May heyday of his young manhood once went off with a band of Romanys, and passed weeks in their tents,--no bad thing, either, for anybody. I was more than once tempted to tell him the strange fact that, though he had been among the black people and thought he had learned their language, what they had imposed upon him for that

was not Romany, but cant, or English thieves' slang. For what is given,
in good faith, as the gypsy tongue in "Paul Clifford" and the "Disowned,"
is only the same old mumping **kennick** which was palmed off on Bampfylde
Moore Carew; or which he palmed on his readers, as the secret of the
Roms. But what is the use or humanity of disillusioning an author by
correcting an error forty years old. If one could have corrected it in
the proof, **a la bonne heure**! Besides, it was of no particular
consequence to anybody whether the characters in "Paul Clifford" called a
clergyman a **patter-cove** or a **rashai**. It is a supreme moment of
triumph for a man when he discovers that his specialty--whatever it
be--is not of such value as to be worth troubling anybody with it. As
for Everybody, **he** is fair game.

The boat went up the Thames, and I remember that the river was, that
morning, unusually beautiful. It is graceful, as in an outline, even
when leaden with November mists, or iron-gray in the drizzle of December,
but under the golden sunlight of June it is lovely. It becomes every
year, with gay boating parties in semi-fancy dresses, more of a carnival,
in which the carnivalers and their carnivalentines assume a more decided
character. It is very strange to see this tendency of the age to unfold
itself in new festival forms, when those who believe that there can never
be any poetry or picturing in life but in the past are wailing over the
vanishing of May-poles and old English sports. There may be, from time
to time, a pause between the acts; the curtain may be down a little
longer than usual; but in the long run the world-old play of the Peoples'
Holiday will go on, as it has been going ever since Satan suggested that
little apple-stealing excursion to Eve, which, as explained by the
Talmudists, was manifestly the direct cause of all the flirtations and
other dreadful doings in all little outings down to the present day, in
the drawing-room or "on the leads," world without end.

And as the boat went along by Weybridge we passed a bank by which was a
small gypsy camp; tents and wagons, donkeys and all, reflected in the

silent stream, as much as were the swans in the fore-water. And in the camp was a tall, handsome, wild beauty, named Britannia, who knew me well; a damsel fond of larking, with as much genuine devil's gunpowder in her as would have made an entire pack or a Chinese hundred of sixty-four of the small crackers known as fast girls, in or around society. She was a splendid creature, long and lithe and lissom, but well rounded, of a figure suggestive of leaping hedges; and as the sun shone on her white teeth and burning black eyes, there was a hint of biting, too, about her. She lay coiled and basking, in feline fashion, in the sun; but at sight of me on the boat, up she bounded, and ran along the bank, easily keeping up with the steamer, and crying out to me in Romanes.

Now it just so happened that I by no means felt certain that *all* of the company present were such genial Bohemians as to appreciate anything like the joyous intimacy which Britannia was manifesting, as she, Atalanta-like, coursed along. Consequently, I was not delighted with her attentions.

"What a fine girl!" said Mr. Roebuck. "How well she would look on the stage! She seems to know you."

"Certainly," said one of the ladies, "or she would not be speaking her language. Why don't you answer her? Let us hear a conversation."

Thus adjured, I answered,--

"*Miri pen, miri kushti pen, beng lel tute, ma rakker sa drovan! Or ma rakker Romaneskas. Man dikesa te rania shan akai. Miri kameli--man kair mandy ladge!*" (My sister, my nice, sweet sister!--devil take you! don't hallo at me like that! Or else don't talk Romany. Don't you see there are ladies here? My dear, don't put me to shame!)

"*Pen the rani ta wusser mandy a trin-grushi--who--op, hallo!*"
(Tell the lady to shy me a shilling--whoop!) cried the fast damsel.

"*Pa miri duvels kam, pen--o bero se ta duro. Mandy'll de tute a pash-korauna keratti if tu tevel ja. Gorgie shan i foki kavakoi!*"
(For the Lord's sake, sister!--the boat is too far from shore. I'll give you half a crown this evening if you'll clear out. These be Gentiles, these here.)

"It seems to be a melodious language," said Mr. Roebuck, greatly amused. "What are you saying?"

"I am telling her to hold her tongue, and go."

"But how on earth does it happen that you speak such a language?" inquired a lady. "I always thought that the gypsies only talked a kind of English slang, and this sounds like a foreign tongue."

All this time Britannia, like the Cork Leg, never tired, but kept on the chase, neck and neck, till we reached a lock, when, with a merry laugh like a child, she turned on her track and left us.

"Mr. L.'s proficiency in Romany," said Mr. Roebuck, "is well known to me. I have heard him spoken of as the successor to George Borrow."

"That," I replied, "I do not deserve. There are other gentlemen in England who are by far my superiors in knowledge of the people."

And I spoke very sincerely. Apropos of Mr. George Borrow, I knew him, and a grand old fellow he was,--a fresh and hearty giant, holding his six feet two or three inches as uprightly at eighty as he ever had at eighteen. I believe that was his age, but may be wrong. Borrow was like one of the old Norse heroes, whom he so much admired, or an old-fashioned gypsy bruiser, full of craft and merry tricks. One of these he played on me, and I bear him no malice for it. The manner of the joke was this: I had written a book on the English gypsies and their language; but before I announced it, I wrote a letter to Father George, telling him that I proposed to print it, and asking his permission to dedicate it to him. He did not answer the letter, but "worked the tip" promptly enough, for he immediately announced in the newspapers on the following Monday his "Word-Book of the Romany Language," "with many pieces in gypsy, illustrative of the way of speaking and thinking of the English gypsies, with specimens of their poetry, and an account of various things relating to gypsy life in England." This was exactly what I had told him that my book would contain; for I intended originally to publish a vocabulary. Father George covered the track by not answering my letter; but I subsequently ascertained that it had been faithfully delivered to him by a gentleman from whom I obtained the information.

It was like the contest between Hildebrand the elder and his son:--

> "A ready trick tried Hildebrand,
> That old, gray-bearded man;
> For when the younger raised to strike,
> Beneath his sword he ran."

And, like the son, I had no ill feeling about it. My obligations to him for "Lavengro" and the "Romany Rye" and his other works are such as I owe to few men. I have enjoyed gypsying more than any sport in the world, and I owe my love of it all to George Borrow. I have since heard that a part of Mr. Borrow's "Romano Lavo-Lil" had been in manuscript for thirty years, and that it might never have been published but for my own work. I hope that this is true; for I am sincerely proud to think that I may have been in any way, directly or indirectly, the cause of his giving it to the world. I would gladly enough have burnt my own book, as I said, with a hearty laugh, when I saw the announcement of the "Lavo-Lil," if it would have pleased the old Romany rye, and I never spoke a truer word. He would not have believed it; but it would have been true, all the same.

I well remember the first time I met George Borrow. It was in the British Museum, and I was introduced to him by Mrs. Estelle Lewis,--now dead,--the well known-friend of Edgar A. Poe. He was seated at a table, and had a large old German folio open before him. We talked about gypsies, and I told him that I had unquestionably found the word for "green," *shelno*, in use among the English Romany. He assented, and said that he knew it. I mention this as a proof of the manner in which the "Romano Lavo-Lil" must have been hurried, because he declares in it that there is no English gypsy word for "green." In this work he asserts that the English gypsy speech does not probably amount to fourteen hundred words. It is a weakness with the Romany rye fraternity to believe that there are no words in gypsy which they to not know. I am sure that my own collection contains nearly four thousand Anglo-Romany terms, many of which I feared were doubtful, but which I am constantly verifying. America is a far better place in which to study the language than England. As an old Scotch gypsy said to me lately, the deepest and cleverest old gypsies all come over here to America, where they have grown rich, and built the old language up again.

I knew a gentleman in London who was a man of extraordinary energy. Having been utterly ruined, at seventy years of age, by a relative, he left England, was absent two or three years in a foreign country, during which time he made in business some fifty thousand pounds, and, returning, settled down in England. He had been in youth for a long time the most intimate friend of George Borrow, who was, he said, a very wild and eccentric youth. One night, when skylarking about London, Borrow was pursued by the police, as he wished to be, even as Panurge so planned as to be chased by the night-watch. He was very tall and strong in those days, a trained shoulder-hitter, and could run like a deer. He was hunted to the Thames, "and there they thought they had him." But the

Romany rye made for the edge, and, leaping into the wan water, like the Squyre in the old ballad, swam to the other side, and escaped.

I have conversed with Mr. Borrow on many subjects,--horses, gypsies, and Old Irish. Anent which latter subject I have heard him declare that he doubted whether there was any man living who could really read an old Irish manuscript. I have seen the same statement made by another writer. My personal impressions of Mr. Borrow were very agreeable, and I was pleased to learn afterwards from Mrs. Lewis that he had expressed himself warmly as regarded myself. As he was not invariably disposed to like those whom be met, it is a source of great pleasure to me to reflect that I have nothing but pleasant memories of the good old Romany rye, the Nestor of gypsy gentlemen. It is commonly reported among gypsies that Mr. Borrow was one by blood, and that his real name was Boro, or great. This is not true. He was of pure English extraction.

When I first met "George Eliot" and G. H. Lewes, at their house in North Bank, the lady turned the conversation almost at once to gypsies. They spoke of having visited the Zincali in Spain, and of several very curious meetings with the **Chabos**. Mr. Lewes, in fact, seldom met me--and we met very often about town, and at many places, especially at the Trubners'--without conversing on the Romanys. The subject evidently had for him a special fascination. I believe that I have elsewhere mentioned that after I returned from Russia, and had given him, by particular request, an account of my visits to the gypsies of St. Petersburg and Moscow, he was much struck by the fact that I had chiromanced to the Romany clan of the latter city. To tell the fortunes of gypsy girls was, he thought, the refinement of presumption. "There was in this world nothing so impudent as a gypsy when determined to tell a fortune; and the idea of not one, but many gypsy girls believing earnestly in my palmistry was like a righteous retribution."

The late Tom Taylor had, while a student at Cambridge, been **aficionado**, or smitten, with gypsies, and made a manuscript vocabulary of Romany words, which he allowed me to use, and from which I obtained several which were new to me. This fact should make all smart gypsy scholars "take tent" and heed as to believing that they know everything. I have many Anglo-Romany words--purely Hindi as to origin--which I have verified again and again, yet which have never appeared in print. Thus far the Romany vocabulary field has been merely scratched over.

Who that knows London knoweth not Sir Patrick Colquhoun? I made his acquaintance in 1848, when, coming over from student-life in Paris and the Revolution, I was most kindly treated by his family. A glorious, tough, widely experienced man he was even in early youth. For then he already bore the enviable reputation of being the first amateur sculler on the Thames, the first gentleman light-weight boxer in England, a graduate with honors of Cambridge, a Doctor Ph. of Heidelberg, a diplomat, and a linguist who knew Arabic, Persian, and Gaelic, Modern Greek and the Omnium Botherum tongues. They don't make such men nowadays, or, if they do, they leave out the genial element.

Years had passed, and I had returned to London in 1870, and found Sir Patrick living, as of yore, in the Temple, where I once and yet again and again dined with him. It was in the early days of this new spring of English life that we found ourselves by chance at a boat-race on the Thames. It was on the Thames, by his invitation, that I had twenty years before first seen an English regatta, and had a place in the gayly decked, superbly luncheoned barge of his club. It is a curious point in English character that the cleverest people do not realize or understand how festive and genial they really are, or how gayly and picturesquely they conduct their sports. It is a generally accepted doctrine with them that they do this kind of thing better in France; they believe sincerely that they take their own amusements sadly; it is the tone, the style, with the wearily-witty, dreary clowns of the weekly press, in their watery imitations of Thackeray's worst, to ridicule all English festivity

and merry-making, as though sunshine had faded out of life, and God and
Nature were dead, and in their place a great wind-bag Jesuit-Mallock were
crying, in tones tainted with sulphuretted hydrogen, "*Ah bah*!" Reader
mine, I have seen many a fete in my time, all the way from illuminations
of Paris to the Khedive's fifteen-million-dollar spree in 1873 and the
last grand flash of the Roman-candle carnival of 1846, but for true,
hearty enjoyment and quiet beauty give me a merry party on the Thames.
Give me, I say, its sparkling waters, its green banks, the joyous,
beautiful girls, the hearty, handsome men. Give me the boats, darting
like fishes, the gay cries. And oh--oh!--give me the Alsopp's ale in a
quart mug, and not a remark save of approbation when I empty it.

I had met Sir Patrick in the crowd, and our conversation turned on
gypsies. When living before-time in Roumania, he had Romany servants,
and learned a little of their language. Yes, he was inclined to be
"affected" into the race, and thereupon we went gypsying. Truly, we had
not far to seek, for just outside the crowd a large and flourishing
community of the black-blood had set itself up in the *pivlioi*
(cocoa-nut) or *kashta* (stick) business, and as it was late in the
afternoon, and the entire business-world was about as drunk as mere beer
could make it, the scene was not unlively. At that time I was new to
England, and unknown to every gypsy on the ground. In after-days I
learned to know them well, very well, for they were chiefly Coopers and
their congeners, who came to speak of me as *their* rye and own special
property or proprietor,--an allegiance which involved on one side an
amount of shillings and beer which concentrated might have set up a
charity, but which was duly reciprocated on the other by jocular tenures
of cocoa-nuts, baskets, and choice and deep words in the language of
Egypt.

As we approached the cock-shy, where sticks were cast at cocoa-nuts, a
young gypsy *chai*, whom I learned to know in after-days as Athalia
Cooper, asked me to buy some sticks. A penny a throw, all the cocoa-nuts

I could hit to be my own. I declined; she became urgent, jolly, riotous, insistive. I endured it well, for I held the winning cards. *Qui minus propere*, *minus prospere*. And then, as her voice rose *crescendo* into a bawl, so that all the Romanys around laughed aloud to see the green Gorgio so chaffed and bothered, I bent me low, and whispered softly in her ear a single monosyllable.

Why are all those sticks dropped so suddenly? Why does Athalia in a second become sober, and stand up staring at me, all her chaff and urgency forgotten. Quite polite and earnest now. But there is joy behind in her heart. This *is* a game, a jolly game, and no mistake. And uplifting her voice again, as the voice of one who findeth an exceeding great treasure even in the wilderness, she cried aloud,--"*It's a Romany rye*!"

The spiciest and saltest and rosiest of Sir Patrick's own stories, told after dinner over his own old port to a special conventicle of clergymen about town, was never received with such a roar of delight as that cry of Athalia's was by the Romany clan. Up went three sheers at the find; further afield went the shout proclaiming the discovery of an aristocratic stranger of their race, a *rye*, who was to them as wheat,--a gypsy gentleman. Neglecting business, they threw down their sticks, and left their cocoanuts to grin in solitude; the *dyes* turned aside from fortune-telling to see what strange fortune had sent such a visitor. In ten minutes Sir Patrick and I were surrounded by such a circle of sudden admirers and vehement applauders, as it seldom happens to any mortal to acquire--out of Ireland--at such exceedingly short notice and on such easy terms.

They were not particular as to what sort of a gypsy I was, or where I came from, or any nonsense of that sort, you know. It was about *cerevisia vincit omnia*, or the beery time of day with them, and they cared not for anything. I was extremely welcome; in short, there was poetry in me. I had come down on them by a way that was dark and a trick that was vain, in the path of mystery, and dropped on Athalia and picked her up. It was gypsily done and very creditable to me, and even Sir Patrick was regarded as one to be honored as an accomplice. It is a charming novelty in every life to have the better class of one's own kind come into it, and nobody feels so keenly as a jolly Romany that ***jucundum nihil est nisi quod reficit varietas***--naught pleases us without variety.

Then and there I drew to me the first threads of what became in after-days a strange and varied skein of humanity. There was the Thames upon a holiday. Now I look back to it, I ask, ***Ubi sunt***? (Where are they all?) Joshua Cooper, as good and earnest a Rom as ever lived, in his grave, with more than one of those who made my acquaintance by hurrahing for me. Some in America, some wandering wide. Yet there by Weybridge still the Thames runs on.

By that sweet river I made many a song. One of these, to the tune of "Waves in Sunlight Dancing," rises and falls in memory like a fitful fairy coming and going in green shadows, and that it may not perish utterly I here give it a place:--

AVELLA PARL O PANI.

Av' kushto parl o pani,
Av' kushto mir' akai!
Mi kameli chovihani,
Avel ke tiro rye!

Shan raklia rinkenidiri,
Mukkellan rinkeni se;
Kek rakli 'dre i temia
Se rinkenidiri mi.

Shan dudnidiri yakka,
Mukkelan dudeni;
Kek yakk peshel' sa kushti
Pa miro kameli zi.

Shan balia longi diri,
Mukk 'lende bori 'pre,
Kek waveri raklia balia,
Te lian man opre.

Yoi lela angustrini,
I miri tacheni,
Kek wavei mush jinella,
Sa dovo covva se.

Adre, adre o doeyav
Patrinia pellelan,
Kenna yek chumer kerdo
O wavero well' an.

Te wenna butidiri,
Ke jana sig akoi
Sa sig sa yeck si gillo
Shan waveri adoi.

Avella parl o pani,
Avella sig akai!
Mi kamli tani-rani
Avell' ke tiro rye!

* * * * *

COME OVER THE RIVER

O love, come o'er the water,
O love, where'er you be!
My own sweetheart, my darling,
Come over the river to me!

If any girls are fairer,
Then fairer let them be;
No maid in all the country
Is half so fair to me.

If other eyes are brighter,
Then brighter let them shine;
I know that none are lighter
Upon this heart of mine.

If other's locks are longer,
Then longer let them grow;
Hers are the only fish-lines
Which ever caught me so.

She wears upon her finger
A ring we know so well,
And we and that ring only
Know what the ring can tell.

From trees into the water
Leaves fall and float away,
So kisses come and leave us,
A thousand in a day.

Yet though they come by thousands,

Yet still they show their face;
As soon as one has left us
Another fills its place.

O love, come o'er the water,
O lore, where'er you be!
My own sweetheart, my darling,
Come over the river to me!

WELSH GYPSIES.

I. MAT WOODS THE FIDDLER.

The gypsies of Wales are to those of England what the Welsh themselves
are to the English; more antique and quaint, therefore to a collector of
human bric-a-brac more curious. The Welsh Rom is specially grateful for
kindness or courtesy; he is deeper as to language, and preserves many of
the picturesque traits of his race which are now so rapidly vanishing.
But then he has such excellent opportunity for gypsying. In Wales there
are yet thousands of acres of wild land, deep ravines, rocky corners, and
roadside nooks, where he can boil the kettle and ***hatch the tan***, or
pitch his tent, undisturbed by the rural policeman. For it is a charming
country, where no one need weary in summer, when the days are long, or in
early autumn,--

"When the barley is ripe,
And the frog doth pipe,

> In golden stripe
> And green all dressed;
> When the red apples
> Roll in the chest."

Then it is pleasant walking in Wales, and there too at times, between hedge-rows, you may meet with the Romany.

I was at Aberystwith by the sea, and one afternoon we went, a party of three gentlemen and three ladies, in a char-a-banc, or wagonette, to drive. It was a pleasant afternoon, and we had many a fine view of distant mountains, on whose sides were mines of lead with silver, and of which there were legends from the time of Queen Elizabeth. The hills looked leaden and blue in the distance, while the glancing sea far beyond recalled silver,--for the alchemy of imagery, at least, is never wanting to supply ideal metals, though the real may show a sad *deficit* in the returns.

As we drove we suddenly overtook a singular party, the first of whom was the leader, who had lagged behind. He was a handsome, slender, very dark young man, carrying a violin. Before him went a little open cart, in which lay an old woman, and by her a harp. With it walked a good-looking gypsy girl, and another young man, not a gypsy. He was by far the handsomest young fellow, in form and features, whom I ever met among the agricultural class in England; we called him a peasant Apollo. It became evident that the passional affinity which had drawn this rustic to the gypsy girl, and to the roads, was according to the law of natural selection, for they were wonderfully well matched. The young man had the grace inseparable from a fine figure and a handsome face, while the girl was tall, lithe, and pantherine, with the diavolesque charm which, though often attributed by fast-fashionable novelists to their heroines, is really never found except among the lowborn beauties of nature. It is the beauty of the Imp and of the Serpent; it fades with letters; it dies in the drawing-room or on the stage. You are mistaken when you think you see it coming out of the synagogue, unless it be a very vulgar one. Your Lahova has it not, despite her black eyes, for she is too clever and too conscious; the devil-beauty never knows how to read, she is unstudied and no actress. Rachel and the Bernhardt have it not, any more than Saint Agnes or Miss Blanche Lapin. It is not of good or of evil, or of culture, which is both; it is all and only of nature, and it does not know itself.

As the wagonette stopped I greeted the young man at first in English, then in Romany. When he heard the gypsy tongue he started, his countenance expressing the utmost surprise and delight. As if he could hardly believe in such a phenomenon he inquired, "***Romany***?" and as I nodded assent, he clasped my hand, the tears coming into his eyes. Such manifestations are not common among gypsies, but I can remember how one, the wife of black Ben Lee, was thus surprised and affected. How well I recall the time and scene,--by the Thames, in the late twilight, when every tree and twig was violet black against the amber sky, where the birds were chirp-chattering themselves to roost and rest, and the river rippled and murmured a duet with the evening breeze. I was walking homeward to Oatlands when I met the tawny Sinaminta, bearing her little stock of baskets to the tent and van which I had just quitted, and where Ben and his beautiful little boy were lighting the ***al fresco*** fire. "I have prayed to see this day!" exclaimed the gypsy woman. "I have so wanted to see the Romany rye of the Coopers. And I laid by a little ***delaben***, a small present, for you when we should meet. It's a photograph of Ben and me and our child." I might have forgotten the evening and the amber sky, rippling river and dark-green hedge-rows, but for this strange meeting and greeting of an unknown friend, but a few kind words fixed them all for life. That must be indeed a wonderful landscape which humanity does not make more impressive.

I spoke but a few words to the gypsy with the violin, and we drove on to a little wayside inn, where we alighted and rested. After a while the gypsies came along.

"And now, if you will, let us have a real frolic," I said to my friends. A word was enough. A quart of ale, and the fiddle was set going, and I sang in Romany, and the rustic landlord and his household wondered what sort of guests we could be. That they had never before entertained such a mixed party I can well believe. Here, on one hand, were indubitable swells, above their usual range; there, on the other, were the dusky vagabonds of the road; and it could be no common condescending patronage, for I was speaking neither Welsh nor English, and our friendly fraternity was evident. Yes, many a time, in England, have I seen the civil landlady or the neat-handed Phillis awed with bewilderment, as I have introduced Plato Buckland, or the most disreputable-looking but oily--yea, glycerine-politeful--old Windsor Frog, into the parlor, and conversed with him in mystic words. Such an event is a rare joy to the gypsy. For he loves to be lifted up among men; he will tell you with pride of the times when he was pointed at, and people said, "*He's* the man!" and how a real gentleman once invited him into his house and gave him a glass of wine. But to enter the best room of the familiar tavern, to order, in politest but imperative tones, "beer"--sixpenny beer--for himself and "the other gentleman," is indeed bliss. Then, in addition to the honor of moving in distinguished society, before the very eyes and in the high places of those who have hitherto always considered him as a lowly cuss, the Romany realizes far more than the common peasant the contrast-contradiction, or the humor of the drama, its bit of mystification, and especially the mystification of the house-folk. This is unto him the high hour of the soul, and it is not forgotten. It passes unto the golden legends of the heart, and you are tenderly enshrined in it.

Once, when I was wandering afoot with old Cooper, we stopped at an inn, and in a room by ourselves ordered luncheon. The gypsy might have had poultry of the best; he preferred cold pork. While the attendant was in the room, he sat with exemplary dignity at the table; but as the girl left, he followed her step sounds with his ears, like a dog, moved his head, glanced at me with a nod, turned sideways from the table, and, putting his plate on his knees, proceeded to eat without a fork.

"For it isn't proper for me to eat at the table with you, or *as* you do."

The Welsh gypsy played well, and his sister touched the harp and sang, the ale circulated, and the villagers, assembling, gazed in a crowd into the hall. Then the girl danced solo, just as I have seen her sisters do in Egypt and in Russia, to her brother's fiddling. Even so of old, Syrian and Egyptian girls haunted gardens and taverns, and danced *pas seul* all over the Roman empire, even unto Spain, behaving so gypsily that wise men have conjectured that they were gypsies in very truth. And who shall say they were not? For it is possible that prehistorically, and beyond all records of Persian Luri and Syrian Ballerine and Egyptian Almeh, there was all over the East an outflowing of these children of art from one common primeval Indian stock. From one fraternity, in Italy, at the present day, those itinerant pests, the hand-organ players, proceed to the ends of the earth and to the gold-diggings thereof, and time will yet show that before all time, or in its early dawn, there were root-born Romany itinerants singing, piping, and dancing unto all the known world; yea, and into the unknown darkness beyond, *in partibus infidelium*.

A gentleman who was in our party had been long in the East. I had known him in Alexandria during the carnival, and he had lived long time *outre mer*, in India. Hearing me use the gypsy numerals--*yeck, dui, trin, shtor, panj*,--he proceeded to count in Hindustani or Persian, in which the same words from one to ten are almost identical with Romany. All of this was carefully noted by the old gypsy mother,--as, also, that my friend is of dark complexion, with sparkling black eyes. Reduced in dress, or diluted down to worn corduroy and a red tie, he might easily pass muster, among the Sons of the Road, as one of them.

And now the ladies must, of course, have their fortunes told, and this, I could observe, greatly astonished the gypsies in their secret souls, though they put a cool face on it. That we, ourselves, were some kind of a mysterious high-caste Romany they had already concluded, and what faith could we put in *dukkerin*? But as it would indubitably bring forth shillings to their benefit, they wisely raised no questions, but calmly took this windfall, which had fallen as it were, from the skies, even as they had accepted the beer, which had come, like a providential rain, unto them, in the thirst of a dry journey.

It is customary for all gypsy sorceresses to take those who are to be fortune-told aside, and, if possible, into a room by themselves. This is done partly to enhance the mystery of the proceeding, and partly to avoid the presence of witnesses to what is really an illegal act. And as the old sorceress led a lady into the little parlor, the gypsy man, whose name was Mat, glanced up at me, with a droll, puzzled expression, and said, "Patchessa *tu* adovo?" (Do *you* believe in that?) With a wink, I answered, "Why not? I, too, tell fortunes myself." **Anch io sono pittore**. It seemed to satisfy him, for he replied, with a nod-wink, and proceeded to pour forth the balance of his thoughts, if he had any, into the music of his violin.

When the ladies had all been instructed as to their future, my friend, who had been in the East, must needs have his destiny made known unto him. He did not believe in this sort of thing, you know,--of course not. But he had lived a long time among Orientals, and he just happened to wish to know how certain speculations would fall out, and he loves, above all things, a lark, or anything out of the common. So he went in. And when alone with the sybil, she began to talk to him in Romany.

"Oh, I say, now, old lady, stow that!" he exclaimed. "I don't understand you."

"You don't understand me!" exclaimed the fortune-teller. "Perhaps you didn't understand your own mother when she talked Romany to you. What's the use of your tryin' to make yourself out a Gorgio to *me*? Don't I know our people? Didn't your friend there talk Romanes? Isn't he all Romaneskas? And didn't I hear you with my own ears count up to ten in Romany? And now, after that, you would deny your own blood and people! Yes, you've dwelt in Gorgines so long that you think your eyes are blue and your hair is yellow, my son, and you have been far over the sea; but wherever you went you knew Romanes, if you don't know your own color. But you shall hear your fortune. There is lead in the mines and silver in the lead, and wealth for him who is to win it, and that will be a dark man who has been nine times over the sea, and eaten his bread under the black tents, and been three times near death, once from a horse, and once from a man, and once through a woman. And you will know something you don't know now before a month is over, and something will be found that is now hidden, and has been hidden since the world was made. And there's a good fortune coming to the man it was made for, before the oldest tree that's a-growing was a seed, and that's a man as knows how to count Romanes up to ten, and many a more thing beside that, that he's learned beyond the great water."

And so we went our ways, the harp and violin sounds growing fainter as we receded, till they were like the buzzing of bees in drying clover, and the twilight grew rosier brown. I never met Mat Woods again, though I often heard of his fame as a fiddler. Whether my Anglo-Indian friend found the fortune so vaguely predicted is to me as yet unknown. But I believe that the prediction encouraged him. That there are evils in palmistry, and sin in card-drawing, and iniquity in coffee-grounding, and vice in all the planets, is established by statute, and yet withal I incline to believe that the art of prediction cheers up many a despondent soul, and does some little good, even as good ale, despite the wickedness of drinking, makes some hearts merry and others stronger. If there are foolish maids who have had their heads turned by being told of coming noblemen and prospective swells, who loved the ground they trod on, and were waiting to woo and win and wed, and if the same maidens herein described have thereby, in the manner set forth, been led by the aforesaid devices unto their great injury, as written in the above indictment, it may also **per contra** and on the other hand be pleaded that divers girls, to wit, those who believe in prediction, have, by encouragement and hope to them held out of legally marrying sundry young men of good estate, been induced to behave better than they would otherwise have done, and led by this hope have acted more morally than was their wont, and thereby lifted themselves above the lowly state of vulgarity, and even of vice, in which they would otherwise have groveled, hoveled, or cottaged. And there have been men who, cherishing in their hearts a prediction, or, what amounts to the same thing, a conviction, or a set fancy, have persevered in hope until the hope was realized. You, O Christian, who believe in a millennium, you, O Jew, who expect a Messiah, and await the fulfillment of your **dukkerin**, are both in the right, for both will come true when you **make** them do so.

II. THE PIOUS WASHERWOMAN.

There is not much in life pleasanter than a long ramble on the road in leaf-green, sun-gold summer. Then it is Nature's merry-time, when fowls in woods them maken blithe, and the crow preaches from the fence to his friends afield, and the honeysuckle winketh to the wild rose in the hedge when she is wooed by the little buzzy bee. In such times it is good for the heart to wander over the hills and far away, into haunts known of old, where perhaps some semi-Saxon church nestles in a hollow behind a

hill, where grass o'ergrows each mouldering tomb, and the brook, as it
ripples by in a darksome aldered hollow, speaks in a language which man
knows no more, but which is answered in the same forgotten tongue by the
thousand-year yew as it rustles in the breeze. And when there are Runic
stones in this garden of God, where He raises souls, I often fancy that
this old dialect is written in their rhythmic lines. The yew-trees were
planted by law, lang-syne, to yield bows to the realm, and now archery is
dead and Martini-Henry has taken its place, but the yews still live, and
the Runic fine art of the twisted lines on the tombs, after a thousand
years' sleep, is beginning to revive. Every thing at such a time speaks
of joy and resurrection--tree and tomb and bird and flower and bee.

These are all memories of a walk from the town of Aberystwith, in Wales,
which walk leads by an ancient church, in the soul garden of which are
two Runic cross tombstones. One day I went farther afield to a more
ancient shrine, on the top of a high mountain. This was to the summit of
Cader Idris, sixteen miles off. On this summit there is a Druidical
circle, of which the stones, themselves to ruin grown, are strange and
death-like old. Legend says that this is the burial-place of Taliesin,
the first of Welsh bards, the primeval poet of Celtic time. Whoever
sleeps on the grave will awake either a madman or a poet, or is at any
rate unsafe to become one or the other. I went, with two friends, afoot
on this little pilgrimage. Both were professors at one of the great
universities. The elder is a gentleman of great benevolence, learning,
and gentleness; the other, a younger man, has been well polished and
sharpened by travel in many lands. It is rumored that he has preached
Islam in a mosque unto the Moslem even unto taking up a collection, which
is the final test of the faith which reaches forth into a bright
eternity. That he can be, as I have elsewhere noted, a Persian unto
Persians, and a Romany among Roms, and a professional among the
hanky-pankorites, is likewise on the cards, as surely as that he knows
the roads and all the devices and little games of them that dwell
thereon. Though elegant enough in his court dress and rapier when he

kisses the hand of our sovereign lady the queen, he appears such an
abandoned rough when he goes a-fishing that the innocent and guileless
gypsies, little suspecting that a *rye* lies *perdu* in his wrap-rascal,
will then confide in him as if he and in-doors had never been acquainted.

We had taken with us a sparing lunch of thin sandwiches and a frugal
flask of modest, blushing brandy, which we diluted at a stingy little
fountain spring which dropped economically through a rift in the rock, as
if its nymph were conscious that such a delicious drink should not be
wasted. As it was, it refreshed us, and we were resting in a blessed
repose under the green leaves, when we heard footsteps, and an old woman
came walking by.

She was the ideal of decent and extreme poverty. I never saw anybody who
was at once so poor and so clean. In her face and in her thin garments
was marked the mute, resolute struggle between need and self-respect,
which, to him who understands it, is as brave as any battle between life
and death. She walked on as if she would have gone past without a word,
but when we greeted her she paused, and spoke respectfully. Without
forwardness she told her sad and simple story: how she belonged to the
Wesleyan confession, how her daughter was dying in the hospital at
Caernarvon; how she had walked sixty miles to see her, and hoped to get
there in time to close her eyes. In reply to a question as to her means,
she admitted that they were exhausted, but that she could get through
without money; she did not beg. And then came naturally enough the rest
of the little artless narrative, as it generally happens among the simple
annals of the poor: how she had been for forty years a washerwoman, and
had a letter from her clergyman.

There was a tear in the eye of the elder professor, and his hand was in
his pocket. The younger smoked in silence. I was greatly moved
myself,--perhaps bewildered would be the better word,--when, all at once,
as the old woman turned in the sunlight, I caught the expression *of the*

corner of an eye!

My friend Salaman, who boasts that he is of the last of the Sadducees,--that strange, ancient, and secret sect, who disguise themselves as the **Neu Reformirte**,--declares that the Sephardim may be distinguished from the Ashkenazim as readily as from the confounded Goyim, by the corners of their eyes. This he illustrated by pointing out to me, as they walked by in the cool of the evening, the difference between the eyes of Fraulein Eleonora Kohn and Senorita Linda Abarbanel and divers and sundry other young ladies,--the result being that I received in return thirty-six distinct *oeillades*, several of which expressed indignation, and in all of which there was evidently an entire misconception of my object in looking at them. Now the eyes of the Sephardesses are unquestionably fascinating; and here it may be recalled that, in the Middle Ages, witches were also recognized by having exactly the same corners, or peaks, to the eye. This is an ancient mystery of darksome lore, that the enchantress always has the bird-peaked eye, which betokens danger to somebody, be she of the Sephardim, or an ordinary witch or enchantress, or a gypsy.

Now, as the old Wesleyan washerwoman turned around in the sunshine, I saw the witch-pointed eye and the glint of the Romany. And then I glanced at her hands, and saw that they had not been long familiar with wash-tubs; for, though clean, they were brown, and had never been blanched with an age of soap-suds. And I spoke suddenly, and said,--

"**Can tute rakker Romanes**, **miri dye**?" (Can you speak Romany, my mother?) And she answered, as if bewildered,--

"The Lord forbid, sir, that I should talk any of them wicked languages."

The younger professor's eyes expressed dawning delight. I followed my shot with,--

"*Tute needn't be attrash to rakker. Mandy's been apre the drom mi-kokero*." (You needn't be afraid to speak. I have been upon the road myself.)

And, still more confused, she answered in English,--

"Why, sir, you be upon the road now!"

"It seems to me, old lady," remarked the younger professor, "that you understand Romany very well for one who has been for forty years in the Methodist communion."

It may be observed that he here confounded washing with worshiping.

The face of the true believer was at this point a fine study. All her confidence had deserted her. Whether she thought we were of her kind in disguise, or that, in the unknown higher world of respectability, there might be gypsies of corresponding rank, even as there might be gypsy angels among the celestial hierarchies, I cannot with confidence assert. About a week ago a philologist and purist told me that there is no exact synonym in English for the word *flabbergasted*, as it expresses a peculiar state of bewilderment as yet unnamed by scholars, and it exactly sets forth the condition in which our virtuous poverty appeared. She was, indeed, flabbergasted. *Cornix scorpum rapuit*,--the owl had come down on the rabbits, and lo! they had fangs. I resumed,--

"Now, old lady, here is a penny. You are a very poor person, and I pity you so much that I give you this penny for your poverty. But there is a pocketful where this came from, and you shall have the lot if you'll *rakker*,"--that is, talk gypsy.

And at that touch of the Ithuriel spear the old toad flashed up into the

Romany devil, as with gleaming eyes and a witch-like grin she cried in a mixture of gypsy and tinker languages,--

"Gents, I'll have tute jin when you tharis mandy you rakker a reg'lar fly old bewer." Which means, "Gentlemen, I'll have you know, when you talk to me, you talk to a reg'lar shrewd old female thief."

The face of the elder professor was a study of astonishment for Lavater. His fingers relaxed their grasp of the shilling, his hand was drawn from his pocket, and his glance, like Bill Nye's, remarked: "***Can*** this be?" He tells the story to this day, and always adds, "I ***never*** was so astonished in my life." But the venerable washerwoman was also changed, and, the mask once thrown aside, she became as festive as a witch on the Brocken. Truly, it is a great comfort to cease playing a part, particularly a pious one, and be at home and at ease among your like; and better still if they be swells. This was the delight of Anderson's ugly duck when it got among the swans, "and, blest sensation, felt genteel." And to show her gratitude, the sorceress, who really seemed to have grown several shades darker, insisted on telling our fortunes. I think it was to give vent to her feelings in defiance of the law that she did this; certain it was that just then, under the circumstances, it was the only way available in which the law could be broken. And as it was, indeed, by heath and hill that the priestess of the hidden spell bade the Palmer from over the sea hold out his palm. And she began in the usual sing-song tone, mocking the style of gypsy fortune-tellers, and satirizing herself. And thus she spoke,--

"You're born under a lucky star, my good gentleman, and you're a married man; but there's a black-eyed young lady that's in love with you."

"Oh, mother of all the thieves!" I cried, "you've put the ***dukkerin*** on the wrong man. I'm the one that the dark girls go after."

"Yes, my good gentleman. She's in love with you both."

"And now tell my fortune!" I exclaimed, and with a grim expression, casting up my palm, I said,--

"***Pen mengy if mandy'll be bitchade padel for chorin a gry***, ***or nasherdo for merin a gav-mush***." (Tell me if I am to be transported for stealing a horse, or hung for killing a policeman.)

The old woman's face changed. "You'll never need to steal a horse. The man that knows what you know never need be poor like me. I know who *you* are *now*; you're not one of these tourists. You're the boro Romany rye [the tall gypsy gentleman]. And go your way, and brag about it in your house,--and well you may,--that Old Moll of the Roads couldn't take you in, and that you found her out. Never another *rye* but you will ever say that again. Never."

And she went dancing away in the sunshine, capering backwards along the road, merrily shaking the pennies in her hand for music, while she sang something in gypsy,--witch to the last, vanishing as witches only can. And there came over me a feeling as of the very olden time, and some memory of another witch, who had said to another man, "*Thou* art no traveler, Great master, I know thee now;" and who, when he called her the mother of the giants, replied, "Go thy way, and boast at home that no man will ever waken me again with spells. Never." That was the parting of Odin and the Vala sorceress, and it was the story of oldest time; and so the myth of ancient days becomes a tattered parody, and thus runs the world away to Romanys and rags--when the gods are gone.

When I laughed at the younger professor for confounding forty years in the church with as many at the wash-tub, he replied,--

"Cleanliness is with me so near to godliness that it is not remarkable that in my hurry I mistook one for the other."

So we went on and climbed Cader Idris, and found the ancient grave of
rocks in a mystic circle, whose meaning lies buried with the last Druid,
who would perhaps have told you they were--

> "Seats of stone nevir hewin with mennes hand
> But wrocht by Nature as it ane house had bene
> For Nymphes, goddis of floudes and woodis grene."

And we saw afar the beautiful scene, "where fluddes rynnys in the foaming
sea," as Gawain Douglas sings, and where, between the fresh water and
salt, stands a village, even where it stood in earliest Cymric
prehistoric dawn, and the spot where ran the weir in which the prince who
was in grief because his weir yielded no fish, at last fished up a poet,
even as Pharaoh's daughter fished out a prophet. I shall not soon forget
that summer day, nor the dream-like panorama, nor the ancient grave; nor
how the younger professor lay down on the seat of stone nevir hewin with
mennes hand, and declared he had a nap,--just enough to make him a poet.
To prove which he wrote a long poem on the finding of Taliesin in the
nets, and sent it to the Aberystwith newspaper; while I, not to be
behindhand, wrote another, in imitation of the triplets of Llydwarch Hen,
which were so greatly admired as tributes to Welsh poetry that they were
forthwith translated faithfully into lines of consonants, touched up with
so many *w*'s that they looked like saws; and they circulated even unto
Llandudno, and, for aught I know, may be sung at Eistedfodds, now and
ever, to the twanging of small harps,--*in soecula saeculorum*. Truly,
the day which had begun with a witch ended fitly enough at the tomb of a
prophet poet.

III. THE GYPSIES AT ABERYSTWITH.

Aberystwith is a little fishing-village, which has of late years first
bloomed as a railway-station, and then fruited into prosperity as a
bathing-place. Like many **parvenus**, it makes a great display of its
Norman ancestor, the old castle, saying little about the long centuries
of plebeian obscurity in which it was once buried. This castle, after
being woefully neglected during the days when nobody cared for its early
respectability, has been suddenly remembered, now that better times have
come, and, though not restored, has been made comely with grass banks,
benches, and gravel walks, reminding one of an Irish grandfather in
America, taken out on a Sunday with "the childher," and looking "gintale"
in the clean shirt and whole coat unknown to him for many a decade in
Tipperary. Of course the castle and the wealth, or the hotels and
parade, are well to the fore, or boldly displayed, as Englishly as
possible, while the little Welsh town shrinks quietly into the hollow
behind. And being new to prosperity, Aberystwith is also a little
muddled as to propriety. It would regard with horror the idea of
allowing ladies and gentlemen to bathe together, even though completely
clad; but it sees nothing out of the way when gentlemen in pre-fig-leaf
costume disport themselves, bathing just before the young ladies'
boarding-school and the chief hotel, or running joyous races on the
beach. I shall never forget the amazement and horror with which an
Aberystwithienne learned that in distant lands ladies and gentlemen went
into the water arm in arm, although dressed. But when it was urged that
the Aberystwith system was somewhat peculiar, she replied, "Oh, **that** is
a very different thing!"

On which words for a text a curious sermon might be preached to the
Philistiny souls who live perfectly reconciled to absurd paradoxes,
simply because they are accustomed to them. Now, of all human beings, I

think the gypsies are freest from trouble with paradoxes as to things
being different or alike, and the least afflicted with moral problems,
burning questions, social puzzles, or any other kind of mental rubbish.
They are even freer than savages or the heathen in this respect, since of
all human beings the Fijian, New Zealander, Mpongwe, or Esquimaux is most
terribly tortured with the laws of etiquette, religion, social position,
and propriety. Among many of these heathen unfortunates the meeting with
an equal involves fifteen minutes of bowing, re-bowing, surre-bowing, and
rejoinder-bowing, with complementary complimenting, according to old
custom, while the worship of Mrs. Grundy through a superior requires a
half hour wearisome beyond belief. "In Fiji," says Miss C. F. Gordon
Cumming, "strict etiquette rules every action of life, and the most
trifling mistake in such matters would cause as great dissatisfaction as
a breach in the order of precedence at a European ceremonial." In
dividing cold baked missionary at a dinner, especially if a chief be
present, the host committing the least mistake as to helping the proper
guest to the proper piece in the proper way would find himself promptly
put down in the *menu*. In Fiji, as in all other countries, this
punctilio is nothing but the direct result of ceaseless effort on the
part of the upper classes to distinguish themselves from the lower.
Cannibalism is a joint sprout from the same root; "the devourers of the
poor" are the scorners of the humble and lowly, and they are all grains
of the same corn, of the devil's planting, all the world over. Perhaps
the quaintest error which haunts the world in England and America is that
so much of this stuff as is taught by rule or fashion as laws for "the
elite" is the very nucleus of enlightenment and refinement, instead of
its being a remnant of barbarism. And when we reflect on the degree to
which this naive and child-like faith exists in the United States, as
shown by the enormous amount of information in certain newspapers as to
what is the latest thing necessary to be done, acted, or suffered in
order to be socially saved, I surmise that some future historian will
record that we, being an envious people, turned out the Chinese, because
we could not endure the presence among us of a race so vastly our

superiors in all that constituted the true principles of culture and
"custom."

Arthur Mitchell, in inquiring What is Civilization? {209} remarks that
"all the things which gather round or grow upon a high state of
civilization are not necessarily true parts of it. These
conventionalities are often regarded as its very essence." And it is
true that the greater the fool or snob, the deeper is the conviction that
the conventional is the core of "culture." "'It is not genteel,' 'in
good form,' or 'the mode,' to do this or do that, or say this or say
that." "Such things are spoken of as marks of a high civilization, or by
those who do not confound civilization with culture as differentiators
between the cultured and the uncultured." Dr. Mitchell "neither praises
nor condemns these things;" but it is well for a man, while he is about
it, to know his own mind, and I, for myself, condemn them with all my
heart and soul, whenever anybody declares that such brass counters in the
game of life are real gold, and insists that I shall accept them as such.
For small play in a very small way with small people, I would endure
them; but many men and nearly all women make their capital of them. And
whatever may be said in their favor, it cannot be denied that they
constantly lead to lying and heartlessness. Even Dr. Mitchell, while he
says he does not condemn them, proceeds immediately to declare that
"while we submit to them they constitute a sort of tyranny, under which
we fret and secretly pine for escape. Does not the exquisite of Rotten
Row weary for his flannel shirt and shooting-jacket? Do not
'well-constituted' men want to fish and shoot or kill something,
themselves, by climbing mountains, when they can find nothing else? In
short, does it not appear that these conventionalities are irksome, and
are disregarded when the chance presents itself? And does it not seem as
if there were something in human nature pulling men back to a rude and
simple life?" To find that **men** suffer under the conventionalities,
"adds, on the whole," says our canny, prudent Scot, "to the
respectability of human nature." ***Tu ha ragione*** (right you are), Dr.

Mitchell, there. For the conventional, whether found among Fijians as they were, or in Mayfair as it is, whenever it is vexatious and merely serves as a cordon to separate "sassiety" from society, detracts from the respectability of humanity, and is in itself vulgar. If every man in society were a gentleman and every woman a lady, there would be no more conventionalism. **Usus est tyrannus** (custom is a tyrant), or, as the Talmud proverb saith, "Custom is the plague of wise men, but is the idol of fools." And he was a wise Jew, whoever he was, who declared it.

But let us return to our black sheep, the gypsy. While happy in not being conventional, and while rejoicing, or at least unconsciously enjoying freedom from the bonds of etiquette, he agrees with the Chinese, red Indians, May Fairies, and Fifth Avenoodles in manifesting under the most trying circumstances that imperturbability which was once declared by an eminent Philadelphian to be "the Corinthian ornament of a gentleman." He who said this builded better than he knew, for the ornament in question, if purely Corinthian, is simply brass. One morning I was sauntering with the Palmer in Aberystwith, when we met with a young and good-looking gypsy woman, with whom we entered into conversation, learning that she was a Bosville, and acquiring other items of news as to Egypt and the roads, and then left.

We had not gone far before we found a tinker. He who catches a tinker has got hold of half a gypsy and a whole cosmopolite, however bad the catch may be. He did not understand the greeting **Sarishan**!--he really could not remember to have heard it. He did not know any gypsies,--"he could not get along with them." They were a bad lot. He had seen some gypsies three weeks before on the road. They were curious dark people, who lived in tents. He could not talk Romany.

This was really pitiable. It was too much. The Palmer informed him that he was wasting his best opportunities, and that it was a great pity that any man who lived on the roads should be so ignorant. The tinker never winked. In the goodness of our hearts we even offered to give him lessons in the **kalo jib**, or black language. The grinder was as calm as a Belgravian image. And as we turned to depart the professor said,--

"**Mandy'd del tute a shahori to pi moro kammaben**, *if tute jinned sa mandi pukkers*." (I'd give you a sixpence to drink our health, if you knew what I am saying.)

With undisturbed gravity the tinker replied,--

"Now I come to think of it, I do remember to have heard somethin' in the parst like that. It's a conwivial expression arskin' me if I won't have a tanner for ale. Which I will."

"Now since you take such an interest in gypsies," I answered, "it is a pity that you should know so little about them. I have seen them since you have. I saw a nice young woman, one of the Bosvilles here, not half an hour ago. Shall I introduce you?"

"That young woman," remarked the tinker, with the same immovable countenance, "is my wife. And I've come down here, by app'intment, to meet some Romany pals."

And having politely accepted his sixpence, the griddler went his way, tinkling his bell, along the road. He did not disturb himself that his first speeches did not agree with his last; he was not in the habit of being disturbed about anything, and he knew that no one ever learned Romany without learning with it not to be astonished at any little inconsistencies. Serene and polished as a piece of tin in the sunshine, he would not stoop to be put out by trifles. He was a typical tinker. He knew that the world had made up proverbs expressing the utmost indifference either for a tinker's blessing or a tinker's curse, and he retaliated by not caring a curse whether the world blessed or banned him.

In all ages and in all lands the tinker has always been the type of this droning indifference, which goes through life bagpiping its single melody, or whistling, like the serene Marquis de Crabs, "Toujours Santerre."

"Es ist und bleibt das alte Lied
Von dem versoff'nen Pfannenschmied,
Und wer's nicht weiter singen kann,
Der fang's von Vorne wieder an."

'T will ever be the same old song
Of tipsy tinkers all day long,
And he who cannot sing it more
May sing it over, as before.

I should have liked to know John Bunyan. As a half-blood gypsy tinker he must have been self-contained and pleasant. He had his wits about him, too, in a very Romanly way. When confined in prison he made a flute or pipe out of the leg of his three legged-stool, and would play on it to pass time. When the jailer entered to stop the noise, John replaced the leg in the stool, and sat on it looking innocent as only a gypsy tinker could,--calm as a summer morning. I commend the subject for a picture. Very recently, that is, in the beginning of 1881, a man of the same tinkering kind, and possibly of the same blood as Honest John, confined in the prison of Moyamensing, Philadelphia, did nearly the same thing, only that instead of making his stool leg into a musical pipe he converted it into a pipe for tobacco. But when the watchman, led by the smell, entered his cell, there was no pipe to be found; only a deeply injured man complaining that "somebody, had been smokin' outside, and it had blowed into his cell through the door-winder from the corridore, and p'isoned the atmosphere. And he didn't like it." And thus history repeats itself. 'T is all very well for the sticklers for Wesleyan gentility to deny that John Bunyan was a gypsy, but he who in his life cannot read Romany between the lines knows not the jib nor the cut thereof. Tough was J. B., "and de-vil-ish sly," and altogether a much better man than many suppose him to have been.

The tinker lived with his wife in a "tramps' lodging-house" in the town. To those Americans who know such places by the abominable dens which are occasionally reported by American grand juries, the term will suggest something much worse than it is. In England the average tramp's lodging is cleaner, better regulated, and more orderly than many Western "hotels." The police look closely after it, and do not allow more than a certain number in a room. They see that it is frequently cleaned, and that clean sheets are frequently put on the beds. One or two hand-organs in the hall, with a tinker's barrow or wheel, proclaimed the character of the lodgers, and in the sitting-room there were to be found, of an evening, gypsies, laborers with their families seeking work or itinerant musicians. I can recall a powerful and tall young man, with a badly expressive face, one-legged, and well dressed as a sailor. He was a beggar, who measured the good or evil of all mankind by what they gave him. He was very bitter as to the bad. Yet this house was in its way upper class. It was not a den of despair, dirt, and misery, and even the Italians who came there were obliged to be decent and clean. It would not have been appropriate to have written for them on the door, "***Voi che intrate lasciate ogni speranza***." (He who enters here leaves soap behind.) The most painful fact which struck me, in my many visits, was the intelligence and decency of some of the boarders. There was more than one who conversed in a manner which indicated an excellent early education; more than one who read the newspaper aloud and commented on it to the company, as any gentleman might have done. Indeed, the painful part of life as shown among these poor people was the manifest fact that so many of them had come down from a higher position, or were qualified for it. And this is characteristic of such places. In his "London Labour and the London Poor," vol. i. p. 217, Mahew tells of a low lodging-house "in which there were at one time five university men, three surgeons, and several sorts of broken-down clerks." The majority of these cases are the result of parents having risen from poverty and raised their families to "gentility." The sons are deprived by their bringing up of the vulgar pluck and coarse energy by which the father rose, and yet are expected to make their way in the world, with nothing but a so-called "education," which is too often less a help than a hindrance. In the race of life no man is so heavily handicapped as a young "gentleman." The humblest and raggedest of all the inmates of this house were two men who got their living by **shelkin gallopas** (or selling ferns), as it is called in the Shelta, or tinker's and tramp's slang. One of these, whom I have described in another chapter as teaching me this dialect, could conjugate a French verb; we thought he had studied law. The other was a poor old fellow called Krooty, who could give the Latin names for all the plants which he gathered and sold, and who would repeat poetry very appropriately, proving sufficiently that he had read it. Both the fern-sellers spoke better English than divers Lord Mayors and Knights to whom I have listened, for they neither omitted *h* like the lowly, nor *r* like the lofty ones of London.

The tinker's wife was afflicted with a nervous disorder, which caused her great suffering, and made it almost impossible for her to sell goods, or contribute anything to the joint support. Her husband always treated her with the greatest kindness; I have seldom seen an instance in which a man was more indulgent and gentle. He made no display whatever of his feelings; it was only little by little that I found out what a heart this imperturbable rough of the road possessed. Now the Palmer, who was always engaged in some wild act of unconscious benevolence, bought for her some medicine, and gave her an order on the first physician in the town for proper advice; the result being a decided amelioration of her health. And I never knew any human being to be more sincerely grateful than the tinker was for this kindness. Ascertaining that I had tools for wood-carving, he insisted on presenting me with crocus powder, "to put an edge on." He had a remarkably fine whetstone, "the best in England; it

was worth half a sovereign," and this he often and vainly begged me to
accept. And he had a peculiar little trick of relieving his kindly
feelings. Whenever we dropped in of an evening to the lodging-house, he
would cunningly borrow my knife, and then disappear. Presently the
whiz-whiz, *st'st* of his wheel would be heard without, and then the
artful dodger would reappear with a triumphant smile, and with the knife
sharpened to a razor edge. Anent which gratitude I shall have more to
say anon.

One day I was walking on the Front, when I overtook a gypsy van, loaded
with baskets and mats, lumbering along. The proprietor, who was a
stranger to me, was also slightly or lightly lumbering in his gait, being
cheerfully beery, while his berry brown wife, with a little
three-year-old boy, peddled wares from door to door. Both were amazed
and pleased at being accosted in Romany. In the course of conversation
they showed great anxiety as to their child, who had long suffered from
some disorder which caused them great alarm. The man's first name was
Anselo, though it was painted Onslow on his vehicle. Mr. Anselo, though
himself just come to town, was at once deeply impressed with the duty of
hospitality to a Romany rye. I had called him *pal*, and this in
gypsydom involves the shaking of hands, and with the better class an
extra display of courtesy. He produced half a crown, and declared his
willingness to devote it all to beer for my benefit. I declined, but he
repeated his offer several times,--not with any annoying display, but
with a courteous earnestness, intended to set forth a sweet sincerity.
As I bade him good-by, he put the crown-piece into one eye, and as he
danced backward, gypsy fashion up the street and vanished in the sunny
purple twilight towards the sea I could see him winking with the other,
and hear him cry, "Don't say no--now's the last chance--do I hear a bid?"

We found this family in due time at the lodging-house, where the little
boy proved to be indeed seriously ill, and we at once discovered that the
parents, in their ignorance, had quite misunderstood his malady and were

aggravating it by mal-treatment. To these poor people the good Palmer
also gave an order on the old physician, who declared that the boy must
have died in a few days, had he not taken charge of him. As it was, the
little fellow was speedily cured. There was, it appeared, some kind of
consanguinity between the tinker or his wife and the Anselo family.
These good people, anxious to do anything, yet able to do little,
consulted together as to showing their gratitude, and noting that we were
specially desirous of collecting old gypsy words gave us all they could
think of, and without informing us of their intention, which indeed we
only learned by accident a long time after, sent a messenger many miles
to bring to Aberystwith a certain Bosville, who was famed as being deep
in Romany lore, and in possession of many ancient words. Which was
indeed true, he having been the first to teach us *pisali*, meaning a
saddle, and in which Professor Cowell, of Cambridge, promptly detected
the Sanskrit for sit-upon, the same double meaning also existing in
boshto; or, as old Mrs. Buckland said to me at Oaklands Park, in
Philadelphia, "a *pisali* is the same thing with a *boshto*."

"What will gain thy faith?" said Quentin Durward to Hayradden Maugrabhin.
"Kindness," answered the gypsy.

The joint families, solely with intent to please us, although they never
said a word about it, next sent for a young Romany, one of the Lees, and
his wife whom they supposed we would like to meet. Walking along the
Front, I met the tinker's wife with the handsomest Romany girl I ever
beheld. In a London ball-room or on the stage she would have been a
really startling beauty. This was young Mrs. Lee. Her husband was a
clever violinist, and it was very remarkable that when he gave himself up
to playing, with *abandon* or self-forgetfulness, there came into his
melodies the same wild gypsy expression, the same chords and tones, which
abound in the music of the Austrian Tsigane. It was not my imagination
which prompted the recognition; the Palmer also observed it, without
thinking it remarkable. From the playing of both Mat Woods and young

Lee, I am sure that there has survived among the Welsh gypsies some of the spirit of their old Eastern music, just as in the solo dancing of Mat's sister there was precisely the same kind of step which I had seen in Moscow. Among the hundreds of the race whom I have met in Great Britain, I have never known any young people who were so purely Romany as these. The tinker and Anselo with his wife had judged wisely that we would be pleased with this picturesque couple. They always seemed to me in the house like two wild birds, and tropical ones at that, in a cage. There was a tawny-gold, black and scarlet tone about them and their garb, an Indian Spanish duskiness and glow which I loved to look at.

Every proceeding of the tinker and Anselo was veiled in mystery and hidden in the obscurity so dear to such grown-up children, but as I observed after a few days that Lee did nothing beyond acting as assistant to the tinker at the wheel, I surmised that the visit was solely for our benefit. As the tinker was devoted to his poor wife, so was Anselo and his dame devoted to their child. He was, indeed, a brave little fellow, and frequently manifested the precocious pluck and sturdiness so greatly admired by the Romanys of the road; and when he would take a whip and lead the horse, or in other ways show his courage, the delight of his parents was in its turn delightful. They would look at the child as if charmed, and then at one another with feelings too deep for words, and then at me for sympathetic admiration.

The keeper of the house where they lodged was in his way a character and a linguist. Welsh was his native tongue and English his second best. He also knew others, such as Romany, of which he was proud, and the Shelta or Minklas of the tinkers, of which he was not. The only language which he knew of which he was really ashamed was Italian, and though he could maintain a common conversation in it he always denied that he remembered more than a few words. For it was not as the tongue of Dante, but as the lingo of organ-grinders and such "catenone" that he knew it, and I think that the Palmer and I lost dignity in his eyes by inadvertently admitting that it was familiar to us. "I shouldn't have thought it," was all his comment on the discovery, but I knew his thought, and it was that we had made ourselves unnecessarily familiar with vulgarity.

It is not every one who is aware of the extent to which Italian is known by the lower orders in London. It is not spoken as a language; but many of its words, sadly mangled, are mixed with English as a jargon. Thus the Italian *scappare*, to escape, or run away, has become *scarper*; and a dweller in the Seven Dials has been heard to say he would "*scarper* with the *feele* of the *donna* of the *cassey*;" which means, run away with the daughter of the landlady of the house, and which, as the editor of the Slang Dictionary pens, is almost pure Italian,--*scappare colla figlia della donna*, *della casa*. Most costermongers call a penny a *saltee*, from *soldo*; a crown, a *caroon*; and one half, *madza*, from *mezza*. They count as follows:--

ITALIAN.

Oney saltee, a penny Uno soldo.
Dooey saltee, twopence
    Dui soldi.
Tray saltee, threepence
    Tre soldi.
Quarterer saltee, fourpence
    Quattro soldi.
Chinker saltee, fivepence
    Cinque soldi.
Say saltee, sixpence
    Sei soldi.
Say oney saltee, or setter
    Sette soldi.
saltee, sevenpence
Say dooee saltee, or otter

> Otto soldi.
saltee, eightpence
Say tray saltee, or nobba saltee,
> Nove soldi.
ninepence
Say quarterer saltee, or dacha
> Dieci soldi.
(datsha) saltee, tenpence
Say chinker saltee, or dacha one
> Dieci uno soldi
saltee, elevenpence
Oney beong, one shilling
> Uno bianco.
A beong say saltee, one shilling
> Uno bianco sei soldi.
and sixpence
Madza caroon, half a crown Mezza corona.

Mr. Hotten says that he could never discover the derivation of **beong**, or **beonk**. It is very plainly the Italian **bianco**, white, which, like **blanc** in French and **blank** in German, is often applied slangily to a silver coin. It is as if one had said, "a shiner." Apropos of which word there is something curious to be noted. It came forth in evidence, a few years ago in England, that burglars or other thieves always carried with them a piece of coal; and on this disclosure, a certain writer, in his printed collection of curiosities, comments as if it were a superstition, remarking that the coal is carried for an amulet. But the truth is that the thief has no such idea. The coal is simply a sign for money; and when the bearer meets with a man whom he thinks may be a "fence," or a purchaser of stolen goods, he shows the coal, which is as much as to say, Have you money? Money, in vulgar gypsy, is **wongur**, a corruption of the better word **angar**, which also means a hot coal; and **braise**, in French **argot**, has the same double meaning. I may be wrong, but I suspect that *rat*, a dollar in Hebrew, or at least in Schmussen, has its root in common with *ratzafim*, coals, and possibly *poschit*, a farthing, with *pecham*, coal. In the six kinds of fire mentioned in the Talmud, {222} there is no identification of coals with money; but in the German legends of Rubezahl, there is a tale of a charcoal-burner who found them changed to gold. Coins are called shiners because they shine like glowing coals, and I dare say that the simile exists in many more languages.

One twilight we found in the public sitting-room of the lodging-house a couple whom I can never forget. It was an elderly gypsy and his wife. The husband was himself characteristic; the wife was more than merely picturesque. I have never met such a superb old Romany as she was; indeed, I doubt if I ever saw any woman of her age, in any land or any range of life, with a more magnificently proud expression or such unaffected dignity. It was the whole poem of "Crescentius" living in modern time in other form.

When a scholar associates much with gypsies there is developed in him in due time a perception or intuition of certain kinds of men or minds, which it is as difficult to describe as it is wonderful. He who has read Matthew Arnold's "Gipsy Scholar" may, however, find therein many apt words for it. I mean very seriously what I say; I mean that through the Romany the demon of Socrates acquires distinctness; I mean that a faculty is developed which is as strange as divination, and which is greatly akin to it. The gypsies themselves apply it directly to palmistry; were they well educated they would feel it in higher forms. It may be reached among other races and in other modes, and Nature is always offering it to us freely; but it seems to live, or at least to be most developed, among the Romany. It comes upon the possessor far more powerfully when in contact with certain lives than with others, and with the sympathetic it takes in at a glance that which may employ it at intervals for years to think out.

And by this *duk* I read in a few words in the Romany woman an eagle soul, caged between the bars of poverty, ignorance, and custom; but a great soul for all that. Both she and her husband were of the old type of their race, now so rare in England, though commoner in America. They spoke Romany with inflection and conjugation; they remembered the old rhymes and old words, which I quoted freely, with the Palmer. Little by little, the old man seemed to be deeply impressed, indeed awed, by our utterly inexplicable knowledge. I wore a velveteen coat, and had on a broad, soft felt hat.

"You talk as the old Romanys did," said the old man. "I hear you use words which I once heard from old men who died when I was a boy. I thought those words were lying in graves which have long been green. I hear songs and sayings which I never expected to hear again. You talk like gypsies, and such gypsies as I never meet now; and you look like Gorgios. But when I was still young, a few of the oldest Romany *chals* still wore hats such as you have; and when I first looked at you, I thought of them. I don't understand you. It is strange, very strange."

"It is the Romany *soul*," said his wife. "People take to what is in them; if a bird were born a fox, it would love to fly."

I wondered what flights she would have taken if she had wings. But I understood why the old man had spoken as he did; for, knowing that we had intelligent listeners, the Palmer and I had brought forth all our best and quaintest Romany curios, and these rural Welsh wanderers were not, like their English pals, familiar with Romany ryes. And I was moved to like them, and nobody perceives this sooner than a gypsy. The old couple were the parents of young Lee, and said they had come to visit him; but I think that it was rather to see us that we owed their presence in Aberystwith. For the tinker and Anselo were at this time engaged, in their secret and owl-like manner, as befitted men who were up to all

manner of ways that were dark, in collecting the most interesting
specimens of Romanys, for our especial study; and whenever this could be
managed so that it appeared entirely accidental and a surprise, then they
retired into their shadowed souls and chuckled with fiendish glee at
having managed things so charmingly. But it will be long ere I forget
how the old man's eye looked into the past as he recalled,--

> "The hat of antique shape and coat of gray,
> The same the gypsies wore,"

and went far away back through my words to words heard in the olden time,
by fires long since burnt out, beneath the flame-gilt branches of forests
which have sailed away as ships, farther than woods e'er went from
Dunsinane, and been wrecked in Southern seas. But though I could not
tell exactly what was in every room, I knew into what house his soul had
gone; and it was for this that the scholar-gypsy went from Oxford halls
"to learn strange arts and join a gypsy tribe." His friends had gone
from earth long since, and were laid to sleep; some, perhaps, far in the
wold and wild, amid the rocks, where fox and wild bird were their
visitors; but for an instant they rose again from their graves, and I
knew them.

"They could do wonders by the power of the imagination," says Glanvil of
the gypsies; "their fancy binding that of others." Understand by
imagination and fancy all that Glanvil really meant, and I agree with
him. It is a matter of history that, since the Aryan morning of mankind,
the Romanys have been chiromancing, and, following it, trying to read
people's minds and bind them to belief. Thousands of years of
transmitted hereditary influences always result in something; it has
really resulted with the gypsies in an instinctive, though undeveloped,
intuitive perception, which a sympathetic mind acquires from them,--nay,
is compelled to acquire, out of mere self-defense; and when gained, it
manifests itself in many forms,

"But it needs heaven-sent moments for this skill."

AMERICAN GYPSIES.

I. GYPSIES IN PHILADELPHIA.

It is true that the American gypsy has grown more vigorous in this country, and, like many plants, has thriven better for being trans--I was about to write incautiously **ported**, but, on second thought, say **planted**. Strangely enough, he is more Romany than ever. I have had many opportunities of studying both the elders from England and the younger gypsies, born of English parents, and I have found that there is unquestionably a great improvement in the race here, even from a gypsy stand-point. The young sapling, under more favorable influences, has pushed out from the old root, and grown stronger. The causes for this are varied. Gypsies, like peacocks, thrive best when allowed to range afar. ***Il faut leur donner le clef des champs*** (you must give them the key of the fields), as I once heard an old Frenchman, employed on Delmonico's Long Island farm, lang syne, say of that splendid poultry. And what a range they have, from the Atlantic to the Pacific! Marry, sir, 't is like roaming from sunrise to sunset, east and west, "and from the aurora borealis to a Southern blue-jay," and no man shall make them afraid. Wood! "Well, 't is a ***kushto tem for kasht***" (a fair land for timber), as a very decent **Romani-chal** said to me one afternoon. It was thinking of him which led me to these remarks.

I had gone with my niece--who speaks Romany--out to a gypsyry by Oaklands Park, and found there one of our good people, with his wife and children, in a tent. Hard by was the wagon and the horse, and, after the usual initiatory amazement at being accosted in the **kalo jib**, or black language, had been survived, we settled down into conversation. It was a fine autumnal day, Indian-summery,--the many in one of all that is fine in weather all the world over, put into a single glorious sense,--a sense of bracing air and sunshine not over-bold or bright, and purple, tawny hues in western skies, and dim, sweet feelings of the olden time. And as we sat lounging in lowly seats, and talked about the people and their ways, it seemed to me as if I were again in Devonshire or Surrey. Our host--for every gypsy who is visited treats you as a guest, thus much Oriental politeness being deeply set in him--had been in America from boyhood, but he seemed to be perfectly acquainted with all whom I had known over the sea. Only one thing he had not heard, the death of old Gentilla Cooper, of the Devil's Dyke, near Brighton, for I had just received a letter from England announcing the sad news.

"Yes, this America is a good country for travelers. *We can go South in winter*. Aye, the land is big enough to go to a warm side in winter, and a cool one in summer. But I don't go South, because I don't like the people; I don't get along with them. *Some Romanys do*. Yes, but I'm not on that horse, I hear that the old country's getting to be a hard place for our people. Yes, just as you say, there's no *tan to hatch*, no place to stay in there, unless you pay as much as if you went to a hotel. 'T isn't so here. Some places they're uncivil, but mostly we can get wood and water, and a place for a tent, and a bite for the old *gry* [horse]. The country people like to see us come, in many places. They're more high-minded and hon'rable here than they are in England. If we can cheat them in horse-dealin' they stand it as gentlemen always ought to do among themselves in such games. Horse-dealin' is horse-stealin', in a way, among real gentlemen. If I can Jew you or you do me, it's all square in gamblin', and nobody has any call to complain. Therefore, I allow that Americans are higher up as gentlemen than what they are in England. It is not all of one side, like a jug-handle, either. Many of these American farmers can cheat me, and have done it, and are proud of it. Oh, yes; they're much higher toned here. In England, if you put off a **bavolengro** [broken-winded horse] on a fellow he comes after you with a **chinamangri** [writ]. Here he goes like a man and swindles somebody else with the *gry*, instead of sneaking off to a magistrate.

"Yes," he continued, "England's a little country, very little, indeed, but it is astonishing how many Romanys come out of it over here. ***Do I notice any change in them after coming***? I do. When they first come, they drink liquor or beer all the time. After a while they stop heavy drinking."

I may here observe that even in England the gypsy, although his getting drunk is too often regulated or limited simply by his means, seldom shows in his person the results of long-continued intemperance. Living in the open air, taking much exercise, constantly practicing boxing, rough riding, and other manly sports, he is "as hard as nails," and generally lives to a hearty old age. As he very much prefers beer to spirits, it may be a question whether excess in such drinking is really any serious injury to him. The ancestors of the common English peasants have for a thousand, it may be for two thousand, years or more all got drunk on beer, whenever they could afford it, and yet a more powerful human being than the English peasant does not exist. It may be that the weaklings all die at an early age. This I cannot deny, nor that those who survive are simply so tough that beer cannot kill them. What this gypsy said of the impartial and liberal manner in which he and his kind are received by the farmers is also true. I once conversed on this subject with a gentleman farmer, and his remarks were much like those of the Rom. I inferred from what he said that the coming of a party of gypsy horse-dealers into his neighborhood was welcomed much as the passengers on a Southern steamboat were wont of old to welcome the proprietor of a portable faro bank. "I think," said he, "that the last time the gypsies were here they left more than they took away." An old Rom told me once that in some parts of New Jersey they were obliged to watch their tents and wagons very carefully for fear of the country people. I do not answer for the truth of this. It speaks vast volumes for the cleverness of gypsies that they can actually make a living by trading horses in New Spain.

It is very true that in many parts of America the wanderers are welcomed with *feux de joie*, or with salutes of shot-guns,--the guns, unfortunately, being shotted and aimed at them. I have mentioned in another chapter, on a Gypsy Magic Spell, that once in Tennessee, when an old Romany mother had succeeded in hoaxing a farmer's wife out of all she had in the world, the neighboring farmers took the witch, and, with a view to preventing effectually further depredation, caused her to pass "through flames material and temporal unto flames immaterial and eternal;" that is to say, they burned her alive. But the gypsy would much prefer having to deal with lynchers than with lawyers. Like the hedge-hog, which is typically a gypsy animal, he likes better to be eaten by those of his own kind than to be crushed into dirt by those who do not understand him. This story of the hedge-hog was cited from my first gypsy book by Sir Charles Dilke, in a speech in which he made an application of it to certain conservatives who remained blindly suffering by their own party. It will hold good forever. Gypsies never flourished so in Europe as during the days when every man's hand was against them. It is said that they raided and plundered about Scotland for fifty years before they were definitely discovered to be mere marauders, for the Scots themselves were so much given up to similar pursuits that the gypsies passed unnoticed.

The American gypsies do not beg, like their English brothers, and particularly their English sisters. This fact speaks volumes for their greater prosperity and for the influence which association with a proud race has on the poorest people. Our friends at Oaklands always welcomed us as guests. On another occasion when we went there, I said to my niece, "If we find strangers who do not know us, do not speak at first in Romany. Let us astonish them." We came to a tent, before which sat a very dark, old-fashioned gypsy woman. I paused before her, and said in English,--

"Can you tell a fortune for a young lady?"

"She don't want her fortune told," replied the old woman, suspiciously and cautiously, or it may be with a view of drawing us on. "No, I can't tell fortunes."

At this the young lady was so astonished that, without thinking of what she was saying, or in what language, she cried,--

"*Dordi*! *Can't tute pen dukkerin*?" (Look! Can't you tell fortunes?)

This unaffected outburst had a greater effect than the most deeply studied theatrical situation could have brought about. The old dame stared at me and at the lady as if bewildered, and cried,--

"In the name of God, what kind of gypsies are *you*?"

"Oh! *mendui shom bori chovihani*!" cried L., laughing; "we are a great witch and a wizard, and if you can't tell me my fortune, I'll tell yours. Hold out your hand, and cross mine with a dollar, and I'll tell you as big a lie as you ever *penned* a *galderli Gorgio* [a green Gentile]."

"Well," exclaimed the gypsy, "I'll believe that you can tell fortunes or do anything! *Dordi*! *dordi*! but this is wonderful. Yet you're not

the first Romany *rani* [lady] I ever met. There's one in Delaware: a
boridiri [very great] lady she is, and true Romany,--*flick o the jib
te rinkeni adosta* [quick of tongue and fair of face]. Well, I am glad
to see you." "Who is that talking there?" cried a man's voice from
within the tent. He had heard Romany, and he spoke it, and came out
expecting to see familiar faces. His own was a study, as his glance
encountered mine. As soon as he understood that I came as a friend, he
gave way to infinite joy, mingled with sincerest grief that he had not at
hand the means of displaying hospitality to such distinguished Romanys as
we evidently were. He bewailed the absence of strong drink. Would we
have some tea made? Would I accompany him to the next tavern, and have
some beer? All at once a happy thought struck him. He went into the
tent and brought out a piece of tobacco, which I was compelled to accept.
Refusal would have been unkind, for it was given from the very heart.
George Borrow tells us that, in Spain, a poor gypsy once brought him a
pomegranate as a first acquaintanceship token. A gypsy is a gypsy
wherever you find him.

These were very nice people. The old dame took a great liking to L., and
showed it in pleasant manners. The couple were both English, and liked
to talk with me of the old country and the many mutual friends whom we
had left behind. On another visit, L. brought a scarlet silk
handkerchief, which she had bound round her head and tied under her chin
in a very gypsy manner. It excited, as I anticipated, great admiration
from the old dame.

"*Ah kenna tute dikks rinkeni*--now you look nice. That's the way a
Romany lady ought to wear it! Don't she look just as Alfi used to look?"
she cried to her husband. "Just such eyes and hair!"

Here L. took off the *diklo*, or handkerchief, and passed it round the
gypsy woman's head, and tied it under her chin, saying,--

"I am sure it becomes you much more than it does me. Now you look nice:--

> "'Red and yellow for Romany,
> And blue and pink for the Gorgiee.'"

We rose to depart, the old dame offered back to L. her handkerchief, and, on being told to keep it, was greatly pleased. I saw that the way in which it was given had won her heart.

"Did you hear what the old woman said while she was telling your fortune?" asked L., after we had left the tent.

"Now, I think of it, I remember that she or you had hold of my hand, while I was talking with the old man, and he was making merry with my whisky. I was turned away, and around so that I never noticed what you two were saying."

"She **penned** your **dukkerin**, and it was wonderful. She said that she must tell it."

And here L. told me what the old **dye** had insisted on reading in my hand. It was simply very remarkable, and embraced an apparent knowledge of the past, which would make any credulous person believe in her happy predictions of the future.

"Ah, well," I said, "I suppose the **dukk** told it to her. She may be an eye-reader. A hint dropped here and there, unconsciously, the expression of the face, and a life's practice will make anybody a witch. And if there ever was a witch's eye, she has it."

"I would like to have her picture," said L., "in that **lullo diklo** [red handkerchief]. She looked like all the sorceresses of Thessaly and Egypt in one, and, as Bulwer says of the Witch of Vesuvius, was all the more terrible for having been beautiful."

Some time after this we went, with Britannia Lee a-gypsying, not figuratively, but literally, over the river into New Jersey. And our first greeting, as we touched the ground, was of good omen, and from a great man, for it was Walt Whitman. It is not often that even a poet meets with three sincerer admirers than the venerable bard encountered on this occasion; so, of course, we stopped and talked, and L. had the pleasure of being the first to communicate to Bon Gualtier certain pleasant things which had recently been printed of him by a distinguished English author, which is always an agreeable task. Blessed upon the mountains, or at the Camden ferryboat, or anywhere, are the feet of anybody who bringeth glad tidings.

"Well, are you going to see gypsies?"

"We are. We three gypsies be. By the abattoir. *Au revoir*."

And on we went to the place where I had first found gypsies in America. All was at first so still that it seemed if no one could be camped in the spot.

"*Se kekno adoi*." (There's nobody there.)

"*Dordi!*" cried Britannia, "*Dikkava me o tuv te tan te wardo*. [I see a smoke, a tent, a wagon.] I declare, it is my *puro pal*, my old friend, W."

And we drew near the tent and greeted its owner, who was equally astonished and delighted at seeing such distinguished Romany *tani ranis*, or gypsy young ladies, and brought forth his wife and three really beautiful children to do the honors. W. was a good specimen of an

American-born gypsy, strong, healthy, clean, and temperate, none the worse for wear in out-of-dooring, through tropical summers and terrible winters. Like all American Romanys, he was more straightforward than most of his race in Europe. All Romanys are polite, but many of the European kind are most uncomfortably and unconsciously naive. Strange that the most innocent people should be those who most offend morality. I knew a lady once--Heaven grant that I may never meet with such another!--who had been perfectly educated in entire purity of soul. And I never knew any *devergondee* who could so shock, shame, and pain decent people as this Agnes did in her sweet ignorance.

"I shall never forget the first day you came to my camp," said W. to Britannia. "Ah, you astonished me then. You might have knocked me down with a feather. And I didn't know what to say. You came in a carriage with two other ladies. And you jumped out first, and walked up to me, and cried, '*Sa'shan*!' That stunned me, but I answered, '*Sa'shan*.' Then I didn't speak Romanes to you, for I didn't know but what you kept it a secret from the other two ladies, and I didn't wish to betray you. And when you began to talk it as deep as any old Romany I ever heard, and pronounced it so rich and beautiful, I thought I'd never heard the like. I thought you must be a witch."

"*Awer me shom chovihani*" (but I am a witch), cried the lady. "*Mukka men ja adre o tan*." (Let us go into the tent.) So we entered, and sat round the fire, and asked news of all the wanderers of the roads, and the young ladies, having filled their pockets with sweets, produced them for the children, and we were as much at home as we had ever been in any salon; for it was a familiar scene to us all, though it would, perhaps, have been a strange one to the reader, had he by chance, walking that lonely way in the twilight, looked into the tent and asked his way, and there found two young ladies--*bien mises*--with their escort, all very much at their ease, and talking Romany as if they had never known any other tongue from the cradle.

"What is the charm of all this?" It is that if one has a soul, and does
not live entirely reflected from the little thoughts and little ways of a
thousand other little people, it is well to have at all times in his
heart some strong hold of nature. No matter how much we may be lost in
society, dinners, balls, business, we should never forget that there is
an eternal sky with stars over it all, a vast, mysterious earth with
terrible secrets beneath us, seas, mountains, rivers, and forests away
and around; and that it is from these and what is theirs, and not from
gas-lit, stifling follies, that all strength and true beauty must come.
To this life, odd as he is, the gypsy belongs, and to be sometimes at
home with him by wood and wold takes us for a time from "the world." If
I express myself vaguely and imperfectly, it is only to those who know
not the charm of nature, its ineffable soothing sympathy,--its life, its
love. Gypsies, like children, feel this enchantment as the older grown
do not. To them it is a song without words; would they be happier if the
world brought them to know it as words without song, without music or
melody? I never read a right old English ballad of sumere when the
leaves are grene or the not-broune maid, with its rustling as of sprays
quivering to the song of the wode-wale, without thinking or feeling
deeply how those who wrote them would have been bound to the Romany. It
is ridiculous to say that gypsies are not "educated" to nature and art,
when, in fact, they live it. I sometimes suspect that aesthetic culture
takes more true love of nature out of the soul than it inspires. One
would not say anything of a wild bird or deer being deficient in a sense
of that beauty of which it is a part. There are infinite grades, kinds,
or varieties of feeling of nature, and every man is perfectly satisfied
that his is the true one. For my own part, I am not sure that a rabbit,
in the dewy grass, does not feel the beauty of nature quite as much as
Mr. Ruskin, and much more than I do.

No poet has so far set forth the charm of gypsy life better than Lenau
has done, in his highly-colored, quickly-expressive ballad of "Die drei

Zigeuner," of which I here give a translation into English and another into Anglo-American Romany.

THE THREE GYPSIES.

I saw three gypsy men, one day,
Camped in a field together,
As my wagon went its weary way,
All over the sand and heather.

And one of the three whom I saw there
Had his fiddle just before him,
And played for himself a stormy air,
While the evening-red shone o'er him.

And the second puffed his pipe again
Serenely and undaunted,
As if he at least of earthly men
Had all the luck that he wanted.

In sleep and comfort the last was laid,
In a tree his cymbal {238} lying,
Over its strings the breezes played,
O'er his heart a dream went flying.

Ragged enough were all the three,
Their garments in holes and tatters;
But they seemed to defy right sturdily
The world and all worldly matters.

Thrice to the soul they seemed to say,
When earthly trouble tries it,
How to fiddle, sleep it, and smoke it away,

And so in three ways despise it.

And ever anon I look around,
As my wagon onward presses,
At the gypsy faces darkly browned,
And the long black flying tresses.

TRIN ROMANI CHALIA.

Dikdom me trin geeria
Sar yeckno a tacho Rom,
Sa miro wardo ghias adur
Apre a wafedo drom.

O yeckto sos boshengero,
Yuv kellde pes-kokero,
O kamlo-dud te perele
Sos lullo apre lo.

O duito sar a swagele
Dikde 'pre lestes tuv,
Ne kamde kumi, penava me
'Dre sar o miduvels puv.

O trinto sovade kushto-bak
Lest 'zimbel adre rukk se,
O bavol kelld' pre i tavia,
O sutto 'pre leskro zi.

Te sar i lengheri rudaben
Shan katterdi-chingerdo
Awer me penav' i Romani chals
Ne kesserden chi pa lo.

Trin dromia lende sikkerden kan
Sar dikela wafedo,
Ta bosher, tuver te sove-a-le
Aja sa bachtalo.

Dikdom palal, sa ghiom adur
Talla yeckno Romani chal
'Pre lengheri kali-brauni mui,
Te lengheri kali bal.

II. THE CROCUS-PITCHER. {241}
(PHILADELPHIA.)

It was a fine spring noon, and the corner of Fourth and Library streets
in Philadelphia was like a rock in the turn of a rapid river, so great
was the crowd of busy business men which flowed past. Just out of the
current a man paused, put down a parcel which he carried, turned it into
a table, placed on it several vials, produced a bundle of hand-bills, and
began, in the language of his tribe, to *cant*--that is, *cantare*, to
sing--the virtues of a medicine which was certainly *patent* in being
spread out by him to extremest thinness. In an instant there were a
hundred people round him. He seemed to be well known and waited for. I
saw at a glance what he was. The dark eye and brown face indicated a
touch of the *diddikai*, or one with a little gypsy blood in his veins,
while his fluent patter and unabashed boldness showed a long familiarity
with race-grounds and the road, or with the Cheap-Jack and Dutch auction
business, and other pursuits requiring unlimited eloquence and impudence.
How many a man of learning, nay of genius, might have paused and envied

that vagabond the gifts which were worth so little to their possessor! But what was remarkable about him was that instead of endeavoring to conceal any gypsy indications, they were manifestly exaggerated. He wore a broad-brimmed hat and ear-rings and a red embroidered waistcoat of the most forcible old Romany pattern, which was soon explained by his words.

"Sorry to keep you waiting," he said. "I am always sorry to detain a select and genteel audience. But I was detained myself by a very interesting incident. I was invited to lunch with a wealthy German gentleman; a very wealthy German, I say, one of the pillars of your city and front door-step of your council, and who would be the steeple of your exchange, if it had one. And on arriving at his house he remarked, 'Toctor, by tam you koom yust in goot dime, for mine frau und die cook ish bote fall sick mit some-ding in a hoory, und I kess she'll die pooty quick-sudden.' Unfortunately I had with me, gentlemen, but a single dose of my world-famous Gypsy's Elixir and Romany Pharmacopheionepenthe. (That is the name, gentlemen, but as I detest quackery I term it simply the Gypsy's Elixir.) When the German gentleman learned that in all probability but one life could be saved he said, 'Veil, denn, doctor, subbose you gifes dat dose to de cook. For mine frau ish so goot dat it's all right mit her. She's reaty to tie. But de boor gook ish a sinner, ash I knows, und not reaty for de next world. And dere ish no vomans in town dat can gook mine sauer-kraut ash she do.' Fortunately, gentlemen, I found in an unknown corner of a forgotten pocket an unsuspected bottle of the Gypsy's Elixir, and both interesting lives were saved with such promptitude, punctuality, neatness and dispatch that the cook proceeded immediately to conclude the preparation of our meal--(thank you sir,--one dollar, if you please, sir. You say I only charged half a dollar yesterday! That was for a smaller bottle, sir. Same size, as this, was it? Ah, yes, I gave you a large bottle by mistake,--so you owe me fifty cents. Never mind, don't give it back. I'll take the half dollar.")

All of this had been spoken with the utmost volubility. As I listened I almost fancied myself again in England, and at a country fair. Taking in his audience at a glance, I saw his eye rest on me ere it flitted, and he resumed,--

"We gypsies are, as you know, a remarkable race, and possessed of certain rare secrets, which have all been formulated, concentrated, dictated, and plenipotentiarated into this idealized Elixir. If I were a mountebank or a charlatan I would claim that it cures a hundred diseases. Charlatan is a French word for a quack. I speak French, gentlemen; I speak nine languages, and can tell you the Hebrew for an old umbrella. The Gypsy's Elixir cures colds, gout, all nervous affections, with such cutaneous disorders as are diseases of the skin, debility, sterility, hostility, and all the illities that flesh is heir to except what it can't, such as small-pox and cholera. It has cured cholera, but it don't claim to do it. Others claim to cure, but can't. I am not a charlatan, but an Ann-Eliza. That is the difference between me and a lady, as the pig said when he astonished his missus by blushing at her remarks to the postman. (*Better have another bottle*, *sir*. *Haven't you the change*? *Never mind*, *you can owe me fifty cents*. *I know a gentleman when I see one*.) I was recently Down East in Maine, where they are so patriotic, they all put the stars and stripes into their beds for sheets, have the Fourth of July three hundred and sixty-five times in the year, and eat the Declaration of Independence for breakfast. And they wouldn't buy a bottle of my Gypsy's Elixir till they heard it was good for the Constitution, whereupon they immediately purchased my entire stock. Don't lose time in securing this invaluable blessing to those who feel occasional pains in the lungs. This is not taradiddle. I am engaged to lecture this afternoon before the Medical Association of Germantown, as on Wednesday before the University of Baltimore; for though I sell medicine here in the streets, it is only, upon my word of honor, that the poor may benefit, and the lowly as well as the learned know how to prize the philanthropic and eccentric gypsy."

He run on with his patter for some time in this vein, and sold several vials of his panacea, and then in due time ceased, and went into a bar-room, which I also entered. I found him in what looked like prospective trouble, for a policeman was insisting on purchasing his medicine, and on having one of his hand-bills. He was remonstrating, when I quietly said to him in Romany, "Don't trouble yourself; you were not making any disturbance." He took no apparent notice of what I said beyond an almost imperceptible wink, but soon left the room, and when I had followed him into the street, and we were out of ear-shot, he suddenly turned on me and said,--

"Well, you *are* a swell, for a Romany. How do you do it up to such a high peg?"

"Do what?"

"Do the whole lay,--look so gorgeous?"

"Why, I'm no better dressed than you are,--not so well, if you come to that *vongree*" (waistcoat).

"'T isn't *that*,--'t isn't the clothes. It's the air and the style. Anybody'd believe you'd had no end of an education. I could make ten dollars a patter if I could do it as natural as you do. Perhaps you'd like to come in on halves with me as a bonnet. *No*? Well, I suppose you have a better line. You've been lucky. I tell you, you astonished me when you *rakkered*, though I spotted you in the crowd for one who was off the color of the common Gorgios,--or, as the Yahudi say, the *Goyim*. No, I carn't *rakker*, or none to speak of, and noways as deep as you, though I was born in a tent on Battersea Common and grew up a fly fakir. What's the drab made of that I sell in these bottles? Why, the old fake, of course,--you needn't say *you* don't know that. *Italic good*

English. Yes, I know I do. A fakir is bothered out of his life and
chaffed out of half his business when he drops his *h*'s. A man can do
anything when he must, and I must talk fluently and correctly to succeed
in such a business. ***Would I like a drop of something***? You paid for
the last, now you must take a drop with me. ***Do I know of any Romany's
in town***? Lots of them. There is a ken in Lombard Street with a regular
fly mort,--but on second thoughts we won't go there,--*and*--oh, I say--a
very nice place in --- Street. The landlord is a Yahud; his wife can
rakker you, I'm sure. ***She's*** a good lot, too."

And while on the way I will explain that my acquaintance was not to be
regarded as a real gypsy. He was one of that large nomadic class with a
tinge of gypsy blood who have grown up as waifs and strays, and who,
having some innate cleverness, do the best they can to live without
breaking the law--much. They deserve pity, for they have never been
cared for; they owe nothing to society for kindness, and yet they are
held even more strictly to account by the law than if they had been
regularly Sunday-schooled from babyhood. This man when he spoke of
Romanys did not mean real gypsies; he used the word as it occurs in
Ainsworth's song of

> "Nix my dolly, pals fake away.
> And here I am both tight and free,
> A regular rollicking Romany."

For he meant *Bohemian* in its widest and wildest sense, and to him all
that was apart from the world was *his* world, whether it was Rom or
Yahudi, and whether it conversed in Romany or Schmussen, or any other
tongue unknown to the Gentiles. He had indeed no home, and had never
known one.

It was not difficult to perceive that the place to which he led me was
devoted in the off hours to some other business besides the selling of

liquor. It was neat and quiet, in fact rather sleepy; but its card, which was handed to me, stated in a large capital head-line that it was OPEN ALL NIGHT, and that there was pool at all hours. I conjectured that a little game might also be performed there at all hours, and that, like the fountain of Jupiter Ammon, it became livelier as it grew later, and that it certainly would not be on the full boil before midnight.

"*Scheiker fur mich*, *der Isch will jain soreff shaskenen*" (Beer for me and brandy for him), I said to the landlord, who at once shook my hand and saluted me with *Sholem*! Even so did Ben Daoud of Jerusalem, not long ago. Ben knew me not, and I was buying a pocket-book of him at his open-air stand in Market Street, and talking German, while he was endeavoring to convince me that I ought to give five cents more for it than I had given for a similar case the day before, on the ground that it was of a different color, or under color that the leather had a different ground, I forget which. In talking I let fall the word *kesef* (silver). In an instant Ben had taken my hand, and said *Sholem aleichum*, and "Can you talk Spanish?"--which was to show that he was superfine Sephardi, and not common Ashkenaz.

"Yes," resumed the crocus-fakir; "a man must be able to talk English very fluently, pronounce it correctly, and, above all things, keep his temper, if he would do anything that requires chanting or pattering. *How did I learn it*? A man can learn to do anything when it's business and his living depends on it. The people who crowd around me in the streets cannot pronounce English decently; not one in a thousand here can say *laugh*, except as a sheep says it. Suppose that you are a Cheap Jack selling things from a van. About once in an hour some tipsy fellow tries to chaff you. He hears your tongue going, and that sets his off. He hears the people laugh at your jokes, and he wants them to laugh at his. When you say you're selling to raise money for a burned-out widow, he asks if she isn't your wife. Then you answer him, 'No, but the kind-hearted old woman who found you on the door-step and brought you up

to the begging business.' If you say you are selling goods under cost,
it's very likely some yokel will cry out, 'Stolen, hey?' And you patter
as quick as lightning, 'Very likely; I thought your wife sold 'em to me
too cheap for the good of somebody's clothes-line.' If you show yourself
his superior in language awd wit, the people will buy better; they always
prefer a gentleman to a cad. Bless me! why, a swell in a dress-coat and
kid gloves, with good patter and hatter, can sell a hundred rat-traps
while a dusty cad in a flash kingsman would sell one. As for the
replies, most of them are old ones. As the men who interrupt you are
nearly all of the same kind, and have heads of very much the same make,
with an equal number of corners, it follows that they all say nearly the
same things. Why, I've heard two duffers cry out the same thing at once
to me. So you soon have answers cut and dried for them. We call 'em
cocks, because they're just like half-penny ballads, all ready printed,
while the pitcher always has the one you want ready at his finger-ends.
It is the same in all canting. I knew a man once who got his living by
singing of evenings in the gaffs to the piano, and making up verses on
the gentlemen and ladies as they came in; and very nice verses he made,
too,--always as smooth as butter. *How do you do it*? I asked him one
day. 'Well, you wouldn't believe it,' said he; 'but they're mostly
cocks. The best ones I buy for a tanner [sixpence] apiece. If a tall
gentleman with a big beard comes in, I strike a deep chord and sing,--

> "'This tall and handsome party,
> With such a lot of hair,
> Who seems so grand and hearty,
> Must be a *militaire*;
> We like to see a swell come
> Who looks so *distingue*,
> So let us bid him welcome,
> And hope he'll find us gay.'

"The last half can be used for anybody. That's the way the improvisatory business is managed for visitors. Why, it's the same with fortune-telling. ***You have noticed that***. Well, if the Gorgios had, it would have been all up with the fake long ago. The old woman has the same sort of girls come to her with the same old stories, over and over again, and she has a hundred dodges and gets a hundred straight tips where nobody else would see anything; and of course she has the same replies all ready. There is nothing like being glib. And there's really a great deal of the same in the regular doctor business, as I know, coming close on to it and calling myself one. Why, I've been called into a regular consultation in Chicago, where I had an office,--'pon my honor I was, and no great honor neither. It was all patter, and I pattered 'em dumb."

I began to think that the fakir could talk forever and ever faster. If he excelled in his business, he evidently practiced at all times to do so. I intimated as much, and he at once proceeded fluently to illustrate this point also.

"You hear men say every day that if they only had an education they would do great things. What it would all come to with most of them is that they would ***talk*** so as to shut other men up and astonish 'em. They have not an idea above that. I never had any schooling but the roads and race-grounds, but I can talk the hat off a lawyer, and that's all I can do. Any man of them could talk well if he tried; but none of them will try, and as they go through life, telling you how clever they'd have been if somebody else had only done something for them, instead of doing something for themselves. So you must be going. Well, I hope I shall see you again. Just come up when you're going by and say that your wife was raised from the dead by my Elixir, and that it's the best medicine you ever had. And if you want to see some regular tent gypsies, there's a camp of them now just four miles from here; real old style Romanys. Go out on the road four miles, and you'll find them just off the side,--anybody will show you the place. ***Sarishan***!"

I was sorry to read in the newspaper, a few days after, that the fakir had been really arrested and imprisoned for selling a quack medicine. For in this land of liberty it makes an enormous difference whether you sell by advertisement in the newspapers or on the sidewalk, which shows that there is one law for the rich and another for the poor, even in a republic.

III. GYPSIES IN CAMP (NEW JERSEY.)

The Weather had put on his very worst clothes, and was never so hard at work for the agricultural interests, or so little inclined to see visitors, as on the Sunday afternoon when I started gypsying. The rain and the wind were fighting one with another, and both with the mud, even as the Jews in Jerusalem fought with themselves, and both with the Romans,--which was the time when the *Shaket*, or butcher, killed the ox who drank the water which quenched the fire which the reader has often heard all about, yet not knowing, perhaps, that the house which Jack built was the Holy Temple of Jerusalem. It was with such reflections that I beguiled time on a long walk, for which I was not unfitly equipped in corduroy trousers, with a long Ulster and a most disreputable cap befitting a stable-boy. The rig, however, kept out the wet, and I was too recently from England to care much that it was raining. I had seen the sun on color about thirty times altogether during the past year, and so had not as yet learned to miss him. It is on record that when the Shah was in England a lady said to him, "Can it be possible, your highness, that there are in your dominions people who worship the sun?" "Yes," replied the monarch, musingly; "and so would you, if you could only see him."

The houses became fewer as I went on, till at last I reached the place
near which I knew the gypsies must be camped. As is their custom in
England, they had so established themselves as not to be seen from the
road. The instinct which they display in thus getting near people, and
yet keeping out of their sight, even as rats do, is remarkable. I
thought I knew the town of Brighton, in England, thoroughly, and had
explored all its nooks, and wondered that I had never found any gypsies
there. One day I went out with a Romany acquaintance, who, in a short
time, took me to half a dozen tenting-places, round corners in mysterious
by-ways. It often happens that the spots which they select to ***hatch the
tan***, or pitch the tent, are picturesque bits, such as artists love, and
all gypsies are fully appreciative of beauty in this respect. It is not
a week, as I write, since I heard an old horse-dealing veteran of the
roads apologize to me with real feeling for the want of a view near his
tent, just as any other man might have excused the absence of pictures
from his walls. The most beautiful spot for miles around Williamsport,
in Pennsylvania, a river dell, which any artist would give a day to
visit, is the favorite camping-ground of the Romany. Woods and water,
rocks and loneliness, make it lovely by day, and when, at eventide, the
fire of the wanderers lights up the scene, it also lights up in the soul
many a memory of tents in the wilderness, of pictures in the Louvre, of
Arabs and of Wouvermanns and belated walks by the Thames, and of Salvator
Rosa. Ask me why I haunt gypsydom. It has put me into a thousand
sympathies with nature and art, which I had never known without it. The
Romany, like the red Indian, and all who dwell by wood and wold as
outlawes wont to do, are the best human links to bind us to their
home-scenery, and lead us into its inner life. What constitutes the
antithetic charm of those wonderful lines,

> "Afar in the desert, I love to ride,
> With the silent bush-boy alone by my side,"

but the presence of the savage who belongs to the scene, and whose *being* binds the poet to it, and blends him with it as the flux causes the fire to melt the gold?

I left the road, turned the corner, and saw before me the low, round tents, with smoke rising from the tops, dark at first and spreading into light gray, like scalp-locks and feathers upon Indian heads. Near them were the gayly-painted vans, in which I at once observed a difference from the more substantial-looking old-country *vardo*. The whole scene was so English that I felt a flutter at the heart: it was a bit from over the sea; it seemed as if hedge-rows should have been round, and an old Gothic steeple looking over the trees. I thought of the last gypsy camp I had seen near Henley-on-Thames, and wished Plato Buckland were with me to share the fun which one was always sure to have on such an occasion in his eccentric company. But now Plato was, like his father in the song,

> "*Duro pardel the boro pani*,"
> Far away over the broad-rolling sea,

and I must introduce myself. There was not a sign of life about, save in a sorrowful hen, who looked as if she felt bitterly what it was to be a Pariah among poultry and a down-pin, and who cluttered as if she might have had a history of being borne from her bower in the dark midnight by desperate African reivers, of a wild moonlit flitting and crossing black roaring torrents, drawn all the while by the neck, as a Turcoman pulls a Persian prisoner on an "alaman," with a rope, into captivity, and finally of being sold unto the Egyptians. I drew near a tent: all was silent, as it always is in a *tan* when the foot-fall of the stranger is heard; but I knew that it was packed with inhabitants.

I called in Romany my greeting, and bade somebody come out. And there appeared a powerfully built, dark-browed, good-looking man of thirty, who was as gypsy as Plato himself. He greeted me very civilly, but with some surprise, and asked me what he could do for me.

"Ask me in out of the rain, pal," I replied. "You don't suppose I've come four miles to see you and stop out here, do you?"

This was, indeed, reasonable, and I was invited to enter, which I did, and found myself in a scene which would have charmed Callot or Goya. There was no door or window to the black tent; what light there was came through a few rifts and rents and mingled with the dull gleam of a smoldering fire, producing a perfect Rembrandt blending of rosy-red with dreamy half-darkness. It was a real witch-aura, and the denizens were worthy of it. As my eyes gradually grew to the gloom, I saw that on one side four brown old Romany sorceresses were "**beshing apre ye pus**" (sitting on the straw), as the song has it, with deeper masses of darkness behind them, in which other forms were barely visible. Their black eyes all flashed up together at me, like those of a row of eagles in a cage; and I saw in a second that, with men and all I was in a party who were anything but milksops; in fact, with as regularly determined a lot of hard old Romanys as ever battered a policeman. I confess that a feeling like a thrill of joy came over me--a memory of old days and by-gone scenes over the sea--when I saw this, and knew they were not *diddikais*, or half-breed mumpers. On the other side, several young people, among them three or four good-looking girls, were eating their four-o'clock meal from a canvas spread on the ground. There were perhaps twenty persons in the place, including the children who swarmed about.

Even in a gypsy tent something depends on the style of a self-introduction by a perfect stranger. Stepping forward, I divested myself of my Ulster, and handed it to a nice damsel, giving her special injunction to fold it up and lay it by. My *mise en scène* appeared to meet with approbation, and I stood forth and remarked,--

"Here I am, glad to see you; and if you want to see a regular *Romany rye* [gypsy gentleman], just over from England, now's your chance.

Sarishan!"

And I received, as I expected, a cordial welcome. I was invited to sit down and eat, but excused myself as having just come from **habben**, or food, and settled myself to a cigar. But while everybody was polite, I felt that under it all there was a reserve, a chill. I was altogether too heavy a mystery. I knew my friends, and they did not know me. Something, however, now took place which went far to promote conviviality. The tent-flap was lifted, and there entered an elderly woman, who, as a gypsy, might have been the other four in one, she was so quadruply dark, so fourfold uncanny, so too-too witch-like in her eyes. The others had so far been reserved as to speaking Romany; she, glancing at me keenly, began at once to talk it very fluently, without a word of English, with the intention of testing me; but as I understood her perfectly, and replied with a burning gush of the same language, being, indeed, glad to have at last "got into my plate," we were friends in a minute. I did not know then that I was talking with a celebrity whose name has even been groomily recorded in an English book; but I found at once that she was truly "a character." She had manifestly been sent for to test the stranger, and I knew this, and made myself agreeable, and was evidently found **tacho**, or all right. It being a rule, in fact, with few exceptions, that when you really like people, in a friendly way, and are glad to be among them, they never fail to find it out, and the jury always comes to a favorable verdict.

And so we sat and talked on in the monotone in which Romany is generally spoken, like an Indian song, while, like an Indian drum, the rain pattered an accompaniment on the tightly drawn tent. Those who live in cities, and who are always realizing self, and thinking how they think, and are while awake given up to introverting vanity, never **live** in song. To do this one must be a child, an Indian, a dweller in fields and green forests, a brother of the rain and road-puddles and rolling streams, and a friend of the rustling leaves and the summer orchestra of frogs and crickets and rippling grass. Those who hear this music and think to it never think about it; those who live only in books never sing to it in soul. As there are dreams which ***will not*** be remembered or known to ***reason***, so this music shrinks from it. It is wonderful how beauty perishes like a shade-grown flower before the sunlight of analysis. It is dying out all the world over in women, under the influence of cleverness and "style;" it is perishing in poetry and art before criticism; it is wearing away from manliness, through priggishness; it is being crushed out of true gentleness of heart and nobility of soul by the pessimist puppyism of miching Mallockos. But nature is eternal and will return. When man has run one of his phases of culture fairly to the end, and when the fruit is followed by a rattling rococo husk, then comes a winter sleep, from which he awakens to grow again as a child-flower. We are at the very worst of such a time; but there is a morning redness far away, which shows that the darkness is ending, the winter past, the rain is over and gone. Arise, and come away!

"Sossi kair'd tute to av'akai pardel o boro pani?" (And what made you come here across the broad water?) said the good old dame confidentially and kindly, in the same low monotone. "Si lesti chorin a gry?" (Was it stealing a horse?)

Dum, ***dum***, ***dum***, ***patter***, ***patter***, ***dum***! played the rain.

"Avali I dikked your romus kaliko" (I saw your husband yesterday), remarked some one aside to a girl.

Dum, ***dum***, ***dum***, ***patter***, ***patter***, ***dum***!

"No, mother deari, it was not a horse, for I am on a better, higher lay."

Dum, ***dum***, ***dum***, ***patter***, ***patter***, ***dum***!

"He is a first-rate dog, but mine's as good."

Dum, *dum*, *dum*, *patter*, *dum*!

"Tacho! There's money to be made by a gentleman like you by telling fortunes."

Dum, *dum*, *dum*, *patter*, *dum*!

"Yes, a five-hundred-dollar hit sometimes. But *dye*, I work upon a better lay."

Dum, *dum*, *dum*, *patter*, *dum*!

"Perhaps you are *a boro drabengro*" (a great physician).

Dum, *dum*, *dum*, *patter*, *dum*!

"It was away among the rocks that he fell into the reeds, half in the water, and kept still till they went by."

"If any one is ill among you, I may be of use."

Dum, *dum*, *dum*, *patter*, *dum*!

"And what a wind! It blows as if the good Lord were singing! Kushti chirus se atch a-kerri." (This is a pleasant day to be at home.)

Dum, *dum*, *dum*, *patter*, *dum*!

"I thought you were a doctor, for you were going about in the town with the one who sells medicine. I heard of it."

Dum, *dum*, *dum*, *patter*, *dum*!

"Do not hurry away! Come again and see us. I think the Coopers are all out in Ohio."

Dum, *dum*, *dum*, *patter*, *dum*!

The cold wind and slight rain seemed refreshing and even welcome, as I went out into the cold air. The captain showed me his stock of fourteen horses and mules, and we interchanged views as to the best method of managing certain maladies in such stock. I had been most kindly entertained; indeed, with the home kindliness which good people in the country show to some hitherto unseen and unknown relative who descends to them from the great world of the city. Not but that my friends did not know cities and men as well as Ulysses, but even Ulysses sometimes met with a marvel. In after days I became quite familiar with the several families who made the camp, and visited them in sunshine. But they always occur to me in memory as in a deep Rembrandt picture, a wonderful picture, and their voices as in vocal chiaroscuro; singing to the wind without and the rain on the tent,--

Dum, *dum*, *dum*, *patter*, *dum*!

IV. HOUSE GYPSIES IN PHILADELPHIA

This chapter was written by my niece through marriage, Miss Elizabeth Robins. It is a part of an article which was published in "The Century," and it sets forth certain wanderings in seeking old houses in the city of Philadelphia.

All along the lower part of Race Street, saith the lady, are wholesale
stores and warehouses of every description. Some carts belonging to one
of them had just been unloaded. The stevedores who do this--all
negroes--were resting while they waited for the next load. They were
great powerful men, selected for their strength, and were of many hues,
from *cafe au lait*, or coffee much milked, up to the browned or
black-scorched berry itself, while the very *athletae* were coal-black.
They wore blue overalls, and on their heads they had thrown old
coffee-bags, which, resting on their foreheads, passed behind their ears
and hung loosely down their backs. It was in fact the *haik* or
bag-cloak of the East, and it made a wonderfully effective Arab costume.
One of them was half leaning, half sitting, on a pile of bags; his
Herculean arms were folded, and he had unconsciously assumed an air of
dignity and defiance. He might have passed for an African chief. When
we see such men in Egypt or other sunny countries *outre mer*, we become
artistically eloquent; but it rarely occurs to sketchers and
word-painters to do much business in the home-market.

The mixture of races in our cities is rapidly increasing, and we hardly
notice it. Yet it is coming to pass that a large part of our population
is German and Irish, and that our streets within ten years have become
fuller of Italian fruit dealers and organ-grinders, so that *Cives sum
Romanus* (I am a Roman citizen), when abroad, now means either "I possess
a monkey" or "I sell pea-nuts." Jews from Jerusalem peddle pocket-books
on our sidewalks, Chinamen are monoplizing our washing and ironing, while
among laboring classes are thousands of Scandinavians, Bohemians, and
other Slaves. The prim provincial element which predominated in my
younger years is yielding before this influx of foreigners, and Quaker
monotony and stern conservatism are vanishing, while Philadelphia becomes
year by year more cosmopolite.

As we left the handsome negroes and continued our walk on Water Street an

Italian passed us. He was indeed very dirty and dilapidated; his clothes were of the poorest, and he carried a rag-picker's bag over his shoulder; but his face, as he turned it towards us, was really beautiful.

"*Siete Italiano*?" (Are you an Italian?) asked my uncle.

"*Si*, *signore*" (Yes, sir), he answered, showing all his white teeth, and opening his big brown eyes very wide.

"*E come lei piace questo paese*?" (And how do you like this country?)

"Not at all. It is too cold," was his frank answer, and laughing good-humoredly he continued his search through the gutters. He would have made a good model for an artist, for he had what we do not always see in Italians, the real southern beauty of face and expression. Two or three weeks after this encounter, we were astonished at meeting on Chestnut Street a little man, decently dressed, who at once manifested the most extraordinary and extravagant symptoms of delighted recognition. Never saw I mortal so grin-full, so bowing. As we went on and crossed the street, and looked back, he was waving his hat in the air with one hand, while he made gestures of delight with the other. It was the little Italian rag-picker.

Then along and afar, till we met a woman, decently enough dressed, with jet-black eyes and hair, and looking not unlike a gypsy. "A Romany!" I cried with delight. Her red shawl made me think of gypsies, and when I caught her eye I saw the indescrible flash of the *kalorat*, or black blood. It is very curious that Hindus, Persians, and gypsies have in common an expression of the eye which distinguishes them from all other Oriental races, and chief in this expression is the Romany. Captain Newbold, who first investigated the gypsies of Egypt, declares that, however disguised, he could always detect them by their glance, which is unlike that of any other human being, though something resembling it is often seen in the ruder type of the rural American. I believe myself that there is something in the gypsy eye which is inexplicable, and which enables its possessor to see farther through that strange mill-stone, the human soul, than I can explain. Any one who has ever seen an old fortune-teller of "the people" keeping some simple-minded maiden by the hand, while she holds her by her glittering eye, like the Ancient Mariner, with a basilisk stare, will agree with me. As Scheele de Vere writes, "It must not be forgotten that the human eye has, beyond question, often a power which far transcends the ordinary purposes of sight, and approaches the boundaries of magic."

But one glance, and my companion whispered, "Answer me in Romany when I speak, and don't seem to notice her." And then, in loud tone, he remarked, while looking across the street,--

"*Adovo's a kushto puro rinkeno ker adoi*." (That is a nice old pretty house there.)

"*Avali*, *rya*" (Yes, sir), I replied.

There was a perceptible movement by the woman in the red shawl to keep within ear-shot of us. Mine uncle resumed,--

"*Boro kushto covva se ta rakker a jib te kek Gorgio iinella*." (It's nice to talk a language that no Gentile knows.)

The red shawl was on the trail. "*Je crois que ca mord*," remarked my uncle. We allowed our artist guide to pass on, when, as I expected, I felt a twitch at my outer garment. I turned, and the witch eyes, distended with awe and amazement, were glaring into mine, while she said, in a hurried whisper,--

"Wasn't it Romanes?"

"*Avah*," I replied, "*mendui rakker sarja adovo jib. Butikumi ryeskro lis se denna Gorgines*." (Yes, we always talk that language. Much more genteel it is than English.)

"*Te adovo wavero rye*?" (And that *other* gentleman?) with a glance of suspicion at our artist friend.

"*Sar tacho*" (He's all right), remarked mine uncle, which I greatly fear meant, when correctly translated in a Christian sense, "He's all wrong." But there is a natural sympathy and intelligence between Bohemians of every grade, all the world over, and I never knew a gypsy who did not understand an artist. One glance satisfied her that he was quite worthy of our society.

"And where are you *tannin kenna*?" (tenting now), I inquired.

"We are not tenting at this time of year; we're *kairin*," *i.e.*, houseing, or home-ing. It is a good verb, and might be introduced into English.

"And where is your house?"

"There, right by Mammy Sauerkraut's Row. Come in and sit down."

I need not give the Romany which was spoken, but will simply translate. The house was like all the others. We passed through a close, dark passage, in which lay canvas and poles, a kettle and a *sarshta*, or the iron which is stuck into the ground, and by which a kettle hangs. The old-fashioned tripod, popularly supposed to be used by gypsies, in all probability never existed, since the Roms of India to-day use the *sarshta*, as mine uncle tells me he learned from a *ci-devant* Indian gypsy Dacoit, or wandering thief, who was one of his intimates in London.

We entered an inner room, and I was at once struck by its general indescribable unlikeness to ordinary rooms. Architects declare that the type of the tent is to be distinctly found in all Chinese and Arab or Turkish architecture; it is also as marked in a gypsy's house--when he gets one. This room, which was evidently the common home of a large family, suggested, in its arrangement of furniture and the manner in which its occupants sat around the tent and the wagon. There was a bed, it is true but there was a roll of sail-cloth, which evidently did duty for sleeping on at night, but which now, rolled up, acted the part described by Goldsmith:--

> "A thing contrived a double part to play,
> A bed by night, a sofa during day."

There was one chair and a saddle, a stove and a chest of drawers. I observed an engraving hanging up which I have several times seen in gypsy tents. It represents a very dark Italian youth. It is a favorite also with Roman Catholics, because the boy has a consecrated medal. The gypsies, however, believe that the boy stole the medal. The Catholics think the picture is that of a Roman boy, because the inscription says so; and the gypsies call it a Romany, so that all are satisfied. There were some eight or nine children in the room, and among them more than one whose resemblance to the dark-skinned saint might have given color enough to the theory that he was

> "One whose blood
> Had rolled through gypsies ever since the flood."

There was also a girl, of the pantherine type, and one damsel of about ten, who had light hair and fair complexion, but whose air was gypsy and whose youthful countenance suggested not the golden, but the brazenest, age of life. Scarcely was I seated in the only chair, when this little maiden, after keenly scrutinizing my appearance, and apparently taking in the situation, came up to me and said,--

"Yer come here to have yer fortune told. I'll tell it to yer for five cents."

"*Can tute pen dukkerin aja*?" (Can you tell fortunes already?) I inquired. And if that damsel had been lifted at that instant by the hair into the infinite glory of the seventh sphere, her countenance could not have manifested more amazement. She stood *bouche beante*, stock still staring, open-mouthed wide. I believe one might have put a brandy ball into it, or a "bull's eye," without her jaws closing on the dainty. It was a stare of twenty-four carats, and fourth proof.

"This here *rye*" remarked mine uncle, affably, in middle English, "is a hartist. He puts 'is heart into all he does; *that's* why. He ain't Romanes, but he may be trusted. He's come here, that wot he has, to draw this 'ere Mammy Sauerkraut's Row, because it's interestin'. He ain't a tax-gatherer. *We* don't approve o' payin' taxes, none of hus. We practices heconomy, and dislike the po-lice. Who was Mammy Sauerkraut?"

"I know!" cried the youthful would-be fortune-teller. "She was a witch."

"*Tool yer chib*!" (Hold your tongue!) cried the parent. "Don't bother the lady with stories about *chovihanis*" (witches).

"But that's just what I want to hear!" I cried. "Go on, my little dear, about Mammy Sauerkraut, and you will get your five cents yet, if you only give me enough of it."

"Well, then, Mammy Sauerkraut was a witch, and a little black girl who lives next door told me so. And Mammy Sauerkraut used to change herself into a pig of nights, and that's why they called her Sauerkraut. This was because they had pig ketchers going about in those times, and once they ketched a pig that belonged to her, and to be revenged on them she used to look like a pig, and they would follow her clear out of town way up the river, and she'd run, and they'd run after her, till by and by fire would begin to fly out of her bristles, and she jumped into the river and sizzed."

This I thought worthy of the five cents. Then my uncle began to put questions in Romany.

"Where is Ansélo W.? He that was *staruben* for a *gry*?" (imprisoned for a horse).

"*Staruben apopli*." (Imprisoned again.)

"I am sorry for it, sister Nell. He used to play the fiddle well. I wot he was a canty chiel', and dearly lo'ed the whusky, oh!"

"Yes, he was too fond of that. How well he could play!"

"Yes," said my uncle, "he could. And I have sung to his fiddling when the *tatto-pani* [hot water, *i.e.*, spirits] boiled within us, and made us gay, oh, my golden sister! That's the way we Hungarian gypsy gentlemen always call the ladies of our people. I sang in Romany."

"I'd like to hear you sing now," remarked a dark, handsome young man, who had just made a mysterious appearance out of the surrounding shadows.

"It's a *kamaben gilli*" (a love-song), said the *rye*; "and it is beautiful, deep old Romanes,--enough to make you cry."

There was the long sound of a violin, clear as the note of a horn. I had not observed that the dark young man had found one to his hand, and, as he accompanied, my uncle sang; and I give the lyric as he afterwards gave it to me, both in Romany and English. As he frankly admitted, it was his own composition.

KE TEINALI.

Tu shan miri pireni
Me kamava tute,
Kamlidiri, rinkeni,
Kames mande buti?

Sa o miro kushto gry
Taders miri wardi,--
Sa o boro buno rye
Rikkers lesto stardi.

Sa o bokro dre o char
Hawala adovo,--
Sa i choramengeri
Lels o ryas luvoo,--

Sa o sasto levinor
Kairs amandy matto,--
Sa o yag adre o tan
Kairs o geero tatto,--

Sa i puri Romni chai
Pens o kushto dukkrin,--
Sa i Gorgi dinneli,
Patsers lakis pukkrin,--

Tute taders tiro rom,
Sims o gry, o wardi,

Tute chores o zi adrom
Rikkers sa i stardi.

Tute haws te chores m'ri all,
Tutes dukkered buti
Tu shan miro jivaben
Me t'vel paller tute.

Paller tute sarasa
Pardel puv te pani,
Trinali--o krallisa!
Miri chovihani!

TO TRINALI.

Now thou art my darling girl,
And I love thee dearly;
Oh, beloved and my fair,
Lov'st thou me sincerely?

As my good old trusty horse
Draws his load or bears it;
As a gallant cavalier
Cocks his hat and wears it;

As a sheep devours the grass
When the day is sunny;
As a thief who has the chance
Takes away our money;

As strong ale when taken down
Makes the strongest tipsy;
As a fire within a tent

Warms a shivering gypsy;

As a gypsy grandmother
Tells a fortune neatly;
As the Gentile trusts in her,
And is done completely,--

So you draw me here and there,
Where you like you take me;
Or you sport me like a hat,--
What you will you make me.

So you steal and gnaw my heart
For to that I'm fated!
And by you, my gypsy Kate,
I'm intoxicated.

And I own you are a witch,
I am beaten hollow;
Where thou goest in this world
I am bound to follow,--

Follow thee, where'er it be,
Over land and water,
Trinali, my gypsy queen!
Witch and witch's daughter!

"Well, that *is* deep Romanes," said the woman, admiringly. "It's beautiful."

"*I* should think it was," remarked the violinist. "Why, I didn't understand more than one half of it. But what I caught I understood." Which, I reflected, as he uttered it, is perhaps exactly the case with far more than half the readers of all poetry. They run on in a semi-sensuous mental condition, soothed by cadence and lulled by rhyme, reading as they run for want of thought. Are there not poets of the present day who mean that you shall read them thus, and who cast their gold ornaments hollow, as jewelers do, lest they should be too heavy?

"My children," said Meister Karl, "I could go on all day with Romany songs; and I can count up to a hundred in the black language. I know three words for a mouse, three for a monkey, and three for the shadow which falleth at noonday. And I know how to **pen dukkerin**, **lel dudikabin te chiv o manzin apre latti**." {270}

"Well, the man who knows **that** is up to **drab** [medicine], and hasn't much more to learn," said the young man. "When a **rye's** a Rom he's anywhere at home."

"So **kushto bak**!" (Good luck!) I said, rising to go. "We will come again!"

"Yes, we will come again," said Meister Karl. "Look for me with the roses at the races, and tell me the horse to bet on. You'll find my **patteran** [a mark or sign to show which way a gypsy has traveled] at the next church-door, or may be on the public-house step. Child of the old Egyptians, mother of all the witches, sister of the stars, daughter of darkness, farewell!"

This bewildering speech was received with admiring awe, and we departed. I should have liked to hear the comments on us which passed that evening among the gypsy denizens of Mammy Sauerkraut's Row.

V. A GYPSY LETTER.

All the gypsies in the country are not upon the roads. Many of them live in houses, and that very respectably, nay, even aristocratically. Yea, and it may be, O reader, that thou hast met them and knowest them not, any more than thou knowest many other deep secrets of the hearts and lives of those who live around thee. Dark are the ways of the Romany, strange his paths, even when reclaimed from the tent and the van. It is, however, intelligible enough that the Rom converted to the true faith of broadcloth garments by Poole, or dresses by Worth, as well as to the holy gospel of daily baths and *savon au violet*, should say as little as possible of his origin. For the majority of the world being snobs, they continually insist that all blood unlike their own is base, and the child of the *kalorat*, knowing this, sayeth naught, and ever carefully keeps the lid of silence on the pot of his birth. And as no being that ever was, is, or will be ever enjoyed holding a secret, playing a part, or otherwise entering into the deepest mystery of life--which is to make a joke of it--so thoroughly as a gypsy, it follows that the being respectable has to him a raciness and drollery and pungency and point which passeth faith. It has often occurred to me, and the older I grow the more I find it true, that the *real* pleasure which bank presidents, moral politicians, not a few clergymen, and most other highly representative good men take in having a high character is the exquisite secret consciousness of its being utterly undeserved. They love acting. Let no man say that the love of the drama is founded on the artificial or sham. I have heard the Reverend Histriomastix war and batter this on the pulpit; but the utterance *per se* was an actual, living lie. He was acting while he preached. Love or hunger is not more an innate passion than acting. The child in the nursery, the savage by the Nyanza or in Alaska, the multitude of great cities, all love to bemask and seem what they are not. Crush out carnivals and masked balls and theatres, and lo, you! the disguising and acting and masking show themselves in the whole community. Mawworm and Aminidab Sleek then play a role in every household, and every child becomes a wretched little Roscius. Verily I say unto you, the fewer actors the more acting; the fewer theatres the more stages, and the worse. Lay it to heart, study it deeply, you who believe that the stage is an open door to hell, for the chances are ninety and nine to one that if this be true *you* will end by consciously or unconsciously keeping a private little gate thereunto. Beloved, put this in thy pipe and fumigate it, that acting in some form is a human instinct which cannot be extinguished, which never has been and never will be; and this being so, is it not better, with Dr. Bellows, to try to put it into proper form than to crush it? Truly it has been proved that with this, as with a certain other unquenchable penchant of humanity, when you suppress a score of professionals you create a thousand zealous amateurs. There was never in this world a stage on which mere acting was more skillfully carried out than in all England under Cromwell, or in Philadelphia under the Quakers. Eccentric dresses, artificial forms of language, separate and "peculiar" expressions of character unlike those of "the world," were all only giving a form to that craving for being odd and queer which forms the soul of masking and acting. Of course people who act all the time object to the stage. *Le diable ne veut pas de miroir*.

The gypsy of society not always, but yet frequently, retains a keen interest in his wild ancestry. He keeps up the language; it is a delightful secret; he loves now and then to take a look at "the old thing." Closely allied to the converted sinners are the *aficionados*, or the ladies and gentlemen born with unconquerable Bohemian tastes, which may be accounted for by their having been themselves gypsies in preexistent lives. No one can explain how or why it is that the *aficion* comes upon them. It is *in* them. I know a very learned man in England, a gentleman of high position, one whose name is familiar to

my readers. He could never explain or understand why from early
childhood he had felt himself drawn towards the wanderers. When he was
only ten years old he saved up all his little store of pence wherewith to
pay a tinker to give him lessons in Romany, in which tongue he is now a
Past Grand. I know ladies in England and in America, both of the blood
and otherwise, who would give up a ball of the highest flight in society,
to sit an hour in a gypsy tent, and on whom a whispered word of Romany
acts like wild-fire. Great as my experience has been I can really no
more explain the intensity of this yearning, this *rapport*, than I can
fly. My own fancy for gypsydom is faint and feeble compared to what I
have found in many others. It is in them like the love for opium, for
music, for love itself, or for acting. I confess that there is to me a
nameless charm in the strangely, softly flowing language, which gives a
sweeter sound to every foreign word which it adopts, just as the melody
of a forest stream is said to make more musical the songs of the birds
who dwell beside it. Thus Wentzel becomes Wenselo and Anselo; Arthur,
Artaros; London, Lundra; Sylvester, Westaros. Such a phrase as "*Dordi*!
dovelo adoi?" (See! what is that there?) could not be surpassed for
mere beauty of sound.

It is apropos of living double lives, and playing parts, and the charm of
stealing away unseen, like naughty children, to romp with the tabooed
offspring of outlawed neighbors, that I write this, to introduce a letter
from a lady, who has kindly permitted me to publish it. It tells its own
story of two existences, two souls in one. I give it as it was written,
first in Romany, and then in English:--

Febmunti 1*st*.

MIRO KAMLO PAL,--Tu tevel mishto ta shun te latcherdum me akovo
kurikus tacho Romany tan akai adre o gav. Buti kamaben lis sas ta
dikk mori foki apopli; buti kushti ta shun moro jib. Mi-duvel atch
apa mande, si ne shomas pash naflo o Gorginess, vonk' akovo vias. O

waver divvus sa me viom fon a swell saleskro haben, dikdom me dui
Romani chia beshin alay apre a longo skamin adre --- Square. Kalor
yakkor, kalor balyor, lullo diklas apre i sherria, te lender trushnia
aglal lender piria. Mi-duvel, shomas pash divio sar kamaben ta dikav
lender! Avo! kairdum o wardomengro hatch i graia te sheldom avri,
"***Come here***!" Yon penden te me sos a rani ta dukker te vian sig
adosta. Awer me saldom te pendom adre Romanis: "Sarishan miri
dearis! Tute don't jin mandy's a Romany!" Yon nastis patser lende
kania nera yakkor. "Mi-duvel! Sa se tiro nav? putchde yeck. "Miro
nav se Britannia Lee." Kenna-sig yon diktas te me sos tachi, te
penden amengi lender navia shanas M. te D. Lis sos duro pa lende ta
jin sa a Romani rani astis jiv amen Gorgios, te dikk sa Gorgious,
awer te vel kushti Romani aja, te tevel buoino lakis kaloratt. Buti
rakkerdem apre mori foki, buti nevvi, buti savo sos rumado, te beeno,
te puredo, savo sos vino fon o puro tem, te butikumi aja kekkeno sos
rakkerben sa gudli. M. pende amengi, "Mandy don't jin how tute can
jiv among dem Gorgies." Pukerdom anpali: "Mandy dont jiv, mandy mers
kairin amen lender." Yon mangades mande ta well ta dikk a len, adre
lendes ker apre o chumba kai atchena pa o wen. Pende M., "Av miri
pen ta ha a bitti sar mendi. Tute jins the chais are only kerri
aratti te Kurrkus."

Sunday sala miri pen te me ghion adoi te latchedon o ker. O tan sos
bitto, awer sa i Romanis pende, dikde boro adosta paller jivin adre o
wardo. M. sos adoi te lakis roms dye, a kushti puri chai. A. sar
shtor chavia. M. kerde haben sa mendui viom adoi. I puri dye sos
mishto ta dikk mande, yoi kamde ta jin sar trustal mande. Rakkerdem
buti aja, te yoi pende te yoi ne kekker latchde a Romani rani denna
mande. Pendom me ke laki shan adre society kumi Romani rania, awer i
galderli Gorgios ne jinena lis.

Yoi pende sa miri pen dikde simlo Lusha Cooper, te siggerde lakis
kaloratt butider denna me. "Tute don't favor the Coopers, miri

dearie! Tute pens tiri dye rummerd a mush navvered Smith. Was adovo the Smith as lelled kellin te kurin booths pasher Lundra Bridge? Sos tute beeno adre Anglaterra?" Pukkerdom me ke puri dye sar jinav me trustal miri kokeri te simensi. Tu jinsa shan kek Gorgies sa longi-bavoli apre genealogies, sa i puri Romani dyia. Vonka foki nastis chin lende adre lilia, rikkerena lende aduro adre lendros sherria. *Que la main droit perd recueille la gauche*.

"Does tute jin any of the ---'s?" pende M. "Tute dikks sim ta ---'s juva." "Ne kekker, yois too pauno,' pens A. "It's chomani adre the look of her," pende M.

Dikkpali miro pal. Tu jinsa te --- sos i chi savo dudikabinde manush, navdo --- buti wongur. Vanka yoi sos lino apre, o Beshomengro pende ta ker laki chiv apre a shuba sims Gorgios te adenne lelled laki adre a tan sar desh te dui gorgi chaia. --- astissa pen i chai savo chorde lestis lovvo. Vanka yoi vias adre o tan, yoi ghias sig keti laki, te pende: "Jinava me laki talla lakis longi vangusti, te rinkeni mui. Yoi sos stardi dui beshya, awer o Gorgio kekker las leski vongur pali."

Savo-chirus mendi rakkerden o wuder pirido, te trin manushia vian adre.... Pali lenders sarishans, M. shelde avri: "Av ta misali, rikker yer skammins longo tute! Mrs. Lee, why didn't tute bring yer rom?" "Adenna me shom kek rumadi." "Mi-duvel, Britannia!" pende --- "M. pende amengy te tu sos rumado." "M. didn't dukker tacho vonka yoi dukkerd adovo. Yois a dinneli," pendom me. Te adenne sar mendi saden atut M. Haben sos kushto, loim a kani, ballovas te puvengros, te kushto curro levina. Liom mendi kushto paiass dre moro puro Romany dromus. Rinkenodiro sos, kerde mande pash ta ruv, shomas sa kushto-bakno ta atch yecker apopli men mori foki. Sos "Britannia!" akai, te "Britannia!" doi, te sar sa adre o puro cheirus, vonka chavi shomas. Ne patserava me ta Dante chinde:--

"Nessun maggior dolore
Che ricordarsi dei tempi felici."

Talla me shomas kushto-bakno ta pen apre o puro chirus. Sar lende
piden miro kamaben Romaneskaes, sar gudlo; talla H. Yov pende nastis
ker lis, pa yuv kenna lias tabuti. Kushto dikin Romnichal yuv. Tu
tevel jin lesti sarakai pa Romani, yuv se sa kalo. Te avec l'air
indefinnissable du vrai Bohemien. Yuv patserde me ta piav miro
sastopen wavescro chirus. Kana shomas pa misali, geero vias keti
ian; dukkeriben kamde yov. Hunali sos i puri dye te pendes amergi,
"Beng lel o puro jukel for wellin vanka mendi shom hain, te kenna tu
shan akai, miri Britannia Yov ne tevel lel kek kushto bak. Mandy'll
pen leste a wafedo dukkerin." Adoi A. putcherde mengy, "Does tute
dukker or sa does tute ker." "Miri pen, mandy'll pen tute tacho.
Mandy dukkers te dudikabins te kers buti covvas. Shom a tachi Romani
chovihani." "Tacho! tacho!" saden butider. Miri pen te me rikkerdem
a boro matto-morricley pa i chavis. Yon beshden alay apre o purj,
hais lis. Rinkeno *picture* sas, pendom dikkav mande te miri penia
te pralia kenna shomas bitti. Latcherdom me a tani kali chavi of
panj besh chorin levina avri miro curro. Dikde, sar lakis bori kali
yakka te kali balia simno tikno Bacchante, sa yoi prasterde adrom.

Pendom parako pa moro kushto-bakeno chirus--"kushto bak" te "kushto
divvus." Mendi diom moro tachopen ta well apopli, te kan viom kerri.
Patserava dikk tute akai talla o prasterin o ye graia. Kushto bak te
kushto ratti.

Sarja tiro pen,

BRITANNIA LEE.

TRANSLATION.

February 1*st*.

MY DEAR FRIEND,--You will be glad to learn that I, within the week, found a real Romany family (place) here in this town. Charming it was to find our folk again; pleasant it was to listen to our tongue. The Lord be on me! but I was half sick of Gentiles and their ways till this occurred. The other day, as I was returning from a highly aristocratic breakfast, where we had winter strawberries with the *creme de la creme*, I saw two gypsy women sitting on a bench in --- Square. Black eyes, black hair, red kerchiefs on their heads, their baskets on the ground before their feet. Dear Lord! but I was half wild with delight at seeing them. Aye, I made the coachman stop the horses, and cried aloud, "Come here!" They thought I was a lady to fortune-tell, and came quickly. But I laughed, and said in Romany, "How are you, my dears? You don't know that I am a gypsy." They could not trust their very ears or eyes! At length one said, "My God! what *is* your name?" "My name's Britannia Lee," and, at a glance, they saw that I was to be trusted, and a Romany. Their names, they said, were M. and D. It was hard (far) for them to understand how a Romany lady *could* live among Gentiles, and look so Gorgious, and yet be a true gypsy withal, and proud of her dark blood. Much they talked about our people; much news I heard,--much as to who was married and born and buried, who was come from the old country, and much more. Oh, *never* was such news so sweet to me! M. said, "I don't know how you *can* live among the Gentiles." I answered, "I don't live; I *die*, living in their houses with them." They begged me then to come and see them in their home, upon the hill, where they are wintering. M. said, "Come, my sister, and eat a little with us. You know that the women are only at home at night and on Sunday."

Sunday morning, sister and I went there, and found the house. It was a little place, but, as they said, after the life in wagons it seemed large. M. was there, and her husband's mother, a nice old woman; also A., with four children. M. was cooking as we entered. The old mother was glad to see us; she wished to know all about us. All talked, indeed, and that quite rapidly, and she said that I was the first Romany lady {279} she had ever seen. I said to her that in society are many gypsy ladies to be found, but that the wretched Gentiles do not know it.

She said that my sister looked like Lusha Cooper, and showed her dark blood more than I do. "You don't favor the Coopers, my dearie. You say your mother married a Smith. Was that the Smith who kept a dancing and boxing place near London Bridge? Were you born in England?" I told the old mother all I knew about myself and my relations. You know that no Gorgios are so long-winded on genealogies as old mothers in Rom. When people don't write them down in their family Bibles, they carry them, extended, in their heads. *Que la main droit perd recueille la gauche*.

"Do you know any of the ---'s?" said M. "You look like ---'s wife." "No; she's too pale," said A. "It's something in the look of her," said M.

Reflect, my brother. You know that --- was the woman who "cleaned out" a man named --- of a very large sum {280} by "dukkeripen" and "dudikaþin." "When she was arrested, the justice made her dress like any Gorgio, and placed her among twelve Gentile women. The man who had been robbed was to point out who among them had stolen his money. When she came into the room, he went at once to her, and said, 'I know her by her long skinny fingers and handsome face.' She was imprisoned for two years, but the Gorgio never recovered his money."

What time we reasoned thus, the door undid, and three men entered. After their greetings, M. cried, "Come to table; bring your chairs with you!" "Mrs. Lee, why didn't you bring your husband?" "Because I am not married." "Lord! Britannia! Why, M. told me that you were." "Ah, M. didn't fortune right when she fortuned that. She's a fool," quoth I. And then we all laughed like children. The food was good: chickens and ham and fried potatoes, with a glass of sound ale. We were gay as flies in summer, in the real old Romany way. 'T was "Britannia" here, "Britannia" there, as in the merry days when we were young. Little do I believe in Dante's words,--

"Nessun maggior dolore,
Che ricordarsi dei tempi felici."

"There is no greater grief
Than to remember by-gone happy days."

For it is always happiness to me to think of good old times when I was glad. All drank my health, **Romaneskaes**, together, with a shout,--all save H., who said he had already had too much. Good-looking gypsy, that! You'd know him anywhere for Romany, he is so dark,--**avec l'air indefinissable du vrai Bohemien**. He promised to drink my health another time.

As we sat, a gentleman came in below, wishing to have his fortune told. I remember to have read that the Pythoness of Delphian oracle prepared herself for **dukkerin**, or presaging, by taking a few drops of cherry-laurel water. (I have had it prescribed for my eyes as R **aq. laur. cerasi. fiat lotio**,--possibly to enable me to see into the future.) Perhaps it was the cherry-brandy beloved of British

matrons and Brighton school-girls, taken at Mutton's. Mais revenons
a nos moutons. The old mother had taken, not cherry-laurel water,
nor even cherry-brandy, but joly good ale, and olde, which, far from
fitting her to reveal the darksome lore of futurity, had rendered her
loath to leave the festive board of the present. Wrathful was the
sybil, furious as the Vala when waked by Odin, angry as Thor when he
missed his hammer, to miss her merriment. "May the devil take the
old dog for coming when we are eating, and when thou art here, my
Britannia! Little good fortune will he hear this day. Evil shall be
the best I'll promise him." Thus spake the sorceress, and out she
went to keep her word. Truly it was a splendid picture this of "The
Enraged Witch," as painted by Hexenmeister von Teufel, of
Hollenstadt,--her viper eyes flashing infernal light and most
unchristian fire, shaking *les noirs serpents de ses cheveux*, as she
went forth. I know how, in an instant, her face was beautiful with
welcome, smiling like a Neapolitan at a cent; but the poor believer
caught it hot, all the same, and had a sleepless night over his
future fate. I wonder if the Pythoness of old, when summoned from a
petit souper, or a holy prophet called out of bed of a cold night,
to decide by royal command on the fate of Israel, ever "took it out"
on the untimely king by promising him a lively, unhappy time of it.
Truly it is fine to be behind the scenes and see how they work the
oracle. For the gentleman who came to consult my witch was a man of
might in the secrets of state, and one whom I have met in high
society. And, oh! *if* he had known who it was that was up-stairs,
laughing at him for a fool!

While she was forth, A. asked me, "Do you tell fortunes, or *what*?"
"My sister," I replied, "I'll tell thee the truth. I do tell
fortunes. I keep a house for the purchase of stolen goods. I am
largely engaged in making counterfeit money and all kinds of forgery.
I am interested in burglary. I lie, swear, cheat, and steal, and get
drunk on Sunday. And I do many other things. I am a real Romany

witch." This little confession of faith brought down the house. "Bravo! bravo!" they cried, laughing.

Sister and I had brought a great tipsy-cake for the children, and they were all sitting under a table, eating it. It was a pretty picture. I thought I saw in it myself and all my sisters and brothers as we were once. Just such little gypsies and duckling Romanys! And now! And then! What a comedy some lives are,--yea, such lives as mine! And now it is *you* who are behind the scenes; anon, I shall change with you. *Va Pierre*, *vient Pierette*. Then I surprised a little brown maiden imp of five summers stealing my beer, and as she was caught in the act, and tore away shrieking with laughter, she looked, with her great black eyes and flowing jetty curling locks, like a perfect little Bacchante.

Then we said, "Thank you for the happy time!" "Good luck!" and "Good day!" giving our promises to come again. So we went home all well. I hope to see you at the races here. Good luck and good-night also to you.

Always your friend,

BRITANNIA LEE

I have somewhat abbreviated the Romany text of this letter, and Miss Lee herself has somewhat polished and enlarged the translation, which is strictly fit and proper, she being a very different person in English from what she is in gypsy, as are most of her kind. This letter may be, to many, a strange lesson, a quaint essay, a social problem, a fable, an epigram, or a frolic,--just as they choose to take it. To me it is a poem. Thou, my friend, canst easily understand why all that is wild and strange, out-of-doors, far away by night, is worthy of being Tennysoned or Whitmanned. If there be given unto thee stupendous blasted trees, looking in the moonlight like the pillars of a vast and ghostly temple; the fall of cataracts down awful rocks; the wind wailing in wondrous language or whistling Indian melody all night on heath, rocks, and hills, over ancient graves and through lonely caves, bearing with it the hoot of the night-owl; while over all the stars look down in eternal mystery, like eyes reading the great riddle of the night which thou knowest not,--this is to thee like Ariel's song. To me and to us there are men and women who are in life as the wild river and the night-owl, as the blasted tree and the wind over ancient graves. No man is educated until he has arrived at that state of thought when a picture is quite the same as a book, an old gray-beard jug as a manuscript, men, women, and children as libraries. It was but yester morn that I read a cuneiform inscription printed by doves' feet in the snow, finding a meaning where in by-gone years I should have seen only a quaint resemblance. For in this by the *ornithomanteia* known of old to the Chaldean sages I saw that it was neither from arrow-heads or wedges which gave the letters to the old Assyrians. When thou art at this point, then Nature is equal in all her types, and the city, as the forest, full of endless beauty and piquancy,--*in saecula saeculorum*.

I had written the foregoing, and had enveloped and directed it to be mailed, when I met in a lady-book entitled "Magyarland" with the following passages:--

> "The gypsy girl in this family was a pretty young woman, with masses of raven hair and a clear skin, but, notwithstanding her neat dress and civilized surroundings, we recognized her immediately. It is, in truth, not until one sees the Romany translated to an entirely new form of existence, and under circumstances inconsistent with their ordinary lives, that one realizes how completely different they are from the rest of mankind in form and feature. Instead of disguising, the garb of civilization only enhances the type, and renders it the more apparent. No matter what dress they may assume, no matter what

may be their calling, no matter whether they are dwellers in tents or houses, it is impossible for gypsies to disguise their origin. Taken from their customary surroundings, they become at once an anomaly and an anachronism, and present such an instance of the absurdity of attempting to invert the order of nature that we feel more than ever how utterly different they are from the human race; that there is a key to their strange life which we do not possess,--a secret free masonry that renders them more isolated than the veriest savages dwelling in the African wilds,--and a hidden mystery hanging over them and their origin that we shall never comprehend. They are indeed a people so entirely separate and distinct that, in whatever clime or quarter of the globe they may be met with, they are instantly recognized; for with them forty centuries of association with civilized races have not succeeded in obliterating one single sign."

* * * * *

"Alas!" cried the princess; "I can never, never find the door of the enchanted cavern, nor enter the golden cavern, nor solve its wonderful mystery. It has been closed for thousands of years, and it will remain closed forever."

"What flowers are those which thou holdest?" asked the hermit.

"Only primroses or Mary's-keys, {285} and tulips," replied the princess.

"Touch the rock with them," said the hermit, "and the door will open."

* * * * *

The lady writer of "Magyarland" held in her hand all the while, and knew it not, a beautiful primrose, which might have opened for her the mysterious Romany cavern. On a Danube steamboat she saw a little blind boy sitting all day all alone: only a little Slavonian peasant boy, "an odd, quaint little specimen of humanity, with loose brown garments, cut precisely like those of a grown-up man, and his bits of feet in little raw-hide moccasins." However, with a tender, gentle heart she began to pet the little waif. And the captain told her what the boy was. "He is a *guslar*, or minstrel, as they call them in Croatia. The Yougo-Slavs dedicate all male children who are born blind, from infancy, to the Muses. As soon as they are old enough to handle anything, a small mandolin is given them, which they are taught to play; after which they are taken every day into the woods, where they are left till evening to commune in their little hearts with nature. In due time they become poets, or at any rate rhapsodists, singing of the things they never saw, and when grown up are sent forth to earn their livelihood, like the troubadours of old, by singing from place to place, and asking alms by the wayside.

"It is not difficult for a Slav to become a poet; he takes in poetic sentiment as a river does water from its source. The first sounds he is conscious of are the words of his mother singing to him as she rocks his cradle. Then, as she watches the dawning of intelligence in his infant face, her mother language is that of poetry, which she improvises at the moment, and though he never saw the flowers nor the snow-capped mountains, nor the flowing streams and rivers, he describes them out of his inner consciousness, and the influence which the varied sounds of nature have upon his mind."

Rock and river and greenwood tree, sweet-spiced spring flower, rustling grass, and bird-singing nature and freedom,--this is the secret of the poets' song and of the Romany, and there is no other mystery in either. He who sleeps on graves rises mad or a poet; all who lie on the earth, which is the grave and cradle of nature, and who live *al fresco*, understand gypsies as well as my lady Britannia Lee. Nay, when some natures take to the Romany they become like the Norman knights of the Pale, who were more Paddyfied than the Paddies themselves. These become leaders among the gypsies, who recognize the fact that one renegade is more zealous than ten Turks. As for the "mystery" of the history of the gypsies, it is time, sweet friends, that 't were ended. When we know that there is to-day, in India, a sect and set of Vauriens, who are there considered Gipsissimae, and who call themselves, with their wives and language and being, Rom, Romni, and Romnipana, even as they do in England; and when we know, moreover, that their faces proclaim them to be Indian, and that they have been a wandering caste since the dawn of Hindu history, we have, I trow, little more to seek. As for the rest, you may read it in the great book of Out-of Doors, *capitulo nullo folio nigro*, or wherever you choose to open it, written as distinctly, plainly, and sweetly as the imprint of a school-boy's knife and fork on a mince-pie, or in the uprolled rapture of the eyes of Britannia when she inhaleth the perfume of a fresh bunch of Florentine violets. *Ite missa est*.

GYPSIES IN THE EAST.

Noon in Cairo.

A silent old court-yard, half sun and half shadow in which quaintly graceful, strangely curving columns seem to have taken from long companionship with trees something of their inner life, while the palms, their neighbors, from long in-door existence, look as if they had in turn acquired household or animal instincts, if not human sympathies. And as the younger the race the more it seeks for poets and orators to express

in thought what it only feels, so these dumb pillars and plants found
their poet and orator in the fountain which sang or spoke for them
strangely and sweetly all night and day, uttering for them not only their
waking thoughts, but their dreams. It gave a voice, too, to the ancient
Persian tiles and the Cufic inscriptions which had seen the caliphs, and
it told endless stories of Zobeide and Mesrour and Haroun al Raschid.

Beyond the door which, when opened, gave this sight was a dark ancient
archway twenty yards long, which opened on the glaring, dusty street,
where camels with their drivers and screaming *sais*, or carriage-runners
and donkey-boys and crying venders, kept up the wonted Oriental din. But
just within the archway, in its duskiest corner, there sat all day a
living picture, a dark and handsome woman, apparently thirty years old,
who was unveiled. She had before her a cloth and a few shells; sometimes
an Egyptian of the lower class stopped, and there would be a grave
consultation, and the shells would be thrown, and then further solemn
conference and a payment of money and a departure. And it was world-old
Egyptian, or Chaldean, as to custom, for the woman was a Rhagarin, or
gypsy, and she was one of the diviners who sit by the wayside, casting
shells for auspices, even as shells and arrows were cast of old, to be
cursed by Israel.

It is not remarkable that among the myriad *manteias* of olden days there
should have been one by shells. The sound of the sea as heard in the
nautilus or conch, when

> "It remembers its august abode
> And murmurs as the ocean murmurs there,"

is very strange to children, and I can remember how in childhood I
listened with perfect faith to the distant roaring, and marveled at the
mystery of the ocean song being thus forever kept alive, inland. Shells
seem so much like work of human hands, and are often so marked as with

letters, that it is not strange that faith soon found the supernatural in them. The magic shell of all others is the cowrie. Why the Roman ladies called it *porcella*, or little pig, because it has a pig's back, is the objective explanation of its name, and how from its gloss that name, or porcellana, was transferred to porcelain, is in books. But there is another side to the shell, and another or esoteric meaning to "piggy," which was also known to the *dames du temps jadis*, to Archipiada and Thais, *qui fut la belle Romaine*,--and this inner meaning makes of it a type of birth or creation. Now all that symbolizes fertility, birth, pleasure, warmth, light, and love is opposed to barrenness, cold, death, and evil; whence it follows that the very sight of a shell, and especially of a cowrie, frightens away the devils as well as a horse-shoe, which by the way has also its cryptic meaning. Hence it was selected to cast for luck, a world-old custom, which still lingers in the game of props; and for the same reason it is hung on donkeys, the devil being still scared away by the sight of a cowrie, even as he was scared away of old by its prototype, as told by Rabelais.

As the sibyls sat in caves, so the sorceress sat in the dark archway, immovable when not sought, mysterious as are all her kind, and something to wonder at. It was after passing her, and feeling by quick intuition what she was, that the court-yard became a fairy-land, and the fountain its poet, and the palm-trees Tamar maids. There are people who believe there is no mystery, that an analysis of the gypsy sorceress would have shown an ignorant outcast; but while nature gives chiaro-oscuro and beauty, and while God is the Unknown, I believe that the more light there is cast by science the more stupendous will be the new abysses of darkness revealed. These natures must be taken with the *life* in them, not dead,--and their life is mystery. The Hungarian gypsy lives in an intense mystery, yes, in true magic in his singing. You may say that he cannot, like Orpheus, move rocks or tame beasts with his music. If he could he could do no more than astonish and move us, and he does that now, and the *why* is as deep a mystery as that would be.

So far is it from being only a degrading superstition in those who
believe that mortals like themselves can predict the future, that it
seems, on the contrary ennobling. It is precisely because man feels a
mystery within himself that he admits it may be higher in others; if
spirits whisper to him in dreams and airy passages of trembling light, or
in the music never heard but ever felt below, what may not be revealed to
others? You may tell me if you will that prophecies are all rubbish and
magic a lie, and it may be so,--nay, *is* so, but the awful mystery of
the Unknown without a name and the yearning to penetrate it *is*, and is
all the more, because I have found all prophecies and jugglings and
thaumaturgy fail to bridge over the abyss. It is since I have read with
love and faith the evolutionists and physiologists of the most advanced
type that the Unknown has become to me most wonderful, and that I have
seen the light which never shone on sea or land as I never saw it before.
And therefore to me the gypsy and all the races who live in freedom and
near to nature are more poetic than ever. For which reason, after the
laws of acoustics have fully explained to me why the nautilus sounds like
a far off-ocean dirge, the unutterable longing *to know more* seizes upon
me,

> "Till my heart is full of longing
> For the secret of the sea,
> And the heart of the great ocean
> Sends a thrilling pulse through me."

That gypsy fortune-teller, sitting in the shadow, is, moreover,
interesting as a living manifestation of a dead past. As in one of her
own shells when petrified we should have the ancient form without its
color, all the old elements being displaced by new ones, so we have the
old magic shape, though every atom in it is different; the same, yet not
the same Life in the future, and the divination thereof, was a
stupendous, ever-present reality to the ancient Egyptian, and the sole

inspiration of humanity when it produced few but tremendous results. It is when we see it in such living forms that it is most interesting. As in Western wilds we can tell exactly by the outline of the forests where the borders of ancient inland seas once ran, so in the great greenwood of history we can trace by the richness or absence of foliage and flower the vanished landmarks of poetry, or perceive where the enchantment whose charm has now flown like the snow of the foregone year once reigned in beauty. So a line of lilies has shown me where the sea-foam once fell, and pine-trees sang of masts preceding them.

> "I sometimes think that never blows so red
> The rose as where some buried Caesar bled;
> That every hyacinth the garden wears
> Dropt in her lap from some once lovely head." {292}

The memory of that court-yard reminds me that I possess two Persian tiles, each with a story. There is a house in Cairo which is said to be more or less contemporary with the prophet, and it is inhabited by an old white-bearded emir, more or less a descendant of the prophet. This old gentleman once gave as a precious souvenir to an American lady two of the beautiful old tiles from his house, whereof I had one. In the eyes of a Muslim there is a degree of sanctity attached to this tile, as one on which the eyes of the prophet may have rested,--or at least the eyes of those who were nearer to him than we are. Long after I returned from Cairo I wrote and published a fairy-book called Johnnykin, {292} in which occurred the following lines:--

> Trust not the Ghoul, love,
> Heed not his smile;
> *Out of the Mosque, love,*
> *He stole the tile*.

One day my friend the Palmer from over the sea came to me with a present.

It was a beautiful Persian tile.

"Where did you get it?" I asked.

"I stole it out of a mosque in Syria."

"Did you ever read my Johnnykin?"

"Of course not."

"I know you never did." Here I repeated the verse. "But you remember what the Persian poet says:--

> "'And never since the vine-clad earth was young
> Was some great crime committed on the earth,
> But that some poet prophesied the deed.'"

"True, and also what the great Tsigane poet sang:--

> "'O manush te lela sossi choredo,
> Wafodiro se te choramengro.'

> "He who takes the stolen ring,
> Is worse than he who stole the thing."

"And it would have been better for you, while you were *dukkerin* or prophesying, to have prophesied about something more valuable than a tile."

And so it came to pass that the two Persian tiles, one given by a descendant of the Prophet, and the other the subject of a prophecy, rest in my cabinet side by side.

In Egypt, as in Austria, or Syria, or Persia, or India, the gypsies are
the popular musicians. I had long sought for the derivation of the word
banjo, and one day I found that the Oriental gypsies called a gourd by
that name. Walking one day with the Palmer in Cambridge, we saw in a
window a very fine Hindu lute, or in fact a real banjo made of a gourd.
We inquired, and found that it belonged to a mutual friend, Mr. Charles
Brookfield, one of the best fellows living, and who, on being forthwith
"requisitioned" by the unanimous voice of all who sympathized with me in
my need, sent me the instrument. "He did not think it right," he said,
"to keep it, when Philology wanted it. If it had been any other
party,--but he always had a particular respect and awe of her." I do not
assert that this discovery settles the origin of the word **banjo**, but
the coincidence is, to say the least, remarkable.

I saw many gypsies in Egypt, but learned little from them. What I found
I stated in a work called the "Egyptian Sketch Book." It was to this
effect: My first information was derived from the late Khedive Ismael,
who during an interview with me said, "There are in Egypt many people
known as Rhagarin, or Ghagarin, who are probably the same as the gypsies
of Europe. They are wanderers, who live in tents, and are regarded with
contempt even by the peasantry. Their women tell fortunes, tattoo, and
sell small wares; the men work in iron. They are all adroit thieves, and
noted as such. The men may sometimes be seen going round the country
with monkeys. In fact, they appear to be in all respects the same people
as the gypsies of Europe."

I habitually employed, while in Cairo, the same donkey-driver, an
intelligent and well-behaved man named Mahomet, who spoke English fairly.
On asking him if he could show me any Rhagarin, he replied that there was
a fair or market held every Saturday at Boulac, where I would be sure to
meet with women of the tribe. The men, he said, seldom ventured into the
city, because they were subject to much insult and ill-treatment from the
common people.

On the day appointed I rode to Boulac. The market was very interesting.
I saw no European or Frangi there, except my companion, Baron de Cosson,
who afterwards traveled far into the White Nile country, and who had with
his brother Edward many remarkable adventures in Abyssinia, which were
well recorded by the latter in a book. All around were thousands of
blue-skirted and red-tarbouched or white-turbaned Egyptians, buying or
selling, or else amusing themselves, but with an excess of outcry and
hallo which indicates their grown child character. There were dealers in
donkeys and horses roaring aloud, "He is for ten napoleons! Had I asked
twenty you would have gladly given me fifteen!" "O true believers, here
is a Syrian steed which will give renown to the purchaser!" Strolling
loosely about were dealers in sugar-cane and pea-nuts, which are called
gooba in Africa as in America, pipe peddlers and venders of rosaries,
jugglers and minstrels. At last we came to a middle-aged woman seated on
the ground behind a basket containing beads, glass armlets, and such
trinkets. She was dressed like any Arab-woman of the lower class, but
was not veiled, and on her chin blue lines were tattooed. Her features
and expression were, however, gypsy, and not Egyptian. And as she sat
there quietly I wondered how a woman could feel in her heart who was
looked down upon with infinite scorn by an Egyptian, who might justly be
looked down on in his turn with sublime contempt by an average American
Methodist colored whitewasher who "took de 'Ledger.'" Yet there was in
the woman the quiet expression which associates itself with
respectability, and it is worth remarking that whenever a race is greatly
looked down on by another from the stand-point of mere color, as in
America, or mere religion, as in Mahometan lands, it always contains
proportionally a larger number of ***decent*** people than are to be found
among those who immediately oppress it. An average Chinese is as a human
being far superior to a hoodlum, and a man of color to the white man who
cannot speak of him or to him except as a "naygur" or a "nigger." It is
when a man realizes that he is superior in ***nothing*** else save race,
color, religion, family, inherited fortune, and their contingent

advantages that he develops most readily into the prig and snob.

I spoke to the woman in Romany, using such words as would have been intelligible to any of her race in any other country; but she did not understand me, and declared that she could speak nothing but Arabic. At my request Mahomet explained to her that I had come from a distant country in Orobba, or Europe, where there were many Rhagarin, who said that their fathers came from Egypt, and that I wished to know if any in the old country could speak the old language. She replied that the Rhagarin of Montesinos could still speak it; but that her people in Egypt had lost the tongue. Mahomet, in translating, here remarked that Montesinos meant Mount Sinai or Syria. I then asked her if the Rhagarin had no peculiar name for themselves, and she answered, "Yes; we call ourselves Tataren."

This at least was satisfactory. All over Southern Germany and in Norway the gypsies are called Tartaren, and though the word means Tartars, and is misapplied, it indicates the race. The woman seemed to be much gratified at the interest I manifested in her people. I gave her a double piaster, and asked for its value in blue glass armlets. She gave me four, and as I turned to depart called me back, and with a good-natured smile handed me four more as a present. This generosity was very gypsy-like, and very unlike the habitual meanness of the ordinary Egyptian.

After this Mahomet took me to a number of Rhagarin. They all resembled the one whom I had seen, and all were sellers of small articles and fortune-tellers. They all differed slightly from common Egyptians in appearance, and were more unlike them in not being importunate for money, nor disagreeable in their manners. But though they were as certainly gypsies as old Charlotte Cooper herself, none of them could speak Romany. I used to amuse myself by imagining what some of my English gypsy friends would have done if turned loose in Cairo among their cousins. How naturally old Charlotte would have waylaid and "dukkered" and amazed the English ladies in the Muskee, and how easily that reprobate old amiable cosmopolite, the Windsor Frog, would have mingled with the motley mob of donkey-boys and tourists before Shepherd's Hotel, and appointed himself an *attache* to their excursions to the Pyramids, and drunk their pale ale or anything else to their healths, and then at the end of the day have claimed a wage for his politeness! And how well the climate would have agreed with them, and how they would have agreed that it was of all lands the best for *tannin*, or tenting out, in the world!

The gypsiest-looking gypsy in Cairo, with whom I became somewhat familiar, was a boy of sixteen, a snake-charmer; a dark and even handsome youth, but with eyes of such wild wickedness that no one who had ever seen him excited could hope that he would ever become as other human beings. I believe that he had come, as do all of his calling, from a snake-catching line of ancestors, and that he had taken in from them, as did Elsie Venner, the serpent nature. They had gone snaking, generation after generation, from the days of the serpent worship of old, it may be back to the old Serpent himself; and this tawny, sinuous, active thing of evil, this boy, without the least sense of sympathy for any pain, who devoured a cobra alive with as much indifference as he had just shown in petting it, was the result. He was a human snake. I had long before reading the wonderfully original work of Doctor Holmes reflected deeply on the moral and immoral influences which serpent worship of old, in Syria and other lands, must have had upon its followers. But Elsie Venner sets forth the serpent nature as benumbed or suspended by cold New England winters and New England religions, moral and social influences; the Ophites of old and the Cairene gypsy showed the boy as warmed to life in lands whose winters are as burning summers. Elsie Venner is not sensual, and sensuality is the leading trait of the human-serpent nature. Herein lies an error, just as a sculptor would err who should present Lady Godiva as fully draped, or Sappho merely as a sweet singer of Lesbos, or Antinous only as a fine young man. He who would harrow hell and rake out the devil, and then exhibit to us an ordinary sinner, or an *opera bouffe* "Mefistofele," as the result, reminds one of the seven Suabians who went to hunt a monster,--"*a Ungeheuer*,"--and returned with a hare. Elsie Venner is not a hare; she is a wonderful creation; but she is a winter-snake. I confess that I have no patience, however, with those who pretend to show us summer-snakes, and would fain dabble with vice; who are amateurs in the diabolical, and drawing-room dilettanti in damnation. Such, as I have said before, are the aesthetic adorers of Villon, whom the old *roue* himself would have most despised, and the admirers of "Faustine," whom Faustina would have picked up between her thumb and finger, and eyed with serene contempt before throwing them out of the window. A future age will have for these would-be wickeds, who are only monks half turned inside out, more laughter than we now indulge in at Chloe and Strephon.

I always regarded my young friend Abdullah as a natural child of the devil and a serpent-souled young sinner, and he never disappointed me in my opinion of him. I never in my life felt any antipathy to serpents, and he evidently regarded me as a *sapengro*, or snake-master. The first day I met him he put into my hands a cobra which had the fangs extracted, and then handled an asp which still had its poison teeth. On his asking me if I was afraid of it, and my telling him "No," he gave it to me, and after I had petted it, he always manifested an understanding,--I cannot say sympathy. I should have liked to see that boy's sister, if he ever had one, and was not hatched out from some egg found in the desert by an Egyptian incubus or incubator. She must have been a charming young lady, and his mother must have been a beauty, especially when in court-dress,--with her broom *et praeterea nihil*. But neither, alas, could be ever seen by me, for it is written in the "Gittin" that there are three hundred species of male demons, but what the female herself is like is known to no one.

Abdullah first made his appearance before me at Shepherd's Hotel, and despite his amazing natural impudence, which appeared to such splendid advantage in the street that I always thought he must be a lineal descendant of the brazen serpent himself, he evinced a certain timidity which was to me inexplicable, until I recalled that the big snake of Irish legends had shown the same modesty when Saint Patrick wanted him to enter the chest which he had prepared for his prison. "Sure, it's a nate little house I've made for yees," said the saint, "wid an iligant parlor." "I don't like the look av it at all, at all," says the sarpent, as he squinted at it suspiciously, "and I'm loath to *inter* it."

Abdullah looked at the parlor as if he too were loath to "inter" it; but he was in charge of one in whom his race instinctively trust, so I led him in. His apparel was simple: it consisted of a coarse shirt, very short, with a belt around the waist, and an old tarbouch on his head. Between the shirt and his bare skin, as in a bag, was about a half peck of cobras, asps, vipers, and similar squirming property; while between his cap and his hair were generally stowed one or two enormous living scorpions, and any small serpents that he could not trust to dwell with the larger ones. When I asked Abdullah where he contrived to get such vast scorpions and such lively serpents, he replied, "Out in the desert." I arranged, in fact, to go out with him some day a-snaking and scorp'ing, and have ever since regretted that I did not avail myself of the opportunity. He showed off his snakes to the ladies, and concluded by offering to eat the largest one alive before our eyes for a dollar, which price he speedily reduced to a half. There was a young New England lady present who was very anxious to witness this performance; but as I informed Abdullah that if he attempted anything of the kind I would kick him out-of-doors, snakes and all, he ceased to offer to show himself a cannibal. Perhaps he had learned what Rabbi Simon ben Yochai taught, that it is a good deed to smash the heads of the best of serpents, even as it is a duty to kill the best of Goyim. And if by Goyim he meant Philistines, I agree with him.

I often met Abdullah after that, and helped him to several very good
exhibitions. Two or three things I learned from him. One was that the
cobra, when wide awake, yet not too violently excited, lifts its head and
maintains a curious swaying motion, which, when accompanied by music, may
readily be mistaken for dancing acquired from a teacher. The Hindu
sappa-wallahs make people believe that this "dancing" is really the
result of tuition, and that it is influenced by music. Later, I found
that the common people in Egypt continue to believe that the snakes which
Abdullah and his tribe exhibit are as dangerous and deadly as can be, and
that they are managed by magic. Whether they believe, as it was held of
old by the Rabbis, that serpents are to be tamed by sorcery only on the
Sabbath, I never learned.

Abdullah was crafty enough for a whole generation of snakes, but in the
wisdom attributed to serpents he was woefully wanting. He would run by
my side in the street as I rode, expecting that I would pause to accept a
large wiggling scorpion as a gift, or purchase a viper, I suppose for a
riding-whip or a necktie. One day when I was in a jam of about a hundred
donkey-boys, trying to outride the roaring mob, and all of a fever with
heat and dust, Abdullah spied me, and, joining the mob, kept running by
my side, crying in maddening monotony, "Snake, sah! Scorpion, sah! Very
fine snake to-day, sah!"--just as if his serpents were edible delicacies,
which were for that day particularly fresh and nice.

There are three kinds of gypsies in Egypt,--the Rhagarin, the Helebis,
and the Nauar. They have secret jargons among themselves; but as I
ascertained subsequently from specimens given by Captain Newboldt {302a}
and Seetzen, as quoted by Pott, {302b} their language is made up of
Arabic "back-slang," Turkish and Greek, with a very little Romany,--so
little that it is not wonderful that I could not converse with them in
it. The Syrian gypsies, or Nuri, who are seen with bears and monkeys in
Cairo, are strangers in the land. With them a conversation is not
difficult. It is remarkable that while English, German, and Turkish or

Syrian gypsy look so different and difficult as printed in books, it is on the whole an easy matter to get on with them in conversation. The roots being the same, a little management soon supplies the rest.

Abdullah was a Helebi. The last time I saw him I was sitting on the balcony of Shepherd's Hotel, in the early evening, with an American, who had never seen a snake-charmer. I called the boy, and inadvertently gave him his pay in advance, telling him to show all his stock in trade. But the temptation to swindle was too great, and seizing the coin he rushed back into the darkness. From that hour I beheld him no more. I think I can see that last gleam of his demon eyes as he turned and fled. I met in after-days with other snake-boys, but for an eye which indicated an unadulterated child of the devil, and for general blackguardly behavior to match, I never found anybody like my young friend Abdullah.

The last snake-masters whom I came across were two sailors at the Oriental Seamen's Home in London. And strangely enough, on the day of my visit they had obtained in London, of all places, a very large and profitable job; for they had been employed to draw the teeth of all the poisonous serpents in the Zoological Garden. Whether these practitioners ever applied for or received positions as members of the Dental College I do not know, any more than if they were entitled to practice as surgeons without licenses. Like all the Hindu *sappa-wallahs*, or snake-men, they are what in Europe would be called gypsies.

GYPSY NAMES AND FAMILY CHARACTERISTICS.

The following list gives the names of the principal gypsy families in England, with their characteristics. It was prepared for me by an old,

well-known Romany, of full blood. Those which have (A) appended to them
are known to have representatives in America. For myself, I believe that
gypsies bearing all these names are to be found in both countries. I
would also state that the personal characteristics attributed to certain
families are by no means very strictly applicable, neither do any of them
confine themselves rigidly to any particular part of England. I have
met, for instance, with Bosvilles, Lees, Coopers, Smiths, Bucklands,
etc., in every part of England as well as Wales. I am aware that the
list is imperfect in all respects.

AYRES.

BAILEY (A). Half-bloods. Also called rich. Roam in Sussex.

BARTON. Lower Wiltshire.

BLACK. Hampshire.

BOSVILLE (A). Generally spread, but are specially to be found in
Devonshire. I have found several fine specimens of real Romanys among
the American Bosvilles. In Romany, ***Chumomishto***, that is, Buss (or
Kiss) well.

BROADWAY (A). Somerset.

BUCKLAND. In Gloucestershire, but abounding over England. Sometimes
called ***Chokamengro***, that is Tailor.

BURTON (A). Wiltshire.

CHAPMAN (A). Half-blood, and are commonly spoken of as a rich clan.
Travel all over England.

CHILCOTT (vul. CHILCOCK).

CLARKE. Half-blood. Portsmouth.

COOPER (A). Chiefly found in Berkshire and Windsor. In Romany, *Vardo mescro*.

DAVIES.

DICKENS. Half-blood.

DIGHTON. Blackheath.

DRAPER. Hertfordshire.

FINCH.

FULLER. Hardly half-blood, but talk Romany.

GRAY. Essex. In Romany, *Gry*, or horse.

HARE (A). Chiefly in Hampshire.

HAZARD. Half-blood. Windsor.

HERNE. Oxfordshire and London. "Of this name there are," says Borrow (Romano Lavo-Lil), "two gypsy renderings: (1.) Rosar-mescro or Ratzie-mescro, that is, *duck*-fellow; the duck being substituted for the *heron*, for which there is no word in Romany, this being done because there is a resemblance in the sound of Heron and Herne. (2.) Balor-engre, or Hairy People, the translator having confounded Herne with Haaren, Old English for hairs."

HICKS. Half-blood. Berkshire.

HUGHES. Wiltshire.

INGRAHAM (A). Wales and Birmingham, or in the Kalo tem or Black Country.

JAMES. Half-blood.

JENKINS. Wiltshire.

JONES. Half-blood. Headquarters at Battersea, near London.

LEE (A). The same in most respects as the Smiths, but are even more widely extended. I have met with several of the most decided type of pure-blooded, old-fashioned gypsies among Lees in America. They are sometimes among themselves called *purum*, a *lee-k*, from the fancied resemblance of the words.

LEWIS. Hampshire.

LOCKE. Somerset and Gloucestershire.

LOVEL. Known in Romany as Kamlo, or Kamescro, that is, lover. London, but are found everywhere.

LOVERIDGE. Travel in Oxfordshire; are in London at Shepherd's Bush.

MARSHALL. As much Scotch as English, especially in Dumfriesshire and Galloway, in which latter region, in Saint Cuthbert's church-yard, lies buried the "old man" of the race, who died at the age of one hundred and seven. In Romany Makkado-tan-engree, that is, Fellows of the Marshes. Also known as Bungoror, cork-fellows and Chikkenemengree, china or earthenware (lit. dirt or clay) men, from their cutting corks, and peddling pottery, or mending china.

MATTHEWS. Half-blood. Surrey.

NORTH.

PETULENGRO, or SMITH. The Romany name Petulengro means Master of the Horseshoe; that is, Smith. The gypsy who made this list declared that he had been acquainted with Jasper Petulengro, of Borrow's Lavengro, and that he died near Norwich about sixty years ago. The Smiths are general as travelers, but are chiefly to be found in the East of England.

PIKE. Berkshire.

PINFOLD, or PENFOLD. Half and quarter blood. Widely extended, but most at home in London.

ROLLIN (ROLAND?). Half-blood. Chiefly about London.

SCAMP. Chiefly in Kent. A small clan. Mr. Borrow derives this name from the Sanskrit Ksump, to go. I trust that it has not a more recent and purely English derivation.

SHAW.

SMALL (A). Found in West England, chiefly in Somerset and Devonshire.

STANLEY (A). One of the most extended clans, but said to be chiefly found in Devonshire. They sometimes call themselves in joke Beshalay, that is, Sit-Down, from the word ***stan***, suggesting standing up in connection with lay. Also Bangor, or Baromescre, that is, Stone (stan) people. Thus "Stony-lea" was probably their first name. Also called Kashtengrees, Woodmen, from the New Forest.

TAYLOR. A clan described as *diddikai*, or half-bloods. Chiefly in London. This clan should be the only one known as *Chokamengro*.

TURNER.

WALKER. Half-blood. Travel about Surrey.

WELLS (A). Half-blood. Somerset.

WHARTON. WORTON. I have only met the Whartons in America.

WHEELER. Pure and half-blood. Battersea.

WHITE.

"Adre o Lavines tem o Romanies see WOODS, ROBERTS, WILLIAMS, and JONES.
In Wales the gypsies are Woods, Roberts, Williams, and Jones." {307a}

CHARACTERISTICS. {307b}

Of these gypsies the BAILIES are fair.

The BIRDS are in Norfolk and Suffolk.

The BLACKS are dark, stout, and strong.

The BOSVILLES are rather short, fair, stout, and heavy.

The BROADWAYS are fair, of medium height and good figures.

The BUCKLANDS are thin, dark, and tallish.

The BUNCES travel in the South of England.

The BURTONS are short, dark, and very active.

The CHAPMANS are fair.

The CLARKES are fair and well-sized men.

The COOPERS are short, dark, and very active.

The DIGHTONS are very dark and stout.

The DRAPERS are very tall and large and dark.

The FAAS are at Kirk Yetholm, in Scotland.

The GRAYS are very large and fair.

The GREENES are small and dark.

The GREGORIES range from Surrey to Suffolk.

The HARES are large, stout, and dark.

The HAZARDS are tall and fair.

The HERNES (Herons) are very large and dark.

The HICKS are very large, strong, and fair.

The HUGHES are short, stubby, and dark.

The INGRAHAMS are fair and all of medium height.

The JENKINS are dark, not large, and active.

The JONES are fair and of middling height.

The LANES are fair and of medium height.

The LEES are dark, tall, and stout.

The LEWIS are dark and of medium height.

The LIGHTS are half-bloods, and travel in Middlesex.

The LOCKES are shortish, dark, and large.

The LOVELLS are dark and large.

The MACES are about Norwich.

The MATTHEWS are thick, short, and stout, fair, and good fighters.

The MILLERS are at Battersea.

NORTH. Are to be found at Shepherd's Bush.

The OLIVERS are in Kent.

The PIKES are light and very tall.

The PINFOLDS are light, rather tall, not heavy. (Are really a Norfolk family. F. Groome.)

The ROLANDS are rather large and dark.

The SCAMPS are very dark and stout.

The SHAWS travel in Middlesex.

The SMALLS are tall, stout, and fair.

The SMITHS are dark, rather tall, slender, and active.

The STANLEYS are tall, dark, and handsome.

The TAYLORS are short, stout, and dark.

The TURNERS are also in Norfolk and Suffolk.

The WALKERS are stout and fair.

The WELLS are very light and tall.

The WHEELERS are thin and fair.

The WHITES are short and light.

The YOUNGS are very dark. They travel in the northern counties, and belong both to Scotland and England.

* * * * *

The following is a collection of the more remarkable "fore" or Christian names of Romanys:--

MASCULINE NAMES.

Opi Boswell.

Wanselo, or Anselo. I was once of the opinion that this name was
originally Lancelot, but as Mr. Borrow has found Wentzlow, *i.e.*,
Wenceslas, in England, the latter is probably the original. I have found
it changed to Onslow, as the name painted on a Romany van in Aberystwith,
but it was pronounced Anselo.

Pastor-rumis.

Spico.

Jineral, *i.e.*, General Cooper.

Horferus and Horfer. Either Arthur or Orpheus. His name was then
changed to Wacker-doll, and finally settled into Wacker.

Plato or Platos Buckland.

Wine-Vinegar Cooper. The original name of the child bearing this
extraordinary name was Owen. He died soon after birth, and was in
consequence always spoken of as Wine-Vinegar,--Wine for the joy which his
parents had at his birth, and Vinegar to signify their grief at his loss.

Gilderoy Buckland. Silvanus Boswell.

Lancelot Cooper. Sylvester, Vester, Wester, Westarus and 'Starus.

Oscar Buckland.

Dimiti Buckland. Liberty.

Piramus Boswell. Goliath.

Reconcile. Octavius.

Justerinus. Render Smith.

Faunio.

Shek-esu. I am assured on good authority that a gypsy had a child baptized by this name.

Artaros. Sacki.

Culvato (Claude). Spysell.

Divervus. Spico.

Lasho, *i.e.*, Louis.

Vesuvius. I do not know whether any child was actually called by this burning cognomen, but I remember that a gypsy, hearing two gentlemen talking about Mount Vesuvius, was greatly impressed by the name, and consulted with them as to the propriety of giving it to his little boy.

Wisdom. Loverin.

Inverto. Mantis.

Studaveres Lovel. Happy Boswell.

FEMININE NAMES.

Selinda, Slinda, Linda, Slindi. Delilah.

Mia. Prudence.

Mizelia, Mizelli, Mizela. Providence.

Lina. Eve.

Pendivella. Athaliah.

Jewranum, *i.e.*, Geranium. Gentilla, Gentie.

Virginia. Synfie. Probably Cynthia.

Suby, Azuba. Sybie. Probably from Sibyl.

Isaia.

Richenda. Canairis.

Kiomi. Fenella.

Liberina. Floure, Flower, Flora.

Malindi. Kisaiya.

Otchame. Orlenda.

Renee. Reyora, Regina.

Sinaminta. Syeira. Probably Cyra.

Y-yra or Yeira. Truffeni.

Delira, Deleera. Ocean Solis.

Marili Stanley. Penelli. Possibly from Fenella.

Britannia.

Glani. Segel Buckland.

Zuba. Morella Knightly.

Sybarini Cooper. Eza.

Esmeralda Locke. Lenda.

Penti. Collia.

Reservi. This extraordinary name was derived from a reservoir, by which some gypsies were camped, and where a child was born.

Lementina. Casello (Celia).

Rodi. Catseye.

Alabina. Trainette.

Dosia. Perpinia.

Lavi. Dora.

Silvina. Starlina.

Richenda. Bazena.

Marbelenni. Bena.

Ashena. Ewri.

Vashti. Koket.

Youregh. Lusho.

GYPSY STORIES IN ROMANY, WITH TRANSLATION.

MERLINOS TE TRINALI.

"Miro koko, pen mandy a rinkeno gudlo?"

Avali miri chavi. Me 'tvel pen tute dui te shyan trin, vonka tute 'atches sar pukeno. Shun amengi. Yeckorus adre o Lavines tem sos a boro chovihan, navdo Merlinos. Gusvero mush sos Merlinos, buti seeri covva yuv asti kair. Jindas yuv ta pur yeck jivnipen adre o waver, saster adre o rupp, te o rupp adre sonakai. Fino covva sos adovo te sos miro. Te longoduro fon leste jivdes a bori chovihani, Trinali sos lakis nav. Boridiri chovihani sos Trinali, buti manushe seerdas yoi, buti ryor purdas yoi adre mylia te balor, te ne kesserdas yeck haura pa sar lender dush.

Yeck divvus Merlinos lias lester chovihaneskro ran te jas aduro ta latcher i chovihani te pessur laki drovan pa sar lakis wafropen. Te pa adovo tacho divvus i rani Trinali shundas sa Merlinos boro ruslo sorelo chovihan se, te pendas, "Sossi ajafra mush? Me dukkerava leste or yuv tevel mer mande, s'up mi o beng! me shom te seer leste. Mukkamen dikk savo lela kumi shunaben, te savo se o jinescrodiro?" Te adoi o Merlinos jas apre o dromus, sarodivvus akonyo, sarja adre o kamescro dud, te Trinali jas adre o wesh sarja adre o ratinus, o tam, o kalopen, o shure, denne yoi sos chovihani. Kennasig, yan latcherde yeckawaver, awer Merlinos ne jindas yoi sos Trinali, te Trinali ne jindas adovo manush se Merlinos. Te yuv sos buti kamelo ke laki, te yoi apopli; kennasig yandui ankairde ta kam yeckawaver butidiro. Vonka yeck jinella adovo te o waver jinella lis, kek boro chirus tvel i dui sosti jinavit. Merlinos te Trinali pende "me kamava tute," sig ketenes, te chumerde yeckawaver, te beshde alay rikkerend adre o simno pelashta te rakkerde kushto bak.

Te adenna Merlinos pukkerdas laki, yuv jas ta dusher a buti wafodi chovihani, te Trinali pendas lesko o simno covva, sa yoi sos ruzno ta kair o simno keti a boro chovihano. Te i dui ankairede ta manger yeckawaver ta mukk o covva ja, te yoi te yuv shomas atrash o nasherin lende pireno te pireni. Awer Merlinos pendas, "Mandy sovahalldom pa o kam ta pur laki pa sar lakis jivaben adre o waves truppo." Te yoi ruvvedas te pendas, "Sovahalldas me pa o chone ta pur adovo chovihano adre a wavero, sim's tute." Denna Merlinos putcherdas, "Sasi lesters nav?" Yoi pendas, "Merlinos." Yuv rakkeredas palall, "Me shom leste, sasi tiro nav?" Yoi shelledas avri, "Trinali!"

Kenna vanka chovihanis sovahallan chumeny apre o kam te i choni, yan
sosti keravit or mer. Te denna Merlinos pendas, "Jinesa tu sa ta kair
akovo pennis sar kushto te tacho?" "Kekker miro kamlo pireno," pendas i
chori chovihani sa yoi ruvdas." "Denna me shom kumi jinescro, ne tute,"
pendas Merlinos. "Shukar te kushto covva se akovo, miri romni. Me bevel
pur tute adre mande, te mande adre tute. Te vonka mendui shom romadi
mendui tevel yeck."

Sa yeck mush ta divvus kenna penella yoi siggerdas leste, te awavero pens
yuv siggerdas laki. Ne jinava me miri kameli. Ne dikkdas tu kekker a
dui sherescro haura? Avail! Wusser lis uppar, te vanka lis pellalay
pukk amengy savo rikk se alay. Welsher pendas man adovo. Welsheri
pennena sarja tachopen.

MERLIN AND TRINALI.

"My uncle, tell me a pretty story!"

Yes, my child. I will tell you two, and perhaps three, if you keep very
quiet. Listen to me. Once in Wales there was a great wizard named
Merlin. Many magic things he could do. He knew how to change one living
being into another, iron into silver, and silver into gold. A fine thing
that would be if it were mine. And afar from him lived a great witch.
Trinali was her name. A great witch was Trinali. Many men did she
enchant, many gentlemen did she change into asses and pigs, and never
cared a copper for all their sufferings.

One day Merlin took his magic rod, and went afar to find the witch, and
pay her severely for all her wickedness. And on that very [true] day the

lady Trinali heard how Merlin was [is] a great, powerful wizard, and said, "What sort of a man is this? I will punish him or he shall kill me, deuce help me! I will bewitch him. Let us see who has the most cleverness and who is the most knowing." And then Merlin went on the road all day alone, always in sunshine; and Trinali went in the forest, always in the shade, the darkness, the gloom, for she was a black witch. Soon they found one another, but Merlin did not know [that] she was Trinali, and Trinal, did not know that man was [is to be] Merlin. And he was very pleasant to her, and she to him again. Very soon the two began to love one another very much. When one knows that and the other knows it, both will soon know it. Merlin and Trinali said "I love thee" both together, and kissed one another, and sat down wrapped in the same cloak, and conversed happily.

Then Merlin told her he was going to punish a very wicked witch; and Trinali told him the same thing, how she was bold [daring] to do the same thing to a great wizard. And the two began to beg one another to let the thing go, and she and he were afraid of losing lover and sweetheart. But Merlin said, "I swore by the sun to change her for her whole life into another form" [body]; and she wept and said, "I swore by the moon to change that wizard into another [person] even as you did." Then Merlin inquired, "What is his name?" She said, "Merlin." He replied, "I am he; what is your name?" She cried aloud, "Trinali."

Now when witches swear anything on the sun or the moon, they must do it or die. Then Merlin said, "Do you know how to make this business all nice and right?" "Not at all, my dear love," said the poor witch, as she wept. "Then I am cleverer than you," said Merlin. "An easy and nice thing it is, my bride. For I will change you into me, and myself into you. And when we are married we two will be one."

So one man says nowadays that she conquered him, and another that he conquered her. I do not know [which it was], my dear. Did you ever see a two-headed halfpenny? *Yes*? Throw it up, and when it falls down ask me which side is under. A Welsher told me that story. Welshers always tell the truth.

O PUV-SUVER.

Yeckorus sims buti kedivvus, sos rakli, te yoi sos kushti partanengri, te yoi astis kair a rinkeno plachta, yeck sar divvus. Te covakai chi kamdas rye butidiro, awer yeck divvus lakis pireno sos stardo adre staruben. Te vonka yoi shundas lis, yoi hushtiedas apre te jas keti krallis te mangerdas leste choruknes ta mukk lakis pireno ja piro. Te krallis patserdas laki tevel yoi kairdas leste a rinkeno plachta, yeck sar divvus pa kurikus, hafta plachta pa hafta divvus, yuv tvel ferdel leste, te de leste tachaben ta ja 'vri. I tani rani siggerdas ta keravit, te pa shov divvus yoi taderedas adrom, kushti zi, pa lis te sarkon chirus adre o shab yoi bitcherdas plachta keta krallis. Awer avella yeck divvus yoi sos kinlo, te pendes yoi nei kamdas kair butsi 'dovo divvus si sos brishnu te yoi nestis shiri a sappa dre o kamlo dud. Adenn' o krallis pendas te yoi nestis kair butsi hafta divvus lava lakis pireno, o rye sosti hatch staramescro te yoi ne mukkdas kamaben adosta pa leste. Te i rakli sos sa hunnalo te tukno dre lakis zi yoi merdas o ruvvin te lias puraben adre o puv-suver. Te keti divvus kenna yoi pandella apre lakris tavia, vonka kam peshella, te i cuttor pani tu dikess' apre lende shan o panni fon lakis yakka yoi ruvdas pa lakris pireno.

Te tu vel hatch kaulo yeck lilieskro divvus tu astis nasher sar o kairoben fon o chollo kurikus, miri chavi. Tu peness' tu kamess' to shun waveri gudli. Sar tacho. Me tevel puker tute rinkno gudlo apre kali foki. Repper tute sarkon me penava sa me repper das lis fon miro babus.

THE SPIDER. {317}

Once there was a girl, as there are many to-day, and she was a good
needle-worker, and could make a beautiful cloak in one day. And that
[there] girl loved a gentleman very much; but one day her sweetheart was
shut up in prison, and when she heard it she hastened and went to the
king, and begged him humbly to let her love go free. And the king
promised her if she would make him a fine cloak,--one every day for a
week, seven cloaks for seven days,--he would forgive him, and give him
leave to go free. The young lady hastened to do it, and for six days she
worked hard [lit. pulled away] cheerfully at it, and always in the
evening she sent a cloak to the king. But it came [happened] one day
that she was tired, and said [that] she did not wish to work because it
was rainy, and she could not dry or bleach the cloth [?] in the sunlight.
Then the king said that if she could not work seven days to get her lover
the gentleman must remain imprisoned, for she did not love him as she
should [did not let love enough on him]. And the maid was so angry and
vexed in her heart [or soul] that she died of grief, and was changed into
a spider. And to this day she spreads out her threads when the sun
shines, and the dew-drops which you see on them are the tears which she
has wept for her lover.

If you remain idle one summer day you may lose a whole week's work, my
dear. You say that you would like to hear more stories! All right. I
will tell you a nice story about lazy people. {317b} Remember all I tell
you, as I remembered it from my grandfather.

GORGIO, KALO-MANUSH, TE ROM.

Yeckorus pa ankairoben, kon i manushia nanei lavia, o boro Duvel jas
pirian. Sa si asar? Shun miri chavi, me givellis tute:--

> Buti beshia kedivrus kenna
> Adre o tem ankairoben,
> O boro Duvel jas 'vri aja,
> Ta dikk i mushia miraben.

Sa yuv pirridas, dikkdas trin mushia pash o dromescro rikk, hatchin keti
chomano mush te vel de lendis navia, te len putcherde o boro Duvel ta
navver lende. Dordi, o yeckto mush sos pano, te o boro Duvel pukkerdas
kavodoi, "Gorgio." Te yuv sikkerdas leste kokero keti dovo, te suderdas
leste buti kameli sa jewries, te rinkeni rudaben, te jas *gorgeous*. Te
o wavescro geero sos kalo sa skunya, te o boro Duvel pendas, "Nigger!" te
yuv *nikkeredas* adrom, sa sujery te muzhili, te yuv se *nikkerin* sarja
keti kenna, adre o kamescro dud, te yuv's kalo-kalo ta kair butsi, nanei
tu serbers leste keti lis, te tazzers lis. Te o trinto mush sos brauuo,
te yuv beshdas pukeno, tuvin leste's swagler, keti o boro Duvel
rakkerdas, "Rom!" te adenna o mush hatchedas apre, te pendas buti kamelo,
"Parraco Rya tiro kushtaben; me te vel mishto piav tiro sastopen!" Te
jas romeli a *roamin* langs i lescro romni, te kekker dukkerdas lester
kokerus, ne kesserdas pa chichi fon adennadoi keti kenna, te jas adral o
sweti, te kekker hatchedas pukenus, te nanei hudder ta keravit ket' o
boro Duvel penell' o lav. Tacho adovo se sa tiri yakka, miri kamli.

GORGIO, {319a} BLACK MAN, AND GYPSY.

Once in the creation, when men had no names, the Lord went walking. How was that? Listen, my child, I will sing it to you:--

> Many a year has passed away
> Since the world was first begun,
> That the great Lord went out one day
> To see how men's lives went on.

As he walked along he saw three men by the roadside, waiting till some man would give them names; and they asked the Lord to name them. See! the first man was white, and the Lord called him Gorgio. Then he adapted himself to that name, and adorned himself with jewelry and fine clothes, and went **gorgeous**. And the other man was black and the Lord called him Nigger, and he lounged away [**nikker**, to lounge, loiter; an attempted pun], so idle and foul; and he is always lounging till now in the sunshine, and he is too lazy [**kalo-kalo**, black-black, or lazy-lazy, that is, too black or too lazy] to work unless you compel and punish him. And the third man was brown, and he sat quiet, smoking his pipe, till the Lord said, Rom! [gypsy, or "roam"]; and then that man arose and said, very politely, "Thank you, Lord, for your kindness. I'd be glad to drink your health." And he went, Romany fashion, a-roaming {319b} with his romni [wife], and never troubled himself about anything from that time till to-day, and went through the world, and never rested and never wished to until the Lord speaks the word. That is all as true as your eyes, my dear!

YAG-BAR TE SASTER.
SA O KAM SOS ANKERDO.

"Pen mandy a waver gudlo trustal o ankairoben!"

Ne shomas adoi, awer shundom buti apa lis fon miro babus. Foki pende
mengy sa o chollo-tem {320} sos kerdo fon o kam, awer i Romany chalia
savo keren sar chingernes, pen o kam sos kerdo fon o boro tem. Wafedo
gry se adovo te nestis ja sigan te anpali o kushto drom. Yeckorus 'dre o
puro chirus, te kenna, sos a bori pureni chovihani te kerdas sirini
covvas, te jivdas sar akonyo adre o heb adre o ratti. Yeck divvus yoi
latchedas yag-bar adre o puv, te tilldas es apre te pukkeredas lestes nav
pale, "Yag-bar." Te pash a bittus yoi latchedas a bitto kushto-saster,
te haderdas lis apre te putchedas lestis nav, te lis rakkerdas apopli,
"Saster." Chivdasi dui 'dre lakis putsi, te pendas Yag-bar, "Tu sosti
rummer o rye, Saster!" Te yan kerdavit, awer yeck divvus i dui ankairede
ta chinger, te Saster des lestis juva Yag-bar a tatto-yek adre o yakk, te
kairedas i chingari ta mukker avri, te hotcher i puri juva's putsi. Sa
yoi wusserdas hotcherni putsi adre o hev, te pendas lis ta kessur adrom
keti avenna o mush sari juva kun kekker chingerd chichi. I chingari shan
staria, te dovo yag se o kam, te lis nanei jillo avri keti kenna, te lis
tevel hotcher anduro buti beshia pa sar jinova me keti chingerben. Tacho
si? Ne shomas adoi.

FLINT AND STEEL.
OR HOW THE SUN WAS CREATED.

"Tell me another story about the creation!"

I was not there at the time, but I heard a great deal about it from my
grandfather. All he did there was to turn the wheel. People tell me
that the world was made from the sun, but gypsies, who do everything all
contrary, say that the sun was made from the earth. A bad horse is that
which will not travel either way on a road. Once in the old time, as
[there may be] now, was a great old witch, who made enchantments, and
lived all alone in the sky in the night. One day she found a flint in a
field, and picked her up, and the stone told her that her name was Flint.
And after a bit she found a small piece of steel, and picked him up, and
asked his name, and he replied, "Steel" [iron]. She put the two in her
pocket, and said to Flint, "You must marry Master Steel." So they did,
but one day the two began to quarrel, and Steel gave his wife Flint a hot
one [a severe blow] in the eye, and made sparks fly, and set fire to the
old woman's pocket. So she threw the burning pocket up into the sky, and
told it to stay there until a man and his wife who had never quarreled
should come there. The sparks [from Flint's eye] are the stars, and the
fire is the sun, and it has not gone out as yet, and it will burn on many
a year, for all I know to the contrary. Is it true? I was not there.

O MANUSH KON JIVDAS ADRE O CHONE (SHONE).

"Pen mandy a waver gudlo apa o chone?"

Avail miri deari. Adre o puro chirus butidosta manushia jivvede
kushti-bakeno 'dre o chone, sar chichi ta kair awer ta rikker ap o yag so
kerela o dud. Awer, amen i foki jivdas buti wafodo muleno manush, kon
dusherdas te lias witchaben atut sar i waveri deari manushia, te yuv
kairedas lis sa's ta shikker lende sar adrom, te chivdas len avri o
chone. Te kenna o sig o i foki shan jillo, yuv pendas: "Kenna akovi

dinneli juckalis shan jillo, me te vel jiv mashni te kushto, sar
akonyus." Awer pash o bitto, o yag ankairdas ta hatch alay, te akovo
geero latchdas se yuv ne kamdas ta hatch adre o ratti te merav shillino,
yuv sosti ja sarja pa kosht. Te kanna i waveri foki shanas adoi, yan ne
kerden o rikkaben te wadderin i kashta adre o divvusko chirus, awer kenna
asti lel lis sar apre sustis pikkia, sar i ratti, te sar o divvus. Sa i
foki akai apre o chollo-tem dikena adovo manush keti divvus kenna, sar
pordo o koshter te bittered, te muserd te gumeri, te guberin keti leskro
noko kokero, te kunerin akonyus pash lestis yag. Te i chori mushia te
yuv badderedas adrom, yul [yan] jassed sar atut te trustal o hev akai, te
adoi, te hatchede up buti pa lender kokeros; te adovi shan i starya, te
chirkia, te bitti dudapen tu dikessa sarakai.

"Se adovo sar tacho?" Akovi se kumi te me jinova. Awer kanna sa tu
penessa me astis dikk o manush dre o chone savo rikkela kasht apre lestes
dumo, yuv sosti keravit ta chiv adre o yag, te yuv ne tevel dukker lestes
kokero ta kair adovo te yuv sus rumado or lias palyor, sa lis se kammaben
adosta o mush chingerd lestis palya te nassered lende sar anduro. Tacho.

THE MAN WHO LIVED IN THE MOON.

"Tell me another story about the moon."

Yes, my dear. In the old time many men lived happily in the moon, with
nothing to do but keep up the fire which makes the light. But among the
folk lived a very wicked, obstinate man, who troubled and hated all the
other nice [dear] people, and he managed it so as to drive them all away,
and put them out of the moon. And when the mass of the folk were gone,
he said, "Now those stupid dogs have gone, I will live comfortably and
well, all alone." But after a bit the fire began to burn down, and that

man found that if he did not want to be in the darkness [night] and die
of cold he must go all the time for wood. And when the other people were
there, they never did any carrying or splitting wood in the day-time, but
now he had to take it all on his shoulders, all night and all day. So
the people here on our earth see that man to this day all burdened [full]
of wood, and bitter and grumbling to himself, and lurking alone by his
fire. And the poor people whom he had driven away went all across and
around heaven, here and there, and set up in business for themselves, and
they are the stars and planets and lesser lights which you see all about.

ROMANY TACHIPEN.

Taken down accurately from an old gypsy. Common dialect, or
"half-and-half" language.

"Rya, tute kams mandy to pukker tute the tachopen--awo? Se's a boro or a
kusi covva, mandy'll rakker tacho, s'up mi-duvel, apre mi meriben, bengis
adre man'nys see if mandy pens a bitto huckaben! An' sa se adduvvel?
Did mandy ever chore a kani adre mi jiv? and what do the Romany chals
kair o' the poris, 'cause kekker ever dikked chichi pash of a Romany tan?
Kek rya,--mandy *never* chored a kani an' adre sixty beshes kenna 'at
mandy's been apre the drumyors, an' sar dovo chirus mandy never dikked or
shuned or jinned of a Romany chal's chorin yeck. What's adduvel tute
pens?--that Petulengro kaliko divvus penned tute yuv rikkered a
yagengeree to muller kanis! Avail rya--tacho se aja--the mush penned
adre his kokero see *weshni* kanis. But kek *kairescro* kanis. Romanis
kekker chores lendy."

GYPSY TRUTH.

"Master, you want me to tell you all the truth,--yes? If it's a big or a little thing, I'll tell the truth, so help me God, upon my life! The devil be in my soul if I tell the least lie! And what is it? Did I ever in all my life steal a chicken? and what do the gypsies do with the feathers, because nobody ever saw any near a gypsy tent? Never, sir,--I *never* stole a chicken; and in all the sixty years that I've been on the roads, in all that time I never saw or heard or knew of a gypsy's stealing one. What's that you say?--that Petulengro told you yesterday that he carried a gun to kill *chickens*! Ah yes, sir,--that is true, too. The man meant in his heart wood chickens [that is, pheasants]. But not *domestic* chickens. Gypsies never steal *them*." {324}

CHOVIHANIPEN.

"Miri diri bibi, me kamava butidiro tevel chovihani. Kamava ta dukker geeris te ta jin kunjerni cola. Tu sosti sikker mengi sarakovi."

"Oh miri kamli! vonka tu vissa te vel chovihani, te i Gorgie jinena lis, tu lesa buti tugnus. Sar i chavi tevel shellavri, te kair a gudli te wusser baria kanna dikena tute, te shyan i bori foki merena tute. Awer kushti se ta jin garini covva, kushti se vonka chori churkni juva te sar i sweti chungen' apre, jinela sa ta kair lende wafodopen ta pessur sar lenghis dush. Te man tevel sikker tute chomany chovihaneskes. Shun! Vonka tu kamesa pen o dukkerin, lesa tu sar tiro man {325} ta latcher ajafera a manush te manushi lis se. De lende o yack, chiv lis drovan opa lakis yakka tevel se rakli. Vonka se pash trasherdo yoi tevel pen buti

talla jinaben. Kanna tu sos kedo lis sorkon cherus tu astis risser buti
dinneli chaia sa tav trustal tiro angushtri. Kenna-sig tiri yakka dikena
pensa sappa, te vonka tu shan hoini tu tevel dikk pens' o puro beng. O
pashno covva miri deari se ta jin sa ta plasser, te kamer, te masher
foki. Vanka rakli lela chumeni kek-siglo adre lakis mui, tu sastis pen
laki adovo sikerela buti bak. Kanna lela lulli te safrani balia, pen
laki adovo se tatcho sigaben yoi sasti lel buti sonakei. Kanna lakis
koria wena ketenes, dovo sikerela yoi tevel ketni buti barveli rya. Pen
sarja vonka tu dikesa o latch apre lakis cham, talla lakis kor, te
vaniso, adovos sigaben yoi tevel a bori rani. Ma kessur tu ki lo se,
'pre o truppo te pre o bull, pen laki sarja o latch adoi se sigaben o
boridirines. Hammer laki apre. Te dikessa tu yoi lela bitti wastia te
bitti piria, pen laki trustal a rye ko se divius pa rinkeni piria, te sa
o rinkeno wast anela kumi bacht te rinkno mui. Hammerin te kamerin te
masherin te shorin shan o pash o dukkerin. Se kek rakli te kekno mush
adre mi duvel's chollo-tem savo ne se boino te hunkari pa chomani, te si
tu astis latcher sa se tu susti lel lender wongur. Stastis, latcher sar
o rakkerben apre foki.

"Awer miri bibi, adovos sar hokkanipen. Me kamava buti ta sikker tachni
chovihanipen. Pen mandy si nanei tachi chovahanis, te sa yol dikena."

"O tachi chovihani miri chavi, lela yakka pensa chiriclo, o kunsus se
rikkeredo apre pensa bongo chiv. Buti Yahudi, te nebollongeri lena jafri
yakka. Te cho'hani balia shan rikkerdi pa lakis ankairoben te surri, te
adenna risserdi. Vonka Gorgikani cho'hani lena shelni yakka, adulli shan
i trasheni.

"Me penava tuki chomani sirines. Vonka tu latchesa o pori te o sasterni
krafni, te anpali tu latchesa cuttor fon papiros, tu sastis chin apre lis
sar o pori savo tu kamesa, te ha lis te tu lesa lis. Awer tu sasti chin
sar tiro noko ratt. Si tu latchessa pash o lon-doeyav o boro
matcheskro-bar, te o puro curro, chiv lis keti kan, shunesa godli. Tevel

tastis kana pordo chone peshela, besh sar nangi adre lakis dud hefta
ratti, te shundes adre lis, sarrati o gudli te vel tachodiro, te anpale
tu shunesa i feris rakerena sig adosta. Vonka tu keresa hev sar o bar
adre o mulleskri-tan, jasa tu adoi yeck ratti pash a waver te kenna-sig
tu shunesa sa i mulia rakerena. Sorkon-chirus penena ki lovo se garrido.
Sastis lel o bar te risser lis apre o mulleskri-tan, talla hev si kedo.

"Me penava tuki apopli chomani cho'haunes. Le vini o sar covva te
suverena apre o pani, pa lenia, pa doeyav. Te asar i paneskri mullos kon
jivena adre o pani rakkerena keti puveskri chovihanis. Si manush dikela
pano panna, te partan te diklo apre o pani te lela lis, adovo sikela
astis lel a pireni, o yuzhior te o kushtidir o partan se, o kushtidir i
rakli. Si latchesa ran apre o pani, dovo sikela sastis kur tiro wafedo
geero. Chokka or curro apre o pani penela tu tevel sig atch kamelo sar
tiri pireni, te pireno. Te safrani ruzhia pa pani dukerena sonaki, te
pauni, rupp, te loli, kammaben."

"Kana latchesa klisin, dovo se buti bacht. Vonka haderesa lis apre, pen
o manusheskro te rakleskri nav, te yan wena kamlo o tute. Butidir bacht
si lullo dori te tav. Rikker lis, sikela kushti kamaben. Man nasher lis
avri tiro zi miri chavi."

"Nanei, bibi, kekker."

WITCHCRAFT. {327}

"My dear aunt, I wish very much to be a witch. I would like to enchant
people and to know secret things. You can teach me all that."

"Oh, my darling! if you come to be a witch, and the Gentiles know it, you will have much trouble. All the children will cry aloud, and make a noise and throw stones at you when they see you, and perhaps the grown-up people will kill you. But it is nice to know secret things; pleasant for a poor old humble woman whom all the world spits upon to know how to do them evil and pay them for their cruelty. And I *will* teach you something of witchcraft. Listen! When thou wilt tell a fortune, put all thy heart into finding out what kind of a man or woman thou hast to deal with. Look [keenly], fix thy glance sharply, especially if it be a girl. When she is half-frightened, she will tell you much without knowing it. When thou shalt have often done this thou wilt be able to twist many a silly girl like twine around thy fingers. Soon thy eyes will look like a snake's, and when thou art angry thou wilt look like the old devil. Half the business, my dear, is to know how to please and flatter and allure people. When a girl has anything unusual in her face, you must tell her that it signifies extraordinary luck. If she have red or yellow hair, tell her that is a true sign that she will have much gold. When her eyebrows meet, that shows she will be united to many rich gentlemen. Tell her always, when you see a mole on her cheek or her forehead or anything, that is a sign she will become a great lady. Never mind where it is, on her body,--tell her always that a mole or fleck is a sign of greatness. *Praise her up*. And if you see that she has small hands or feet, tell her about a gentleman who is wild about pretty feet, and how a pretty hand brings more luck than a pretty face. Praising and petting and alluring and crying-up are half of fortune-telling. There is no girl and no man in all the Lord's earth who is not proud and vain about something, and if you can find it out you can get their money. If you can, pick up all the gossip about people."

"But, my aunt, that is all humbug. I wish much to learn real witchcraft. Tell me if there are no real witches, and how they look."

"A real witch, my child, has eyes like a bird, the corner turned up like the point of a curved pointed knife. Many Jews and un-Christians have such eyes. And witches' hairs are drawn out from the beginning [roots] and straight, and then curled [at the ends]. When Gentile witches have green eyes they are the most [to be] dreaded.

"I will tell you something magical. When you find a pen or an iron nail, and then a piece of paper, you should write on it with the pen all thou wishest, and eat it, and thou wilt get thy wish. But thou must write all in thy own blood. If thou findest by the sea a great shell or an old pitcher [cup, etc.], put it to your ear: you will hear a noise. If you can, when the full moon shines sit quite naked in her light and listen to it; every night the noise will become more distinct, and then thou wilt hear the fairies talking plainly enough. When you make a hole with a stone in a tomb go there night after night, and erelong thou wilt hear what the dead are saying. Often they tell where money is buried. You must take a stone and turn it around in the tomb till a hole is there.

"I will tell you something more witchly. Observe [take care] of everything that swims on water, on rivers or the sea. For so the water-spirits who live in the water speak to the earth's witches. If a man sees cloth on the water and gets it, that shows he will get a sweetheart; the cleaner and nicer the cloth, the better the maid. If you find a staff [stick or rod] on the water, that shows you will beat your enemy. A shoe or cup floating on the water means that you will soon be loved by your sweetheart. And yellow flowers [floating] on the water foretell gold, and white, silver, and red, love.

"When you find a key, that is much luck. When you pick [lift it] up, utter a male or female name, and the person will become your own. Very lucky is a red string or ribbon. Keep it. It foretells happy love. Do not let this run away from thy soul, my child."

"No, aunt, never."

THE ORIGIN OF THE GYPSIES.

This chapter contains in abridged form the substance of papers on the origin of the gypsies and their language, read before the London Philological Society; also of another paper read before the Oriental Congress at Florence in 1878; and a *resume* of these published in the London *Saturday Review*.

It has been repeated until the remark has become accepted as a sort of truism, that the gypsies are a mysterious race, and that nothing is known of their origin. And a few years ago this was true; but within those years so much has been discovered that at present there is really no more mystery attached to the beginning of these nomads than is peculiar to many other peoples. What these discoveries or grounds of belief are I shall proceed to give briefly, my limits not permitting the detailed citation of authorities. First, then, there appears to be every reason for believing with Captain Richard Burton that the Jats of Northwestern India furnished so large a proportion of the emigrants or exiles who, from the tenth century, went out of India westward, that there is very little risk in assuming it as an hypothesis, at least, that they formed the *Hauptstamm* of the gypsies of Europe. What other elements entered into these, with whom we are all familiar, will be considered presently. These gypsies came from India, where caste is established and callings are hereditary even among out-castes. It is not assuming too much to suppose that, as they evinced a marked aptitude for certain pursuits and an inveterate attachment to certain habits, their ancestors had in these respects resembled them for ages. These pursuits and habits were that

They were tinkers, smiths, and farriers.

They dealt in horses, and were naturally familiar with them.

They were without religion.

They were unscrupulous thieves.

Their women were fortune-tellers, especially by chiromancy.

They ate without scruple animals which had died a natural death, being especially fond of the pig, which, when it has thus been "butchered by God," is still regarded even by prosperous gypsies in England as a delicacy.

They flayed animals, carried corpses, and showed such aptness for these and similar detested callings that in several European countries they long monopolized them.

They made and sold mats, baskets, and small articles of wood.

They have shown great skill as dancers, musicians, singers, acrobats; and it is a rule almost without exception that there is hardly a traveling company of such performers or a theatre, in Europe or America, in which there is not at least one person with some Romany blood.

Their hair remains black to advanced age, and they retain it longer than do Europeans or ordinary Orientals.

They speak an Aryan tongue, which agrees in the main with that of the Jats, but which contains words gathered from other Indian sources. This is a consideration of the utmost importance, as by it alone can we determine what was the agglomeration of tribes in India which formed the Western gypsy.

Admitting these as the peculiar pursuits of the race, the next step
should be to consider what are the principal nomadic tribes of gypsies in
India and Persia, and how far their occupations agree with those of the
Romany of Europe. That the Jats probably supplied the main stock has
been admitted. This was a bold race of Northwestern India, which at one
time had such power as to obtain important victories over the caliphs.
They were broken and dispersed in the eleventh century by Mahmoud, many
thousands of them wandering to the West. They were without religion, "of
the horse, horsey," and notorious thieves. In this they agree with the
European gypsy. But they are not habitual eaters of **mullo balor**, or
"dead pork;" they do not devour everything like dogs. We cannot
ascertain that the Jat is specially a musician, a dancer, a mat and
basket maker, a rope-dancer, a bear-leader, or a peddler. We do not know
whether they are peculiar in India among the Indians for keeping their
hair unchanged to old age, as do pure-blood English gypsies. All of
these things are, however, markedly characteristic of certain different
kinds of wanderers, or gypsies, in India. From this we conclude,
hypothetically, that the Jat warriors were supplemented by other
tribes,--chief among these may have been the Dom,--and that the Jat
element has at present disappeared, and been supplanted by the lower
type.

The Doms are a race of gypsies found from Central India to the far
northern frontier, where a portion of their early ancestry appears as the
Domarr, and are supposed to be pre-Aryan. In "The People of India,"
edited by J. Forbes Watson and J. W. Kaye (India Museum, 1868), we are
told that the appearance and modes of life of the Doms indicate a marked
difference from those of the people who surround them (in Behar). The
Hindus admit their claim to antiquity. Their designation in the Shastras
is Sopuckh, meaning dog-eater. They are wanderers; they make baskets and
mats, and are inveterate drinkers of spirits, spending all their earnings
on it. They have almost a monopoly as to burning corpses and handling

all dead bodies. They eat all animals which have died a natural death, and are particularly fond of pork of this description. "Notwithstanding profligate habits, many of them attain the age of eighty or ninety; and it is not till sixty or sixty-five that their hair begins to get white." The Domarr are a mountain race, nomads, shepherds, and robbers. Travelers speak of them as "gypsies." A specimen which we have of their language would, with the exception of one word, which is probably an error of the transcriber, be intelligible to any English gypsy, and be called pure Romany. Finally, the ordinary Dom calls himself a Dom, his wife a Domni, and the being a Dom, or the collective gypsydom, Domnipana. *D* in Hindustani is found as *r* in English gypsy speech,--*e.g.*, *doi*, a wooden spoon, is known in Europe as *roi*. Now in common Romany we have, even in London,--

Rom . . . A gypsy.

Romni . . . A gypsy wife.

Romnipen . . . Gypsydom.

Of this word *rom* I shall have more to say. It may be observed that there are in the Indian *Dom* certain distinctly-marked and degrading features, characteristic of the European gypsy, which are out of keeping with the habits of warriors, and of a daring Aryan race which withstood the caliphs. Grubbing in filth as if by instinct, handling corpses, making baskets, eating carrion, being given to drunkenness, does not agree with anything we can learn of the Jats. Yet the European gypsies are all this, and at the same time "horsey" like the Jats. Is it not extremely probable that during the "out-wandering" the Dom communicated his name and habits to his fellow-emigrants?

The marked musical talent characteristic of the Slavonian and other European gypsies appears to link them with the Luri of Persia. These are distinctly gypsies; that is to say, they are wanderers, thieves, fortune-tellers, and minstrels. The Shah-Nameh of Firdusi tells us that about the year 420 A.D. Shankal, the Maharajah of India, sent to Behram Gour, a ruler of the Sassanian dynasty in Persia, ten thousand minstrels, male and female, called **Luri**. Though lands were allotted to them, with corn and cattle, they became from the beginning irreclaimable vagabonds. Of their descendants, as they now exist, Sir Henry Pottinger says:--

> "They bear a marked affinity to the gypsies of Europe. {335} They speak a dialect peculiar to themselves, have a king to each troupe, and are notorious for kidnapping and pilfering. Their principal
>
> pastimes are drinking, dancing, and music. . . . They are invariably attended by half a dozen of bears and monkeys that are broke in to perform all manner of grotesque tricks. In each company there are always two or three members who profess . . . modes of divining, which procure them a ready admission into every society."

This account, especially with the mention of trained bears and monkeys, identifies them with the Ricinari, or bear-leading gypsies of Syria (also called Nuri), Turkey, and Roumania. A party of these lately came to England. We have seen these Syrian Ricinari in Egypt. They are unquestionably gypsies, and it is probable that many of them accompanied the early migration of Jats and Doms.

The Nats or Nuts are Indian wanderers, who, as Dr. J. Forbes Watson declares, in "The People of India," "correspond to the European gypsy tribes," and were in their origin probably identical with the Luri. They are musicians, dancers, conjurers, acrobats, fortune-tellers, blacksmiths, robbers, and dwellers in tents. They eat everything, except garlic. There are also in India the Banjari, who are spoken of by travelers as "gypsies." They are traveling merchants or peddlers. Among all these wanderers there is a current slang of the roads, as in England.

This slang extends even into Persia. Each tribe has its own, but the name for the generally spoken *lingua franca* is **Rom**.

It has never been pointed out, however, by any writer, that there is in Northern and Central India a distinct tribe, which is regarded, even by the Nats and Doms and Jats themselves, as peculiarly and distinctly gypsy. There are, however, such wanderers, and the manner in which I became aware of their existence was, to say the least, remarkable. I was going one day along the Marylebone Road when I met a very dark man, poorly clad, whom I took for a gypsy; and no wonder, as his eyes had the very expression of the purest blood of the oldest families. To him I said,--

"*Rakessa tu Romanes*?" (Can you talk gypsy?)

"I know what you mean," he answered in English. "You ask me if I can talk gypsy. I know what those people are. But I'm a Mahometan Hindu from Calcutta. I get my living by making curry powder. Here is my card." Saying this he handed me a piece of paper, with his name written on it: **John Nano**.

"When I say to you, '**Rakessa tu Romanes**?' what does it mean?"

"It means, 'Can you talk Rom?' But *rakessa* is not a Hindu word. It's Panjabi."

I met John Nano several times afterwards and visited him in his lodgings, and had him carefully examined and cross-questioned and pumped by Professor Palmer of Cambridge, who is proficient in Eastern tongues. He conversed with John in Hindustani, and the result of our examination was that John declared he had in his youth lived a very loose life, and belonged to a tribe of wanderers who were to all the other wanderers on the roads in India what regular gypsies are to the English Gorgio hawkers and tramps. These people were, he declared, "the *real* gypsies of India, and just like the gypsies here. People in India called them Trablus, which means Syrians, but they were full-blood Hindus, and not Syrians." And here I may observe that this word Trablus which is thus applied to Syria, is derived from Tripoli. John was very sure that his gypsies were Indian. They had a peculiar language, consisting of words which were not generally intelligible. "Could he remember any of these words?" Yes. One of them was *manro*, which meant bread. Now *manro* is all over Europe the gypsy word for bread. John Nano, who spoke several tongues, said that he did not know it in any Indian dialect except in that of his gypsies. These gypsies called themselves and their language *Rom*. Rom meant in India a real gypsy. And Rom was the general slang of the road, and it came from the Roms or Trablus. Once he had written all his autobiography in a book. This is generally done by intelligent Mahometans. This manuscript had unfortunately been burned by his English wife, who told us that she had done so "because she was tired of seeing a book lying about which she could not read."

Reader, think of losing such a life! The autobiography of an Indian gypsy,--an abyss of adventure and darksome mysteries, illuminated, it may be, with vivid flashes of Dacoitee, while in the distance rumbled the thunder of Thuggism! Lost, lost, irreparably lost forever! And in this book John had embodied a vocabulary of the real Indian Romany dialect. Nothing was wanting to complete our woe. John thought at first that he had lent it to a friend who had never returned it. But his wife remembered burning it. Of one thing John was positive: Rom was as distinctively gypsy talk in India as in England, and the Trablus are the true Romanys of India.

What here suggests itself is, how these Indian gypsies came to be called *Syrian*. The gypsies which roam over Syria are evidently of Indian origin; their language and physiognomy both declare it plainly. I offer as an hypothesis that bands of gypsies who have roamed from India to

Syria have, after returning, been called Trablus, or Syrians, just as I have known Germans, after returning from the father-land to America, to be called Americans. One thing, however, is at least certain. The Rom are the very gypsies of gypsies in India. They are thieves, fortune-tellers, and vagrants. But whether they have or had any connection with the migration to the West we cannot establish. Their language and their name would seem to indicate it; but then it must be borne in mind that the word *rom*, like *dom*, is one of wide dissemination, *dum* being a Syrian gypsy word for the race. And the very great majority of even English gypsy words are Hindi, with an admixture of Persian, and do not belong to a slang of any kind. As in India, *churi* is a knife, *nak* the nose, *balia* hairs, and so on, with others which would be among the first to be furnished with slang equivalents. And yet these very gypsies are *Rom*, and the wife is a *Romni*, and they use words which are not Hindu in common with European gypsies. It is therefore not improbable that in these Trablus, so called through popular ignorance, as they are called Tartars in Egypt and Germany, we have a portion at least of the real stock. It is to be desired that some resident in India would investigate the Trablus. It will probably be found that they are Hindus who have roamed from India to Syria and back again, here and there, until they are regarded as foreigners in both countries.

Next to the word *rom* itself, the most interesting in Romany is *zingan*, or *tchenkan*, which is used in twenty or thirty different forms by the people of every country, except England, to indicate the gypsy. An incredible amount of far-fetched erudition has been wasted in pursuing this philological *ignis fatuus*. That there are leather-working and saddle-working gypsies in Persia who call themselves Zingan is a fair basis for an origin of the word; but then there are Tchangar gypsies of Jat affinity in the Punjab. Wonderful it is that in this war of words no philologist has paid any attention to what the gypsies themselves say about it. What they do say is sufficiently interesting, as it is told in the form of a legend which is intrinsically curious and probably ancient. It is given as follows in "The People of Turkey," by a Consul's Daughter and Wife, edited by Mr. Stanley Lane Poole, London, 1878: "Although the gypsies are not persecuted in Turkey, the antipathy and disdain felt for them evinces itself in many ways, and appears to be founded upon a strange legend current in the country. This legend says that when the gypsy nation were driven out of their country (India), and arrived at Mekran, they constructed a wonderful machine to which a wheel was attached." From the context of this imperfectly told story, it would appear as if the gypsies could not travel farther until this wheel should revolve:--

"Nobody appeared to be able to turn it, till in the midst of their vain efforts some evil spirit presented himself under the disguise of a sage, and informed the chief, whose name was Chen, that the wheel would be made to turn only when he had married his sister Guin. The chief accepted the advice, the wheel turned round, and the name of the tribe after this incident became that of the combined names of the brother and sister, Chenguin, the appellation of all the gypsies of Turkey at the present day."

The legend goes on to state that in consequence of this unnatural marriage the gypsies were cursed and condemned by a Mahometan saint to wander forever on the face of the earth. The real meaning of the myth--for myth it is--is very apparent. ***Chen*** is a Romany word, generally pronounced ***chone***, meaning the moon; {341a} while ***guin*** is almost universally given as ***gan*** or ***kan***. That is to say, Chen-gan or -kan, or Zin-kan, is much commoner than Chen-guin. Now ***kan*** is a common gypsy word for the sun. George Borrow gives it as such, and I myself have heard Romanys call the sun ***kan***, though ***kam*** is commoner, and is usually assumed to be right. Chen-kan means, therefore, moon-sun. And it may be remarked in this connection, that the neighboring Roumanian gypsies, who are nearly allied to the Turkish, have a wild legend stating that the sun was a youth who, having fallen in love with his own sister, was condemned as the sun to wander forever in pursuit of her, after she was turned into the moon. A similar legend exists in Greenland {341b} and in the island of Borneo, and it was known to the old Irish. It is in fact a spontaneous myth, or one of the kind which grow up from causes common to all races. It would be natural, to any imaginative savage, to regard the sun and moon as brother and sister. The next step would be to think of the one as regularly pursuing the other over the heavens, and to this chase an erotic cause would naturally be assigned. And as the pursuit is interminable, the pursuer never attaining his aim, it would be in time regarded as a penance. Hence it comes that in the most distant and different lands we have the same old story of the brother and the sister, just as the Wild Hunter pursues his bride.

It was very natural that the gypsies, observing that the sun and moon were always apparently wandering, should have identified their own nomadic life with that of these luminaries. That they have a tendency to assimilate the idea of a wanderer and pilgrim to that of the Romany, or to *Romanipen*, is shown by the assertion once made to me by an English gypsy that his people regarded Christ as one of themselves, because he was always poor, and went wandering about on a donkey, and was persecuted by the Gorgios. It may be very rationally objected by those to whom the term "solar myth" is as a red rag, that the story, to prove anything, must first be proved itself. This will probably not be far to seek. Everything about it indicates an Indian origin, and if it can be found among any of the wanderers in India, it may well be accepted as the possible origin of the greatly disputed word *zingan*. It is quite as plausible as Dr. Miklosich's very far-fetched derivation from the Acingani,--[Greek text],--an unclean, heretical Christian sect, who dwelt in Phrygia and Lycaonia from the seventh till the eleventh century. The mention of Mekran indicates clearly that the moon story came from India before the Romany could have obtained any Greek name. And if gypsies call themselves or are called Jen-gan, or Chenkan, or Zingan, in the

East, especially if they were so called by Persian poets, it is extremely unlikely that they ever received such a name from the Gorgios of Europe. It is really extraordinary that all the philologists who have toiled to derive the word *zingan* from a Greek or Western source have never reflected that if it was applied to the race at an early time in India or Persia all their speculations must fall to the ground.

One last word of John Nano, who was so called from two similar Indian words, meaning "the pet of his grandfather." I have in my possession a strange Hindu knife, with an enormously broad blade, perhaps five or six inches broad towards the end, with a long handle richly mounted in the purest bronze with a little silver. I never could ascertain till 1 knew him what it had been used for. Even the old ex-king of Oude, when he examined it, went wrong on it. Not so John Nano.

"I know well enough what that knife is. I have seen it before,--years ago. It is very old, and it was long in use; it was the knife used by the public executioner in Bhotan. It is Bhotani."

By the knife hangs the ivory-handled court-dagger which belonged to Francis II. of France, the first husband of Mary Queen of Scots. I wonder which could tell the strangest story of the past!

"It has cut off many a head," said John Nano, "and I have seen it before!"

I do not think that I have gone too far in attaching importance to the gypsy legend of the origin of the word *chen-kan* or *zingan*. It is their own, and therefore entitled to preference over the theories of mere scholars; it is Indian and ancient, and there is much to confirm it. When I read the substance of this chapter before the Philological Society of London, Prince Lucien Bonaparte,--who is beyond question a great philologist, and one distinguished for vast research,--who was in the chair, seemed, in his comments on my paper, to consider this sun and moon legend as frivolous. And it is true enough that German symbolizers have given us the sun myth to such an extent that the mere mention of it in philology causes a recoil. Then, again, there is the law of humanity that the pioneer, the gatherer of raw material, who is seldom collector and critic together, is always assailed. Columbus always gets the chains and Amerigo Vespucci the glory. But the legend itself is undeniably of the gypsies and Indian.

It is remarkable that there are certain catch-words, or test-words, among old gypsies with which they try new acquaintances. One of these is *kekkavi*, a kettle; another, *chinamangri*, a bill-hook, or chopper (also a letter), for which there is also another word. But I have found several very deep mothers in sorcery who have given me the word for sun, *kam*, as a precious secret, but little known. Now the word really is very well known, but the mystery attached to it, as to *chone* or *shule*, the moon, would seem to indicate that at one time these words had a peculiar significance. Once the darkest-colored English gypsy I ever met, wishing to sound the depth of my Romany, asked me for the words for sun and moon, making more account of my knowledge of them than of many more far less known.

As it will interest the reader, I will here give the ballad of the sun and the moon, which exists both in Romany and Roumani, or Roumanian, in the translation which I take from "A Winter in the City of Pleasure" (that is Bucharest), by Florence K. Berger,--a most agreeable book, and one containing two Chapters on the Tzigane, or gypsies.

THE SUN AND THE MOON.

Brother, one day the Sun resolved to marry. During nine years, drawn by nine fiery horses, he had rolled by heaven and earth as fast as the wind or a flying arrow.

But it was in vain that he fatigued his horses. Nowhere could he find a love worthy of him. Nowhere in the universe was one who equaled in beauty his sister Helen, the beautiful Helen with silver tresses.

The Sun went to meet her, and thus addressed her: "My dear little sister Helen, Helen of the silver tresses, let us be betrothed, for we are made for one another.

"We are alike not only in our hair and our features, but also in our beauty. I have locks of gold, and thou hast locks of silver. My face is shining and splendid, and thine is soft and radiant."

"O my brother, light of the world, thou who art pure of all stain, one has never seen a brother and sister married together, because it would be a shameful sin."

At this rebuke the Sun hid himself, and mounted up higher to the throne of God, bent before Him, and spoke:--

"Lord our Father, the time has arrived for me to wed. But, alas! I cannot find a love in the world worthy of me except the beautiful Helen, Helen of the silver hair!"

God heard him, and, taking him by the hand, led him into hell to affright his heart, and then into paradise to enchant his soul.

Then He spake to him, and while He was speaking the Sun began to shine brightly and the clouds passed over:--

"Radiant Sun! Thou who art free from all stain, thou hast been through hell and hast entered paradise. Choose between the two."

The Sun replied, recklessly, "I choose hell, if I may have, for a life, Helen, Helen of the shining silver hair."

The Sun descended from the high heaven to his sister Helen, and ordered preparation for his wedding. He put on her forehead the waving gold chaplet of the bride, he put on her head a royal crown, he put on her body a transparent robe all embroidered with fine pearls, and they all went into the church together.

But woe to him, and woe to her! During the service the lights were extinguished, the bells cracked while ringing, the seats turned themselves upside down, the tower shook to its base, the priests lost their voices, and the sacred robes were torn off their backs.

The bride was convulsed with fear. For suddenly, woe to her! an invisible hand grasped her up, and, having borne her on high, threw her into the sea, where she was at once changed into a beautiful silver fish.

The Sun grew pale and rose into the heaven. Then descending to the west, he plunged into the sea to search for his sister Helen, Helen of the shining silver hair.

However, the Lord God (sanctified in heaven and upon the earth) took the fish in his hand, cast it forth into the sky, and changed it anew into the moon.

Then He spoke. And while God was speaking the entire universe trembled, the peaks of the mountains bowed down, and men shivered with fear.

"Thou, Helen of the long silver tresses, and thou resplendent Sun, who are both free from all stain, I condemn you for eternity to follow each other with your eyes through space, without being ever able to meet or to reach each other upon the road of heaven. Pursue one another for all time in traveling around the skies and lighting up the world."

     * * * * *

Fallen from a high estate by sin, wicked, and therefore wandering: it was with such a story of being penitent pilgrims, doomed for a certain space to walk the earth, that the gypsies entered Europe from India, into Islam and into Christendom, each time modifying the story to suit the religion of the country which they invaded. Now I think that this sun and moon legend is far from being frivolous, and that it conforms wonderfully well with the famous story which they told to the Emperor Sigismund and the Pope and all Europe, that they were destined to wander because they had sinned. When they first entered Europe, the gypsies were full of these legends; they told them to everybody; but they had previously told them to themselves in the form of the Indian sun and moon story. This was the root whence other stories grew. As the tale of the Wandering Jew typifies the Hebrew, so does this of the sun and moon the Romany.

A GYPSY MAGIC SPELL.

There is a meaningless rhyme, very common among children. It is repeated while counting off those who are taking part in a game, and allotting to each a place. It is as follows:--

> "Ekkeri akkery u-kery an
> Fillisi', follasy, Nicolas John
> Queebee-quabee--Irishman.
> Stingle 'em--stangle 'em--buck!"

With a very little alteration in sounds, and not more than children make
of these verses in different places, this may be read as follows:--

> "'Ekkeri, akai-ri, you kair--an.
> Filissin follasy. Nakelas ja'n.
> Kivi, kavi. Irishman.
> Stini--stani--buck!"

This is nonsense, of course, but it is Romany, or gypsy, and may be
translated:--

> "First--here--you begin.
> Castle--gloves. You don't play. Go on!
> *Kivi*--kettle. How are you?
> *Stini*--buck--buck."

The common version of the rhyme begins with:--

> "*One* 'eri--two-ery, ekkeri--an."

But one-ry is the *exact* translation of ekkeri; ek or yek being one.
And it is remarkable that in

> "*Hickory* dickory dock,
> The rat ran up the clock;
> The clock struck *one*,

And down he run,
Hickory dickory dock."

We have hickory or ekkeri again, followed by a significant *one*. It may
be observed that while, the first verses abound in Romany words, I can
find no trace of any in other child-rhymes of the kind. It is also clear
that if we take from the fourth line the *ingle 'em*, *angle 'em*,
evidently added for mere jingle, there remains *stan* or *stani*, "a
buck," followed by the very same word in English.

With the mournful examples of Mr. Bellenden Kerr's efforts to show that
all our old proverbs and tavern signs are Dutch, and Sir William Betham's
Etruscan-Irish, I should be justly regarded as one of the too frequent
seekers for mystery in moonshine if I declared that I positively believed
this to be Romany. Yet it is possible that it contains gypsy words,
especially "fillissi,' follasy," which mean exactly *chateau* and gloves,
and I think it not improbable that it was once a sham charm used by some
Romany fortune-teller to bewilder Gorgios. Let the reader imagine the
burnt-sienna wild-cat eyed old sorceress performing before a credulous
farm-wife and her children the great ceremony of *hakk'ni panki*, which
Mr. Borrow calls *hokkani boro*, but for which there is a far deeper
name,--that of *the great secret*,--which even my best friends among the
Romany tried to conceal from me. This feat is performed by inducing some
woman of largely magnified faith to believe that there is hidden in her
house a magic treasure, which can only be made to come to hand by
depositing in the cellar another treasure, to which it will come by
natural affinity and attraction. "For gold, as you sees, my deari, draws
gold, and so if you ties up all your money in a pocket-handkercher and
leaves it, you'll find it doubled. An' wasn't there the Squire's lady,
and didn't she draw two hundred old gold guineas out of the ground where
they'd laid in a old grave,--and only one guinea she gave me for all my
trouble; an' I hope you'll do better by the poor old gypsy, my deari ---
---."

The gold and all the spoons are tied up,--for, as the enchantress observes, there may be silver too,--and she solemnly repeats over it magical rhymes, while the children, standing around in awe, listen to every word. It is a good subject for a picture. Sometimes the windows are closed, and candles give the only light. The next day the gypsy comes and sees how the charm is working. Could any one look under her cloak he might find another bundle precisely resembling the one containing the treasure. She looks at the precious deposit, repeats her rhyme again, and departs, after carefully charging the housewife that the bundle must not be touched or spoken of for three weeks. "Every word you tell about it, my-deari will be a guinea gone away." Sometimes she exacts an oath on the Bible that nothing shall be said.

Back to the farmer's wife never again. After three weeks another Extraordinary instance of gross credulity appears in the country paper, and is perhaps repeated in a colossal London daily, with a reference to the absence of the school-master. There is wailing and shame in the house,--perhaps great suffering, for it may be that the savings of years have beer swept away. The charm has worked.

But the little sharp-eared children remember it and sing it, and the more meaningless it is in their ears the more mysterious does it sound. And they never talk about the bundle, which when opened was found to contain only sticks, stones, and rags, without repeating it. So it goes from mouth to mouth, until, all mutilated, it passes current for even worse nonsense than it was at first. It may be observed, however,--and the remark will be fully substantiated by any one who knows the language,--that there is a Romany *turn* to even the roughest corners of these rhymes. *Kivi*, *stingli*, *stangli*, are all gypsyish. But, as I have already intimated, this does not appear in any other nonsense verses of the kind. There is nothing of it in

"Intery, mintery, cutery corn"--

or in anything else in Mother Goose. It is alone in its sounds and sense,--or nonsense. But there is not a wanderer of the roads who on hearing it would not explain, "Rya, there's a great deal of Romanes in that ere."

I should also say that the word **na-kelas** or **ne-kelas**, which I here translate differently, was once explained to me at some length by a gypsy as signifying "not speaking," or "keeping quiet."

Now the mystery of mysteries of which I have spoken in the Romany tongue is this. The **hokkani boro**, or great trick, consists of three parts. Firstly, the telling of a fortune, and this is to **pen dukkerin** or **pen durkerin**. The second part is the conveying away of the property, which is to **lel dudikabin**, or to take lightning, possibly connected with the very old English slang term of **bien lightment**. There is evidently a great confusion of words here. And the third is to "**chiv o manzin apre lati**," or to put the oath upon her, which explains itself. When all the deceived are under oath not to utter a word about the trick, the gypsy mother has "a safe thing of it."

The **hokkani boro**, or great trick, was brought by the gypsies from the East. It has been practiced by them all over the world, it is still played every day somewhere. This chapter was written long ago in England. I am now in Philadelphia, and here I read in the "Press" of this city that a Mrs. Brown, whom I sadly and reluctantly believe is the wife of an acquaintance of mine, who walks before the world in other names, was arrested for the same old game of fortune-telling and persuading a simple dame that there was treasure in the house, and all the rest of the grand deception. And Mrs. Brown, good old Mrs. Brown, went to prison, where she will linger until a bribed alderman, or a purchased pardon, or some one of the numerous devices by which justice is evaded in Pennsylvania, delivers her.

Yet it is not a good country, on the whole, for **hokkani boro**, since the people here, especially in the rural districts, have a rough-and-ready way of inflicting justice which interferes sadly with the profits of aldermen and other politicians. Some years ago, in Tennessee, a gypsy woman robbed a farmer by the great trick of all he was worth. Now it is no slander to say that the rural folk of Tennessee greatly resemble Indians in certain respects, and when I saw thousands of them, during the war, mustered out in Nashville, I often thought, as I studied their dark brown faces, high cheek bones, and long straight black hair, that the American is indeed reverting to the aboriginal type. The Tennessee farmer and his neighbors, at any rate, reverted very strongly indeed to the original type when robbed by the gypsies, for they turned out all together, hunted them down, and, having secured the sorceress, burned her alive at the stake. And thus in a single crime and its punishment we have curiously combined a world-old Oriental offense, an European Middle-Age penalty for witchcraft, and the fierce torture of the red Indians.

SHELTA, THE TINKERS' TALK.

"So good a proficient in one quarter of an hour that I can drink with any tinker in his own language during my life."--King Henry the Fourth.

One summer day, in the year 1876, I was returning from a long walk in the beautiful country which lies around Bath, when, on the road near the town, I met with a man who had evidently grown up from childhood into middle age as a beggar and a tramp. I have learned by long experience that there is not a so-called "traveler" of England or of the world, be he beggar, tinker, gypsy, or hawker, from whom something cannot be learned, if one only knows how to use the test-glasses and proper reagents. Most inquirers are chiefly interested in the morals--or immorals--of these nomads. My own researches as regards them are chiefly philological. Therefore, after I had invested twopence in his prospective beer, I addressed him in Romany. Of course he knew a little of it; was there ever an old "traveler" who did not?

"But we are givin' Romanes up very fast,--all of us is," he remarked. "It is a gettin' to be too blown. Everybody knows some Romanes now. But there is *a jib that ain't blown," he remarked reflectively. "Back slang an' cantin' an' rhymin' is grown vulgar, and Italian always* was *the lowest of the lot; thieves* kennick *is genteel alongside of organ-grinder's lingo, you know. Do* you *know anythin' of Italian, sir?"*

"I can rakker *it pretty* flick" (talk it tolerably), was my reply.

"Well I should never a **penned** [thought] sitch a swell gent as you had been down so low in the slums. Now **Romanes** is genteel. I heard there's actilly a book about Romanes to learn it out of. But as for this other jib, its wery hard to talk. It is most all Old Irish, and they calls it Shelter."

This was all that I could learn at that time. It did not impress me much, as I supposed that the man merely meant Old Irish. A year went by, and I found myself at Aberystwith, the beautiful sea-town in Wales, with my friend Professor Palmer--a palmer who has truly been a pilgrim *outre-mer*, even by Galilee's wave, and dwelt as an Arab in the desert. One afternoon we were walking together on that end of the beach which is the antithesis of the old Norman castle; that is, at the other extremity of the town, and by the rocks. And here there was a little crowd, chiefly of young ladies, knitting and novel-reading in the sun, or watching children playing on the sand. All at once there was an alarm, and the whole party fled like partridges, skurrying along and hiding under the lee of the rocks. For a great rock right over our heads was about to be blasted. So the professor and I went on and away, but as we went we observed an eccentric and most miserable figure crouching in a hollow like a little cave to avoid the anticipated falling stones.

"*Dikk o dovo mush adoi a gavverin lester kokero*!" (Look at that man there, hiding himself!) said the professor in Romanes. He wished to call attention to the grotesque figure without hurting the poor fellow's feelings.

"*Yuv's atrash o' ye baryia*" (He is afraid of the stones), I replied.

The man looked up. "I know what you're saying, gentlemen. That's Romany."

"Jump up, then, and come along with us."

He followed. We walked from rock to rock, and over the sand by the sea, to a secluded nook under a cliff. Then, seated around a stone table, we began our conversation, while the ocean, like an importunate beggar, surfed and foamed away, filling up the intervals with its mighty roaring language, which poets only understand or translate:--

> "Thus far, and then no more:"
> Such language speaks the sounding sea
> To the waves upon the shore.

Our new acquaintance was ragged and disreputable. Yet he held in his hand a shilling copy of "Helen's Babies," in which were pressed some fern leaves.

"What do you do for a living?" I asked.

"*Shelkin gallopas* just now," he replied.

"And what is that?"

"Selling ferns. Don't you understand? That's what we call it in *Minklers Thari*. That's tinkers' language. I thought as you knew Romanes you might understand it. The right name for it is *Shelter* or *Shelta*."

Out came our note-books and pencils. So this was the *Shelter* of which I had heard. He was promptly asked to explain what sort of a language it was.

"Well, gentlemen, you must know that I have no great gift for languages. I never could learn even French properly. I can conjugate the verb *etre*,--that is all. I'm an ignorant fellow, and very low. I've been kicked out of the lowest slums in Whitechapel because I was too much of a blackguard for 'em. But I know rhyming slang. Do you know Lord John Russell?"

"Well, I know a little of rhyming, but not that."

"Why, it rhymes to *bustle*."

"I see. *Bustle* is to pick pockets."

"Yes, or anything like it, such as ringing the changes."

Here the professor was "in his plate." He knows perfectly how to ring the changes. It is effected by going into a shop, asking for change for a sovereign, purchasing some trifling article, then, by ostensibly changing your mind as to having the change, so bewilder the shopman as to cheat him out of ten shillings. It is easily done by one who understands it. The professor does not practice this art for the lucre of gain, but he understands it in detail. And of this he gave such proofs to the tramp that the latter was astonished.

"A tinker would like to have a wife who knows as much of that as you do," he remarked. "No woman is fit to be a tinker's wife who can't make ten shillings a day by **glantherin**. **Glantherin** or **glad'herin** is the correct word in Shelter for ringing the changes. As for the language, I believe it's mostly Gaelic, but it's mixed up with Romanes and canting or thieves' slang. Once it was the common language of all the old tinkers. But of late years the old tinkers' families are mostly broken up, and the language is perishing."

Then he proceeded to give us the words in Shelta, or Minklers Thari. They were as follows:--

Shelkin gallopas   Selling ferns.
Soobli, Soobri Brother, friend--a man.
Bewr   Woman.
Gothlin or goch'thlin Child.
Young bewr   Girl.
Durra, or derra   Bread.
Pani   Water (Romany).
Stiff   A warrant (common cant).
Yack   A watch (cant, *i.e.* bull's eye,
       Yack, an eye in Romany).

Mush-faker   Umbrella mender.
Mithani (mithni)   Policeman.
Ghesterman (ghesti) Magistrate.
Needi-mizzlerA tramp.
Dinnessy   Cat.
Stall   Go, travel.
Biyeghin   Stealing.
Biyeg To steal.
Biyeg th'eenik   To steal the thing.
Crack A stick.
Monkery   Country.
Prat   Stop, stay, lodge.
Ned askan   Lodging.
Glantherin (glad'herin)   Money, swindling.

This word has a very peculiar pronunciation.

Sauni or sonniSee.
Strepuck (reepuck)   A harlot.
Strepuck lusk, Luthrum's gothlin   Son of a harlot.
Kurrb yer pee Punch your head or face.
Pee   Face.
Borers and jumpers   Tinkers' tools.
Borers Gimlets.
Jumpers   Cranks.
Ogles Eyes (common slang).
Nyock Head.
Nyock A penny.
Odd   Two.
MidgicA shilling.
Nyo(d)ghee   A pound.
Sai, sy Sixpence.
Charrshom, Cherrshom, TusheroonA crown.

Tre-nyock   Threepence.
Tripo-rauniel A pot of beer.
Thari, Bug   Talk.

Can you thari Shelter? Can you bug Shelta? Can you talk tinkers' language?

Shelter, shelta Tinker's slang.
Larkin Girl.

Curious as perhaps indicating an affinity between the Hindustani *larki*, a girl, and the gypsy *rakli*.

Snips   Scissors (slang).
Dingle fakir   A bell-hanger.
Dunnovans   Potatoes.
Fay (*vulgarly* fee)   Meat.

Our informant declared that there are vulgar forms of certain words.

Gladdher   Ring the changes (cheat in change).

"No minkler would have a bewr who couldn't gladdher."

Reesbin   Prison.
Tre-moon   Three months, a 'drag.'
Rauniel, Runniel   Beer.
Max   Spirits (slang).
Chiv   Knife. (Romany, a pointed knife, *i.e. tongue*.)
Thari   To speak or tell.

"I tharied the soobri I sonnied him." (I told the man I saw him.)

Mushgraw.

Our informant did not know whether this word, of Romany origin, meant, in Shelta, policeman or magistrate.

Scri, scree   To write.

Our informant suggested *scribe* as the origin of this word.

Reader A writ.

"You're readered soobri." (You are put in the "Police Gazette," friend.)

Our informant could give only a single specimen of the Shelta literature. It was as follows:--

> "My name is Barney Mucafee,
> With my borers and jumpers down to my thee (thigh).
> An' it's forty miles I've come to kerrb yer pee."

This vocabulary is, as he declared, an extremely imperfect specimen of the language. He did not claim to speak it well. In its purity it is not mingled with Romany or thieves' slang. Perhaps some student of English dialects may yet succeed in recovering it all. The pronunciation of many of the words is singular, and very different from English or Romany.

Just as the last word was written down, there came up a woman, a female tramp of the most hardened kind. It seldom happens that gentlemen sit down in familiar friendly converse with vagabonds. When they do they are almost always religious people, anxious to talk with the poor for the good of their souls. The talk generally ends with a charitable gift. Such was the view (as the vagabond afterwards told us) which she took of our party. I also infer that she thought we must be very verdant and an easy prey. Almost without preliminary greeting she told us that she was in great straits,--suffering terribly,--and appealed to the man for confirmation, adding that if we would kindly lend her a sovereign it should be faithfully repaid in the morning.

The professor burst out laughing. But the fern-collector gazed at her in wrath and amazement.

"I say, old woman," he cried; "do you know who you're *rakkerin* [speaking] to? This here gentleman is one of the deepest Romany ryes [gypsy gentlemen] a-going. And that there one could *gladdher* you out of your eye-teeth."

She gave one look of dismay,--I shall never forget that look,--and ran away. The witch had chanced upon Arbaces. I think that the tramp had been in his time a man in better position. He was possibly a lawyer's clerk who had fallen into evil ways. He spoke English correctly when not addressing the beggar woman. There was in Aberystwith at the same time another fern-seller, an elderly man, as wretched and as ragged a creature as I ever met. Yet he also spoke English purely, and could give in Latin the names of all the plants which he sold. I have always supposed that the tinkers' language spoken of by Shakespeare was Romany; but I now incline to think it may have been Shelta.

Time passed, and "the levis grene" had fallen thrice from the trees, and I had crossed the sea and was in my native city of Philadelphia. It was a great change after eleven years of Europe, during ten of which I had "homed," as gypsies say, in England. The houses and the roads were old-new to me; there was something familiar-foreign in the voices and ways of those who had been my earliest friends; the very air as it blew hummed tunes which had lost tones in them that made me marvel. Yet even here I soon found traces of something which is the same all the world

over, which goes ever on "as of ever," and that was the wanderer of the
road. Near the city are three distinct gypsyries, where in summer-time
the wagon and the tent may be found; and ever and anon, in my walks about
town, I found interesting varieties of vagabonds from every part of
Europe. Italians of the most Bohemian type, who once had been like
angels,--and truly only in this, that their visits of old were few and
far between,--now swarmed as fruit dealers and boot-blacks in every lane;
Germans were of course at home; Czechs, or Slavs, supposed to be Germans,
gave unlimited facilities for Slavonian practice; while tinkers, almost
unknown in 1860, had in 1880 become marvelously common, and strange to
say were nearly all Austrians of different kinds. And yet not quite all,
and it was lucky for me they were not. For one morning, as I went into
the large garden which lies around the house wherein I wone, I heard by
the honeysuckle and grape-vine a familiar sound,--suggestive of the road
and Romanys and London, and all that is most traveler-esque. It was the
tap, tap, tap of a hammer and the clang of tin, and I knew by the smoke
that so gracefully curled at the end of the garden a tinker was near.
And I advanced to him, and as he glanced up and greeted, I read in his
Irish face long rambles on the roads.

"Good-morning!"

"Good-mornin', sorr!"

"You're an old traveler?"

"I am, sorr."

"Can you rakker Romanes?"

"I can, sorr!"

"*Pen yer nav*." (Tell your name.)

"Owen ---, sorr."

A brief conversation ensued, during which we ascertained that we had many friends in common in the *puro tem* or Ould Country. All at once a thought struck me, and I exclaimed,--

"Do you know any other languages?"

"Yes, sorr: Ould Irish an' Welsh, an' a little Gaelic."

"That's all?"

"Yes, sorr, all av thim."

"All but one?"

"An' what's that wan, sorr?"

"Can you *thari shelta*, *subli*?"

No tinker was ever yet astonished at anything. If he could be he would not be a tinker. If the coals in his stove were to turn to lumps of gold in a twinkle, he would proceed with leisurely action to rake them out and prepare them for sale, and never indicate by a word or a wink that anything remarkable had occurred. But Owen the tinker looked steadily at me for an instant, as if to see what manner of man I might be, and then said,--

"*Shelta*, is it? An' I can talk it. An' there's not six min livin' as can talk it as I do."

"Do you know, I think it's very remarkable that you can talk Shelta."

"An' begorra, I think it's very remarkable, sorr, that ye should know there is such a language."

"Will you give me a lesson?"

"Troth I will."

I went into the house and brought out a note-book. One of the servants brought me a chair. Owen went on soldering a tin dish, and I proceeded to take down from him the following list of words in **Shelta**:

Theddy   Fire (***theinne***. Irish).
StrawnTin.
Blyhunka   Horse.
Leicheen   Girl.
Soobli Male, man.
Binny soobli Boy.
Binny Small.
Chimmel   Stick.
Gh'ratha, grata   Hat.
Griffin, or gruffin   Coat.
Respes Trousers.
Gullemnocks Shoes.
Grascot   Waistcoat.
Skoich, or skoi'   Button.
Numpa   Sovereign, one pound.
Gorhead, or godhed   Money.
MerrihNose (?).
Nyock Head.
Graigh Hair.
Kaine, or kyniEars (Romany, ***kan***).
Melthog   Inner shirt.

Medthel   Black.

Cunnels   Potatoes.

Faihe, or feye Meat (*feoil*. Gaelic).

Muogh   Pig (*muck*. Irish).

Miesli, misli   To go (origin of "mizzle"?)

Mailyas, or moillhas Fingers (*meirleach*, stealers
        Gaelic).

Shaidyog   Policeman.

Respun   To steal.

Shoich Water, blood, liquid.

Alemnoch   Milk.

Raglan, or reglan   Hammer.

Goppa Furnace, smith (*gobha*, a smith.
        Gaelic).

Terry A heating-iron.

Khoi   Pincers.

Chimmes (compare *chimmel*)   Wood or stick.

Mailyas   Arms.

Koras Legs (*cos*, leg. Gaelic).

Skoihopa   Whisky.

Bulla (*ull* as in *gull*) A letter.

Thari Word, language.

Mush   Umbrella (slang).

Lyesken cherps   Telling fortunes.

Loshools   Flowers (*lus*, erb or flower?
        Gaelic).

Dainoch   To lose.

Chaldroch   Knife (*caldock*, sharply pointed.
        Gaelic).

Bog   To get.

Masheen   Cat.

Cambra   Dog.

Laprogh   Goose, duck.

Kaldthog   Hen.

Rumogh   Egg.

Kiena House (**ken**, old gypsy and modern
        cant).

Rawg Wagon.

Gullemnoch Shoes.

Analt To sweep, to broom.

Analken   To wash.

D'erri Bread.

R'ghoglin (gogh'leen)To laugh.

Kradyin   To stop, stay, sit, lodge, remain.

Oura Town.

Lashool   Nice (**lachool**. Irish).

Moinni, or moryeni Good (**min**, pleasant. Gaelic).

Moryenni yook   Good man.

Gyami Bad (**cam**. Gaelic). Probably the
        origin of the common canting term
        gammy, bad.

Ishkimmisk Drunk (**misgeach**. Gaelic)

RoglanA four-wheeled vehicle.

Lorch A two-wheeled vehicle.

Smuggle   Anvil.

Granya   Nail.

Riaglon   Iron.

Gushuk   Vessel of any kind.

Tedhi, thedi Coal; fuel of any kind.

Grawder   Solder.

Tanyok   Halfpenny.

        (Query **tani**, little, Romany, and
        nyok, a head.)

Chlorhin   To hear.

SunainTo see.

Salkaneoch   To taste, take.

Mailyen   To feel (*cumail*, to hold. Gaelic).
Crowder   String.
Sobye (?)
Mislain   Raining (mizzle?).
Goo-ope, guop   Cold.
Skoichen   Rain.
Thomyok   Magistrate.
Shadyog   Police.
Bladhunk   Prison.
Bogh   To get.
Salt   Arrested, taken.
Straihmed   A year.
Gotherna, guttema   Policeman.
[A very rare old word.]
Dyukas, or Jukas   Gorgio, Gentile; one not of the
        class.
Misli   Coming, to come, to send.
To my-deal   To me.
Lychyen   People.
Grannis   Know.
SkolaiaTo write.
Skolaiyami   A good scholar.
Nyok   Head.
Lurk   Eye.
Menoch   Nose.
Glorhoch   Ear.
Koris   Feet.
Tashi shingomai   To read the newspaper.
Gorheid   Money.
Tomgarheid (*i.e.* big money)   Gold.
Skawfer, skawper   Silver.
Tomnumpa   Bank-note.
Terri   Coal.

Ghoi   Put.

Nyadas   Table.

Kradyin   Being, lying.

Tarryin   Rope.

Kor'heh   Box.

Miseli Quick.

Krad'hyi   Slow.

Th-mddusk   Door.

Khaihed   Chair (***khahir***. Irish).

Bord   Table.

Grainyog   Window.

Rumog   Egg.

Aidh   Butter.

Okonneh   A priest. Thus explained in a very
            Irish manner: "***Okonneh***, or ***Koony***,
            is a ***sacred*** man, and ***kuni*** in
            Romany means secret. An' secret and
            sacred, sure, are all the same."

Shliema   Smoke, pipe.

Munches   Tobacco.

Khadyogs   Stones.

Yiesk   Fish (***iasg***. Gaelic).

Cab   Cabbage.

Cherpin   Book. This appears to be vulgar.
            Llyower was on second thought
            declared to be the right word.
            (***Leabhar***, Gaelic.)

Misli dainoch To write a letter; to write; that is,
            send or go.

Misli to my bewr   Write to my woman.

Gritche   Dinner.

Gruppa   Supper.

Goihed   To leave, lay down.

Lurks Eyes.
Ainoch   Thing.
Clisp   To fall, let fall.
Clishpen   To break by letting fall.
Guth, gut   Black.
Gothni, gachlin   Child.
Styemon   Rat.
Krepoch   Cat.
Grannien   With child.
Loshub   Sweet.
Shum   To own.
L'yogh To lose.
Crimum   Sheep.
Khadyog   Stone.
Nglou Nail.
Gial   Yellow, red.
Talosk Weather.
Laprogh   Bird.
Madel Tail.
Carob To cut.
Lubran, luber To hit.
Thom   Violently.
Mish it thom Hit it hard.
Subli, or soobli   Man (***siublach***, a vagrant. Gaelic).

There you are, readers! Make good cheer of it, as Panurge said of what
was beyond him. For what this language really is passeth me and mine.
Of Celtic origin it surely is, for Owen gave me every syllable so
garnished with gutturals that I, being even less of one of the Celtes
than a Chinaman, have not succeeded in writing a single word according to
his pronunciation of it. Thus even Minklers sounds more like ***minkias***,
or ***pikias***, as he gave it.

To the foregoing I add the numerals and a few phrases:--

Hain, or heen One.
Do   Two.
Tri   Three.
Ch'air, or k'hair   Four.
Cood   Five.
She, or shay   Six.
Schaacht, or schach' Seven.
Ocht   Eight.
Ayen, or nai   Nine.
Dy'ai, djai, or dai   Ten.
Hinniadh   Eleven.
Do yed'h   Twelve.
Trin yedh   Thirteen.
K'hair yedh, etc.   Fourteen, etc.
Tat 'th chesin ogomsa   That belongs to me.
Grannis to my deal   It belongs to me.
Dioch maa krady in in this nadas   I am staying here.
Tash emilesh He is staying there.
Boghin the brass   Cooking the food.
My deal is mislin   I am going.
The nidias of the kiena don't The people of the house don't know
granny what we're a tharyin what we're saying.

This was said within hearing of and in reference to a bevy of servants, of every hue save white, who were in full view in the kitchen, and who were manifestly deeply interested and delighted in our interview, as well as in the constant use of my note-book, and our conference in an unknown tongue, since Owen and I spoke frequently in Romany.

That bhoghd out yer mailya You let that fall from your hand.

I also obtained a verse of a ballad, which I may not literally render into pure English:--

> "Cosson kailyah corrum me morro sari,
> Me gul ogalyach mir;
> Rahet manent trasha moroch
> Me tu sosti mo diele."

> "Coming from Galway, tired and weary,
> I met a woman;
> I'll go bail by this time to-morrow,
> You'll have had enough of me."

Me tu sosti, "Thou shalt be (of) me," is Romany, which is freely used in Shelta.

The question which I cannot solve is, On which of the Celtic languages is this jargon based? My informant declares that it is quite independent of Old Irish, Welsh, or Gaelic. In pronunciation it appears to be almost identical with the latter; but while there are Gaelic words in it, it is certain that much examination and inquiry have failed to show that it is contained in that language. That it is "the talk of the ould Picts--thim that built the stone houses like beehives"--is, I confess, too conjectural for a philologist. I have no doubt that when the Picts were suppressed thousands of them must have become wandering outlaws, like the Romany, and that their language in time became a secret tongue of vagabonds on the roads. This is the history of many such lingoes; but unfortunately Owen's opinion, even if it be legendary, will not prove that the Painted People spoke the Shelta tongue. I must call attention, however, to one or two curious points. I have spoken of Shelta as a jargon; but it is, in fact, a language, for it can be spoken grammatically and without using English or Romany. And again, there is a corrupt method of pronouncing it, according to English, while correctly

enunciated it is purely Celtic in sound. More than this I have naught to
say.

Shelta is perhaps the last Old British dialect as yet existing which has
thus far remained undiscovered. There is no hint of it in John Camden
Hotten's Slang Dictionary, nor has it been recognized by the Dialect
Society. Mr. Simson, had he known the "Tinklers" better, would have
found that not Romany, but Shelta, was the really secret language which
they employed, although Romany is also more or less familiar to them all.
To me there is in it something very weird and strange. I cannot well say
why; it seems as if it might be spoken by witches and talking toads, and
uttered by the Druid stones, which are fabled to come down by moonlight
to the water-side to drink, and who will, if surprised during their walk,
answer any questions. Anent which I would fain ask my Spiritualist
friends one which I have long yearned to put. Since you, my dear
ghost-raisers, can call spirits from the vasty deep of the outside-most
beyond, will you not--having many millions from which to call--raise up
one of the Pictish race, and, having brought it in from the ***Ewigkeit***,
take down a vocabulary of the language? Let it be a lady ***par
preference***,--the fair being by far the more fluent in words. Moreover,
it is probable that as the Picts were a painted race, woman among them
must have been very much to the fore, and that Madame Rachels occupied a
high position with rouge, enamels, and other appliances to make them
young and beautiful forever. According to Southey, the British
blue-stocking is descended from these woad-stained ancestresses, which
assertion dimly hints at their having been literary. In which case,
voila notre affaire! for then the business would be promptly done.
Wizards of the secret spells, I adjure ye, raise me a Pictess for the
sake of philology--and the picturesque!

Notes:

{19} From the observations of Frederic Drew (***The Northern Barrier of India***, London, 1877) there can be little doubt that the Dom, or Dum, belong to the pre-Aryan race or races of India. "They are described in the Shastras as Sopukh, or Dog-Eaters" (***Types of India***). I have somewhere met with the statement that the Dom was pre-Aryan, but allowed to rank as Hindoo on account of services rendered to the early conquerors.

{22} Up-stairs in this gentleman's dialect signified up or upon, like ***top*** Pidgin-English.

{23} ***Puccasa***, Sanskrit. Low, inferior. Given by Pliny E. Chase in his ***Sanskrit Analogues*** as the root-word for several inferior animals.

{26} ***A Trip up the Volga to the Fair of Nijni-Novgovod***. By H. A. Munro Butler Johnstone. 1875.

{42} ***Seven Years in the Deserts of America***.

{61} In Old English Romany this is called ***dorrikin***; in common parade, ***dukkerin***. Both forms are really old.

{68} Flower-flag-nation man; that is, American.

{69a} ***Leadee***, reads.

{69b} ***Dly***, dry.

{69c} *Lun*, run.

{82} Diamonds true. *O latcho bar* (in England, *tatcho bar*), "the true or real stone," is the gypsy for a diamond.

{97} Within a mile, Maginn lies buried, without a monument.

{108} *Mashing*, a word of gypsy origin (*mashdva*), meaning fascination by the eye, or taking in.

{125} Goerres, *Christliche Mystik*, i. 296. 1. 23.

{134} *The Saxons in England*, i. 3.

{159} *Peru urphu*! "Increase and multiply!" *Vide* Bodenschatz *Kirchliche Verfassung der Juden*, part IV. ch. 4, sect. 2.

{209} *The Past in the Present*, part 2, lect. 3

{222} *Yoma*, fol. 21, col. 2.

{238} *Zimbel*. The cymbal of the Austrian gypsies is a stringed instrument, like the zitter.

{241} *Crocus*, in common slang an itinerant quack, mountebank, or seller of medicine; *Pitcher*, a street dealer.

{270} A brief *resume* of the most characteristic gypsy mode of obtaining property.

{279} Lady, in gypsy *rani*. The process of degradation is curiously marked in this language. *Rani* (*rawnee*), in Hindi, is a queen. *Rye*, or *rae*, a gentleman, in its native land, is applicable to a nobleman, while *rashai*, a clergyman, even of the smallest dissenting type, rises in the original *rishi* to a saint of the highest order.

{280} This was the very same affair and the same gypsies described and mentioned on page 383 of *In Gypsy Tents*, by Francis Hindes Groome, Edinburgh, 1880. I am well acquainted with them.

{285} *Primulaveris*: in German *Schlussel blume*, that is, key flowers; also Mary's-keys and keys of heaven. Both the primrose and tulip are believed in South Germany to be an Open Sesame to hidden treasure.

{292} Omar Khayyam, *Rubaiyat*.

{293} *Johnnykin and the Goblins*. London: Macmillan.

{302a} Vide *Journal of the Royal Asiatic Society*, vol. xvi. part 2, 1856 p. 285.

{302b} *Die Zigeuner*.

{307a} *The Dialect of the English Gypsies*.

{307b} I beg the reader to bear it in mind that all this is literally as it was given by an old gypsy, and that I am not responsible for its accuracy or inaccuracy.

{317a} Literally, the earth-sewer.

{317b} *Kali foki*. *Kalo* means, as in Hindustani, not only black, but also lazy. Pronounced *kaw-lo*.

{319a} *Gorgio*. Gentile; any man not a gypsy. Possibly from *ghora aji* "Master white man," Hindu. Used as *goi* is applied by Hebrews to the unbelievers.

{319b} *Romeli, rom'ni*. Wandering, gypsying. It is remarkable that *remna*, in Hindu, means to roam.

{320} *Chollo-tem*. Whole country, world.

{324} There is a great moral difference, not only in the gypsy mind, but in that of the peasant, between stealing and poaching. But in fact, as regards the appropriation of poultry of any kind, a young English gypsy has neither more nor less scruple than other poor people of his class.

{325} *Man lana*, Hindostani: to set the heart upon. *Manner*, Eng. Gyp.: to encourage; also, to forbid.

{327} *Chovihan*, m., *chovihani*, fem., often *cho'ian* or *cho'ani*, a witch. Probably from the Hindu *'toanee*, a witch, which has nearly the same pronunciation as the English gypsy word.

{335} *Travels in Beloochistan and Scinde*, p. 153.

{341a} English gypsies also call the moon *shul* and *shone*.

{341b} *Tales and Traditions of the Eskimo*, by Dr. Henry Rink. London 1875, p. 236.

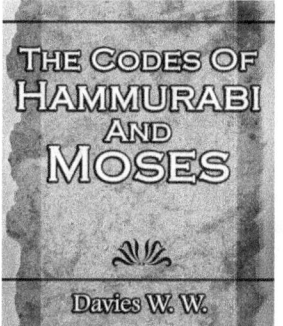

The Codes Of Hammurabi And Moses
W. W. Davies

QTY

The discovery of the Hammurabi Code is one of the greatest achievements of archaeology, and is of paramount interest, not only to the student of the Bible, but also to all those interested in ancient history...

Religion   ISBN: *1-59462-338-4*   Pages:132

MSRP $12.95

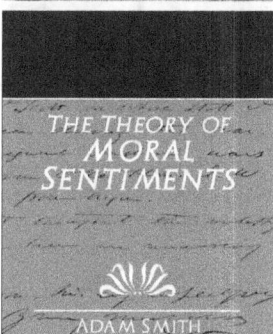

The Theory of Moral Sentiments
Adam Smith

QTY

This work from 1749. contains original theories of conscience amd moral judgment and it is the foundation for systemof morals.

Philosophy ISBN: *1-59462-777-0*   Pages:536

MSRP $19.95

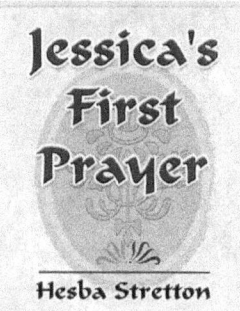

Jessica's First Prayer
Hesba Stretton

QTY

In a screened and secluded corner of one of the many railway-bridges which span the streets of London there could be seen a few years ago, from five o'clock every morning until half past eight, a tidily set-out coffee-stall, consisting of a trestle and board, upon which stood two large tin cans, with a small fire of charcoal burning under each so as to keep the coffee boiling during the early hours of the morning when the work-people were thronging into the city on their way to their daily toil...

Pages:84

Childrens   ISBN: *1-59462-373-2*   *MSRP $9.95*

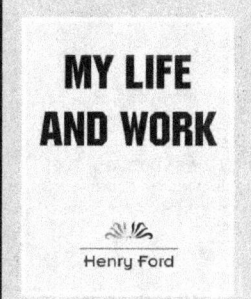

My Life and Work
Henry Ford

QTY

Henry Ford revolutionized the world with his implementation of mass production for the Model T automobile. Gain valuable business insight into his life and work with his own auto-biography... "We have only started on our development of our country we have not as yet, with all our talk of wonderful progress, done more than scratch the surface. The progress has been wonderful enough but..."

Pages:300

Biographies/   ISBN: *1-59462-198-5*   *MSRP $21.95*

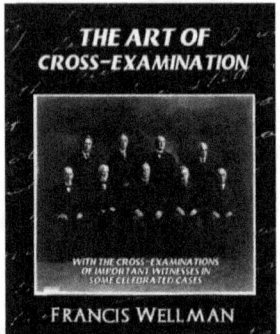

The Art of Cross-Examination
Francis Wellman

QTY

I presume it is the experience of every author, after his first book is published upon an important subject, to be almost overwhelmed with a wealth of ideas and illustrations which could readily have been included in his book, and which to his own mind, at least, seem to make a second edition inevitable. Such certainly was the case with me; and when the first edition had reached its sixth impression in five months, I rejoiced to learn that it seemed to my publishers that the book had met with a sufficiently favorable reception to justify a second and considerably enlarged edition. ..

Reference   **ISBN:** *1-59462-647-2*

Pages:412

MSRP $19.95

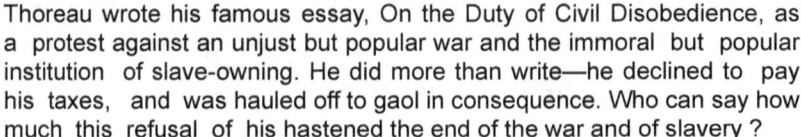

On the Duty of Civil Disobedience
Henry David Thoreau

QTY

Thoreau wrote his famous essay, On the Duty of Civil Disobedience, as a protest against an unjust but popular war and the immoral but popular institution of slave-owning. He did more than write—he declined to pay his taxes, and was hauled off to gaol in consequence. Who can say how much this refusal of his hastened the end of the war and of slavery ?

Law   **ISBN:** *1-59462-747-9*

Pages:48

MSRP $7.45

Dream Psychology Psychoanalysis for Beginners
Sigmund Freud

QTY

Sigmund Freud, born Sigismund Schlomo Freud (May 6, 1856 - September 23, 1939), was a Jewish-Austrian neurologist and psychiatrist who co-founded the psychoanalytic school of psychology. Freud is best known for his theories of the unconscious mind, especially involving the mechanism of repression; his redefinition of sexual desire as mobile and directed towards a wide variety of objects; and his therapeutic techniques, especially his understanding of transference in the therapeutic relationship and the presumed value of dreams as sources of insight into unconscious desires.

Psychology   **ISBN:** *1-59462-905-6*

Pages:196

MSRP $15.45

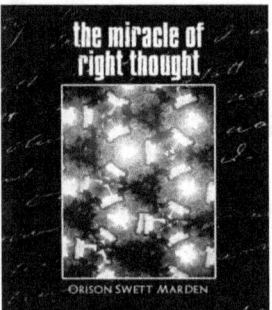

The Miracle of Right Thought
Orison Swett Marden

QTY

Believe with all of your heart that you will do what you were made to do. When the mind has once formed the habit of holding cheerful, happy, prosperous pictures, it will not be easy to form the opposite habit. It does not matter how improbable or how far away this realization may see, or how dark the prospects may be, if we visualize them as best we can, as vividly as possible, hold tenaciously to them and vigorously struggle to attain them, they will gradually become actualized, realized in the life. But a desire, a longing without endeavor, a yearning abandoned or held indifferently will vanish without realization.

Pages:360

Self Help   **ISBN:** *1-59462-644-8*   *MSRP $25.45* www.bookjungle.com *email: sales@bookjungle.com fax: 630-214-0564 mail: Book Jungle PO Box 2226 Champaign, IL 61825*

QTY

The Rosicrucian Cosmo-Conception Mystic Christianity *by Max Heindel* ISBN: *1-59462-188-8* **$38.95**
The Rosicrucian Cosmo-conception is not dogmatic, neither does it appeal to any other authority than the reason of the student. It is: not controversial, but is: sent forth in the, hope that it may help to clear... New Age/Religion Pages 646

Abandonment To Divine Providence *by Jean-Pierre de Caussade* ISBN: *1-59462-228-0* **$25.95**
"The Rev. Jean Pierre de Caussade was one of the most remarkable spiritual writers of the Society of Jesus in France in the 18th Century. His death took place at Toulouse in 1751. His works have gone through many editions and have been republished... Inspirational/Religion Pages 400

Mental Chemistry *by Charles Haanel* ISBN: *1-59462-192-6* **$23.95**
Mental Chemistry allows the change of material conditions by combining and appropriately utilizing the power of the mind. Much like applied chemistry creates something new and unique out of careful combinations of chemicals the mastery of mental chemistry... New Age Pages 354

The Letters of Robert Browning and Elizabeth Barret Barrett 1845-1846 vol II ISBN: *1-59462-193-4* **$35.95**
by Robert Browning and Elizabeth Barrett Biographies Pages 596

Gleanings In Genesis (volume I) *by Arthur W. Pink* ISBN: *1-59462-130-6* **$27.45**
Appropriately has Genesis been termed "the seed plot of the Bible" for in it we have, in germ form, almost all of the great doctrines which are afterwards fully developed in the books of Scripture which follow... Religion/Inspirational Pages 420

The Master Key *by L. W. de Laurence* ISBN: *1-59462-001-6* **$30.95**
In no branch of human knowledge has there been a more lively increase of the spirit of research during the past few years than in the study of Psychology, Concentration and Mental Discipline. The requests for authentic lessons in Thought Control, Mental Discipline and... New Age/Business Pages 422

The Lesser Key Of Solomon Goetia *by L. W. de Laurence* ISBN: *1-59462-092-X* **$9.95**
This translation of the first book of the "Lemegeton" which is now for the first time made accessible to students of Talismanic Magic was done, after careful collation and edition, from numerous Ancient Manuscripts in Hebrew, Latin, and French... New Age/Occult Pages 92

Rubaiyat Of Omar Khayyam *by Edward Fitzgerald* ISBN:*1-59462-332-5* **$13.95**
Edward Fitzgerald, whom the world has already learned, in spite of his own efforts to remain within the shadow of anonymity, to look upon as one of the rarest poets of the century, was born at Bredfield, in Suffolk, on the 31st of March, 1809. He was the third son of John Purcell... Music Pages 172

Ancient Law *by Henry Maine* ISBN: *1-59462-128-4* **$29.95**
The chief object of the following pages is to indicate some of the earliest ideas of mankind, as they are reflected in Ancient Law, and to point out the relation of those ideas to modern thought. Religion/History Pages 452

Far-Away Stories *by William J. Locke* ISBN: *1-59462-129-2* **$19.45**
"Good wine needs no bush, but a collection of mixed vintages does. And this book is just such a collection. Some of the stories I do not want to remain buried for ever in the museum files of dead magazine-numbers an author's not unpardonable vanity..." Fiction Pages 272

Life of David Crockett *by David Crockett* ISBN: *1-59462-250-7* **$27.45**
"Colonel David Crockett was one of the most remarkable men of the times in which he lived. Born in humble life, but gifted with a strong will, an indomitable courage, and unremitting perseverance... Biographies/New Age Pages 424

Lip-Reading *by Edward Nitchie* ISBN: *1-59462-206-X* **$25.95**
Edward B. Nitchie, founder of the New York School for the Hard of Hearing, now the Nitchie School of Lip-Reading, Inc, wrote "LIP-READING Principles and Practice". The development and perfecting of this meritorious work on lip-reading was an undertaking... How-to Pages 400

A Handbook of Suggestive Therapeutics, Applied Hypnotism, Psychic Science ISBN: *1-59462-214-0* **$24.95**
by Henry Munro Health/New Age/Health/Self-help Pages 376

A Doll's House: and Two Other Plays *by Henrik Ibsen* ISBN: *1-59462-112-8* **$19.95**
Henrik Ibsen created this classic when in revolutionary 1848 Rome. Introducing some striking concepts in playwriting for the realist genre, this play has been studied the world over. Fiction/Classics/Plays 308

The Light of Asia *by sir Edwin Arnold* ISBN: *1-59462-204-3* **$13.95**
In this poetic masterpiece, Edwin Arnold describes the life and teachings of Buddha. The man who was to become known as Buddha to the world was born as Prince Gautama of India but he rejected the worldly riches and abandoned the reigns of power when... Religion/History/Biographies Pages 170

The Complete Works of Guy de Maupassant *by Guy de Maupassant* ISBN: *1-59462-157-8* **$16.95**
"For days and days, nights and nights, I had dreamed of that first kiss which was to consecrate our engagement, and I knew not on what spot I should put my lips..." Fiction/Classics Pages 240

The Art of Cross-Examination *by Francis L. Wellman* ISBN: *1-59462-309-0* **$26.95**
Written by a renowned trial lawyer, Wellman imparts his experience and uses case studies to explain how to use psychology to extract desired information through questioning. How-to/Science/Reference Pages 408

Answered or Unanswered? *by Louisa Vaughan* ISBN: *1-59462-248-5* **$10.95**
Miracles of Faith in China Religion Pages 112

The Edinburgh Lectures on Mental Science (1909) *by Thomas* ISBN: *1-59462-008-3* **$11.95**
This book contains the substance of a course of lectures recently given by the writer in the Queen Street Hail, Edinburgh. Its purpose is to indicate the Natural Principles governing the relation between Mental Action and Material Conditions... New Age/Psychology Pages 148

Ayesha *by H. Rider Haggard* ISBN: *1-59462-301-5* **$24.95**
Verily and indeed it is the unexpected that happens! Probably if there was one person upon the earth from whom the Editor of this, and of a certain previous history, did not expect to hear again... Classics Pages 380

Ayala's Angel *by Anthony Trollope* ISBN: *1-59462-352-X* **$29.95**
The two girls were both pretty, but Lucy who was twenty-one who supposed to be simple and comparatively unattractive, whereas Ayala was credited, as her Bombwhat romantic name might show, with poetic charm and a taste for romance. Ayala when her father died was nineteen... Fiction Pages 484

The American Commonwealth *by James Bryce* ISBN: *1-59462-286-8* **$34.45**
An interpretation of American democratic political theory. It examines political mechanics and society from the perspective of Scotsman James Bryce Politics Pages 572

Stories of the Pilgrims *by Margaret P. Pumphrey* ISBN: *1-59462-116-0* **$17.95**
This book explores pilgrims religious oppression in England as well as their escape to Holland and eventual crossing to America on the Mayflower, and their early days in New England... History Pages 268

QTY

The Fasting Cure *by Sinclair Upton*　　　　　　　　　　　　ISBN: *1-59462-222-1*　**$13.95**
In the Cosmopolitan Magazine for May, 1910, and in the Contemporary Review (London) for April, 1910, I published an article dealing with my experiences in fasting. I have written a great many magazine articles, but never one which attracted so much attention... New Age/Self Help/Health Pages 164

Hebrew Astrology *by Sepharial*　　　　　　　　　　　　　ISBN: *1-59462-308-2*　**$13.45**
In these days of advanced thinking it is a matter of common observation that we have left many of the old landmarks behind and that we are now pressing forward to greater heights and to a wider horizon than that which represented the mind-content of our progenitors...　Astrology Pages 144

Thought Vibration or The Law of Attraction in the Thought World　　ISBN: *1-59462-127-6*　**$12.95**
by William Walker Atkinson　　　　　　　　　　　　　　　　　*Psychology/Religion Pages 144*

Optimism *by Helen Keller*　　　　　　　　　　　　　　ISBN: *1-59462-108-X*　**$15.95**
Helen Keller was blind, deaf, and mute since 19 months old, yet famously learned how to overcome these handicaps, communicate with the world, and spread her lectures promoting optimism. An inspiring read for everyone...　Biographies/Inspirational Pages 84

Sara Crewe *by Frances Burnett*　　　　　　　　　　　　ISBN: *1-59462-360-0*　**$9.45**
In the first place, Miss Minchin lived in London. Her home was a large, dull, tall one, in a large, dull square, where all the houses were alike, and all the sparrows were alike, and where all the door-knockers made the same heavy sound...　Childrens/Classic Pages 88

The Autobiography of Benjamin Franklin *by Benjamin Franklin*　　ISBN: *1-59462-135-7*　**$24.95**
The Autobiography of Benjamin Franklin has probably been more extensively read than any other American historical work, and no other book of its kind has had such ups and downs of fortune. Franklin lived for many years in England, where he was agent...　Biographies/History Pages 332

Name	
Email	
Telephone	
Address	
City, State ZIP	

☐ **Credit Card**　　　　　　☐ **Check / Money Order**

Credit Card Number	
Expiration Date	
Signature	

Please Mail to:　Book Jungle
PO Box 2226
Champaign, IL 61825
or Fax to:　　　630-214-0564

ORDERING INFORMATION

web*: www.bookjungle.com*
email*: sales@bookjungle.com*
fax*: 630-214-0564*
mail*: Book Jungle PO Box 2226 Champaign, IL 61825*
or PayPal *to sales@bookjungle.com*

Please contact us for bulk discounts

DIRECT-ORDER TERMS

**20% Discount if You Order
Two or More Books**
Free Domestic Shipping!
Accepted: Master Card, Visa,
Discover, American Express

www.ingramcontent.com/pod-product-compliance
Lightning Source LLC
Chambersburg PA
CBHW081143020726
47504CB00009B/1983